MARKING TIME

TREADING WATER SERIES, BOOK 2

MARIE FORCE

Marking Time
Treading Water Series, Book 2
By: Marie Force
Published by HTJB, Inc.
Copyright 2011. HTJB, Inc.
Cover by Kristina Brinton
Layout by E-book Formatting Fairies
ISBN: 978-1942295266

THE TREADING WATER SERIES

For all the readers who asked for Clare's story—thank you!

PART I
MARKING TIME

Marching in place.

CHAPTER 1

*C*lare checked her watch again. One thirty. *It must be done by now. My husband—or I should say ex-husband—is remarried.*

"Ex-husband," she said with a shudder. Unimaginable. Divorced… Such an ugly word.

She wheeled her chair across her room in the rehabilitation center and gazed out at the steamy August day. Somewhere along the Ten Mile Ocean Drive in historic Newport, Jack had exchanged vows with Andi. *He has a new family now.* Clare had known this day was coming and had set the whole thing in motion by letting him go, but that didn't make it any easier to imagine her Jack married to someone else. "Not my Jack anymore," she said to herself.

The door opened. "Mrs. Harrington?"

Clare didn't correct the nurse. She wasn't "Mrs." any longer. "Yes?"

"They're ready for you in PT."

Taking another long look at the City by the Sea, Clare wondered what Jack was doing right at that moment. Was he kissing his bride? Making a toast? Dancing with one of their daughters? She shook her head, angry to have allowed herself even a brief trip down that road. What did it matter now?

"Let's go." She wheeled herself to the door to let the nurse push her through the long hallways to physical therapy.

~

AFTER DINNER, Clare worked her way into lightweight pajamas. She was proud of her ability to do things for herself, even small things like changing her clothes. Each little victory added up. Rolling the wheelchair across the room she'd called home for the last four months, she eased herself from her chair to the sofa on her own—another recent accomplishment. Her recovery was coming along slowly but surely.

That she had recovered at all was a miracle, or so they all said. No one had expected her to ever emerge from the coma she'd been in for three years after being hit by a car. But four months ago, she'd defied the odds and awakened after a fever doctors had feared would finally end her life. Yep, a real miracle. Everything that happened since then had been somewhat less than miraculous: her twenty-year marriage had disintegrated, and her days were now marked by the struggle to regain her health.

Clare knew she was lucky, but she'd grown tired of hearing that word. Doctors had told her she would most likely be confronted with physical challenges for the rest of her life, including chronic urinary tract infections, a propensity toward pneumonia, fatigue, muscle spasms, and other fallout from three years of inactivity. Oh yeah, what a miracle.

A tearjerker movie on TV caught her attention, and it was a relief to be absorbed into someone else's drama for a change. When someone knocked at her door, Clare muted the television. "Come in," she called and was surprised to see Jack's sister, Frannie Booth.

"May I come in?"

"Of course," Clare said to her former sister-in-law. "Come sit."

Frannie crossed the room to sit next to Clare on the sofa. She wore her auburn hair in an elegant twist left over from her brother's wedding.

"I didn't expect to see you, especially tonight," Clare said, admiring the yellow floral silk dress Frannie had worn to the wedding. "You look fabulous."

"Thanks. I was thinking of you and thought I'd stop by to see how you're doing."

"I'm fine, but you didn't have to come."

"I wanted to."

"How was it?" Clare tried to sound casual as she twirled a lock of her unruly blonde hair around a finger.

"It was lovely but a little more exciting than we'd planned. Andi's water broke during the reception. They had twin boys right there at the hotel. The doctor said they appear to be identical."

"Oh." Clare struggled to hide the surge of emotion. Jack had sons.

"It all happened so fast." Frannie shook her head and smiled. "Apparently, she'd been in labor all night and didn't realize it because she'd had back pain."

Clare worked at keeping her expression neutral as she absorbed the news that the babies had arrived a month early. "They're all fine?"

"Yes."

"The girls must've been excited," Clare said, referring to her daughters.

"They were."

"What're their names?"

"They named them for Jack and the grandfathers, John Joseph Harrington the fourth, and Robert Franklin Harrington. Johnny and Robby."

Despite her best efforts, Clare's eyes flooded with tears. "Johnny and Robby," she whispered.

"I'm sorry to upset you."

Clare wiped her eyes. "It's okay."

"I've wanted to come for weeks to say…what you did…letting him go…" Frannie had a look of awe on her face. "It was so selfless."

"It was the only thing I could do. It was selfish more than anything."

"No, it wasn't. It was amazing. I don't know that I could've done it."

A stab of pain hit Clare just below her broken heart. "I don't want to talk about that anymore. It's over and done with. But I'm glad you're here for another reason."

"What's that?"

"I've had lots of time to think," Clare said with a small grin. "I don't know if I ever adequately thanked you for what you did while I was sick. I mean for you to give up a year and a half of your life to take care of my kids—"

"Taking care of your girls was a pleasure. You don't have to thank me. You'd have done the same for me. So you're really doing okay?"

Clare raised a suspicious eyebrow. "Did Jack send you to check on me?"

"Not this time. I think he's so stunned by the babies arriving in the middle of his wedding, he doesn't even know his own name right now."

They shared a laugh.

"I'm sure," Clare said. "I'm doing fine. Don't worry about me."

"I also came because I have something for you." Frannie reached into her bag for a leather-bound book. She held it against her chest for a moment as she collected her thoughts. "Shortly after I moved in with Jack and the girls, I started keeping a journal. It was odd because I'd never had one before, but I suddenly had a need to write things down. Anyway, I debated for a long time about whether I should share it with you. And then I realized that most of the time I was keeping it, I was doing it for you. I was writing it for you."

"Did you think I'd recover? No one seemed to think I would."

"No, I didn't think so. But for some reason I started writing things down, and when I read it over recently, I understood I'd done it for you, like I was talking to you. I didn't consciously set out to do that. Oh, I'm not explaining it well."

"No, you are. Can I see it?"

She handed the book to Clare. "I know you'll be so happy to get back some of the time you lost with the girls by reading about their lives, but there're other things in there that'll cause you pain. I wish I could spare you that. I didn't give it to you before now because of that."

"You wrote about them, too, didn't you? About Jack and Andi?" Clare asked as she brushed a hand over the leather cover.

"Yes, and I don't know if you should read those parts."

"Maybe I'll skip them. You have no idea how much this means to me."

"I think maybe I do. I'm a mom now, too, remember? If you want to talk about it—any of it—you only have to ask."

"Thank you." Feeling as if she'd been given a priceless gift, Clare reached out to squeeze Frannie's hand. "Thank you so much."

"I hope you'll still be thanking me after you've read it," Frannie said with a grin. "Have you made any plans?"

Clare shrugged. "Not really. They're saying I have maybe another month of rehab, and then I can go home. I'm not sure what's next for me." She twisted her face into an ironic smile. "I find myself at loose ends for the first time in more than twenty years."

"I'm sure you'll figure it out. I know the girls are looking forward to having you at home. Do you need anything?"

"Your brother made sure I'd never want for anything. I got my bank statement the other day, and my eyes almost popped out of my head."

"He doesn't want you to worry about supporting yourself."

"With that kind of money, I'll never have to worry again, that's for sure. He didn't have to do that."

"Yes, he did."

Clare smiled. "I'm glad you came, Frannie. Will you come again and bring your babies? I'd love to see them."

"You bet."

"COME ON, Clare, give me one more step. Just one more."

Sweat rolled down her face as she struggled against the crutches. "You're a sadist, Jeffrey."

"You love me. You know you do."

Clare put her last bit of energy into that final step and then rested against his outstretched arms.

"Right," she panted. "Just keep reminding me."

Behind them, someone applauded.

Clare turned to find her doctor watching. "Great, an audience," she grumbled and swiped at the sweat on her face.

Dr. Paul Langston came across the room. "That was outstanding. I counted at least fifty steps."

"I counted fifty-five," Jeffrey said.

"I don't remember sending you an invite, Dr. Paul. What're you doing here?" Clare thanked Jeffrey when he eased her into her wheelchair.

"I came to check on my star patient. Do I need an invitation?"

She took a long drink from her water bottle. "Not if you're going to charm me."

Dr. Langston tapped a toe against the chair. "I'm thinking we're just about ready to kiss this baby good-bye and talk about sending you home."

Her stomach clenched with anxiety. "Already? I thought you said another month?"

"You've gotten used to us, huh? Can't live without me?"

"Yeah, something like that," she said with a grin. He was a dreamboat with close-cropped blond hair and mischievous blue eyes. Too bad he was also ten years younger than her. "You're easy enough on the eyes, I guess."

He hooted. "Such flattery! It's going straight to my head. I'll take Miss Congeniality back to her room," he told Jeffrey.

"See you tomorrow, Clare," Jeffrey said.

"Can't wait."

"You've been doing so well," Dr. Langston said as they rolled along the corridor. "The nurses tell me you're showering and dressing on your own and relying on them less every day." He stopped next to a bench in the hallway and sat to bring himself to her eye level. "I thought you were busting to get out of here. What gives?"

She shrugged.

"Is it what's waiting for you at home?"

She raised an eyebrow. "Don't you mean what's not waiting for me?"

"Have you talked to Dr. Baker about it?" he asked, referring to Clare's psychiatrist.

"Here and there, but we've been more focused on the attack and all that. I haven't wanted to talk about the untimely demise of my marriage. I'm just a bundle of unresolved issues," she said with the good-natured grin that had made her a favorite among the medical team that had cared for her over the last four months.

"I think we should set a date." Dr. Langston folded his arms over his white coat. "Two weeks from today?"

"Are you sure? That's awfully soon."

"Your daughters are waiting for you. Don't you want to get home to them?"

"They're happy living with their father right now."

"They'll be thrilled to have you home again. They've waited a long time."

"I'm sure they're more than used to being without me. How do I get back three years with them?" She bit back the urge to weep.

"You can't. All you can do is go forward from here. I'm going to be honest with you, Clare. None of us imagined you'd get this far. You've defied the odds. Don't let yourself down by giving up now."

She smiled. "You're tossing me out, huh?"

"I'm afraid so."

"You've all been so great. I'll miss you."

He got up from the bench. "Nah, you'll be too busy enjoying your fabulous new life to give us a thought."

"Somehow I doubt that." She twisted her hands in her lap. The idea of going home filled her with apprehension.

He squatted down so she could see him. "Talk to Dr. Baker. Tell him how you feel about going home. Let him help you."

"I will. Thanks, Paul."

~

AN ITEM in the *Newport Daily News* caught Clare's eye the next day:

Prominent City Architect Welcomes Double Delivery

NEWPORT—(August 27) It's not every day that twins interrupt their parents' wedding, but that's what happened Tuesday.

Jack Harrington, co-owner of the Newport architectural firm Harrington Booth Associates, and his wife Andi welcomed twin sons, John Joseph Harrington IV and Robert Franklin Harrington. The twins arrived in the midst of their parents' wedding at the Infinity Newport Hotel where their mother is the general manager. The hotel, which opened in December, was designed and built by Harrington Booth Associates.

"We thought we were just having a wedding, but I guess the babies didn't want to miss it," said Jamie Booth, Mr. Harrington's business partner and brother-in-law. Mr. Booth is married to Mr. Harrington's sister, Frannie. The Booths are also the parents of twins, one-year-old Owen and Olivia. "Andi and the babies are doing great," Mr. Booth reported.

The new twins are the grandsons of John and Madeline Harrington of Greenwich, Conn., Betty Franklin of Chicago, Ill., and the late Robert Franklin. They join sisters Jill, Kate, and Maggie, and a brother, Eric.

CLARE READ IT A SECOND TIME. It was still so hard to believe that Jack was now married to someone else and had twin babies with her— twin sons, no less. And it was splashed all over the news. Anyone who didn't already know she and Jack had recently gotten divorced did now.

Knowing how much her daughters loved babies, she could imagine their delight with their new brothers. No doubt she would hear all about it when they came to visit. Thinking back to the girls being born brought a smile to Clare's face. Jill had just turned nineteen and was beginning her sophomore year at Brown University in Providence. Kate would be eighteen in November, and they had agreed to let her go to Nashville for a year after her birthday to pursue a career in country music. And Clare's "baby," Maggie, would be thirteen in December.

Clare reached over to the table next to the sofa to pick up the book Frannie had left. She had spent a few days working up the courage to look at it, and now the curiosity was overwhelming. Opening the book, she flipped to the first page, taking comfort in the familiarity of Frannie's precise penmanship. The first item was dated June 20.

It's late and the girls are finally in bed. They were wound up today —the last day of school. We now have an 11th grader, a 10th grader, and a 4th grader. I'm thrilled to see them excited and happy for a change. It's been a while.

July 26

Jack sits by Clare's bedside hour after hour, day after day. He talks to her until he's hoarse and weak with fatigue. I look at him and wonder how he'll ever live without her. But he's not ready to think about that. I don't know if he'll ever be.

CLARE BRUSHED a tear from her cheek and read several entries about the girls' activities that summer. Jill had babysat for a neighborhood family, and Kate had gone to sleepaway camp for the first time. They went to the beach a lot, and Jamie took them out on the sailboat he owned with Jack.

August 19

Jill is sweet sixteen today, and it's her first birthday without her mom. She was weepy during the day but enjoyed the party we had for her after dinner. The nurses who care for Clare have become part of the family, and Jill invited them to have cake with us.

ENOUGH, Clare thought as she closed the book and wiped her tears. That's enough for today.

CHAPTER 2

*J*ack brought Maggie in for a visit, and she burst into the room, chatting a mile a minute while her father hung back.

Clare hugged Maggie and waved him in as her heart hammered. *How long will it take for that to stop?* Tall with thick dark hair and gray eyes, he looked exhausted but happy. In fact he looked terrific, but then he always did. "Congratulations."

"Thanks," he said. "How are you?"

Before Clare could answer, Maggie picked up the stream of chatter again in an obvious attempt to offset the awkwardness between her parents. She had gotten tall over the summer, and her sleek dark hair —so much like her father's—hung down her back. "You're not going to *believe* who showed her face at the beach today." Maggie rolled her blue eyes as her parents looked on in amusement.

"Who?" Clare asked.

"Hailey Harper. Ugh, we're all so *over* her. After what she pulled in school last year…" Maggie shook her head with disgust.

"Maggie, be nice," Jack said.

"Whatever. She's the one with the problem. Hey, can I get ice cream?" Her eyes lit up, and Hailey was forgotten.

"Sure." Jack took a ten-dollar bill from his wallet. "Get Mom some, too."

"Rocky road?" Maggie asked Clare.

"But of course," Clare said with a smile. "Thanks."

"Whew," Jack said as Maggie flew from the room, headed for the hospital cafeteria. He came in to sit with Clare. "She's a whirling dervish these days."

"She always was." Clare noticed his new platinum wedding ring and wondered what he'd done with the gold one she'd given him. "Some kind of excitement for you this week. Everyone's doing well?"

"Yes, but I haven't slept in four days," he said with the wry grin that was all Jack. It had never failed to stop her heart. "The one-two punch is something else. It's nonstop."

"I can only imagine." Clare forced herself to be cheerful. "And Andi? She's well?"

"She's tired and sore, but she's doing fine, considering she's had no sleep and seems to be feeding one baby or the other around the clock."

"Hell of a honeymoon, huh?" Clare joked.

He smiled and shrugged.

"Please pass along my congratulations to her, too."

"I will. So how are you doing?"

"Apparently, well enough to go home."

His eyes lit up with delight. "Really? When?"

"They're saying early September."

"Wow. That's great, Clare."

"I suppose so."

"You don't sound happy about it."

"I am." She brushed some imaginary lint off her jeans as she stole a glimpse of him. *God, he's gorgeous.* He always had been, from the day they met on Block Island twenty-two summers ago.

"We need to get the house ready," he said. "I'll send some guys over to adapt the downstairs bathroom and set you up with a bedroom on the first floor until you can manage the stairs."

"You don't have to do that. I can take care of it. You've got enough going on."

"Let me handle it. It's no trouble at all."

Knowing he had easy access to what she needed done to the house, she nodded. "Okay. Thanks."

"Remember what I told you—whatever you need. You only have to ask."

"This is so weird," she said softly, giving voice to the tension between them. They'd been divorced for only two weeks, and he was already remarried with new twin babies. It boggled the mind.

"It probably will be for a while, but it's bound to get easier. For both of us."

"I hope so. We have to stay focused on the girls, especially Maggie."

"Always." He reached over to squeeze her hand.

Maggie came in juggling two dripping cones. "Hurry, Mom, it's running." She thrust the cone at Clare and handed Jack his change.

He stood up. "I need to get back. When we left, the babies were sleeping, but that never lasts long. Kate will be by to get you in a little while, Maggie." Hesitantly, he bent to kiss Clare's cheek. "I'll be in touch about the house."

"Thanks, Jack."

"It's no problem. See you later, Mags."

After he had gone, Clare turned to Maggie as they licked their cones. "So tell me about the babies. It's so exciting, huh?"

Her face lit up. "Oh, God, Mom, they're *unbelievable*. They have shiny black hair and these tiny scrunched-up faces..." She trailed off and went back to her cone.

"It's okay to be excited about your new brothers, honey."

Maggie's cheeks colored. "I don't mean to be insensitive."

Clare was amazed by her youngest daughter's sudden maturity. She'd left behind a little girl three years ago and had returned to find a young woman. At times like this, the metamorphosis was startling. "You're not being insensitive. You have two new baby brothers. Of course you're thrilled."

Maggie brightened. "They're awesome." She bit into her cone. "Actually, I have three little brothers now."

"I know." Clare had heard all about Maggie's close bond with Eric,

Andi's son from her first marriage. Maggie had learned sign language to communicate with the hearing-impaired boy and was now almost fluent.

"Dad's adopting Eric."

"That's a nice thing for him to do."

"He doesn't know his own father, so Dad's like his dad already."

"He's just making it official," Clare said with a smile. *Oh, how this hurt.* Jack's life was all set, and hers was in shambles. She reminded herself that it had been her decision to let him go. Now she just had to find a way to live with it. "So the doctors are sending me home in about two weeks."

Maggie's eyes lit up. "Really?"

Clare nodded. "I'm hoping you'll want to spend some time with me." *I sound so pathetic. How will I ever compete with three new brothers?*

"I'll come to your house to catch up on my sleep," Maggie teased.

Clare laughed and finished her cone. "Oh, I see. You'll be using me?"

"Definitely." Maggie giggled. "So Dad bought a house on Ocean Drive."

Kate and Maggie had been staying with Jack and Andi at the hotel since the babies were born. He had moved out of what was now Clare's house just before their divorce became final. "Did he?"

"Yeah, some gray place, gray house or something," Maggie said with a shrug.

"Oh, Gray Hall." Clare had been a Realtor before her accident and was well aware of the estate. "That's a great old house, right on the water."

Maggie rolled her eyes. "Of course it is. You know how weird he is about that."

"Yes, I do," Clare said, smiling at Jack's need to live on the water.

"Anyway, I guess we're moving in at the end of next week. Living at the hotel is getting kind of old, and they want to get settled with the babies and all."

"I can imagine they do. When I get home, we'll work something out so you can spend time with both of us, okay?"

"Sure. I'm glad you're getting to come home."

"Me, too. We've got a lot of catching up to do."

The door opened, and Kate came in. Clare was always amazed at how much her middle daughter resembled her, with the same unruly blonde hair and bright blue eyes. It was like seeing herself at eighteen except Kate had Jack's height, which gave her a coltish stride as she crossed the room to plant a kiss on her mother's forehead.

"What've you been eating, brat?" Kate asked her sister. "It's all over your face."

"Don't call her that, Kate," Clare admonished, sending an empathetic smile to Maggie.

"That's okay, Mom. I'd fall over and die of shock if she called me Maggie."

Kate's eyes twinkled. "Really? Maggie, Maggie, Maggie. Damn, it didn't work."

"Ha-ha," Maggie said, using a wet paper towel to wipe the ice cream off her face.

"I see some things never change," Clare said, delighted by her girls.

"Mom's coming home the week after next," Maggie told her sister.

"That's great! I'm glad you'll be home for a while before I leave."

Clare nodded. "Me, too." She didn't like to think about Kate's impending departure for Nashville. Jack had made that decision before her recovery, and he had convinced Clare to give it a try for a year. He had promised her he would see to all the details, including making sure Kate had a safe place to live. Clare was glad she had a couple of months yet before she had to deal with that.

"Sorry, Mom, but we've got to go," Kate said with a kiss to her mother's cheek. "I'm working tomorrow, so I need to hit the sack." She had been playing the guitar and singing at the Infinity Newport Hotel's outdoor bars all summer.

"That's okay. I'm glad to see you, even just for a minute."

"I'll call you tomorrow," Maggie promised, kissing her mother good night.

"I'll look forward to it." Clare waved as the door closed behind them. Watching them go, she was hit by a sense of panic, wondering if they felt closer now to their stepmother than they did to her, wondering if she'd ever get back the close bond she'd shared with each of her daughters.

CHAPTER 3

*N*ovember 22
Today is Thanksgiving, and my goal is to help the girls remember all the many blessings of their lives, despite their loss. Mother, Dad, Jamie, and his parents are coming for dinner, and I hope having them here will help Jack. I feel Clare's absence so acutely today. The holidays were her favorite time of the year, and she always made them special for the rest of us. Just getting out of bed to face this day took effort for me. I can't imagine how Jack and the girls must feel.

JANUARY 1

I don't know when I've ever been so glad to say good-bye to a year! Jill and Kate were invited to a slumber party for New Year's Eve, and I encouraged them to go. It's good for them to spend time with their friends. After Maggie went to bed, Jack and I tied one on and watched the ball drop at Times Square. When I looked over at him at midnight, there were tears running down his face. His pain is so intense. Christmas was a horror show around here. They didn't want a tree or decorations. I tried to cajole them, but Jack told me to let it go. No one was in the mood.

. . .

THE PHONE RANG, startling her. Clare set aside the journal and took a deep breath to calm her emotions before she answered.

"Hello?"

"Hi, Clare. It's Janice Hayes."

"Hi, Janice. It's so nice to hear from you."

"How are you?"

"I'm actually getting ready to go home. One more week."

"Oh, that's wonderful news! Cooper and I have been keeping tabs on you."

Cooper Hayes had been Jack's attorney for years. The four of them had socialized on many occasions, and he'd handled their divorce. It was nice to know she hadn't been forgotten by her old friend. "Thank you, it's good to hear your voice."

"I've wanted to come by to see you, but Jack said you weren't taking visitors at the hospital."

"Yes, well, I kind of wanted to get back to my old self before I greeted the world. Why don't you come by the house when I get home? I'd love to see you."

"I'd like that. Coop told me what happened, that you were—"

"I was raped, and he threatened to kill one of my kids if I told anyone." Clare saved her friend from having to say the words. "I didn't tell anyone, and the stress was horrible." She paused before she continued, knowing she might as well tell her friend the rest. "That day, in the parking lot, when the car was coming at me... I'm ashamed to say I saw it as a way out. I let that car hit me, Janice." Clare had only recently been able to speak of it after months of intense therapy. "I did a terrible thing to my girls by letting that happen right in front of them."

"I'm so sorry, Clare," Janice said in a whisper, and Clare could tell she was crying. "The man who hurt you—"

"He's doing a life sentence in California. Apparently, he was a career felon."

"Thank God they got him. I saw the piece in the paper about Jack getting married. I just can't imagine how you must be feeling. You two were always so in love. We envied you."

"Yes," Clare said with a sigh. "On top of everything else, while I was in a coma, my husband fell in love with someone else and was expecting twins with her by the time I recovered. Needless to say, it was quite a shock."

"I'm sure it was terrible for you. Are you all right?"

"I'm doing better. It worked out the way it was meant to."

"What you've been through, all of you… If there's anything I can do for you, I hope you won't hesitate to call."

"I'll need all the friends I can muster over the next few months. I do hope you'll come by."

"I will. I promise."

They ended the call, and Clare set the phone down on the table next to her bed. *I guess that's the first of many times I'll have that conversation.*

SHE WENT HOME on a Saturday so the girls could be with her when she left the hospital. Jill came from college in Providence, and Clare's mother, Anna, was there from Hartford for the big day.

The halls of the rehabilitation center were lined with staffers applauding their star patient as she was taken on one last wheelchair ride to the front door. Embarrassed by the attention, Clare emerged into the late summer humidity, handed her crutches to Kate, and eased herself into the passenger seat of her own beloved burgundy Volvo. She had paid cash for it with the proceeds of the first house she ever sold and had hung on to it despite Jack's many attempts to get her to upgrade. When she closed her door and looked over, she was startled to see Jill behind the wheel.

Jill laughed. "Yes, Mother, I drive now."

"I do, too," Kate said from the backseat where she sat with Maggie and their grandmother.

"Me, too," Maggie said, and everyone laughed.

"Of course, I knew you guys were driving, but having you drive me is another story," Clare said. "This'll take some getting used to, ladies."

"That's okay," Jill said.

"Go slow, Jill, you don't want me to have a heart attack on my first day out of the hospital."

Anna reached out to pat her daughter's shoulder. "Relax, honey, they're both excellent drivers."

"Thanks, Gram, I think she needed to hear that," Jill said with amusement as she pulled away from the hospital. "What do you think, Mom? Shall we take the scenic route?"

"Absolutely." Clare rolled down the window to let in the breeze. She'd been out of the hospital only once since her recovery in April, to attend Kate's high school graduation in June.

Jill drove through downtown, along Newport Harbor. Clare was quiet during the ride as she drank in the familiar and noticed all the changes wrought by the passage of time—a new lane added to a roadway, the landscaping in front of a favorite restaurant, once-loved shops long gone and replaced by new ones.

"Can we take a ride?" Clare asked as Jill approached the traffic light at the end of America's Cup Avenue, where they would have gone up the hill at Memorial Boulevard to go home.

"Sure, where do you want to go?" Jill asked.

"I'd like to see the hotel." Jack had met Andi while building the hotel, and Clare had been curious about it for months.

"No problem," Jill said, taking a right onto Lower Thames, which would lead them to Ocean Drive.

"Look at all the people." Anna marveled at the tourists crowding the quaint city's sidewalks and cobblestone streets.

"Newport is as popular as ever," Clare said.

They navigated Ocean Drive's winding curves in silence until an elaborate gold-leaf sign announcing "Infinity Newport" appeared in front of them. Sitting at the end of a quarter-mile driveway, the hotel kissed the shore of Rhode Island's Narragansett Bay.

"Oh my." Clare took in the sprawling two-story shingled building with dark green shutters and trim. "Why, it already looks like it's been there for years!"

"I know," Kate said. "I've thought that, too."

"It's magnificent," Clare said.

"Wait 'til you see the inside," Maggie said. "It's awesome."

"We'll save that for another time," Clare said as Jill drove slowly past the hotel. "Dad and Uncle Jamie did a wonderful job. Thanks for showing me."

They fell quiet again as they wound along the ten-mile Ocean Drive on Newport's southern coast.

"Oh, look, that's the house Dad and Andi are buying." Maggie pointed to an ornate wrought-iron gate in front of a two-story gray colonial.

"Is that it? I haven't seen it yet." Jill slowed the car to get a better look. "Wow, it's huge."

"It is," Kate agreed. "There's a little beach out in front, too."

"Very nice." Clare felt suddenly disconnected as her daughters checked out their father's new house. "I think I'm ready to get home, guys."

"Sure, Mom," Jill said, taking the curve to Bellevue Avenue where they passed the city's famous mansions. They drove by the merry-go-round at First Beach, and a few turns later, Jill pulled into the gravel driveway at home.

Kate retrieved Clare's crutches and helped her mother from the car.

Clare took a long look at the house she hadn't seen in more than three years. The only noticeable difference was the landscaping, which had grown and matured in her absence—just like her daughters. She shook off their offers of help and navigated the three small stairs to the front porch. When a flood of memories assailed her, she gestured for the others to go on in.

"I'll be right there." She rested against the porch railing. "Go ahead, honey," she said when Jill hesitated.

Jill went in, and Clare stood riveted, staring at the bright red front door, remembering.

"THREE SMALL STEPS," he had said, taking both her hands to lead her. "One, two, okay, stand there a minute."

Listening to a door opening, she'd been tempted to nudge aside the blindfold he insisted she wear. "Jack, where are we? What's going on?" She felt him come back to her, and before she knew it, he swept her up into his arms. "Jack! What are you doing?"

"Carrying my bride over the threshold."

"Bride? Have you lost your mind?" she asked as he set her down and untied the blindfold. When her eyes had adjusted to the light, she saw high ceilings, shining wood floors, and glass—lots and lots of glass through which there was a dazzling view of the ocean. "What is this place? Where are we?"

He put his arms around her and kissed her. "We're home. Merry Christmas."

"Home?" She looked around again. "I don't understand..."

He took her hand to lead her into the kitchen.

Through French doors, she saw a stone patio around an elaborately tiled in-ground pool. "Did you buy this house, Jack?"

"Not exactly. I built this house."

She whirled around to look again, realizing parts of what she saw were familiar. "Oh, God, you built it. You built my house, didn't you?" she asked in a whisper, her eyes flooding with tears. "The house you drew for me after our wedding?"

He nodded.

She wiped tears from her face. "But how? When? When did you do this?"

"Many late nights with 'clients,' and many, many lies," he said with the devilish grin that still melted her bones after thirteen and a half years together.

"The top, with the circle and the glass, did you do that, too?" she asked, filled with excitement as the details of the plans he'd drawn for "someday" came rushing back to her.

"Of course I did. Want to see?"

She nodded and put her arms around him. Whatever had she done to deserve this man—this amazing, thoughtful, generous man? "I want to see, but first I just want you." She hugged him close to her. "I can't believe you did this."

He pulled back to look down at her. "Did you think I'd forgotten?"

"You've been so busy with the firm. I haven't thought about this in years."

"I've never stopped thinking about it, and when this property came on the market, I snapped it up."

"It's so beautiful, but it must've cost a fortune. Can we afford this?" She tipped her eyes up to his. The firm he and Jamie had founded almost six years ago had been wildly successful, but she didn't think they had this kind of money.

"We can afford it. I did a lot of it myself to keep the cost down, but I don't want to talk about that. Can I show you the rest?"

"Yes." She reached up to caress his face. "In case I forget to say this later, thank you, Jack. This is the best surprise I've ever gotten." She drew him down and kissed him with a thoroughness that left them both breathless.

"Wow," he said when she finally released him. "I need to build you a house more often. Come see." He took her through the kitchen to show her the study, the dining room, and family room, which boasted a huge stone fireplace. Stairs from both the kitchen and the family room led to the second-floor wing he had built for the girls. "They'll each have their own bathroom, which will be critical as we face the teenage years. You'll also be glad to know I gave them each their own water heater, so there won't be any more screaming about hot water."

"You thought of everything." She didn't see one thing she would have changed. Across from the girls' rooms were three more bedrooms.

"One is a guest room with another bathroom, and the other two rooms can be used for a home gym or anything else you want."

"Okay, I'm trying to count bathrooms—"

"Six including ours: one downstairs, four up here, and one more upstairs. Seven bedrooms all together."

Her hand covered her mouth as she peeked into the guest bedroom. "It's so overwhelming." The house had been built to keep

25

the ocean view prominent in almost every room. He'd left all the walls white so she could choose the paint colors.

"You've got to see the best part." He took her hand to guide her to a spiral staircase in the middle of the second floor. "After you."

She walked up the winding stairs, opened the door at the top, and let out a shriek. The top floor was circular with walls made entirely of glass, offering a view of the beach and fresh-water reservoir. A fireplace in the middle divided the bedroom and sitting areas. It was the only room that was furnished with a new king-size cherry sleigh bed and rich leather furniture in the sitting room.

She turned to him with fresh tears in her eyes. "Oh, Jack, it's exactly as you described it."

"You remember?"

"Of course I do. We used to lie in bed in the apartment on Beacon Hill, and you'd describe this to me down to the smallest detail. It's so much better than I ever imagined."

He nudged her toward the spacious master bathroom where he'd put a huge Jacuzzi tub. Everything was marble and shiny new.

"There's one more thing. Come on out here." He opened the sliding door to a small deck that hung over the pool area and rocky shoreline below.

"Oh, look at this!" She marveled at the view. The winter ocean foamed with frigid rage as the gulls dove for lunch in the surf. Off in the distance, a stretch of sandy beach was deserted and barren except for a few hardy runners and their dogs. "It's just so amazing. The most beautiful house I've ever seen."

"I'm glad you like it." The relief showed on his face. "I was kind of worried."

"Like it? I love it! Why were you worried?"

He shrugged and grinned. "I've been married long enough to know how particular women are about their houses."

"You shouldn't have worried. I love every inch of it. I'm so lucky to have such a talented husband." She kissed him again the way she had downstairs and threw her arms around him in sheer delight. "I love it, I love you, and I want to see it again."

He leaned down for another of those kisses she was handing out. "All in good time," he said, leading her back inside and closing the door against the December cold.

She put her hands on his chest to steer him backward to the new bed.

He fell on the bed, pulling her down on top of him. "You know, when they christen a new ship, they break a bottle of champagne over the bow," he said with a glint in his eye.

She kissed him. "Yes, I've heard that."

He wrapped his arms around her. "Do you know how new houses are christened?"

"I think I'm about to find out."

KATE WALKED out the front door. "Mom?"

Clare shook her head and snapped out of her remembrance. "I'm coming."

"Everything okay?"

"Yes, honey, everything's fine. Let's go in, shall we?"

CHAPTER 4

*T*he house was more or less as she remembered it. Furniture had been moved, carpeting replaced, new photos hung, and plants had either died or grown beyond recognition. True to his word, Jack had made her a bedroom in the study, and the downstairs bathroom had been outfitted with handrails. The girls had brought her clothes down from the attic and hung them in the study closet.

Clare's mother planned to spend a month with her, and Sally Coleman, the nurse who'd overseen her care during the coma, would be coming in every day to continue Clare's physical therapy.

The girls had a welcome-home party and made her favorite dinner of steak on the grill with baked potatoes and salad. They were so delighted to have her home that Clare got caught up in their excitement. But as the evening wore on, it became clear to her that nothing was right.

She began to have trouble swallowing her panic. Where was Jack? Would he really never again come bounding in from work full of passion and excitement, bursting to tell her about a design he'd finished, a client he'd landed, or a laugh he'd shared with Jamie?

How was it possible he didn't live here anymore? Or that he'd shared this home, even temporarily, with another woman? How could he have married her? How did this happen? All the emotions she'd managed to keep at bay during the long months in the hospital surged to the surface. Her chest tightened, and she knew she was going to cry in front of the girls if she didn't escape immediately.

Clare stood, and Maggie jumped up to get her crutches. "Thank you for the lovely dinner. Would you please excuse me?" She hobbled into the study and closed the door.

~

MAGGIE TURNED TO HER GRANDMOTHER. "What's wrong with her?"

"I think she's just overwhelmed, honey." Anna reached out to pat her granddaughter's hand. "She's got to get used to a lot of changes in her life."

The phone rang, and Kate got up to answer it.

"Hi, Dad." Kate glanced over at the others. "Yes, she's home. It all went fine." She held the phone to the side with her hand over the mouthpiece. "He wants to talk to Mom. Should I get her?"

"Let me." Anna took the cordless phone from Kate. "Why don't you girls start cleaning up?" She walked into the family room. "Hi, Jack. It's Anna."

"Hi, Anna. Is everything all right?"

"Everything's fine, but I don't think Clare's up to chatting right now. Can I have her give you a call in a day or two?"

"Sure. I just wanted to make sure she has everything she needs. I could come by—"

Through the phone, Anna could hear a baby crying. "I don't think that would be a good idea. She needs some time to get used to the way things are now, and having you here…"

"That's fine, I understand."

"I'm sorry."

"Don't be. You're right. I'll stay away for a while. I'm glad she has you and the girls to lean on right now."

"We'll take good care of her. Don't worry. It was good of you to call."

"It's good of you to still be so nice to me."

"Why wouldn't I be?"

"It's just this whole thing, it's so...well...I guess messy is the best word I can think of."

"It's bound to be for a while, but it'll get better when you've all had some time to adjust. In the meantime, let her call the shots for now, okay?"

"Of course. Please let her know I called."

"I will. By the way, congratulations to you and Andi. I hear you have two beautiful baby boys."

"Thank you. I'm sure you can hear them raising a ruckus."

"You'd better go. Take care of yourself, Jack."

"Bye, Anna."

Anna clicked off the phone and thought about the lovely young man her daughter had been married to. Clare still loved him so much. This whole situation would be easier if she could hate him or blame him for the end of what had been a beautiful marriage. But it wasn't that simple. If it had been, Clare wouldn't hurt like she did.

CLARE DIDN'T LEAVE her room again that evening.

At around ten, her mother knocked on the study door to check on her. "Are you all right?"

Clare looked up from the rocking chair where she sat with Frannie's journal. "I'm fine. I'm sorry about earlier. I'll talk to the girls in the morning."

"There's no need. They understand. Jack called to make sure you got home. I told him you'd call him in a day or two."

"Thanks. I couldn't deal with that tonight."

"That's what I figured. What've you got there?" Anna asked with a nod at the book.

Clare explained about the journal Frannie had kept. "It's helping me to put some pieces together."

"Do you think you should be looking at that tonight? You've had a difficult day."

"It's okay. I'll see you in the morning, Mom. Thanks for everything. I'm glad you're here."

"Just holler if you need anything."

"I will."

Anna closed the door, and Clare went back to the journal, unable to resist feasting on Frannie's words.

FEBRUARY 14

Jamie came over, bringing gifts as he always does. He's forever dropping by to check on us, and he always has something for the girls. Today he brought them everything to make ice cream sundaes. He had roses for me, and the card said, "Thank you for all you're doing to take care of my favorite girls. Love, Jamie." I know I must have blushed fifty shades of red, but it was so sweet of him.

MARCH 22

Maggie told me she's made a new friend. She wasn't sure how to tell her friend about what's wrong with her mother. We had a long talk, but I could tell she's still worried. When I began to notice the girls never bring their friends home anymore, I decided to talk to Jack about making some changes around here. It's time to think about moving Clare somewhere else so the girls can have their home back. Broaching that subject makes me nervous, but he needs to hear it.

MAY 12

A year since Clare's accident...

MAY 31

Today was moving day. Jack bought a condo on the beach for Clare about a mile from home. It was awful to watch them take her from the house she loved so much and to wonder if she'll ever return. I thought Jack was sad before, but this is worse. He's locked himself in his room, and I can't think of anything I can do for him.

JUNE 3

Jack has finally given up his daily vigil at Clare's bedside and is refocused on the girls. Poor Maggie had so many questions for him. He did his best to help her understand that her mother isn't going to get better, but it was agonizing for him—and for her. He's making a real effort to reconnect with the girls, but it's going to take some time. This weekend he's taking them out to the island. They don't really want to go, but he desperately needs to spend some time with them. I'll be hoping it goes well for all of them.

JUNE 17

Jack and the girls seem better since their weekend in Block Island. I'm not sure what happened when they were there, but they've been nicer to him and more accepting of his new role as their only parent. I'm glad for him—for all of them.

JULY 9

Jack finally went back to work today. Thank God.

CLARE CLOSED the book and held it to her chest. There'd been so much pain and heartache. It was like the man who attacked her had set off a tsunami in the lives of everyone she loved. Now that the water had finally receded, she felt as if she'd landed alone on an island with absolutely no idea what she was supposed to do next.

CHAPTER 5

Two weeks after she got home, Anna drove Clare to an appointment with her psychiatrist, Dr. Richard Baker. He'd been working with her since she remembered being raped and had been instrumental in helping her to cope with all the changes in her life since her recovery.

He arrived five minutes late, seeming frazzled.

"Sorry to keep you waiting, Clare." He tossed his briefcase on the desk and shrugged out of his tweed sports coat. "I got called into a consult at the hospital."

"That's more important."

He sat across from her with a pad of paper balanced on his knee. "I'm sorry we were unable to meet before you went home."

She smiled. "I heard you were in Greece."

"My wife surprised me with the trip for our thirtieth anniversary. I didn't realize it would coincide with your release from the hospital. How's everything going?"

She shrugged. "Okay, I guess."

"Just okay?"

"It's very strange being home. Everything's the same—but so different, too."

He made a note on his pad. "Let's talk about what's different."

"Well, Jill doesn't live there anymore. She's in college. Kate's a high school graduate with a job and a car, so I hardly see her."

"What about Maggie?"

"She's been spending a lot of time at Jack's house. There's a lot of excitement there with the babies and all."

He looked up with surprise. "They had the babies already?"

"They arrived a month early, in the midst of their parents' wedding."

Dr. Baker tapped his lip with his pen. "Wow. How do you feel about that?"

Clare shrugged. "I'm happy for them that everything went well."

"That's awfully generous of you. Hold that thought for a minute. Let's go back to Maggie. What kind of custody arrangement have you worked out for her?"

"Nothing formal. We've been doing two nights on, two nights off, with a few deviations."

"How does she get back and forth?"

"Jack usually drives her, but sometimes she comes with Kate."

"So you see him often?"

"Most of the time just to wave to when he drops Maggie off. He's giving me some space at the advice of my mother," Clare said with a wry grin.

"Do you need the space?"

She looked down at her hands, which twisted back and forth in her lap, and nodded.

"You don't want to see him?"

She shook her head and was stunned to realize she was going to cry.

"Clare?"

"I can't stand being in that house," she whispered as a fat tear rolled down her cheek. "I can't *stand* it."

"Because Jack's not there?"

"Mostly that, but *no one's* there. Well, my mother's staying with me, but that's not what I mean. Before all this, my life was about taking care of them. I had my job, but my priority was my family. I don't seem to have a family anymore. My girls went and grew up in my absence, and they don't need me anymore."

"Do you really believe that?"

"They're very self-sufficient. They make their own meals. They even do their own laundry."

"I'm sure you know they'd be doing that by now, even if you hadn't been ill."

"Of course, but I missed the transition, so it just feels like another loss."

"I'm sure it does, but you shouldn't take that to mean they don't need you. Do we ever fully outgrow our mothers?"

"I know I haven't. I don't know what I would've done without mine in the last few months."

"Well, see? There you go. Give them some time to adapt to having you back in their daily lives. They'll start to lean on you again."

"I hope so."

"What about Jack? What're you feeling toward him now that you're home?"

She felt new tears coming and fought a losing battle to contain them. "Being home has put a different spin on our divorce and everything that happened."

"How so?"

"When I was in the hospital, I knew what was going on with him and Andi, but being back in the house we shared—the house he built for me—and realizing he's never coming home again..." She shook her head. "It's just been...very hard."

He handed her a tissue. "Are you regretting your decision to let him go?"

"No." She wiped her tears. "It was the right thing to do. I still believe that being with him when he wanted to be with someone else would've been worse than this. It's just being in *our* place without him that's so unbearable."

"Have you considered moving? You could sell the house and relocate."

She shook her head. "I can't sell that house. I'll never sell it."

"Perhaps you could rent something for a couple of months. Like a transition place."

"Maybe, but not until Kate leaves for Nashville."

"It's something to think about. I can't see putting your recovery in jeopardy because of your environment. You can change that. Maybe you could even get something out of town for a while."

"I can't leave town. I can't do that to Maggie."

"Why not? What's another couple of months if your recovery's at stake? After all the time she had to be without you, I would think she'd want you to do whatever you had to so you can feel better. Her father could provide her with a stable home while you complete your recovery, right?"

"Of course."

"Then maybe you ought to think about it. Just because the doctors were satisfied enough with your physical recovery to send you home doesn't mean you were entirely ready up here." He tapped his head. "Let me ask you this: have you gotten mad with him yet?"

"Mad?"

"With Jack."

"Why would I be mad with him?"

Dr. Baker sat back in his chair and studied her. "Are you serious, Clare? Remember how angry you were when you first recovered and found out about Andi and the babies? Well, now he's married to her and has two new sons with her."

"Yes, but I've gotten past that."

"Have you really? Most women whose husbands of twenty years divorce them for another woman are usually pretty ticked off about it. Add a couple of babies and, well, you get the picture."

"It's not like everything was normal, and he went off and had an affair. I was sick for a long time, and he met someone else. What good will it do me to be mad? What'll that do for my kids?"

"How's it going being stoic? Being the one who lost the most important person in her life and is quietly taking it while everyone

36

else goes about their business? I think you're good and filthy mad, and you have no idea what to do with it."

She shook her head. "I don't feel mad. I feel sad."

"Which is also perfectly normal. Don't get me wrong. I admire what you did. I think you probably did the right thing in the long run by letting him go. But don't cheat yourself out of legitimate feelings. If you feel mad, be mad. If you feel sad, be sad. There's only one way to the other side of this, and that's straight through it. Denying any of your feelings will only make the journey longer."

She nodded and twisted the tissue in her hands.

"I want you to think about a change of scenery. I'm worried about a setback if you remain in the house."

"I'll give it some thought."

"Talk to Maggie. She might surprise you."

She smiled. "I doubt she'd mind staying with her dad for a while. That's where the action is these days."

"Think about what's best for you right now, Clare. It's time to take care of you."

"I'll think about it," she promised.

IF BEING home had caused a mental setback, it did wonders for Clare's physical health. Within a month, she was off crutches and using a cane. She still had a pronounced limp and trouble with stairs, but one day when she was home alone, she forced her unwilling legs up two flights to the top-floor suite she'd once shared with Jack. A rush of emotion hit her the moment she stepped into the room.

The big round room was empty, and she realized she'd never seen it that way before. She opened the door to what used to be Jack's closet and wanted to weep at its gaping barrenness. Walking over to the wide span of windows that overlooked the ocean, she eased herself down to the plush carpet and remembered back to when she and Jack would hustle the girls through their bedtime routine so they could escape up here to relax together.

She gazed out at the water, wanting more than anything to go back to when her girls were small and relied on her for everything, to when Jack was hers and she still believed nothing could ever come between them.

Memories rolled through her mind like home movies, scenes from the past flashing one by one. Wallowing for a moment in the warmth of the recollections, she thought about parties they'd had on the pool deck, waking with Jack to the sound of squealing girls downstairs, holidays with their extended family. The movie ran on, and for a while, she let it.

Finally, she stood up to go back downstairs. "Dr. Baker's right. I've got to get out of here."

CHAPTER 6

*A*nna decided to spend a second month with Clare and kept the two of them so busy that Clare had little time to brood. Clare knew her mother had stayed more to keep her company than to help her. While she still had the limp, Clare soon found she could leave her cane at home. As her strength returned, they took long walks on the beach and went out for dinner with friends who were delighted to see Clare after her long illness. One weekend, her brother Tony and sister Sue came from Connecticut with their families. The girls were home, too. Having a full house was almost like old times.

Almost.

Ten days before Kate was due to leave for Nashville, Dr. Langston cleared Clare to drive. Anna took her to renew her driver's license, and Clare drove them home in her Volvo with the utmost caution, never exceeding thirty miles per hour on the short ride.

The next day, Jack called. She hadn't spoken to him in a couple of weeks. When she heard his voice on the line, her stomach took a nervous dip that made her want to swear with frustration. *Nope, still not over him.* His voice was so familiar and comforting, like a well-worn pair of slippers or a favorite pillow. *Knock it off, Clare. He's not your source of comfort anymore.*

"How are you?" he asked.

"Fine, and you?" They were so sickeningly polite. She wanted to scream.

"Still sleep-deprived. I've had no luck convincing Andi to hire some help. She wants to do it all herself until she goes back to work."

Did his new wife have to be so freaking perfect? Where was the justice? "I don't blame her. You never got anywhere with me on that one either."

He chuckled. "No, I didn't. The reason I'm calling is I was hoping we could sit down with Kate to talk about her move."

"I thought you had that all figured out." She couldn't help her snippy tone. This whole thing had, after all, been his deal with Kate.

"Hell no, I don't have it figured out. That's why I want to talk to her. I want *us* to talk to her."

"Why do you need me? This was always between you and her."

Jack sighed. "This was between her and I before you recovered. Now it's between all of us. I thought you'd want to be part of it." He paused. "I need your help, Clare."

Damn him! Why did he have to say that? He'd gone straight to her Achilles' heel: her need to be needed. "Fine. When do you want to do it?"

"The sooner, the better. We're running out of days. She usually has Thursdays off at the hotel. Would this Thursday work for you, say around four? I'll come over, and I'll ask her to be there."

"That's fine."

"Thanks. Hey, did I hear you're driving again?"

"Just once so far. Dr. Langston cleared me on Friday, and my mother had me at the DMV yesterday before I could chicken out."

"That's wonderful. It'll give you some freedom."

"I suppose. Listen, Jack, there's something else I need to talk to you about."

"What's that?"

She bit her lip and lost her nerve. "Actually, it'll keep until Thursday. I'll just talk to you then."

"Is everything okay?"

Define okay. "Yes, nothing to worry about. I'll see you soon."

~

CLARE TOLD herself she would've spent an hour getting ready even if she wasn't seeing him. She would've given her hair more than the usual five minutes, dusted on a light coat of makeup, and chosen her clothes with special care because she was feeling better, not because her ex-husband was coming over. *Yeah sure, keep telling yourself that,* she thought as she slid into form-fitting jeans and a jaunty yellow top with three-quarter sleeves.

Studying herself in the full-length mirror in the downstairs bathroom, she noticed how the top hugged her breasts and was hit by a reminder of how much Jack had loved her breasts. He had rarely missed an opportunity to touch them, brush against them, or sleep with a hand between them. The memory of that intimacy took her breath away. She backed away from the mirror and wrapped a protective arm around her middle in an effort to regain her equilibrium.

How long had it been since she'd thought about being in bed with Jack? Or sleeping close to him? Or making love with him? Her face heated as a wave of longing cut through her. She yearned for him and the closeness they had always shared.

"Oh, Jack, I miss you so much," she whispered. Tears flooded her eyes as she wondered if he now slept with a hand between Andi's breasts. She shuddered at the thought, wiped her eyes, and opened the bathroom door.

"Clare?" Anna called from the kitchen.

"Coming." Clare leaned against the wall and willed the color in her cheeks to return to normal. With a deep breath, she walked into the kitchen. "Here I am."

"Don't you look nice," Anna said.

"Thanks." Clare picked up an apple from the bowl on the counter and rolled it between her hands.

"What's the occasion?"

Clare's gaze shot up to meet her mother's. She hadn't mentioned the meeting with Jack because she knew her mother was anxious to go home to Hartford for a few days and wouldn't go if she thought she might be needed. "No occasion. What time are you heading out?"

"I'm going now, so I'll be home before dark. Are you sure you'll be okay?" Anna asked, her expression fraught with motherly concern.

"Of course. Maggie will be here over the weekend, and Jill mentioned she might come home, too. I'll be fine, don't worry."

Anna kissed Clare's cheek and picked up her bag. "I'll call you tonight, and I'll be back before you know it."

"Sounds good." Clare saw her mother out the front door. As Anna pulled out of the semicircular gravel driveway, Clare waved and pushed the door closed against the November chill.

She went back into the kitchen and wandered to the full-length window to watch the ocean. Clare had always hated November. They'd often kept the pool open through October. The sailboat Jack owned with Jamie usually came out of the water at the very end of October, too. By November it was all over. Thinking about the boat reminded her of yet another thing that wasn't hers anymore. The churn of the seas gave rise to similar feelings in her as she thought about what she'd had and lost and wondered how she'd ever live without it.

THE DOORBELL RANG at the stroke of four. Clare steeled herself and opened the door with a forced smile on her face, only to be hit again by another intense blow to the belly at the sight of him. His dark hair was wind blown and his face red from the chill. The nervous, uncertain expression on his face tugged at her heart.

"Hi, come on in." She stepped aside and wondered if ringing the bell at the house that used to be his felt weird to him. The all-too-familiar scent of his cologne mixed with the earthy smell of decaying leaves that followed him in. "Can I get you some coffee or something cold?"

"No, thanks, I'm fine." He took off his black wool coat, put it over the back of a chair in the family room, and turned to her. "You look great."

"You look beat."

He grinned. "Such is life for the father of twins. They're killing me. Now I know why people have kids when they're young, not old like me."

She smiled. He didn't look a day over thirty-five. Like her, he was forty-six, but unlike her, he looked as good as he had the day they met. "Do you have a picture?"

He reached for his wallet. "Here you go."

Clare took the photo and walked past him to sit down. "*Oh*, look at them. They're adorable." They each had a full head of shiny dark hair —his hair—eyes that appeared to be hazel, and were clearly identical. She handed the photo back to him. "How do you tell them apart?"

"We put their initials on their diapers with a marker," he said. "Andi ordered ID bracelets with their names on them, but they haven't come in yet." He checked his watch. "I wonder where Kate is? I told her to be here at four."

"She didn't get your punctuality gene. Give her a few minutes and then we can try her cell phone."

"What did you want to talk to me about?"

"Let's talk to Kate first." Clare heard a car door close outside. "Here she comes."

Kate burst through the front door. "Hey, sorry, have you been waiting long?" She kissed them and flopped down on the sofa.

"No, I just got here," Jack said.

"I was out doing a few things and got stuck in a huge line at Target."

Jack groaned. "Ah yes, *Target*, where my daughters spend half my annual income," he said with a grin. "I should buy stock in the company."

"Very funny, Dad, but I spent my own money," Kate said, sticking her tongue out at him.

Jack turned to Clare with a look of disbelief. "Did you hear that? She spent her *own* money? Is that what she said?"

Clare laughed even though she didn't want to be sucked into his easy charm and effortless humor. His amused befuddlement over their daughters had always been something she adored about him. "I think that's what she said. Well, Jack, you called this meeting. What's on your mind?"

"I was just thinking we should talk about your move, Kate, and what happens after you get there."

"I'm glad you asked about that. I've made a few plans I want to tell you about, but first I just want to thank you again for letting me do this. I know it's not easy for you, and you'd rather be sending me to college."

"We want you to be happy," Jack said, reaching over to squeeze her hand. "Why don't you tell us about these plans you've made?"

"I've signed up at Belmont University to take a couple of classes."

"You have?" Clare asked, stunned.

Kate nodded. "Belmont has an excellent Entertainment and Music Business program. I'm not saying I'm going to get a degree, but if this is going to be my business, I figured I'd give it a shot. I'm taking Survey of Music Business and Survey of Recording Technology starting in January."

Jack and Clare exchanged glances as she continued.

"I've also taken my graduation money and some of what I've earned at the hotel to record a demo CD with two covers and two of my own songs. Everything I've read says you should have a demo if you want to get anywhere in Nashville."

"When did you do all this?" Jack asked, incredulous.

"In October. I knew you were busy with the babies and everything. I'm serious about this, Dad."

"I can see that."

"What about living arrangements?" Clare asked.

"I've taken care of that," Jack said. "Jamie and I have a friend from Berkeley, Reid Matthews, who lives just outside of Nashville. I called him a couple of weeks ago, and he said he owns a couple of apartment complexes in the city. He's going to let me know by tomorrow if he has any units open."

"That's great, Dad. Thanks."

"He also offered to be a point of contact for you while you're there. He's a nice guy. You'll like him."

"Sounds like between the two of you, you've got your bases covered," Clare said. "Can we hear your demo?"

"Sure, I've got it in the car. I'll run out and get it."

While they waited for her, Jack looked at Clare in amazement. "Well," he said. "She's your daughter in more than just her looks."

"How do you mean?"

"She's efficient and organized, just like you."

"And she's goal-oriented, like you."

Kate came back in, turned on the CD player, and popped in her demo. She had done covers of Stevie Nicks's "Landslide" and an acoustic guitar version of Willie Nelson's "Always on My Mind," as well as two of her own songs, "Funny," and "Since You Left."

"You sound beautiful, Kate." Clare glanced at Jack, wondering where their daughter had gotten this awesome talent. "It's so impressive."

Jack's eyes were wide with wonder. "I can't believe that's you."

Kate's pleasure showed on her face. "Thanks. I haven't played it for anyone yet. I just couldn't bring myself to do it."

"I don't know why," Clare said. "It's wonderful. I love that song, 'Landslide.'"

"I know. I always think of you when I hear it."

"I'm so proud of you, Kate," Jack said. "You've jumped right into this thing and put a lot of thought into it."

"I only have a year, and I don't want to waste a minute of it. I also answered an ad to work in a nightclub with open-mic nights. If I get the job, hopefully I can perform, too." She checked her watch. "I actually have to run. I'm taking the second half of my coworker's shift at the hotel tonight. It's his wife's birthday."

"One other thing I wanted to mention is I rented a small U-Haul for moving day, and we can attach your car to the back of it," Jack told Kate.

"I was just going to drive there and figure it out when I got there. You can't leave now with the babies and everything."

"It's all worked out. Andi's mother and aunt are coming from Chicago for a week to help out while I get you settled. They get here the day before your birthday. I promised Mom I'd take you myself."

Kate hugged him. "Thank you. You're the best, Dad." She gave her mother a hug as well. "Thank you, too, Mom. I know this isn't what you wanted for me, but I appreciate your support."

"I want whatever you want, honey," Clare said. "I'm so very proud of what a fine young woman you've grown up to be." She only wished she'd been there to see it happen.

"I love you guys. See you later," Kate said with a wave from the door. A moment later, they heard her drive away.

"I have to give you credit, Jack." The room had grown dark, so Clare reached up to flip on a lamp.

"For what?"

"You had to steer Kate and Jill through the toughest years on your own. You did a wonderful job."

"I had a lot of help. I certainly can't take all the credit."

"You can take a good chunk of it since you had to make the big decisions. You did the right thing letting her do this."

"I hope you'll still think so in a year. It's not just the twins keeping me awake at night. It's terrifying to think of that beautiful girl alone in a strange city." He shuddered.

"We just got a good demonstration of how capable she is. She'll be fine."

"Do you want to come with us to Nashville? I should've asked you sooner. I didn't realize you were getting around so well."

"Thanks for asking, but this is something you should do with her. You had the courage to agree to it, so you should take her."

"You're welcome to come if you change your mind."

"I appreciate that, but I've been making some plans of my own. That's what I wanted to talk to you about."

"What kind of plans?"

Gathering her thoughts, she looked down at the floor. When it was just the two of them together in their house, it was easy to forget that he no longer belonged there. "I'm going away for a while. At least I want to, but it all depends on your willingness to have Maggie full time."

Surprise registered on his face. "Going where?"

"To Vermont."

He stared at her as if she had said she was going to the moon. "What's in Vermont?"

"Tony bought a place up there when I was sick," she said, referring to her brother. "He's offered it to me for a few months."

Jack shook his head. "Months? I don't understand."

"No, you wouldn't." She knew she sounded almost snide but didn't care.

"What's that supposed to mean?"

"I can't stand it here!" She waved her hand to indicate the house. "You don't get it because you're not here. You're not *me* trying to live *here* without *you*." The moment she said the words, she wanted to take them back. She didn't want him to know how hard it had been.

He looked stricken. "I don't know what to say."

"Don't say anything. Just tell me you can take care of Maggie for a couple more months. I wouldn't ask you for this if I didn't need it. Really need it. I know you've already had them on your own for three years, but I'm asking for a few more months." She willed herself not to cry.

"It's not about Maggie. Of course I can take her. I just don't see why you can't stay somewhere in town if being in the house isn't working. The girls are just getting used to having you home."

She stood up and went to look out at the patio where the pool was covered for the winter. "If I stay in this town, how long do you think it'll be before I run into you and your new wife in a restaurant or at the grocery store? How long will it be before your wife is getting out again and I come face-to-face with her at the dry cleaners? I need some time to get used to it before I have to see it all the time." Keeping her back to him, she said quietly, "Don't make me beg, Jack."

"I'll take Maggie. Of course I will," he said in a wooden tone. "Will you explain this to her? She won't understand."

"I'll talk to her." Clare turned back to look at him. "I'm not trying to make you feel bad, but I can't see you all the time and expect to get past what's happened between us. I need a break."

"From me?"

"From you and your guilty face, from this house full of painful memories, from your babies and your new wife and your new life. From all of it." It took everything she had not to dissolve into a puddle of tears at the flash of pain that darted across his handsome face.

"I knew it was all too easy." He shook his head as he stood up. "You were so matter-of-fact about our divorce. I wondered when you'd start to hate me."

"I don't hate you, but if I stay here much longer, I might. I don't want that to happen."

"Then go," he said, weary and resigned. "Do what you have to do. I'll take care of Maggie."

"Thank you."

He put his coat on and walked to the front door. "I'm sorry, Clare."

She wanted to scream. *I don't want you to be sorry. I want you to be mine!* But she said nothing as he closed the door behind him.

"Come back," she whimpered, watching his car pull out of the gravel driveway. "Please come back." Only then did she allow herself to cry.

CHAPTER 7

O ver the weekend, Clare organized a girls' night with her daughters, complete with dinner, movies, and manicures.

"Do you like this color on me?" Maggie held up a hand to show off bright red nails.

"It's a bit much," Clare said as she reclined on the sofa and watched her girls. They sat around the coffee table painting their nails. "I liked the purple better."

Maggie reached for the bottle of remover. "Yeah. Me, too."

Knowing she needed to get this over with, Clare sat up and took a deep breath. "There's something I want to talk to you guys about."

Jill blew on her nails and waved her hand around to dry the polish. "What's that?"

"I've been thinking about getting away for a little while."

Kate looked up. "Getting away to where?"

"Remember Uncle Tony telling us about the house he bought in Vermont?" Clare asked, and the girls nodded. "I'm going to go up there for a bit to help him with some work he wants to have done to the house."

Maggie's eyes grew wide. "For how long?"

"Three months, maybe a little longer."

"But why?" Maggie asked, fighting off tears. "You just got home."

Clare reached down to smooth her hair. "I know, sweetheart. But here's the thing: it's really hard for me to be in this house without Dad. I guess I didn't realize just how hard it would be until I was here for a while. I need some time away to adjust to everything that's happened."

"Time away from us?" Jill asked.

"No, honey, this has nothing to do with you guys. I'm hoping you'll come to visit me all the time. You can even go skiing this winter. Maggie, I'd love to have you come with me, but your whole life is here, and I know you'd hate to be in a new school even for a little while. So Dad said he'll bring you to Boston to meet me every couple of weeks, or maybe you can come up with Jill."

"I liked knowing you'd be here even if I wasn't going to be," Kate said sadly.

"No matter where I am, I'm always available to you," Clare said. "I know we have so much time to make up for, and I hate that I feel this need to flee for a while, but I can't deny that I *do* feel it."

"So I'll live with Dad?" Maggie asked.

"Yes, and he's thrilled to know he'll have you to himself for a while," Clare said with a smile. "He said they need your help with the babies."

Maggie nodded gravely. "They *do* need me. Those babies are a handful."

"You'll have a great time being there, and we'll have fun whenever you come up for weekends," Clare said, and Maggie seemed satisfied. "What about you, Jill? Will you come up?"

Jill shrugged. "Sure. If that's where you'll be, I'll come see you and bring Maggie. It sure is better than where you were for the last three years."

Clare's eyes filled. "Anywhere's better than that." She reached out to hug them. "I love you all so much. I know I've already put you through such a terrible ordeal, and I'm asking a lot of you."

"It's okay, Mom," Kate said. "We want you to feel better again."

"I'll fly you up for the weekend whenever you want to come," Clare said, brushing a hand over Kate's soft blonde hair.

"When are you going?" Maggie asked.

"Next week. Right after Kate leaves for Nashville."

"Speaking of that," Kate said. "Dad and Andi are having a birthday-slash-going-away party for me the night before my birthday. I hope you'll come. He's going to call you about it."

Clare's stomach clenched with anxiety. "I don't know, sweetie. I'm not sure I'm up for that."

"You *have* to come, Mom," Kate pleaded. "I want you to come."

Clare bit her thumbnail. "Let me think about it."

CLARE WAS awake half the night trying to imagine herself socializing with Jack and his new wife at their new home. She was sick just thinking about it, so she couldn't imagine what it would be like to actually *be* there. But how could she say no to Kate when she'd missed so much with the girls?

"*Ugh,*" Clare groaned. At four thirty, she gave up on sleep and decided to get up. There was no point in trying to sleep when her head was spinning. As she walked out to the kitchen to make coffee, all she could think about was Kate's face when she'd all but begged her to come to the party.

By the time the girls began appearing just before eleven, Clare had finished a pot of coffee, baked blueberry muffins, and cleaned the kitchen. The work had helped to occupy her mind.

"Morning," Jill grumbled as she came into the kitchen in search of coffee.

Clare poured Jill a cup from the fresh pot she had just made. It still amused her to see the older girls drinking coffee. "Morning, honey. Did you sleep well?"

Jill nodded and inhaled her first sip of coffee.

"What's up for you today?"

"I have to be back to school for a study group meeting at two."

"Have you given any more thought to declaring a major? You have to do that by January, right?"

Jill nodded again. "I'm thinking about pre-law."

Clare raised a surprised eyebrow. "Really? Since when?"

Jill took a muffin and her coffee to the table. "For a while, actually. I'm taking a constitutional law class this semester that I love."

"That's wonderful. You also love to argue, so you'd make a terrific attorney."

Jill grinned. "Dad said the same thing."

That stung. In the past, Clare would have been the first to hear this kind of news.

"Hey, I've been meaning to ask one of you: do you know where my snow boots might be?" Clare asked. "I can't find them anywhere."

"I think Andi put all that stuff down in the basement by the oil tank."

"Oh," Clare said, struck by the reminder that Andi had lived in the house with Jack and the girls for more than a year. "I haven't looked down there. Thanks."

Maggie shuffled into the kitchen with a grouchy look on her face. "Does anyone have a tampon?"

"*Maggie*," Clare gasped. "How long have you had your period?"

"Almost a year. Since right after my birthday."

"I have some," Jill said and went upstairs to get them.

"*God*," Clare groaned as she flopped down onto one of the kitchen chairs. "Have I missed *everything*? It's so early. You were just twelve!"

"Believe me, I know," Maggie said.

"What a thing to go through without your mother," Clare said, filled with regret.

"It's okay, I had—" Maggie stopped herself and blushed.

"You had Andi, didn't you?" Clare asked softly.

Maggie nodded. "She gave me what I needed and took me out to dinner to celebrate. She made a big deal about it. Totally over the top."

Clare could tell Maggie was playing it down to spare her feelings.

"It was nice of her to do that." Clare once again fought off what was becoming a constant urge to weep.

Jill returned with a handful of tampons and handed them to her sister. "Here you go."

"Thanks," Maggie said and shuffled off to the bathroom.

Kate came in with her hair still wet from the shower. "Morning," she said as she reached for a travel mug for her coffee. "I've got to go. I'm working at the hotel at noon, and then they're having a going-away party for me."

"No drinking, right?" Clare asked.

"I don't drink. You can save that speech for Jill," Kate said with a teasing grin for her sister.

"Shut *up*, Kate," Jill said in a singsong voice.

Kate laughed. "Mom, I was thinking about the party at Dad's. I'll understand if you can't come. It's okay."

Clare kissed her middle daughter. "Thanks, baby."

AFTER JILL and Kate had left, Jack called.

"How are you?" he asked tentatively.

"I'm fine. I'm sorry for making such a scene the other day."

"Don't be sorry. I really am fine with having Maggie. I don't want you to think I have any problem with that."

"I know. Thanks."

"Did Kate mention the party we're having Friday night?"

"She did."

"I hope you and your mother can join us."

"I don't know, Jack. I'm not sure that's such a good idea."

"Whatever you think is best. I just wanted you to know you're invited."

"Thank you."

"Do you remember we have an appointment on Tuesday with Cooper to sign the papers for the house?"

"I have it on the calendar."

"There's one thing about that."

"Is there a problem?" She wondered if he was regretting giving her the house in the divorce.

"No, but I've asked Coop to include a provision in the transfer papers that says you can only sell it to me."

Clare felt a flash of temper. "Why? So you can move your new family in here?"

"No, Clare, so I can give it to the girls someday if you don't want it," he said in a controlled tone that told her he was struggling to contain his own anger.

"I'm sorry. That was out of line. I'd never sell this house, and I'd certainly never do it without consulting you first."

He sighed. "I hate this."

She blinked back tears. "I do, too. I think it's good I'm going away for a while, Jack. We could both use the space."

"Maybe. I'll see you Tuesday at two?"

"I'll be there."

"Tell Maggie I'll be by to get her around five today," he added.

"I will."

ON TUESDAY, Clare arrived ahead of Jack at their attorney's office. Cooper Hayes was a strapping ex-football player and a teddy bear of a man who'd been their good friend for years.

"How are you, sweetheart?" he asked as he enveloped Clare in one of his monster hugs.

"I'm good, Coop. Janice came by the other day. It was great to see her."

"She loved seeing you, too."

"How're the boys?" Clare asked, even though she'd gotten the full update from Janice.

"Barry's a sophomore at UNH," he said, referring to the University of New Hampshire. "And Jeff started at Cornell in September. We've got ourselves an empty nest all of a sudden."

"Janice and I shared a few tears over it the other day."

Coop shook his head. "Poor gal, she's been weepy for months now. I need to take her off on a long vacation soon. She needs it."

"And you don't?" Clare asked with a wry smile. Those boys had been Coop's whole world for years.

"You got me," he said with a sad expression. "I'm sorry about all of this, Clare."

She knew he meant her divorce and reached a hand out to him. "Thanks."

Clare's breath got caught in her throat when Jack walked in with a smile and a handshake for Coop. Once again she wondered how long it would take before her heart stopped fluttering every time she saw him or heard his voice. Months? Years? Forever?

He leaned down to kiss her cheek as they said hello.

After they'd caught up for a few minutes, Coop gestured for them to have a seat at the table in his office. "You've discussed the sale provision?"

"Yes," Jack said.

"Okay with you, Clare?" Coop asked.

"Yes," she said, anxious to get it done. All of a sudden, the big room felt small and airless.

"All right, then. I need you both to sign here, here, and here." Coop pointed to the bottom of three pages.

Clare saw Jack hesitate before he signed the first page. A muscle twitched in his cheek, and it saddened her to realize he was emotional about signing away the house he'd built for her. She wanted to reach out to him but curbed the urge.

He scrawled "John J. Harrington" across the bottom of the first page and pushed it over to her.

When they'd signed each page, Coop gathered them up. "You'll receive the deed in about six weeks, Clare. That's all there is to it."

"Thanks, Coop," Jack said, standing to shake his hand.

"Yes, thank you," Clare added. "For everything." He'd handled their divorce with discretion and dispatch.

"No problem," Coop said as he saw them to the door. "Take care of yourselves."

~

CLARE WALKED with Jack to the parking lot. The feelings generated by what they'd just done left Clare feeling bruised. She was the proud owner of a one-of-a-kind million-dollar home, but all she felt was a gnawing, aching emptiness.

"Thank you, Jack," she said, her voice thick with emotion. "I know that wasn't easy for you."

He shrugged. "It's your house. Always was. It was only in my name so I could surprise you with it."

When her eyes burned with tears, Clare wanted to swear out loud. Her body had once again betrayed her fierce desire to show him none of what she felt.

He reached for her hand. "There's something I need to say to you."

Looking up at him, she was stunned to see his eyes had filled, too. "What?" she asked in a whisper.

He appeared to struggle for the right words and for control of his emotions. "This life of ours, it was taken from me, too, Clare," he said in a slow, soft tone. "What we had together—it was mine, too, and just because I have Andi now doesn't mean I don't mourn what I lost with you. What was *stolen* from us. I've just had a lot more time to get used to being without it than you have. I don't want you to think I walked away without a single look back, because I didn't. I couldn't have."

Tears rolled down her cheeks unchecked, brought on by the raw pain she saw on his face.

"I will *always* love you." He wiped away her tears with his thumbs and then wrapped his arms around her. "I needed you to know that."

"Jack." Crying softly, she rested her face on his chest and wallowed in the familiar scent of him. "I don't know what to do without you and our life together. I sound so pathetic even saying it, but I just don't know."

"You'll figure it out. I know you will. Go to Vermont. Do what you need to do, and I'll take care of things here. It's going to be okay, though. Somehow, someway, we'll get through this."

She reached up to caress his face. "I'll always love you, too. Maybe if I can make peace with that, I might just be able to find a life for myself without you."

He hugged her again. "Then go find some peace."

CHAPTER 8

The next week was a flurry of activity as Clare helped Kate pack and make final preparations for her move to Nashville. Jack's college friend, Reid Matthews, had come through with an apartment for Kate in the city's trendy Green Hills neighborhood, which was close to Belmont University where she'd registered for classes.

Friday morning dawned cold and gray, and the weather forecast called for snow flurries. Clare awoke with a sense of dread. The party was that night, and Kate would be leaving with Jack early the next morning.

Clare got up to shower and get dressed. In the kitchen, her mother was already sipping a cup of coffee and reading the morning paper.

"Morning," Anna said.

"Anything in the news?"

"Same old doom and gloom." Anna pushed the paper aside. Her short gray hair was still damp from the shower. "What time's the party tonight?"

"I don't know." Clare poured a cup of coffee and looked out at the stormy-looking ocean.

"We'll have to ask Kate."

"I'm not going."

"Excuse me?"

"I talked to Kate about it. She understands."

"Really?" Anna crossed her arms, and her bright blue eyes narrowed with displeasure. "What exactly does she understand?"

"That I don't feel up to being in the company of her father and his new wife just yet."

Anna snorted. "Grow up, Clare. This isn't about you. This is about your *daughter*—the daughter who had to celebrate *three* birthdays without her mother."

Stunned by her mother's outburst, Clare stared at her. "If you're trying to make me feel guilty, you're succeeding."

"Good. Then you'll come?"

"I didn't say that."

"I've tried to mind my own business during all of this, but I can't sit by and let you do this to Kate. She needs you to be there tonight to show your support and to give her a proper send-off."

"I can't," Clare whispered, remembering the emotional exchange with Jack earlier in the week. "I just *can't*."

Anna stood up. "Fine. You do what you have to do, but you'll regret this, Clare. You'll regret disappointing her."

After her mother left the room, Clare sat back and fumed. *How dare she? What does she know about it? What does* anyone *know about it?* Clare nurtured her anger for several minutes until, all at once, the fury subsided and she was swamped with remorse. Her mother was right. She was being childish and thinking only of herself when her daughter needed her. She went into the family room to find her mother.

"The party's at seven. We'll leave a little before."

"That's fine," Anna said.

CLARE and her mother drove through the gates at Jack's house just after seven. The girls had gone over earlier to help with party preparations. The house was alive with lights and electric candles in every window. Clare parked her car across the driveway from where a small U-Haul sat with Kate's yellow Volkswagen Beetle attached to the back. Clare's grip on the steering wheel tightened when she was hit by a new burst of anxiety.

"Are you all right?" Anna asked.

Clare was finding it hard to breathe. "Sure."

"You're doing this for Kate," Anna reminded her. "Keep that in mind."

"Yes, for Kate." Clare exhaled a long deep breath. "Let's go."

They carried birthday gifts as they crossed the driveway to the stone stairs. Clare rang the bell and heard the chimes echo inside the big house—Jack and Andi's house. *You're doing this for your daughter.*

Kate answered the door. "Mom! You came!" She drew them into the foyer. "Hi, Gram."

"Happy birthday, sweetheart," Anna said with a hug for her grand-daughter.

Kate sparkled with excitement. "Thanks. Let me take your coats."

Clare stole a quick glance around the 1930s-era house. She'd been inside it once before, the last time it was on the market when the listing agent held an open house for other Realtors. At that time, it had been empty and devoid of life, but now the home pulsed with the warmth and energy brought by a family.

She looked up at the elaborate crystal chandelier that hung from the second floor over the black-and-white tiled foyer. A staircase ascended from right to left, framed by a mahogany banister. To the right, Clare remembered a great room that stretched the width of the house. A formal dining room was to the left, and the kitchen was at the end of a hallway under the stairs.

Jack came through the hallway as Kate took their coats. He wore a black cashmere sweater with jeans, and as usual he managed to look casual and elegant at the same time.

He hugged and kissed them both. "Come on in," he said, ushering them into the great room where a fire burned in the fireplace. The room's fifteen-foot ceilings were edged with elaborate mahogany crown molding. Smaller moldings framed the butter-colored walls. The far end of the room was an expanse of glass, and Clare recalled an exquisite ocean view during the day.

Furniture was artfully arranged into two sitting areas by the fire. Tables were laden with food, and a bar had been set up in the far corner. Clare knew Andi had been a decorator at the Infinity Group's corporate headquarters in Chicago before she moved to Rhode Island to live with Jack and manage Infinity's Newport hotel. Clearly, she hadn't lost her flaire for her previous profession. The room was warm and inviting.

"Your home is lovely, Jack," Anna said. "You've been busy."

"We had the party as an incentive to get settled quickly. Upstairs is still a disaster area. Boxes everywhere."

Kate handed her mother a beer and her grandmother a glass of wine and went to answer the door again. She returned a few minutes later with Jack's sister Frannie, her husband Jamie, and their twins Owen and Olivia.

Clare was weak with relief to see Frannie and walked over with Jack to greet them. Jack scooped up the twins, who greeted "Unca Jack" with wet, sloppy kisses.

"You remember Aunt Clare, right?" Frannie said to the fifteen-month-old toddlers. They had visited Clare's house two weeks earlier.

Owen reached out to pat Clare's face. "Clare," he said.

Clare kissed the baby's pudgy hand. Owen and Olivia had their father's bright blue eyes and strawberry-blond hair that was an adorable mix of Frannie's auburn and Jamie's blond.

Jamie hugged Clare and kissed her cheek. "So good to see you," he whispered as he held her close.

Hugging him was like coming home. He had been Jack's best friend since their first day of college, as well as their best man and godfather to all three girls. His marriage to Jack's sister Frannie had been one of the biggest and best surprises to confront Clare after her recovery.

"Jamie Booth, you handsome devil," she whispered. "Don't let go, okay?"

He chuckled. "Never."

When Clare reluctantly released him, she noticed Andi had come into the room.

She extended a hand to them. "Clare, Anna, we're so glad you could come."

Startled by her beauty, Clare shook her hand. The only other time Clare had seen Andi, she'd been seven-months pregnant with the twins. She had obviously bounced back quickly from their birth.

"Thank you for including us," Clare said when she had recovered from the initial shock of seeing Jack and Andi together for the first time—both of them tall, dark and beautiful. *What a striking couple they make.*

As Andi moved on to greet Frannie and Jamie, and with the others occupied with new arrivals, Clare took a moment to study Andi more closely. She was tall—not as tall as Jack—but at least four inches taller than the five-foot five-inch Clare. Her long, dark curls were contained tonight in a simple ponytail, and she managed to look classy and understated in an ivory ribbed turtleneck, well-worn jeans, and black boots. Clare was glad she too had chosen to wear jeans. Andi's soft brown eyes were warm and welcoming as she greeted a group of Kate's friends. Clare knew Andi was thirty-nine, but she didn't look it and didn't show any of the weariness the mother of three-month-old twins must surely feel.

Jill and Maggie came around with hot hors d'oeuvres. They introduced Clare to Andi's mother, Betty, who held one of the twin boys.

"Hello there," Clare said, running a finger along the baby's downy soft cheek.

"That's Johnny," Betty said.

"How can you tell?" Clare asked.

"I just changed him for bed," Betty said with a chuckle. "Otherwise your guess would be as good as mine."

A blond boy dashed through the room, and Betty stopped him with a stern look. She used her free hand to sign a command to the hearing-impaired boy, and he slowed to a walk.

"That's my other grandson, Eric," Betty said to Clare. "He's almost eight and a handful."

"He's adorable." Clare watched Maggie wrap an arm around Eric without missing a beat in her conversation with a friend of Kate's.

Clare moved out of the fray to sit on one of the leather sofas. She watched Jack and Andi circulate through the room, noticing how they moved with the easy grace of a long-married couple. She was forced to look away when Jack put a hand on the small of Andi's back to draw her closer to him. He did it so naturally and unconsciously that Clare ached when she remembered him touching her that way.

The room vibrated with music, voices, and the sound of ice striking crystal.

Frannie sat down next to Clare. "Hanging in?" she asked under her breath.

"By a thread," Clare replied in the same tone.

"You look wonderful. You're all recovered."

"Except for this nagging limp I can't seem to shake."

"You will," Frannie said with a glance across the room at Jamie, who held Olivia as he chatted with Jack and Andi.

"I finished the journal," Clare said. "It was quite a story when Jack met Andi and you and Jamie got together."

Frannie smiled. "That was one hell of a week."

"Tell me about it, Frannie. I read about it, but I want you to tell me."

Frannie raised a skeptical eyebrow. "Really?"

Clare nodded. "This is the first time I've seen them together. It's made me curious more than anything."

Frannie took a deep breath. "Well, it was late August, and Andi came from Chicago to do a site visit in preparation for decorating the Newport hotel. At the time, she was the director of interior design for Infinity. Jack took her around to the mansions, Hammersmith Farm, and some of the other highlights. We went out on the boat and had a cookout at the house for all the designers. It was the first party we'd had at the house since everything happened, and it was fun."

"Your journal said that's when things between you and Jamie

heated up, too." Clare noticed Jack and Frannie's parents, Madeline and John, had arrived, and Clare looked forward to visiting with her former in-laws.

Frannie waved to her parents. "That's right. There'd been this thing between us *forever*, and neither of us ever admitted it to each other or anyone else." Her gaze softened when it landed on her handsome husband.

Clare smiled. "I *always* wondered."

"Did you? We were so surprised to discover we'd both had all these feelings for each other for *years*." Frannie still seemed astounded by it, even more than two years later. "I guess when we saw Jack rejoining the land of the living, it felt like the time was right for us, too."

"You guys seem so happy together."

Frannie smiled. "We are."

"So what happened with Jack and Andi?"

"You're *sure* you want to hear this?"

"It's okay," Clare said with a wave to her mother who was across the room with Jill and Frannie's son, Owen.

"Well, Jack said later it was love at first sight. It was quite overwhelming for him, because he'd only recently given up trying to find help for you and had just been back to work for a month or so at that point. I remember something he said to me that week. I never forgot it. He said, 'I wasn't expecting to meet someone who'd make me want more.' There was this helplessness to him. He worried about what people would say, and he was concerned about the girls." Frannie shrugged. "It was tough for him, Clare. He agonized over it. Don't think he didn't. But he'd suffered so much that I remember being relieved to see a spark of life back in his eyes."

"She went back to Chicago, right?"

Frannie nodded. "But he talked her into coming back to visit for a weekend. They had a wonderful time, but she decided that because of the distance and all the complications it just wasn't going to work out between them. We tried to be supportive and to give him some space, but it was awful. He was so sad again. Strangely enough, it was right around then that Jamie proposed."

"I'm so sorry I missed that part."

"I was, too. I needed you to be my matron of honor."

Clare's eyes filled as she hugged her. "Oh, Frannie."

"The girls did a wonderful job as my bridesmaids, but I never missed you more than I did during the months before my wedding." Frannie dabbed at her eyes and shook off the melancholy. "Anyway, Jack moped around for a week or so after Andi left. Then my mother apparently gave him a talking to about life being too short to miss out on a chance to be happy. The next thing we knew, he was on his way to Chicago. I never heard much about what happened out there, but whatever he did must've worked. They started spending weekends and holidays together. She came with Eric when Quinn got married," Frannie said, referring to Jack's longtime assistant at work. "Then we had a hurricane that kept them here for a week."

"A bad one?" Clare asked.

"Not as bad as it could've been but enough to disrupt travel for days. Long story short, Jack asked her to move here, and Andi's boss sweetened the pot by offering her the job managing the Newport hotel. She and Eric moved here the following February."

"That was after your wedding, right?"

"Right. We got married on New Year's Eve."

"I've wondered about how the girls reacted when he told them she was moving in."

"Well, they'd spent quite a bit of time with her by then, and Maggie, in particular, was just wild about Eric. Kate was very supportive. She said she wanted him to be happy. Jill was upset about it at first, but she came around in time."

Clare glanced at Andi across the room. She had a baby in her arms as she visited with her guests. "She seems hard not to like."

Frannie chuckled. "You're right. She was good with the girls and respected the boundaries. I think that's why it worked out so well."

Jack walked over to them, holding the other baby. "Frannie, can I give Robby to you for a minute?"

She held out her arms. "Of course. Come see Auntie Frannie, big guy."

"Clare, we probably should offer up a toast to our daughter. Are you game?" Jack held out a hand to help her up.

She took his hand. "Only if you do the talking. You're better at that stuff than I am."

Clare stood next to Jack by the fireplace as he clinked a spoon against his glass to quiet the room.

"I want to thank you all for coming tonight. We're here to wish Kate a happy eighteenth birthday and to wish her well as she begins the next phase of her life." He cleared his throat. "In Nashville," he said, appearing to choke on the word as his guests chuckled. "Kate, I find it very hard to believe you're already eighteen, and just to be sure, I got out your birth certificate today." He reached into his pocket to retrieve a piece of paper.

Kate groaned and made a face at him.

Jack held up the birth certificate. "The dates don't lie, so like it or not, it's time for us to let you go. All we can do is hope that when you're a big star you won't forget to come home once in a while. Your mother and I are so proud of you, and we love you very much." He raised his glass. "To Kate."

Kate's cheeks turned red as her guests saluted her. She walked over to hug her father, and Clare was once again startled to witness the new level of intimacy between Jack and the girls. While he'd always been a wonderful father, his relationship with his daughters had clearly grown and deepened during her long illness. Kate pulled back from him and reached for her mother.

"Will you play for us, Kate?" Clare asked as she hugged her daughter.

"I'd love to." Kate looked at her father with a big grin on her face. "I have a song just for you."

"Why am I afraid?" he asked.

"Oh, be *very* afraid," Kate joked and went to find her guitar.

The room quieted again when Kate began to strum the opening notes of the song. "This is by someone I hope to meet someday— Martina McBride—and it's for you, Dad." She launched into the chorus for "Independence Day."

Jack tossed his head back with laughter. "Very funny, Kate."

She gave him a wicked grin as she finished the song. "This one's for everyone else," she said, launching into a haunting rendition of Sarah McLaughlin's "I Will Remember You."

"She sure is something, isn't she?" Madeline Harrington asked Clare.

Clare had been so absorbed in Kate, she hadn't seen Jack walk away. She glanced at her former mother-in-law. "She sure is. She's going to get where she wants to be."

"I'm not sure whether to hope *for* that or *against* it," Madeline said with a sigh.

"You don't approve."

"It's not about approval. I worry—no more or less than you and Jack, I'm sure."

"I have a good feeling about it. I didn't at first, but she inherited Jack's ability to get things done. I don't think I ever really saw that before now."

"You've succeeded in making a doting old grandmother feel better," Madeline said with a smile. "It's so good to have you here with us. Sometimes I still can't believe it. We wished for it for so long."

Touched, Clare squeezed the older woman's hand. "Thank you for all the phone calls and cards and visits. You've always been so good to me."

"I love you, Clare, and I always will. For the rest of my life you *are* my daughter-in-law, and next summer I want to see you at Haven Hill, do you hear me?" Madeline referred to her home on Block Island where they'd summered together for years when the girls were younger.

"I promise," Clare said as she hugged her. "I love you, too, Madeline."

"Well, I told Betty I'd help her get the babies down. It's going to take both grannies to settle those rascals."

Clare chuckled. "Good luck."

Jill walked up to them with a baby brother in one arm and the ice bucket in the other. She handed the baby to her grandmother. "I hear you're on bedtime duty."

"That's right." Madeline held her grandson up to gaze at him. "And which one are you, my love?"

"Robby," Jill said. "I think."

"Does that need a refill?" Clare asked, pointing to the ice bucket. When Jill nodded, Clare took it from her. "I'll do it."

"Thanks, Mom. Right through there," Jill said, pointing the way.

"I'll find it." Clare wove through clusters of people on her way to the hallway off the great room. She pushed open the swinging kitchen door to find Jack resting his forehead against Andi's. Her hands were on his face as she spoke softly to him.

Clare froze. "I'm sorry."

CHAPTER 9

*A*s if she'd touched something hot, Andi's hands fell from her husband's face.

"Clare, come in," Jack said.

Clare felt her cheeks heat with color. "I didn't mean to interrupt."

"You didn't," Andi said graciously. "Do we need more ice?" She took the bucket from Clare. "It's out in the garage. I'll get it."

When Clare turned to go back the way she'd come, Jack stopped her. "Clare."

She turned to him and fought through her embarrassment at having witnessed a tender moment between her ex-husband and his new wife.

"I'm glad you came tonight. I know it means a lot to Kate that you're here."

She nodded. "We're going soon. I still get tired far too easily, and you've got an early morning."

He groaned. "She wants to leave at five."

Clare smiled. "She's not wasting a minute."

"We'd be leaving at midnight if she'd had her way."

"Your mother's worried about Kate."

"Believe me, I know. I've heard *all* about it."

"Well, have a safe trip, and thanks again for taking her."

"I promised I would."

"Make sure she calls me when you get there."

"Will do. When are you leaving for Vermont?"

"In the next few days. I've been so busy getting Kate ready that I haven't packed a thing for myself yet."

"Keep in touch while you're there."

"I will."

Andi came back in with the refilled ice bucket.

Jack took it from her. "I've got it," he said and went back out to the party.

Clare started to follow him but turned back. "Andi?" she said. "I want to thank you for giving this lovely party for Kate."

"It was my pleasure," Andi said with a warm smile.

"And for everything else, too. You've been so good to my girls. I just…well…thank you."

"I love them."

"Yes, I believe you do."

"We're glad you could be here tonight. Jack told me you're planning to go away for a while. We'll take good care of Maggie for you. Don't worry about her."

"I appreciate that. I know it's an imposition with all you have going on."

Andi's eyes danced with amusement. "Are you *kidding* me? She's the *biggest* help with the boys—all of them. I'm lost without her on the days she's at your house."

Clare smiled, imagining Maggie bossing everyone around. "I'm glad she's a help to you."

"Take care of yourself, Clare. We'll take care of Maggie."

"Thank you." *God*, Clare thought, *that was awkward.* Yet she was oddly relieved to know that her daughter was well loved by the woman who'd be helping to care for her while Clare put her life back together.

"MAY I BORROW THE BIRTHDAY GIRL?" Clare asked.

Kate took a last bite of cake and set her plate down on the table. "Excuse me," she said to her friends.

"Is there somewhere we can talk?"

"Come on upstairs." Kate led her mother through a maze of boxes to the far end of the second floor.

Clare tried not to wonder which of the closed doors led to the bedroom Jack shared with Andi.

"Sorry about the mess," Kate said. "We put all our energy into downstairs to get ready for tonight."

"I can't believe how much you've all gotten done in just over a month."

In Kate's room, one last suitcase lay open on the floor. Clare marveled at how quickly Kate had managed to put her unique stamp on the room.

"All ready?" Clare asked as it set in that she wouldn't see her middle daughter again for some time.

"Just about." Kate sat next to her mother on the bed. "Thanks for coming tonight. I know it wasn't easy for you."

"It was a lovely party."

Kate smiled. "Andi did it up."

"Yes, she did. I'll miss you, Kate."

When Kate leaned over to rest her head on her mother's shoulder, Clare realized the girl was crying.

"What, baby?" Clare gathered her daughter into her arms, wishing she could turn back the clock to when Kate was little and relied on her for everything.

"I just feel bad leaving right now."

"Because of me?"

Kate nodded.

Clare ached at the pain she saw on her daughter's face. "Honey, listen. I'll be just fine. I want you to go to Nashville and have this big adventure and enjoy every minute of it. I don't want you to spend one second worrying about me, okay?"

Kate nodded again and wiped her face. "Okay."

"Promise?" Clare tipped up her daughter's chin so she could see her lovely blue eyes.

"I promise."

"I want you to call me all the time. I want to hear all about what you're up to. No detail is too small for your mother."

Kate chuckled. "You got it."

"I love you, Kate. We all do. And we're so proud of you for having the courage to do this."

"I love you, too. I wake up every day and feel so grateful to have you back."

"I'm here for you any time you need me, no matter where I am." Clare hugged her again. "Walk me back down?"

Kate brushed away the last of her tears. "Sure."

DOWNSTAIRS, Clare found her mother sitting with Jack's parents.

"Ready to call it a night, Mom?" Clare asked.

"Whenever you are."

Madeline and John got up to hug them both.

"So great to see you, honey," John said.

"You too."

Maggie came over to them. "Are you leaving?"

"I think so. Want to come home tonight?"

"Let me ask Dad." Maggie dashed off to find Jack.

Right then Clare acknowledged another seismic shift in her life—the girls now deferred to Jack. Clare had always been the boss, and before her accident it wouldn't have occurred to any of them to ask Jack's permission if she was in the room. She'd been absent just long enough for that dynamic to change.

Maggie came back. "Dad wants me to stay here tonight because Grandma and Grandpa are going back to Connecticut tomorrow."

"That's fine, honey. I can come pick you up tomorrow afternoon."

Maggie kissed her mother and grandmother good-bye.

Clare and Anna said their good-byes and walked to the door with

Jack and Andi. It was all so *civilized*, she thought, so goddamned civilized. What would they say, she wondered, if she let loose with the rage she felt boiling in her gut? What would they do if she grabbed Jack by the arm and dragged him out of there?

"It was a great party," Clare said, resisting the urge to take back what had once been hers. "Thank you again."

"Thanks for coming," Andi said.

"Drive carefully tomorrow," Anna said to Jack.

He hugged them both. "I will."

CLARE KEPT quiet on the ride home, trying to absorb it all.

"Nice party," Anna finally said.

"Very," Clare agreed. "You were right, Mom. Thank you for making me go."

"Mothers are always right. Don't you know that by now?"

"You're gloating!" Clare said with a grin. "I have to admit, it wasn't as bad as I thought it would be."

"That's probably because Andi's so nice."

"She really is. If he had to be with someone else, I'm glad it's someone the girls like."

"If they didn't like her, he wouldn't be with her."

"No. No, he wouldn't."

KATE WOKE up at four in the morning, her heart hammering with anticipation. And dread. Her eighteenth birthday—the day she'd been waiting and planning for, but she hadn't expected to be so sad about leaving her family.

She got up to shower. When she was dressed, she tiptoed down the hallway to the nursery next to the room her dad shared with Andi. The babies slept peacefully in the predawn, and Kate was careful not to wake them. She leaned first over Robby's crib and then Johnny's to watch the soft whisper of their breathing. Her eyes filled with tears. They would grow up while she was gone, and she would be a stranger to them on her infrequent trips home.

"Hey," Andi whispered when she came into the room. "You all ready?"

"I hope I didn't disturb you," Kate said with a nod to the baby monitor.

"No. Your dad's up, so I got up, too. Are you all right, Kate?"

Kate turned back to Johnny's crib. "They won't know me," she said as a rush of tears flooded her eyes.

"Oh, sweetie, they *will*. We'll talk about you all the time, and we'll bring them to visit you."

Kate brightened. "You will?"

"Of course. We'll all come."

"I'll miss them," Kate said with a last look at the babies. "I was unprepared for how much I'd love them."

"And I was unprepared for how much *I* love *you*," Andi said.

Kate stepped into her stepmother's outstretched arms. "I love you, too," she whispered.

Jack walked into the room with his hair still wet from the shower to find his daughter silently weeping in his wife's arms. "Hey, hey, what's this all about?" He ushered them into the hallway and closed the door to the nursery.

"Kate's feeling sad about leaving her baby brothers," Andi said as she wiped the tears from Kate's face.

Jack kissed Kate's forehead and hugged her. "We'll send lots of pictures," he promised. "Are you ready to go?"

"Almost," Kate said. "I have a few more good-byes first."

"I'll grab your bag and meet you downstairs when you're ready," Jack said.

"Thanks." Kate opened Eric's bedroom door and crept into the quiet room. She kissed the sleeping boy's warm neck until he woke up with a giggle.

"I'm going now," Kate signed.

His big blue eyes were solemn. "No, I won't let you."

"Take good care of our babies for me, okay?"

He nodded, and Kate held out her arms to him. She hugged him for a long time before she pulled back to look at him. "You are my brother, and I love you, Eric Harrington." Jack's adoption of Andi's son had only become final a week ago, but he had felt like a little brother to Kate for much longer.

"I love you, too," he signed.

"Want to help me wake up Maggie and Jill?"

He grinned and jumped on her back for the ride down the hallway.

KATE WEPT until long after they crossed the Newport Bridge on their way to Interstate 95 south. Saying good-bye to her sisters, her grandparents, Andi, and Eric had been awful. For the first time, Kate questioned the wisdom of what she was doing. She'd been so sure it was what she wanted, but the reality was daunting. However, it was all in motion now, and there was no turning back.

"You okay, hon?" Jack asked.

"I guess so. Leaving was worse than I thought it would be."

"I don't think there's any way to adequately prepare for leaving home."

"I've been so focused on where I'm going that I haven't given much thought to what I'm leaving behind."

"You'll probably be homesick at first, but as you make friends and get into a routine, it'll get easier."

"You sure made things worse by having those babies just before I left," she said with a weak grin. "Thanks for that."

He grimaced. "I'm sorry. Hey! Did anyone remember to say happy birthday?"

She laughed. "No!"

"Happy birthday to you—" he sang.

She held up a hand to stop him. "Leave the singing to me, please." They settled into companionable silence for a while. "Thanks for doing this, Dad. I know it's a bad time for you to be away from home."

"I'm eagerly anticipating *six full* nights of sleep, but don't tell Andi I said that."

Kate laughed. "Your secret's safe with me. So how long will it take to get there?"

"About seventeen hours in a regular car. In this tank, who knows? Probably more like twenty. We'll see how it goes. If we're getting tired, we can stop for the night. I talked to my friend Reid yesterday, and he insisted we use the guesthouse at his place in Brentwood until we move you into your apartment. He said we can get there any time, and it's ready for us."

"That's nice of him."

"He's a good guy. Uncle Jamie and I had a lot of fun with him at Berkeley, but I haven't seen him since then. Jamie was better at keeping in touch with him than I was. In fact, it was Jamie's idea for me to call him."

"Is he an architect, too?"

"I think he keeps up his license, but he's ventured more into real estate development. From what I hear, he's been hugely successful at it."

"Does he have a family?"

"He's got a son, who has to be twenty-five by now. Reid got married the same week we graduated from Berkeley, and his son was born that year. The son is an attorney, and he lives in the same apartment complex where your place will be."

"Is Reid still married?"

Jack shook his head. "His wife died young in a car accident. I remember when it happened. It was really sad because his son was just a little guy at the time."

"That's too bad."

"I'm looking forward to seeing him."

As Kate talked with her dad, she felt her sadness shift back to excitement. She was finally on her way to Nashville.

PART II
FORWARD MARCH

The command that tells the group to begin marching forward.

CHAPTER 10

"**K**ate." Jack nudged her. "Wake up."

She stretched. "Where are we?"

"A couple of miles outside the city. You can see it, though."

As Kate took her first-ever look at Nashville, she wondered if she would find what she was looking for somewhere amid the lights and buildings that made up Music City USA's nighttime skyline.

"What time is it?"

Jack choked back a yawn. "Almost two."

The trip had taken more than twenty-one hours in the U-Haul. They'd shared the driving duties, but he'd stayed wide-awake while she was at the wheel.

"I need some navigating help," Jack said. "Keep an eye out for Interstate 65 south. Reid's place is about twenty miles outside the city."

They crossed the Cumberland River on the way into downtown Nashville on Interstate 40. "Check out the building that looks like Batman," Jack said.

"That's the AT&T building. The blue one's the Tennessee Performing Arts Center."

Amused, Jack glanced over at her. "Is there *anything* you don't already know about this city?"

"I guess I'll find out, but I've read everything I could find." Kate peered out the window as the city unfolded. "There's I-65."

Jack handed her the directions as he merged into the southbound lane. "What exit is it?"

"Umm, seventy-four."

Thirty minutes after they left the city lights behind, they took the final turn on the rural road to Reid's property.

"There's the sign." Kate pointed to the archway over a paved road. The name "Matthews" was carved into a sign at the top of the arch. White split rail fencing ran the length of the road and the long driveway. "Wow," Kate said. "I'll bet this place is something in the daylight." The fence went on until it disappeared into the darkness. Huge trees that might've been oaks lined the driveway.

"Reid said the guesthouse is a mile from the road on the right," Jack said.

They saw the outside light that had been left on for them before they saw the guesthouse itself. "That's the guesthouse?" Kate said. "I had pictured a little cottage."

Jack pulled the U-Haul into the driveway in front of the two-story house. "I guess the main house is another mile and a half up the driveway."

"I can't wait to see that." Kate hopped down from the truck and stretched. She grabbed their bags from behind the seat and followed her father to the door, which was unlocked. "Oh, it's so cute!"

The house was furnished with a combination of antiques and country-style furniture. A stone fireplace dominated the living room.

"Reid left a note," Jack said. "It says, 'Welcome Jack and Kate! Make yourselves at home. Bedrooms are upstairs. Towels are in the bathrooms. Sleep in and come up to the main house for brunch whenever you get up. Look forward to seeing you. Reid.'"

"That's nice," Kate said. "I don't know about you, but I'm beat."

Jack stretched and yawned. "Me, too."

They took their bags upstairs to find bedrooms.

"Dad?" Kate said.

"Yeah?"

"Today was fun. Thanks again for all of this."

He kissed her cheek. "My pleasure. Get some sleep."

WHEN KATE WOKE up the next morning, she couldn't remember where she was. Then it came back to her in bits: the U-Haul, the Batman building, the carved "Matthews" sign, and the larger-than-expected guesthouse. She was finally in Nashville, or, well, twenty miles south of the city. With a big yawn, she looked over at the bedside clock. Ten fifteen. The room was awash with sunlight. Like the living room downstairs, the cozy bedroom was decorated with country touches. Dark wood antique furniture, walls adorned in rose-colored silk, and lace curtains on the windows that complemented the high four-poster bed with the white eyelet duvet.

Kate was stretching out the kinks when her dad knocked on the door.

"Come in," she called.

"Morning," he said. He looked like he, too, had just gotten up.

"Morning. Did you sleep?"

"Oh *yeah*," Jack said with a big smile. "Eight, beautiful, uninterrupted hours."

Kate chuckled. "I'm starving."

"Well, let's shower and get dressed so we can go find Reid. I don't know about you, but I want to see what the main house is like if this counts as the guesthouse."

"I hear ya. Give me thirty minutes."

JACK HAD unhooked Kate's car from the U-Haul by the time she joined him downstairs. Kate was surprised to find that it was almost as cold outside as it had been at home.

He tossed the keys to her so she could drive them up the hill. They were able now to see the rolling green hills that made up Reid's property and the white split rail fence extending as far as she could see.

"Holy shit," she muttered when she caught her first glimpse of the massive Tudor-style home at the top of the hill.

"I'm supposed to tell you not to swear, but holy shit is right."

"It makes Grandma and Grandpa's house in Greenwich look like a shack." Kate parked in the large driveway next to a black Mercedes SUV and a silver Saab.

Before they could ring the bell, the door opened and a uniformed maid greeted them. "Hello, Mr. Harrington, Miss Harrington, I'm Martha. Do come in," she said in a lilting Southern drawl as she waved them into the foyer. "Both Mr. Matthews are here."

As Martha led them into what she called the drawing room, Kate noticed the house screamed of the kind of old money she'd experienced in her grandparents' home. But this house was even more spectacular: antiques, paintings framed in gilded gold, huge mirrors, chandeliers, and rich velvet draperies.

And waiting for them in the drawing room were two of the best looking men Kate had ever seen. Her friends had always claimed her father and Uncle Jamie were "hot." Kate thought they were insane. Her dad and Jamie were *old*! But with her first look at Reid Matthews, she finally got it. He was the same age as her dad, and there was no denying it—he was hot. And the son—*whoa*, Kate thought for the second time that morning, *holy shit*!

Reid walked over to her dad and shook his hand with enthusiasm. "So great to see you, Jack. You haven't changed a bit. I would've known you anywhere."

"You, too. Thanks so much for the hospitality."

As they exchanged greetings, Kate took the opportunity to study Reid. He was tall but not quite as tall as her dad. His light brown hair was sprinkled with shots of silver, and his brown eyes were almond shaped and almost sleepy looking. But it was his cheekbones that took him from plain good-looking straight to hot. Just as she realized she was staring, Jack put his arm around her.

"Reid, this is my daughter, Kate."

"Pleasure to meet you, Kate," Reid said in a honey-coated Southern accent as he shook her hand. "And this is my son, Ashton." The younger man had dark blond hair, green eyes, and a football player's build. The only feature he shared with his father was those amazing cheekbones.

Ashton shook hands with Kate and then Jack. "Pleased to meet you, Kate, sir," he said in the same deep drawl.

Jack guffawed at the word "sir." "Call me Jack, please."

"Y'all must be ready to eat," Reid said. "Martha's cooked up a feast for us, so come on along."

Jack complimented Reid on his home as he led them into the dining room, where the imposing table could easily seat thirty.

"It's a bit much, huh?" Reid said with an amused expression.

"It's amazing," Kate said.

"Ashton is the fourth generation of Matthews men to live here," Reid said. "But he recently escaped to an apartment in the city."

"I ran for my life," Ashton joked.

Martha fussed over them and plied them with fried eggs, biscuits and gravy, grits, sausage, and croissants.

Half an hour later, Jack held up his hands with a groan. "I surrender, Martha. I simply can't eat another bite."

She laughed. "You sure are a charmer, Mr. Jack. Yes, indeedy."

"He always was," Reid said with a wink for Kate. "The girls at Berkeley *loved* your daddy."

"I've always heard it was Jamie who had them hanging all over him," Kate said.

"Jamie was in a league all by himself," Reid said.

Jack laughed. "That's a fact, but as I recall, you did just fine yourself. I can't believe it was twenty-five years ago."

"Seems like yesterday," Reid said wistfully. "Those were the best years. My great escape from Tennessee."

"It was fun," Jack said with a faraway look on his face. His ringing cell phone brought him back to the present. "Excuse me. It's my wife." He got up and left the room.

"Jamie said your dad recently remarried," Reid said to Kate.

"That's right. His wife's name is Andi, and they have three-month-old twins, Johnny and Robby."

"Don't get any ideas, Dad," Ashton teased.

Reid laughed. "Don't worry. That ship has sailed for me."

"I think that's what my dad thought, too," Kate said, and both men laughed.

"So, Kate, Dad says you're here to strike it big," Ashton said with a hint of amusement.

"That's the goal."

He lifted a skeptical eyebrow. "So you can really sing?"

Kate wasn't sure she liked his attitude. "Try me." She folded her arms and tilted her head defiantly.

"What do you mean?"

"I could sing something, but you'd just say it was rehearsed. So tell me what you want to hear."

Ashton appeared to give this considerable thought. "I know," he said with a grin. "Sing 'Crazy' for me."

Ah, a gift. Patsy Cline was one of her favorites. Without breaking eye contact with Ashton, Kate belted out the song with a few twists all her own that she had perfected during the long summer spent singing at the hotel.

"Don't tell me you challenged her," Jack said when he came back into the room.

Reid and Ashton seemed stunned, and Kate knew she probably looked smug. Whatever. He'd pushed her buttons, so she'd let him have it.

"Wow," Reid said.

Ashton sat back in his chair. "Yeah," he said softly. "Wow."

Now Kate was embarrassed. "My Dad tells me you have an apartment I can rent," she said to Reid, trying to ignore the gaze that Ashton continued to direct her way.

"That's right. It's being painted this weekend. You should be able to move in on Monday or Tuesday at the latest. It's fully furnished, and I checked it myself yesterday. Everything's in good shape."

"Thank you," Kate said.

"It's a great place," Ashton said. "You'll like it."

While she wasn't entirely sure she liked *him*, she took his word for it about the apartment complex.

"I'm actually headed back to the city," Ashton said to Kate. "Do you want to come along? I could show you around."

"That'd be great," Kate said, anxious to see the city. "Do you want to go, Dad?"

"I think I'll stay here and catch up with Reid."

"I'll bring her back later," Ashton said to Jack.

Kate handed her car keys to her dad and kissed him on the cheek. "See you in a bit."

AFTER THEY LEFT, Reid took Jack out to show him the stables. "That girl of yours can *sing*, man," Reid said.

"I know. We gave her a guitar when she was twelve. About a year later, she came out of her room and said, 'Listen to this.' We were stunned. She's been playing and singing ever since."

"I know some people in the business. I could make a few calls."

"Thanks, but I don't think that's how she wants to do it. Why don't we see what happens."

"This must not be easy for you."

Jack sighed. "You have *no* idea. I feel better knowing she has you and Ashton to call on if she has any problems."

"We'll take good care of her. Don't worry."

"I appreciate that. I really do."

"There does come a time when we have to let them go their own way. I wasn't happy about Ashton moving into the city, but he needed some space and privacy. He has a right to that."

"He's a nice young man. It couldn't have been easy bringing him up on your own."

"He's my best friend. That boy has never been anything but a total joy to me. I don't know what I would've done without him when Cindy died."

"I sure was sorry to hear about that."

"We had a rough go of it for a while there."

Jack could still see a hint of sadness in his friend's eyes. "You never remarried?"

"Never even came close," Reid said with a shrug. "When you had what I had, well, it's not easy to replace. I understand you've had your own struggles."

"The last few years have been a bit of a roller coaster ride, to say the least."

"Jamie said Kate's mother is almost fully recovered."

"Yes, Clare's doing much better."

"And you're recently remarried?"

Jack nodded. "I met Andi about a year after Clare's accident. By the time she recovered after three years in a coma, Andi was living with us, and we were expecting the twins. It was a tough situation."

"Jesus," Reid said as they leaned against the white fence to watch a trainer work with a black thoroughbred. "I imagine so. What did you do?"

"Well, Clare decided to end our marriage, which I guess was the right thing in light of all that had happened. But it was hard. We'd been married for twenty years—every one of them happy until all this happened."

"So you married Andi."

Jack nodded. "Three months ago. The babies arrived right in the middle of our wedding."

Reid hooted. "You're kidding!"

"Nope," Jack said with a grin. "It was quite a day."

"Let me see, you have Kate and the twins…"

"Jill is nineteen and a sophomore at Brown. Maggie will be thirteen next month, and I adopted Andi's son, Eric, who's almost eight."

"I lost count."

Jack grinned. "Six."

Reid shook his head with amusement. "You sure have been busy since I saw you last. I've read a lot about your firm. You guys have made quite a name for yourselves. And Jamie married your sister. How about that? I remember Frannie visiting you in California."

"She's hardly changed since then. They're great together. They have twins, too. A boy and a girl who're fifteen months."

"God, my life is so boring compared to y'all. All I do is work while the two of you are single-handedly populating the world. Eight kids between you!"

"We have babies, Reid. We're forty-six-years-old, and the two of us are chasing babies. Enjoy the boredom. *Embrace* the boredom."

Reid laughed. "It sure is good to see you."

ASHTON DROVE Kate into the city in his still-new-smelling silver Saab.

"Nice car," she said.

"Thanks, it's the first thing I bought when I graduated from law school in May and went to work."

"Where did you go to school?"

"I stayed right here and went to Vanderbilt for undergrad and law school. I thought about going out of state, but I didn't want to leave my dad. I'm all he has."

He said it so matter-of-factly that Kate's initial assessment of him went up a notch. Maybe he wasn't as arrogant as he had come across earlier. "Where do you work?"

"I'm an associate with a firm downtown that specializes in entertainment law. That's what this town's all about."

"But you don't *have* to work, do you?"

"Do you?"

Kate laughed. "I guess not, but I can't see living off my dad for the rest of my life. He'd never stand for that anyway."

"And you think mine would? He wanted me to come into his company, but I've always wanted to be an attorney."

"What does his company do?"

"Mostly commercial real estate development. The company's called RMD, Reid Matthews Development. You'll see his signs all over town. He has a hand in most of the pies that are baked around here."

"And he has no need for an attorney?"

"He has a stable of them. Maybe someday I'll do that, but I want to do this for now. It's a fun job."

Kate's cell phone rang. "It's my mom," she told him. "Hi, Mom. Sorry I didn't call. We got in at two in the morning."

"Everything went well?" Clare asked.

"Yeah, it was great. No traffic and good weather. Dad's friend Reid's house is amazing. His son Ashton is taking me into the city right now for my first look."

"I'm glad to hear you got there okay. Have a good time, and call me when you get settled."

"I will. When are you heading out?"

"Maybe Wednesday. I'll let you know."

"Okay. Talk to you soon. Love you."

"You too, sweetie."

Kate closed her cell phone and turned back to Ashton. "Sorry about that."

"Don't be." He took the Green Hills exit. "I'll show you where the apartment is."

"Oh, cool."

They drove through a beautiful area peppered with stately old homes, bars, restaurants, and shops.

"There's the Bluebird," Ashton said, pointing to the famous café. "That and Mabel's are the only real music joints in this part of town. The rest are downtown."

"The Bluebird has open-mic nights on Mondays. I want to go tomorrow."

"Do you have original material? You can't do covers there."

"I have a bunch of my own songs."

"Make sure you also bring a signed lease with you. You'll have to prove you live in the city."

Ashton navigated through a busy area before he turned left into the Westchester apartment complex. Six buildings, each with four brick-front town homes, made a square around the parking area. A pool and fitness center sat at the far end of the landscaped parking lot.

"It's really nice," Kate said.

"Home sweet home."

Kate giggled. "I love your accent."

"At least I don't sound like a snotty Yankee."

"Neither do I!"

"All right, darlin', if you say so." His dimpled grin was full of easy charm as the breeze floating through the open window ruffled his blond hair. "Your apartment is in that building, and mine's over there." He pointed to the other side of the parking lot as he turned the car around to head back out of the complex.

He gave her a windshield tour of all the Nashville highlights: the Country Music Hall of Fame, "Music Row" where all the recording companies had offices, the Grand Ole Opry, the Parthenon, and Belmont and Vanderbilt Universities. As they drove through the city, he tossed Tennessee trivia at her.

"Do you know who the three presidents from Tennessee are?"

"That's easy: Andrew Johnson, Andrew Jackson, and James K. Polk."

"Excellent, A-plus. But do you know who the honorary fourth Tennessee president is?"

"Honorary president? What are you talking about?"

"Why, Jack Daniels, of course," he said with a charming smile.

She cracked up. "Funny, I didn't see that in any of my American history books."

"It's a well-kept secret."

They returned to Green Hills to go to Mabel's, where she'd applied for a job before she left Rhode Island.

"A buddy of mine from college bartends here," Ashton said when he'd parked the car on the street. "Let's see if he's working."

Kate followed him into a dark hole in the wall where the smell of smoke and stale beer mixed with music coming from a stage in the back of the large open room. Two bars were doing land-office business on the first floor. A sign on the wall over one of the bars said, "Everyone welcome: Be's, Used to Be's, Might Be's, Never Gonna Be's."

The walls were littered with framed photos of country music royalty, many of them posing with a massive black woman who had to be Mabel herself. Interspersed among the photos were gold records, musical instruments, and framed copies of handwritten songs. Ashton took Kate's hand to keep her with him as they navigated the Sunday afternoon crowd. He led her to the second floor, where a lone guitarist performed on yet another stage.

Ashton tugged Kate along with him and waved to the bartender. "This is Butch Cassidy," Ashton hollered over the noise.

"That is *not* your name," Kate said to the jovial bartender. He had close-cropped curly dark hair and mischievous blue eyes.

Butch grinned and reached out to shake her hand. "What can I say? My mother had a sense of humor."

Not sure whether to believe either of them, Kate shook his hand.

"What can I get you?" Butch asked. They had to yell to be heard over the crowd and the music.

"Couple of beers?" Ashton said, looking at Kate.

"Just a Diet Coke for me."

"Kate is a new transplant from Rhode Island. She's here to strike gold." Ashton had lost the hint of cynicism he'd had before she sang for him.

"Aren't they all?" Butch nodded to the room full of people as he drew a beer for Ashton from the tap. "Wanna be's. Every one of 'em."

"This one might be different," Ashton said with an appreciative glance at Kate. "She's got some pipes."

"Oh yeah? How'd you get hooked up with this guy?" Butch had the same middle Tennessee drawl as Ashton.

"Our dads are friends. I applied for a job here. Who do I need to talk to?"

"Charlie Sledge is the manager. He'll be here tomorrow morning. What's your last name? I'll put in a word for you."

"Harrington."

"Kate Harrington," Butch said. "I'll remember that. Maybe someday I'll be able to say I met you the day you landed in Nashville."

"Maybe so," Kate said, taking in the chaos that was Mabel's, filled with the satisfaction of being *exactly* where she wanted to be.

ON MONDAY, Kate arrived at the five-thirty sign-up time to sing at open-mic night at the Bluebird but didn't make it on stage that night. They gave her a "play next time" ticket. She planned to go back the following Monday, and Reid and Ashton promised to come cheer her on. Jack surprised Kate with tickets to the Tuesday evening show at the Grand Ole Opry and invited the Matthews to go with them. Kate loved the show, which was made up of a talented group of unknowns and a surprise appearance by Vince Gill. Reid said he hadn't been to the Opry in more than fifteen years and thanked Jack and Kate for giving him an excuse to play tourist in his hometown.

With Butch's help, Kate landed a job busing tables at Mabel's and was due to start in a few days.

By the time Friday rolled around, her father had helped to get her settled into the apartment at the Westchester. They turned in the U-Haul and spent the next two days playing tourist. They'd been through the Country Music Hall of Fame, listened to jazz at F. Scott's, visited Belmont Plantation, and made the rounds of the music industry's hot spots, including the Bluebird, the In & Out, and Tootsie's.

Before they left Kate's apartment for the Nashville International Airport, Jack handed her a gift bag.

"What's this?"

"Just a few things to make it possible for me to sleep at night while you're here."

Kate laughed when she pulled a can of mace and a panic button out of the bag. "A safety goody bag. Thank you." He'd already given her a credit card to use for anything she needed.

"I want you to keep that stuff with you all the time, do you hear me?"

She patted his cheek. "I will. I hope you won't be worried every second of every day. You can't do that."

"I'll try to behave and leave you alone, but you have to call. Often. If you don't, I'll worry."

"I have a feeling I'm going to be pretty homesick for a while. You'll get tired of hearing from me."

He pulled her into a tight hug. "Never," he whispered.

Before she could give in to the urge to cry her eyes out, Kate drew back from him. "We'd better go."

They drove the short distance to the airport in silence. Kate took a ticket at the short-term parking lot so she could walk him in.

When she couldn't go any farther with him, he turned to her. "You know where I am if you need anything, right?"

With her hands on his chest, she looked up at him. "I always know where you are. I want you to try very hard not to worry."

"Be careful who you trust here, Kate. This is a tough town. They chew up little girls like you and spit them out. Don't get sucked into all that crap. Reid and Ashton both have my card. They know to call me if they see you heading for any kind of trouble."

"Spies, huh?" Kate asked with a grin. She expected nothing less from him.

"No, friends. Keep in touch with them. They're good people."

"I will." She clung to him much longer than she'd planned to, and when she was finally able to let him go, she wasn't surprised to see tears in his eyes, too. "Do you remember my favorite movie when I was little?"

"Of course I do. I must've watched *The Wizard of Oz* a hundred times with you."

"Then you'll remember what Dorothy said to the Scarecrow when she was leaving Oz. I think I'll miss you most of all."

He hugged her hard and made no attempt to hide his tears. "I love you, I'll miss you, and if I don't go right now, I'll never be able to leave you here."

"I love you, too. Go." She gave him a nudge and watched him move through security.

When he got to the other side, he turned and waved one last time.

She blew him a kiss. Then he was gone, and she was alone in Nashville.

CHAPTER 11

*I*n Rhode Island, Clare made final preparations for her trip
north. Her mother helped her work through a giant to-do
list that included forwarding her mail, temporarily canceling her cable
TV, checking in with Dr. Langston, and having the Volvo serviced.
While she received a clean bill of health, the old Volvo wasn't so lucky.
When the mechanics identified several major problems with the car,
Clare gave in and bought a new one. She chose another burgundy
Volvo with four-wheel drive and a ski rack, so she could bring the
girls' skis with her to Vermont.

By Wednesday, she was finally ready to make the five-hour trek
north. She spent her final night at home with her mother and Maggie.
Her mother left early Wednesday morning to go home to Hartford,
and Clare thanked her profusely for her company and help over the
last few months.

With her new car loaded to the gills, Clare planned to hit the road
after she dropped Maggie off at school.

"I'll see you right after Christmas, okay?" she said to Maggie as
they arrived at school. Maggie and Jill were coming to Vermont for a
week during their holiday vacation.

"I can't wait to ski," Maggie said.

"I'm sorry I'll miss the holidays and your birthday, but we'll celebrate when you come up. I promise."

"Okay. Well, I'd better get in there." Maggie glanced out the window at the flood of students heading into the school.

Clare battled a flood of memories as she leaned over to hug her daughter. "Be good for Dad and Andi. I love you."

"Love you, too. I'll call you."

"You'd better," Clare said with a smile.

Maggie got out, closed the door, and waved from the curb.

Clare indulged in a mini pity-party but pulled herself together by the time she reached the Newport Bridge. It was out of her way to take the bridge north to Boston, but something about that bridge symbolized home and, in this case, leaving home. She could never leave Newport forever, at least not as long as Maggie still lived there, but there was something so necessary about what she was doing that she couldn't help being anxious to get to Vermont and get settled. Dr. Baker's words kept replaying in her mind—*now is the time to take care of you so you can be there for your daughters when they need you.*

The radio kept her company as she left Providence, northern Rhode Island, and southern Massachusetts in her wake. Within ninety minutes, the Boston skyline appeared in the distance, reminding Clare as it always did of Jack taking her to the "Top of the Pru" for the first time. The Prudential building was one of Boston's most recognizable landmarks.

Since her muscles were beginning to stiffen from sitting so long, she decided to stop in the city to take a walk through her old Beacon Hill neighborhood. She took the Storrow Drive exit and parked on Newberry Street. Pulling her winter coat tight around her, Clare set off down Newberry, comforted that little had changed in the pretty, historic area where she and Jack had lived as newlyweds. The narrow cobblestone streets, gas-powered street lamps, and brick-front townhouses were exactly as she remembered them. There were memories here, too, but they were good ones.

Wandering along Beacon Street, Clare came upon the three-story brick house where they'd had an apartment on the third floor.

Standing on the sidewalk looking up, she could still remember every detail of the place. Jack had worked then for Jamie's father, the world-renowned architect Neil Booth, and could walk to his office from their apartment. Clare, who had been a substitute teacher in the Boston school system, often met him halfway home when they would have dinner in one of the cozy restaurants or take a long walk through the Boston Commons. Glancing to the far end of Beacon, she spotted the Citgo sign that hung over the outfield at Fenway Park and remembered spending many a summer evening eating hotdogs and popcorn in the bleachers when the Red Sox played at home.

She recalled Jack's excitement on the night they learned she was finally pregnant. They'd been trying for more than a year and had begun to wonder if something was wrong when along came Jill, followed just over a year later by Kate. She had been pregnant with Jill when they moved to Newport, but Clare had never forgotten those early years in Boston when it had been just her and Jack.

With a wistful last look at the Beacon Street house, she walked back to her car. Energized by her walk, she drove through the city to pick up Interstate 93 north. Oddly enough, though, she felt energized rather than saddened by the visit to their old neighborhood.

Progress.

CLARE ARRIVED IN STOWE, Vermont, just after three that afternoon. Mount Mansfield loomed in the distance as she drove into the picturesque town. The sidewalks were filled with early season skiers wearing snow pants, parkas, hats, and boots. Following her brother Tony's directions, Clare drove to the far end of town, past town hall, the general store, a bookstore, several antique dealers, a coffee shop, a church with a white steeple, and a grocery store.

A minute later, she pulled up to a two-story shingled colonial with a wide front porch and bright red shutters. Clare was pleased that the house was within walking distance of town.

She got out of the car to air that was significantly colder than it had been at home and in Boston. On the front porch, she tipped a clay pot to find the key right where Tony had said it would be. The inside was cozy, if somewhat dilapidated. She could see right away that while the place was warm and inviting, it needed work. The paint looked like it had seen better days, and the hardwood floors were in bad need of refinishing. The kitchen and downstairs bathroom were outdated. The second floor had four bedrooms and two bathrooms and was in slightly better shape but still in need of work.

Shelves around the television in the living room were filled with movies and books left by the former owners who had used the house as a ski rental. The rooms were furnished in what Tony had called "ski house chic," which Clare now realized meant a hodgepodge of furniture, none of which went with anything else. Tony and his wife Miranda had bought the house as an investment with hopes of using it as a weekend getaway. But Tony hadn't counted on getting mired in one of Connecticut's messiest murder trials in decades. As the district attorney in Hartford, he wouldn't be getting away much in the next year, and they were grateful for Clare's willingness to oversee the renovations.

She turned up the heat and went out to unload the car. An hour later she had taken up residence in the second-floor master bedroom, which included a bathroom and a view of the Stowe Community Church's white steeple. After she unpacked, she left a message with the property management firm that cared for the house to let them know she'd arrived. When her stomach let her know it was dinnertime, Clare decided to drive back into town to find something to eat. She would conquer the grocery store in the morning.

A diner called McHugh's looked inviting, so she parked down the block and window-shopped her way to the restaurant. Once inside McHugh's, she sat at the counter, and ordered a cup of coffee and the beef stew from the list of specials.

Clare's mouth watered when the waitress set the bowl of steaming stew down in front of her.

"Enjoy," she said and went to wait on other customers.

When she came back a few minutes later, Clare was nearly done eating. "I hated it."

The waitress laughed. "I see that. Are you new in town?"

"I am. I just arrived this afternoon."

"Where are you staying?"

"My brother has a house on Maple Street. I'm staying there for a few months."

"Well, you picked the right time of year to be in Stowe. This is when all the action happens."

"I'm looking forward to it. My daughters ski, and they'll be up to visit."

"Where are you from?"

"Newport, Rhode Island."

"Oh, I love Newport! I'm Diana Cummings, by the way." She extended her hand to Clare. "I own this dump."

Clare laughed and shook her hand. "This is no dump, and that was the best stew I've ever had. I'm Clare Harrington."

"With compliments like that, I hope you'll be a regular." Diana wiped the counter and refilled Clare's coffee.

"Definitely," Clare said with a warm feeling inside. Diana seemed like someone who could be a friend. "I'm going to have some work done to the house. Can you recommend anyone?"

"What kind of work?"

"Painting, hardwood floors, a new kitchen, and remodeling several bathrooms."

"The best person I can think of would be Aidan O'Malley, but he can be hard to get. He's really popular around here."

"Does he live in Stowe?"

"Just outside of town. I think his card's on the board." Diana gestured to the crowded bulletin board next to the cash register. "You might have to dig a bit to find it."

Clare went over to poke around on the bulletin board. She finally found the card for O'Malley Restorations under several layers of cards for local businesses and wrote down the number.

"Thanks for the info," Clare said as she put her coat on and paid her bill.

"My pleasure. Welcome to Stowe. Come back soon."

"I will," Clare promised.

She went back to the house and attempted to start a fire from the wood stacked on the front porch. When it finally took, she went into the kitchen to call Aidan O'Malley. His answering machine picked up, so she left a message and the phone number at the house. If she didn't hear back from him in the next day or two, she would ask around about other contractors.

Clare also called the girls and her mother to let them know she'd arrived in Stowe. Tony had warned her that cell service could be spotty in the mountains, and she wanted the girls to have the number at the house.

Finished with her calls, she pulled a down comforter around her and settled into the sofa with a book she'd found on the living room shelf. But instead of opening the book, Clare stared into the fire, trying to identify an odd feeling that had been with her all day. After several long moments spent thinking about it, she decided what she felt more than anything else was relief.

CHAPTER 12

*C*lare was bringing in groceries the next morning when the house phone rang.

"This is Aidan O'Malley. You called?"

"Yes, Diana Cummings at McHugh's recommended you. I need to have some work done on my house."

"Inside or out?"

"In." Clare followed his lead by cutting to the chase. "Kitchen, bathrooms, floors, painting."

"I can come by around three today to take a look. Does that work?"

"Three would be fine. It's 22 Maple Street."

"I know that house. An out-of-towner bought it last year. Is that you?"

"I'm from out of town, but I don't own the house. My brother does. I'm helping him with the work."

"All right, then. I'll see you at three."

He was gone before she could say okay or good-bye. *Well, hopefully his renovation skills are better than his phone skills,* Clare thought as she unloaded cereal and pasta from a bag on the kitchen counter.

When everything was put away, she donned her heavy parka to walk into town to take a closer look at the stores on Main Street. She wandered through several antique shops, making mental notes of items that would be perfect for Tony's house when the work was finished. He had given her carte blanche on the restoration and the furnishing, and Clare looked forward to spending his money.

From outside the Book Nook, Clare watched an older woman tape a "Help Wanted" sign in the window. The woman smiled at Clare and waved her inside.

"Come in, come in," she said when Clare opened the door. "You looked frozen standing out there."

A fire burned in a corner woodstove in the cozy shop, which seemed to be designed more for reading books than selling them. Sofas and well-worn chairs were arranged around the woodstove. Bookshelves were so unobtrusive they seemed to be almost an afterthought.

"Can I get you a cup of tea or coffee?" The woman managed to make a flannel shirt and jeans look fashionable. Her long, gray braid made her look older than she actually was. Her pretty heart-shaped face told the true story—that she was closer to fifty than sixty.

"I'd love some coffee, thank you." Clare rubbed her hands together vigorously. She hadn't realized how cold and out of breath she was and had to be careful not to push herself too hard. The last thing she wanted was a setback in her recovery.

"There you are." The woman pointed to a cream and sugar station. "Help yourself."

"Thank you. Your shop is adorable. I could spend a whole day sitting in front of that fire with a good book."

"Feel free to do just that any time you'd like to. I'm Beatrice Simmons, but everyone calls me Bea."

Clare shook her hand. "Clare Harrington."

"Nice to meet you. I don't think I've seen you in here before."

"This is my second day in Stowe."

"Oh! Welcome! Do you like it so far?"

"I love it. Everyone's been so friendly."

"That's Stowe. You couldn't have found a friendlier town to visit. Will you be here long?"

"I'm planning on three months, maybe a little longer. I'm having some work done on a house, and my stay will depend on how long that takes." She told Bea about her brother's house.

"Have you hired anyone yet?"

"Diana at McHugh's recommended Aidan O'Malley. Do you know him?"

Bea chuckled. "Oh, *yes*, I know him. He's a bit of a local celebrity."

Her curiosity piqued, Clare said, "A celebrity? Diana didn't mention that."

"Let's just wait and see what you think of him when you meet him," Bea said with a twinkle in her eye. "You'll have to come back and let me know."

Clare smiled. "That's one way to guarantee a return visit by a potential customer."

"You aren't looking for a job by any chance, are you?"

"Not really. Why? What do you need?"

"I'm desperately seeking some holiday help, a few hours here and there during the crunch periods."

The idea struck Clare as ideal. Working part-time would be a great way to meet people, and it would get her out of the house. She made an impulse decision. "I'll take it."

"You will? Really?"

"I'd love to—but on one condition."

"What's that?"

"I don't want you to pay me. I don't need the money, but I sure could use a diversion."

"I can't do that! Of course I'd have to pay you."

"You'd be doing me as much of a favor as I'd be doing you. Plus, I might be a little rusty since I haven't worked in a while."

"That's no problem. We can get you trained in no time. It's pretty easy, really."

"I should tell you I'm recovering from an accident, so I might need to sit down every now and then."

"Nothing serious, I hope."

Oh, no, nothing serious, just the ruination of my entire life. "It shouldn't keep me from pulling my weight."

"Can you start tomorrow afternoon? We're usually slow after two, so I could get you trained. We'll discuss the issue of payment later."

"I'll be here." Clare shook Bea's hand. "I'll look forward to it."

Bea reached for the sign that Clare had just watched her tape to the window and pulled it down. "Me, too. Thanks, Clare. You're saving my life."

"My pleasure. See you tomorrow."

The bells on the door jangled when Clare left the warmth of the bookstore behind. The blast of cold air was almost shocking—and invigorating. *I have a job. I'm saving someone's life!*

By three thirty, Clare was convinced that Aidan O'Malley wasn't coming and got out the yellow pages to find someone else. The doorbell startled her when it rang at three forty-five. She got up to answer it and encountered the broad back of a tall man talking on one cell phone while another one rang with insistence from its position next to a pager on his belt. Clare could almost taste the anticipation as she waited for the pager to go off, too. It didn't disappoint. Without missing a beat in the heated discussion he was having on the first phone he checked the caller ID on the second one and the LCD on the pager.

He wore a beat-up red down vest over a red plaid flannel shirt with jeans and filthy work boots. A hint of a red bandanna poked through a hole in the back pocket of faded jeans—not that she was looking at the back of his jeans or anything. He just happened to be there on her front porch. Where else was she supposed to look? The cuffs of his flannel shirt were rolled up to reveal a long-sleeved white thermal undershirt. Dark brown hair curled around the edge of what might have been a Red Sox ball cap.

"I have to take another call," he said. "Get over to the cabinet place before the end of the day and get the right order. You can be at the

Millers' by six in the morning to get them installed. They have to be in by this time tomorrow so the floor guys can start." He paused to listen. "Just do it, for Christ's sake." He slapped the phone closed with a curse of aggravation that told her he didn't realize he was being watched.

Watching him juggle fifty things at once brought back memories of her life as a Realtor when there had never been enough hours in the day, and she, too, had been tied to multiple cell phones and a pager. She didn't miss that life and said a silent thank you to the man on her porch for convincing her to let go of the idea that she might one day return to it. *No thanks*, she thought, intrigued by the somewhat major revelation on this, her second day in Vermont. *This place is working wonders!*

After he extricated himself from the second phone call by barking out some more orders, he seemed to finally remember where he was. When he turned around, Clare almost gasped. Standing on her front porch was one deadly gorgeous carpenter, and he was in a foul mood.

"I'm O'Malley. What can I do for you?" His cheeks were rosy, as if he'd been outside all day.

"Come on in," she said. With one quick glance, Clare saw the kindred spirit of a wounded soul in his stormy green eyes. Later she would pick over the meeting to try to understand how she knew, without a shadow of a doubt, that he too had experienced some kind of devastating tragedy.

Rattled, she led him into the house. "The kitchen is back here. I want to start with that. There're three bathrooms to be updated and hardwood floors to be refinished. We'd also like to paint the whole interior."

He released a low whistle. "That's gonna cost you a pretty penny," he said, lifting his hat to pull a pencil out of his hair.

"That's all right. My brother has it to spend."

"Do you have decision-making authority? I hate getting bogged down in decisions by committee."

"I'm it. He doesn't have time to deal with it right now, so I'm doing it for him," Clare said as she followed him from room to room.

Other than an occasional grunt, he didn't say anything else. He made notes, took a few measurements, and grunted some more. He ignored both cell phones and the pager when they rang again.

Clare followed him downstairs.

"What's the plan for the kitchen? Are we gutting?"

"Yes, they want new cabinets, countertops, and appliances."

"Granite?"

"Yes."

He grunted again, twisted his head, seemingly to gauge the number of cabinets that would fit in a reconfigured kitchen, and wrote something in the notebook.

"Same with the bathrooms? Gut and start over?"

"Yes."

He tucked the notebook into his shirt pocket and jammed the pencil back under his hat. "I have what I need. Ten thousand for labor. I'll get you a written estimate for each room within a day or two."

"I'll be getting a couple more quotes."

He shrugged. "Suit yourself."

"If I hire you, how soon could you start?"

"Probably two weeks or so. I'm finishing three other jobs right now and then cutting my crew loose for the winter. I'd do this one myself."

Clare raised a skeptical eyebrow. "Wouldn't you need help?"

"You hire me, the job gets done. Don't worry about how."

His tone bordered on rude, but after witnessing the scene on her front porch, she understood he was more harried than rude.

"Fine. Drop off your estimate when you can."

Both cell phones and the pager rang in concert. He sighed, and with a halfhearted wave, he was gone.

AIDAN SAT in his truck to take both calls. He returned two pages and gave some more orders. *Damned idiots*, he thought of the guys who worked for him. *Can't make a freaking decision on their own.* He couldn't wait to get these last few jobs finished so he could be done with them.

They were going to Florida to work for the winter, which was just fine with Aidan. Good riddance!

He leaned his head against the headrest. *Something has to change.* The dreaded phones and pager sat on his lap, links in a chain holding him to a life he'd stumbled into and no longer wanted. For some time now he'd been thinking about giving up the new construction end of his business so he could focus on the kind of restorations the cute blonde inside was looking to do. O'Malley Restorations had strayed too far from the *restorations.*

Somewhere along the way, he'd become tied to phones, pagers, and idiots. Maybe it was because his thirties were slipping away that he was feeling introspective. *Who knows? Maybe it's the freaking idiots.* As he started the truck, Aidan hoped the blonde—he had her name written down somewhere—hired him. This job could be the new start he desperately needed.

AFTER AIDAN LEFT, Clare used the phone book to identify two more contractors. She left messages for both of them before she wandered over to the window to find Aidan O'Malley's large navy-blue pickup truck still parked in front of the house. She watched him lean his head back in a gesture of weariness that tugged at her heart. He seemed so unhappy that Clare ached for him. It didn't occur to her to wonder why.

CHAPTER 13

$\mathcal{K}$ ate fell into a routine and began to feel at home in her new apartment. She started each day with an hour at the gym followed by at least two hours of guitar practice. The new songs she'd been working on were coming along well, and she hoped to have the chance to debut them soon at the Bluebird.

Ashton and Reid called to check on her with such religious regularity that Kate suspected they had a written schedule. She spent Thanksgiving with them at Reid's house. It had been a relaxing day with great food, board games, and movies. She'd enjoyed their company, even though she missed her own family terribly. Reid had invited her to come out to the house to go riding on Sunday, and she was looking forward to it.

On the days she worked, she left early so she could visit with Butch, the bartender at Mabel's, before her shift. He'd become her only friend there, since most of the women she worked with ignored her.

"I don't know what I ever did to them," Kate lamented to Butch one day before work. She nursed a Diet Coke while he set up the bar.

Butch gave her a sympathetic smile. "You didn't do anything to them, sweetheart. They're threatened by you."

"*By me?* How can they be threatened by *me?*"

"Because they want what you want, and now that they've heard you sing, they know you're better than them."

Charlie, the manager, finally let her on stage the day after she got her first chance to play at the Bluebird. That had been a good couple of days. After her performance, Charlie had gone on and on about how good she was, which Kate could now see led to the sudden increase in her coworkers' hostility. She chewed nervously on her thumbnail. Some of those women were scary. "That's not fair."

"No, it isn't, but that's the way people are in this town." With a glance around to make sure no one was watching, Butch pulled a piece of paper from his pocket. "I grabbed this off the wall for you. One of the city's better house bands is looking for a new female lead singer. I thought you might be interested."

She took the paper from him. "Thanks. What's a house band?"

"They play at house parties around town. Up-and-comers love to perform with them because you never know who'll be at the parties. A lot of people have been discovered that way. The Rafters are really popular, so it could be a good break for you."

She glanced up at him with appreciation. "Thanks, Butch."

He shrugged. "None of the others deserved it. Not after the way they've been treating you."

"You're a good friend." She studied the flyer and learned the band was holding tryouts the next day.

"Have you talked to Ashton?" Butch asked as he unloaded glasses from the dishwasher behind the bar.

"Not in the last few days."

"I think he's got a bad case for you."

Her head whipped up. "*What? Ashton?*"

Butch grinned at her shock. "Open your eyes."

"But we're just friends. I didn't even think he liked me all that much."

"Oh, he likes you all right."

Kate sat back to process this new information. She should be wild about Ashton. He was handsome, successful, funny, and oh, that body of his… But Kate had to admit that it wasn't Ashton she looked forward to hearing from every few days. No, it was his father she loved talking to.

~

REID SURPRISED her the next night by stopping in at Mabel's during her shift. She was startled to see him talking to Butch at the bar. As she watched him from across the room, her heart lurched when he threw his head back to laugh at something Butch said. Reid wore a dark suit and was so devastatingly handsome that Kate couldn't look away. When she finally had a lull in the action, she worked up the nerve to go over and say hello.

"Hey," she said. "What're you doing out on a school night?"

"I had a meeting in town and decided to come by to check on you."

"Do you have to file a written report with my dad?"

"Monthly, and he requires at least one face-to-face meeting with each report," Reid said with a grin.

"What are you drinking?" She wanted to know everything about him.

"One scotch on the rocks for the road."

When he reached for his drink, a gold cuff link peeked out of his suit coat sleeve. There was something so sexy and classy about the little chunk of gold holding his starched white cuff together that her mouth went dry. She fixated on his finger making a path through the condensation on his glass.

"What kind of meeting did you have?" she asked when she finally tore her eyes off his hand.

"Zoning board. We have several projects pending before them."

"Sounds interesting."

He laughed. "Believe me, it's not. What've you been up to?"

"Oh! Get this! I tried out today with a house band called the Rafters. They're auditioning for a new lead singer."

"That's great. How'd it go?"

"Really well, I think. They called me to come back again tomorrow. I'm glad you came by. I was dying to tell you about it."

His smile lit up his handsome face. "That's wonderful, Kate. They're really good. I've seen them play several times at parties."

"You have?"

He nodded.

"I sure hope I get the job."

"I bet you will. Did you walk to work tonight?"

Crooking her head, she grinned. "Should I lie and say no?"

He pretended to make a note on an invisible pad. "It's going in my report—walking in the dark and lying. Multiple demerits."

She laughed. "You'll get me in big trouble."

"I'll walk you home to keep you safe and out of trouble."

"Don't be crazy. I have another hour to go, and you have to work tomorrow."

"I've told you I don't want you walking around by yourself after dark. This *is* a city, you know."

"You sound like my dad. Go home. It's late, and you've already worked twelve hours today."

"Now who's being the parent?" he asked with a playful scowl. "I'll wait."

Kate found it hard to move just then.

"Go," he said. "I'll wait."

WHEN HER SHIFT ended at eleven, she waved good night to Butch and went downstairs ahead of Reid. Once they were outside, she took a deep gulp of fresh air. "The smoke was tough tonight."

"That can't be good for your voice."

"It's not. Even if I don't get the gig with the Rafters, I might quit Mabel's. The smoke sucks, and the people there are kind of shitty."

He stopped walking and turned to her. "Shitty?"

"Mean."

"They're *mean*? To *you*?"

He looked so mad on her behalf that she smiled. "Butch says it's because I sing better than they do."

"Butch is probably right. He's pretty smart about these things."

"I'm not used to people not liking me because of my music, but I suppose it's to be expected here."

"I'm sorry, darlin'. I hate hearing that."

His dismay was so genuine that Kate slipped a hand into the crook of his arm and leaned her head on his shoulder. "Are you gonna beat 'em all up for me?" she asked, mocking his accent.

"I just might have to."

"They're not worth it. Besides, I plan to get my revenge the old-fashioned way."

Amused, he looked down at her. "Oh yeah? How's that?"

"I'm going to be famous."

He laughed. "I have no doubt," he said as they reached the stairs to her townhouse. "Everything okay with the apartment?"

"Yeah, except for the slumlord. He's a major pain."

"You're a real brat, aren't you?"

"Sometimes. The apartment is great, thank you. I love having my own place."

"Just call the slumlord if you ever need anything."

"I'll do that. Are we still on for Sunday?"

"We sure are. You remember how to get there, right?"

"Yep. I'll be out around noon. Is that good?"

"That's perfect. Well, I guess I'll see you then." He kissed her cheek.

"Who's going to walk you back to your car?"

"I think I'll be able to find it."

"This *is* a city you know," she said, imitating his stern lecture from earlier.

He laughed. "You really are a brat."

"Yeah, yeah, put it in your report. Call me from the car. I won't sleep if I have to worry about you getting mugged in the big city."

"All right. Get inside before I go."

At the top of the stairs, she unlocked her door and once inside, waved through the glass door.

He made a twisting motion with his hand.

She rolled her eyes and set the dead bolt. Running upstairs to her living room, she grabbed the portable phone and dialed his cell number.

"Didn't I just leave you?" he asked when he answered.

She could hear the smile in his voice. "I was very concerned about you getting mugged on the way to your car."

"Yet you have no fear of walking home alone on this same street late at night. Ironic, no?"

"You sound so prissy when you use that tone."

"What tone?"

"That tone. Was that a yawn?"

"You're hearing things."

"I told you not to wait for me. Now you'll have to talk to me all the way home so I won't worry about you falling asleep on the road." She heard the double beep of him unlocking his car.

"I'm not going to fall asleep. I'm in the car, so you can go to bed now."

"Talk to me some more, will you?" she asked softly.

"What's the matter, darlin'?"

"Nothing. Just kind of homesick today."

"Did you call home?"

"Yeah, but the babies were crazy so my dad and Andi couldn't talk. Maggie was at her friend's house. I couldn't reach my mom, and Jill was in class."

"I'm sorry. You'll be going home for a couple of days at Christmas, right?"

"Yeah, but that's almost a month away."

"Well, think of it this way—at least you're making some progress here. You've gotten to sing a few times in public, and now there's this possibility with the band."

"That's true."

"I haven't said too much about this, but I know people who could help you get where you want to be—"

"No! I don't want that, Reid. Do you hear me? Don't pull any strings for me."

"Hey, hey. Settle down. I won't do anything you don't want me to do."

"Do you promise? You have to promise me. I don't want it that way."

"I promise. But if I didn't think you had the talent, I wouldn't have offered. You're head and shoulders above the rest. You deserve a break."

"If that's true, then I'll get one. Please, Reid. Don't do it."

"I said I wouldn't."

"Okay."

"Since you're determined to keep me company, will you sing for me?"

"What do you want to hear?"

"Surprise me."

She sang "Time to Fly," one of the songs she had written since she arrived in Nashville. When she was done he didn't say anything. "Uh-oh. I put you to sleep, didn't I?"

"No," he said gruffly. "Definitely not. That was beautiful, Kate. You really have no idea how very talented you are, do you?"

"I don't think about it all that much. It's just something I do. It's so much a part of me."

"You aren't going to need help from me or anyone else."

She let out a nervous laugh as something in his voice stirred feelings she had never experienced quite so acutely before. "I guess we'll see, won't we?"

"That we will. Well, I'm just about home. Time for lights out."

"Thanks for the company."

"Thank *you*. I'll see you soon."

"Good night." She hung up but lay awake for a long time thinking about him and counting the hours until she could see him again.

∼

SUNDAY DAWNED sunny and unseasonably warm. After the intense conversation they'd had the other night, Kate had gone from being excited to see Reid to being nervous, especially since Ashton wouldn't be joining them. He was in Florida for a weekend fishing trip with his law school friends but had called to check on her before he left. She had swallowed her guilt when she assured him she was fine. He promised to call when he got home, but she told him he didn't have to. In light of what Butch had told her, she was concerned about leading Ashton on. He had just laughed and said of course he would call. *Ugh,* she thought as she drove to Reid's house with the window down. *What kind of mess is this shaping up to be?*

Her nerves over seeing Reid shifted into high gear when she reached the entrance to the long driveway. *Don't be ridiculous, Kate. He's old enough to be your father.* She shuddered when she imagined her father's reaction to the crazy crush she had on his friend. She'd only had one serious boyfriend, and that was last year. Ryan was adorable, and she'd imagined herself in love with him. But when her father flipped out after catching them making out, Ryan ran for the hills and never came back. *Just as well. Who wants a boy when you can have a man?*

The man in question appeared when she parked her car next to his black Mercedes SUV. Her heart skipped a crazy beat at the sight of him in worn jeans, cowboy boots, and an oatmeal-colored cotton sweater that had seen better days. For the first time in her life, her mouth watered with lust. *Cool it, Kate,* she said to herself when he reached out to open her door. *Just ride the damned horse and keep it cool.*

His smile sent a flutter through her.

"Hey, you found me."

"With no problem at all," Kate said with more lightness than she felt. She wondered if he would die of shock if she reached up and dragged that beautiful mouth of his down to hers. It was all she could do to resist the urge as he stood close enough to touch, smelling like fresh air and citrus. Her every sense was on full alert, which was also new to her.

Reid walked her to the stables with two bags tossed over his shoulder. "We got a great day to ride. It's never this warm in November."

114

"I talked to my sister this morning. It's snowing in Providence."

"Jill, right?"

Kate was busy watching him walk. "Uh-huh." He startled her when he suddenly turned around to face her.

"Everything okay, Kate?" Studying her with those soft brown eyes, he seemed to see everything she was trying so hard to keep hidden from him.

A keen burst of longing shot through her, and she was certain he could see it. How could he not? "Why do you ask?"

"You seem jittery. Are you nervous or something?"

Her first impulse was to deny it, but she couldn't. "Sort of."

"Why?"

She met his gaze. "I'm not sure."

Neither of them looked away for a long moment during which it became clear to Kate that he had feelings for her, too. Her heart gave a happy lift at what she saw on his face. Desire. Pure and simple.

He held out a hand to her. "Let's ride."

She took his hand as if she'd done it a hundred times before and followed him into the stable where more than a dozen horses peeked out from their stalls to inspect the visitors.

"Oh, they're beautiful!" Kate cried. "Are they all yours?"

"Half of them. The rest belong to friends of Ashton's who board them here."

"That's nice of you."

He shrugged. "It was a good way to keep all the kids coming around when they were in high school and college. They come out most weekends to ride."

"Afternoon, Mr. M," an elderly groom said when he came out of the tack room.

"Hi there, Derek. This is Kate Harrington, a new friend. She might be out to ride now and then when we're not home."

"That'd be fine. We'll make her feel right at home."

"Thank you," Kate said.

"I've saddled up Thunder for you, Mr. M, and Sugar for Miss Kate like you asked." Derek handed Kate a carrot he pulled from his jacket pocket so she could get acquainted with Sugar.

"Thanks, Derek," Reid said a few minutes later when he gave Kate a leg up on the gentle snow-white mare.

While Kate got comfortable in Sugar's saddle, she watched Reid stash two saddlebags on Thunder's back. "He's beautiful," she said. The compliment was rewarded with a loud whicker that made her laugh.

"He must like you," Reid said. "He only talks to people he likes."

They walked the horses out of the gated training area.

"Is Sugar one of yours?"

"No, she belongs to a friend of Ashton's who's away for a few weeks. She asked me to make sure Sugar gets some exercise. Come on, let's give them a workout." He touched his heels to Thunder's side, and the horse bounded into a canter.

Kate followed his lead, urging Sugar into an all-out gallop across the rolling green hills. After they'd gone a good distance, Reid slowed Thunder to a trot and directed him to a creek.

Kate was laughing when she caught up to him. "That was fabulous. I haven't ridden like that in ages."

"Thunder gets ornery if we don't get in a good run every few days."

Thunder snickered, and Kate chuckled with delight. "He's human!"

"I've been convinced of that since he was just a foal." Reid helped Kate down from Sugar, and they walked the horses to the creek for a drink.

"What a beautiful place you have."

"I'm glad you like it. I hope you'll make yourself right at home here any time you need to escape the city."

"Thank you," she said, feeling shy again. Just standing close to him made her light-headed.

He reached up to retrieve the saddlebags from Thunder's back. "Martha packed us some sandwiches. Are you hungry?"

"Sure." Kate followed him to a spot under a large oak tree where he spread a plaid blanket on the grass. He seemed so comfortable in his own skin as he stretched out on the blanket. Kate appreciated being with a man who exuded that kind of easy confidence. She'd grown tired of boys pretending to be men. This was a real man, and it was shocking to acknowledge that she wanted him in a way she had never wanted any of the boys who'd pursued her at home.

"Are you going to sit?" he asked with a grin.

Startled out of her thoughts, Kate kneeled on the far edge of the blanket.

He chewed on a blade of grass and watched her with those eyes that saw everything, even the secrets she was trying desperately to keep from him. "What's with you today, darlin'? You're like a cat on a hot tin roof."

Her cheeks heated. "Nothing."

He watched her for another long moment before he shrugged and opened the second bag. "I hope turkey's okay," he said, handing her one of the thick sandwiches and a diet soda.

"That's fine. Thanks."

Kate stole glances at him while they ate in silence. The more she looked, the harder it became to swallow. She'd never had feelings like these before and had no idea how to handle them. The tension soon became unbearable. She had to get away from him before she embarrassed herself, so she put her sandwich down, got up, and walked back to the creek where she rested her head against Sugar's soft neck. She startled when Reid came up behind her and rested his hands on her shoulders.

"I wish you'd tell me what's bothering you."

"I can't," she whispered.

He turned her to face him. "Now you're worrying me."

Looking up at him, she couldn't resist the urge to caress his face.

His eyes flashed with awareness as he took her hand from his face and kissed the palm. "Kate, honey, you're so beautiful, but you're too young for me. I'm an old man."

"You're not." She rested her head against his chest. "You're perfect." Encircling his neck with her arms, she tilted her face, daring him to kiss her.

He reached up to take her hands and gently extricated himself from her embrace. "Sweetheart, *please.* Your daddy asked me to keep an eye out for you, but I don't think this is what he had in mind."

She tightened her grip on his hands. "I don't want to talk about him."

"This isn't going to happen, Kate."

"It already is."

"It can't."

"Why not? We're both adults."

"You could be my daughter."

"But I'm not," she said, running her finger along his jaw.

"I'm flattered, honey, I really am."

She pulled her hand free of his. "But you're not interested."

"Of course I'm interested, but I'm not going to take advantage of a young girl. That's just not who I am."

"You know what?" she said, suddenly furious. "You can save your whole 'little girl' speech. I stopped being a little girl the day my mother was hit by a car right in front of me, so spare me the bullshit." She swung herself up onto Sugar's back and was gone before he could reply. Back at the stable, she turned Sugar over to a startled Derek. She was on her way to her car when Reid stormed into the yard on Thunder.

He was off the horse before it came to a stop. "Kate! Damn it! *Kate!*"

She reached for the car door, but his hand on hers stopped her.

"Don't go," he said. "Talk to me. Please."

"There's nothing left to say."

His eyes implored her. "Stay."

Over Reid's shoulder, she saw Derek come out to collect Thunder from the yard and discreetly disappear back into the stables.

She looked into Reid's eyes. "If you treat me like a child, you'll break my heart."

His jaw tight with tension, he nodded and took her hand to lead her into the house. "Can I get you anything?"

She shook her head and followed him into the drawing room.

He tugged her down next to him on the sofa. "I'm sorry," he said, cupping her face with his hand. "I don't think of you as a little girl, Kate, and that's the problem. You look like a grown woman, and you act like one. I just can't get past the fact that you're only eighteen. People would call me a dirty old man."

"No one would have to know."

Resting his forehead against hers, he smiled. "Sweetheart, after that scene in the yard, I think Derek's already on to us, and nothing's even happened yet."

His use of the word "yet" stirred hope within her. He was coming around.

"What you said back at the creek, about your mother. Tell me about it." He put an arm around her to draw her to him. When she tensed, he looked down at her. "What is it?"

"What about Martha?"

"She visits her family on Sunday afternoons."

Knowing they were alone, Kate relaxed against him. "I was fourteen," she said, letting her mind wander back to her darkest day. "We had the best life. My parents were awesome—not like a lot of my friends' parents. They were still so in love, and we always knew it. I had my sisters, my friends, school, my music. I was happy, you know?"

He ran a hand over her blonde hair and nodded.

"Then one day my sisters and I went shopping with my mom. As we were leaving the mall, this car came barreling at us. It was totally out of control." Tears rolled down her face.

Reid wiped them away.

"My sisters and I jumped out of the way, but my mom just stood there frozen. We screamed and screamed at her to move, but she didn't. The car hit her, and she went over the top of it. There was blood everywhere." Kate shuddered at the memory. "We heard later that the driver had had a fatal heart attack, which is why the car was going so fast. I can still remember the way my dad looked when he came running into the emergency room. He had this wild look in his eyes that stayed there for a long time afterward. In some ways, it was like we lost them both that day."

Reid tightened his arms around her and rested his cheek against her hair. "I'm sorry, baby," he said in the lilting Southern accent she already loved.

"Nothing was ever the same. She never came out of the coma they induced after the accident. Time went by, and he seemed to get better when he realized sitting by her bed around the clock wasn't going to bring her back. Then he met Andi."

"What did you think of that?"

"I was so relieved to see him happy again that it didn't really bother me. Jill didn't like it at first, but she warmed up eventually. Andi's special. I think in some ways she saved us all."

"That's just what your dad said when he told me about her."

"It's true. She was just what we needed."

"But then your mother recovered."

Kate nodded. "It made me a believer in miracles. After all that time, she just opened her eyes and looked at my dad like five minutes had passed. But Andi was pregnant with the twins by then, so it was complicated."

"Your dad told me. Your mother sounds like a brave woman. Not many people could do what she did. It must've been so hard for her to give him up."

"Yeah, well, I wonder if she isn't having some regrets. It's like everything's sunk in now that she's home from the hospital. She's gone up to Vermont for a few months to get away from it all."

"Did you ever find out why she didn't get out of the way of the car?"

She nodded and slipped an arm around his waist.

He kissed her forehead. "You don't have to tell me if you don't want to."

"I want to, but it's just so awful." She paused and took a deep breath. "She was a Realtor. She was showing a guy a house when he raped her. He said he'd kill one of us if she ever told anyone."

"Christ," Reid whispered.

"So she didn't say a word. She just lived with it. A couple of months after she recovered from the coma, she remembered everything and realized she saw the car as a way out. She thought if she was dead, he would never come after us."

"God almighty."

Kate turned so she could see him. "You know what the worst part is? All that time, all the time she was lost to us, I wondered if I could've pushed her out of the way of the car. I was close enough, but I just assumed she'd move before it was too late."

"Oh, honey, you might've been hit yourself."

"I've never told anyone that," she confessed.

"I'm glad you told me."

"I'm not a little girl, Reid." She tipped her face up to his and kissed him lightly on the lips.

This time he let her.

CHAPTER 14

*A*fter two afternoons at the bookstore, Clare felt confident she could handle her duties behind the counter. The small shop had a surprisingly complex computer system, but Bea was patient as she showed Clare how to ring up sales, record new inventory, and locate items within the store. She learned to keep the coffeepot full and the woodstove stoked. More than anything, she discovered the tiny bookstore was a hub of activity in the small town. Bea knew everyone and introduced her new employee to many of Stowe's year-round residents. She also invited Clare to attend her Thursday-evening book club meeting.

"I'd love to, but I haven't read the book," Clare said.

"Don't worry about it," Bea said. "The book is the least of what we discuss at those meetings. Plus, I want you to meet the rest of my friends."

Clare gladly accepted her invitation.

Aidan O'Malley was scheduled to start work at the house in a few days. The two other quotes she'd gotten had come in lower than his, but Bea had such high praise for his work and his reputation that Clare consulted with her brother, and he agreed the extra money was worth it.

"I just hope he leaves his snarky personality at the door," Clare said to Bea after she decided to hire Aidan.

Bea chuckled. "It's part of the package. He's one sexy devil, isn't he?"

"I didn't notice."

"Liar!"

"You said he's a celebrity around here. With that personality, I can't imagine he has many friends."

"Oh, he has *lots* of friends. He's a celebrity with the women."

"I'm sure he gets around."

"Actually, he doesn't. They chase him relentlessly, but in all the years I've known him, I don't think he's been seriously involved with anyone. His resistance makes him even more appealing to the ladies in town. The thrill of the chase."

"God, I hate that. Women can be so pathetic."

"You may be singing a new tune after you've had him underfoot for a couple of months."

Clare made a face of distaste. "I doubt it."

"We'll see," Bea said with a knowing smile.

CLARE WAS DELIGHTED to find Diana Cummings from the diner among the women who gathered at the Book Nook for the meeting on Thursday. Clare was a frequent customer at McHugh's and enjoyed talking to Diana.

"Hi, Clare," Diana said. "Bea told me she'd roped you into our group."

"It's nice of you to include me."

"Oh, please, it's our pleasure. We get so tired of passing the same old gossip around. We need some fresh blood." Diana had straight red hair and a sprinkling of freckles across the bridge of her nose. Clare figured she was in her mid-thirties. She knew Diana was married but didn't have children yet and was running the business her parents started more than forty years earlier.

Bea opened several bottles of wine while the women dug into the appetizers they had contributed. With the notable exception of Aidan O'Malley, the people in Stowe had been so friendly to her, and tonight was no different. They made Clare feel right at home.

The group of ten women sat in a circle in front of the woodstove. "Okay, Clare, you're on the hot seat tonight," a young blonde named Naomi said. "Tell us your life story."

"You don't have to, Clare," Bea said with a stern look at Naomi.

"No, that's fine. Let's see. I'm from Connecticut originally, but I've lived in Newport, Rhode Island, for almost twenty years. I'm here for a few months to help my brother with some work he's having done on his house on Maple Street."

"I heard you hired Aidan O'Malley," a woman named Jessica said.

"That's right."

"He's *gorgeous*," Jessica said with a wistful expression.

Bea's "I told you so" smirk from across the circle made Clare smile.

"Do you have kids?" Naomi asked.

"Three daughters who are nineteen, eighteen, and thirteen."

"Are you married?" Naomi asked. When Bea shot her another stern look, Naomi said, "What?"

"I'm recently divorced."

"Oh, sorry," Naomi said. "Do we hate him?"

"Naomi!" Diana said. "That's enough. Just because you hate your ex doesn't mean everyone does."

"You'd all *better* hate my ex," Naomi said.

Clare laughed. "No, we don't hate mine."

"It's better that way," one of the others said.

"Yes," Clare agreed.

"Well, let's talk about John Adams," Bea said, shifting the group's focus off Clare and onto the book.

Clare sent Bea a grateful smile. She'd felt better since she arrived in Stowe, and talking about Jack wasn't high on her to-do list just then.

AIDAN O'MALLEY ARRIVED with a thump and a crash at six thirty the following Tuesday morning.

Clare got up to look out the window. From the second floor, she watched him drag a table saw onto her porch. Judging from the way he stalked back to his truck, she figured he was in the usual pleasant mood.

Since Aidan was starting with the kitchen, Clare had moved essential items into one of the spare bedrooms upstairs. She had a coffeemaker, a microwave, and a mini-refrigerator she'd bought to get her through the weeks without a kitchen. Pulling on a robe, she brushed her teeth and ran her fingers through her hair on her way downstairs to let him in.

"Good morning," she said.

"Hey."

At least it wasn't a grunt.

"I had a key made for you so you can come and go." He came with such high praise from Bea that Clare had decided to trust him with the key. It was all part of her determination to acknowledge that just because she'd encountered one monster, not all men were evil.

He took the key and pushed it into the pocket of his faded jeans. "Thanks."

"Big talker, aren't you, O'Malley?"

He stopped what he was doing and stared at her. "Huh?"

"Never mind. I'll get out of your way. Just grunt if you need anything."

She was halfway up the stairs before he grunted out what might've been a chuckle.

THAT AFTERNOON AT THE BOOKSTORE, Bea and Clare sat behind the counter unloading boxes of new inventory that had arrived earlier in the day. The two women kept up a steady stream of chatter during their afternoons together. Bea often said she had no idea how she'd ever managed without Clare. They began to share confidences, which was how Clare knew Bea had never been married or had children but doted on her nieces and nephews. She apologized for the grilling Clare had faced at the book club meeting.

"Don't be sorry. They were just being friendly."

"They're nosy. Especially Naomi. That girl has never had a thought her mouth didn't share."

"They're women. It's what we do."

"Will your girls be coming up to visit soon?"

"My oldest and youngest will be here for a week after Christmas. My middle daughter is living in Nashville this year. She'll be in Rhode Island with her dad's family for Christmas, but she's going back the next day."

"What's she doing in Nashville?"

"The same thing millions of others go there for—she's trying to break in to the music business."

"Wow. Is she that good?"

"She really is."

"It must've been hard for you to let her do that."

"It wasn't exactly my idea. Her father agreed to it when I was..." Clare stopped herself. How did she tell her new friend the rest? "Well, let's just say she worked it out with him."

Bea raised an inquisitive eyebrow.

"It's a long story."

"And it's your business, honey."

"I'll tell you," Clare said haltingly. "I want to tell you. It's just... It's kind of a big deal, and I don't want anyone to feel sorry for me."

Bea studied her for a moment and then got up, turned the Open sign to Closed, and locked the door.

Bea sat in stunned silence, tears rolling unchecked down her face. "I don't know what to say."

Clare squeezed her hand. "You don't have to say anything."

"When you said you'd had an accident, well, it just never occurred to me—"

"Of course it didn't. It's not a story you hear every day."

Bea suddenly snapped out of her stupor. "Why are you comforting me? Come here." She reached out to hug Clare.

"Thanks for listening."

"Thank *you* for trusting me with your story. I'm so sorry for what your family's been through."

"Thank you, but we're all doing better now."

"I can't wait to meet your girls."

Clare smiled. "They'll like you. Despite all this, they're great kids. I have to give Jack credit. He did a good job with them while I was sick."

"I can't believe how generous you are toward him."

"I love him," Clare said with a shrug. "I want him to be happy, and someday things will be better for me, too. I have to believe that, or all of this will have been for nothing."

"You did an admirable thing. You put someone else's happiness ahead of your own. I know good things are ahead for you."

"I'm already happier here than I've been in months. Stowe's been good for me."

Bea squeezed Clare's hand. "We'll take good care of you until you're ready to go home."

AFTER WORK THE NEXT DAY, Clare stopped at McHugh's to pick up vegetable soup for dinner. On an impulse, she ordered a second bowl to go.

Aidan was running a plank through the table saw on the front porch when she arrived at home. He wore protective goggles and sawdust clung to his face and hair. He finished the cut, examined his work, and turned off the saw.

"Hi," she said.

He startled. "Oh, hi. I didn't see you."

"I didn't want to disturb you and cost you a finger. That thing looks pretty sinister."

He held the storm door for her. "It's not so bad."

She went inside.

Carrying the board he had cut, he followed her in.

"I got some soup. Are you hungry?"

"I'm fine."

She held up the bag. "I got extra."

"It does smell good." He ran a hand through his wavy brown hair to brush out the sawdust.

"Stop playing hard to get and come up to my formal dining room." She led him upstairs to the spare bedroom she was using as a makeshift kitchen.

"Let me wash my hands," he said, ducking into the bathroom.

Clare took the soup and plastic spoons out of the bag. The soup's aroma made her mouth water, but she'd come to expect nothing less from Diana.

Aidan came in, and Clare handed him one of the containers. "Want something to drink? I have Diet Coke and two beers," she said, peering into the small fridge.

"I'd love a beer." He took the soup and sat on the sofa.

"Coming right up."

Clare opened the beer for him and took her soup to sit next to him.

"Did you get this at McHugh's?"

"You have to ask?"

"It's good. Thanks."

"No problem."

They ate in silence. It had gotten so quiet that when the phone rang it startled her. "Excuse me." She got up to answer it in her bedroom and was delighted to hear from Maggie, who told her a long story about the goings on at school.

Aidan was finishing his beer when Clare returned to find her soup had gotten cold while she was on the phone.

"Sorry for the interruption. My daughter had a big day at school."

He looked at her with surprise. "You have a daughter?"

"Three of them," she said, retrieving her soup from the microwave.

"Where are they?"

His tone seemed almost accusatory. Clare turned to him. Today he wore a blue flannel shirt with faded jeans. The long-sleeved white thermal undershirt seemed to be a standard part of his uniform. And since he'd been inside all day she decided his rosy cheeks were a permanent feature and not the result of working in the cold. "The oldest is in college in Providence, the middle one lives in Nashville, and the youngest is with her dad in Rhode Island. That was her on the phone."

"Why aren't you with her?"

This time there was no doubt about his tone—or hers. "That's a long story, and I'm not sure it's any of your business."

He got up. "You're right, it isn't. Thanks for the soup." Tossing the beer bottle in the trash, he left the room.

Clare fumed for a minute before she stomped down the stairs to where he was cleaning up his tools in the torn-apart kitchen. "Why do I feel judged?"

He shrugged. "Maybe you feel guilty."

"Are you for *real*? You don't know me at all, and you're making some mighty big assumptions." Clare wouldn't have bothered to engage with him, except he had struck a nerve with the guilty comment.

"All I know is if I had a child, I wouldn't be living away from her."

"It sure is easy to say that when you've never been there."

A flash of naked pain streaked across his handsome face. "You're absolutely right. I'll see you tomorrow."

"Aidan…" Clare went after him, but he was already out the door. A moment later she heard the squeal of his truck's tires.

CHAPTER 15

*C*lare and Aidan went out of their way to avoid each other over the next few days. They said a polite hello in the morning and an equally polite good-bye in the evening. After three days, Clare couldn't take it anymore.

"Aidan, I'm sorry about the other day."

"Forget it," he said as he measured an area over the kitchen sink.

"I can't forget it. I know I said something that hurt you, and I'm sorry."

"I wasn't all that nice to you, either. How you handle your kids is none of my business."

"No, it's not." What was it about him that made her feel like she had to explain herself? "There's more to the story than meets the eye. You shouldn't jump to conclusions."

"Let's just drop it, okay?" He clipped the tape measure onto his belt and held out a hand. "Truce?"

She studied his outstretched hand for a moment before she reached out to shake it. "Truce."

"Have you picked out the cabinets and countertop yet?"

"I have an appointment tomorrow." She walked around to look at what he had done so far. The walls were stripped bare where he had pulled out the old cabinets, and Spackle marked the places where he'd made repairs. The plywood floor was thick with dust and chunks of putty. "I love what you've done with the place."

"You will when it's done."

"So what happened to all your toys?"

His brows knitted with confusion. "What toys?"

"The phones and the pager."

"They're history. I just kept one phone for emergencies."

"What brought that on?"

"Call it a change in direction."

"Good for you."

"I'm getting used to the quiet."

"Well, I'll let you get back to work. I'm off to the bookstore."

"Have a good day at the office. Tell Bea I said hi."

"Thanks, I will." She slipped on her parka for the walk into town and had reached the front door when he called out to her.

"Clare?"

It was the first time he had called her by name. "Yes?"

He came out of the kitchen and handed her a twenty-dollar bill.

"What's this for?"

"Soup's on me tonight."

"Oh," she said. "Okay."

He turned back to the kitchen. "See you later," he said over his shoulder.

"So then he hands me a twenty and says 'soup's on me tonight,'" Clare relayed to Bea when she got to the store. "What does that mean?"

"Sounds like a date to me," Bea said with her trademark "I told you so" smirk.

"It is *not*. He barely speaks to me."

"You had a big fight the other night. How can you say he barely speaks to you?"

"Fighting doesn't count."

"What's wrong with this picture?" Bea asked with amused exasperation. "You were married for twenty years, and you can't tell when a man is interested in you? I've never been married, yet I see it?"

"See *what?*"

Bea took Clare by the shoulders and marched her into the tiny restroom in the back of the store. "Look," she said, standing behind Clare.

"What am I looking at?"

"You're a beautiful woman, Clare. You have all that luscious blonde hair and the most dazzling blue eyes I've ever seen in my life. If an old lady like me can see how gorgeous you are, don't you think Aidan is going to notice it, too?"

Clare reached up to smooth her hair in a self-conscious gesture. "I'm not ready to be thinking about stuff like this. I have enough on my mind as it is."

"Maybe 'stuff like this' is just what you need to get your mind off the rest, huh?"

"I think about that man, the one who hurt me," Clare whispered. "I was able to be with my husband after because it was Jack, and my love for him was so much bigger than the fear. But I can't imagine letting any other man touch me. The thought of it literally makes my skin crawl."

"Maybe when the time comes, you'll feel differently," Bea said, squeezing Clare's shoulders. "Don't worry about that right now. One step at a time. Focus on the soup."

Clare laughed and turned to hug Bea. "I can do that. Focus on the soup."

"Keep saying it," Bea said as she went out to greet a customer.

"Focus on the soup," Clare whispered to herself in the mirror.

~

WHEN CLARE ADDED two pieces of Diana's homemade cheesecake to the soup order, she told herself it was because *she* wanted cheesecake, not because she thought *he* might enjoy it. *You're being such a ninny.*

Clare took her time walking home. The sidewalk was carved out of the foot of snow that fell overnight. She was amused by the casual attitude in town toward what would've been a major snowstorm in Rhode Island. As she walked, she kept reminding herself that soup was soup, and despite what Bea said a bowl of soup did *not* constitute a date. Even someone who'd been out of the dating game for more than twenty years knew that.

But as she turned on to Maple Street, her heart began to beat faster when she spotted Aidan lounging on her front steps drinking a beer like it was seventy degrees outside rather than twenty. She couldn't deny that he appeared to be waiting for her.

"Lying down on the job?" she asked with a raised eyebrow, making a supreme effort to be witty. Her heart almost stopped altogether when she was rewarded with a genuine smile. "You should do that more often."

"What? Lie down on the job?"

"Smile. It looks good on you."

He held her eyes with his for a moment before he shifted his glance to the bag she carried. "What did Diana brew up today?"

"Minestrone."

"Oh, my favorite." He hauled himself up off the stairs and held the front door for her.

Walking past him into the house, she noticed a wet spot on his jeans from the ice on the stairs, not that she was looking at his jeans or anything. "Where did you get the Sam Adams? That's not my brand."

He followed her upstairs to the makeshift dining room. "I bought some. I can't drink that lightweight stuff you like. I got some more of yours, too."

Surprised, she turned to him. "Thanks."

"It's a peace offering," he said as he took one of her beers from the tiny fridge and opened it for her.

"Me bring you peace in form of beer," she joked. "I thought we already made peace. The truce and all that?"

"It occurred to me I never said I was sorry. I was out of line getting on you about your kids, and I *am* sorry."

"Thank you," she said, giving him a suspicious look.

"What?"

"You surprise me, O'Malley."

He chuckled. "How's that?"

"I wouldn't have imagined you to be the apologizing sort."

"Why do I feel judged?" he asked, mimicking her tone from the other night.

Hands on her hips, she stared him down. "Are you trying to jeopardize our truce?"

"No way. I want what you've got in that bag."

"Here's your change and your soup. Thanks for treating."

"My pleasure." He got himself another beer.

Clare sat on the sofa and put her feet up on the coffee table. The leg she'd broken in the accident was aching after the afternoon in the shop. With the Christmas shopping season underway, the store had been busier than usual. She took a long sip of her beer.

He sat on the floor with his back against the sofa but turned so he could see her. "You're a real beer girl, huh?"

"Yep. Always have been. When my husband and I went out he'd have wine, and I'd have beer. He used to tease me about it." Her voice trailed off. She hadn't thought of Jack in days. Where had that memory come from all of a sudden?

"Must've been *some kind* of breakup."

Her gaze darted over to him. "Why do you say that?"

"The look you had on your face when you mentioned him and then the one you got when you realized what you'd said."

Clare wasn't sure if she was annoyed or intrigued to find such startling intelligence beneath his gruff exterior. "I don't want to talk about him."

"Fine, then we won't. Can I ask you something else that's none of my business?"

She shot him a wary look. "If you must."

"Where'd you get the limp?"

"I took a fall."

"What kind of fall?"

"The kind that leaves you with a limp."

"Oh, *that* kind of fall. Why didn't you just say so?"

She couldn't contain a laugh. "Since we're playing twenty questions, do I get to ask a few?"

"Fire away."

"How long have you lived in Stowe?"

"Nine years."

"Ever been married?"

"How do you know I'm not married now?"

"Because you're here eating soup with me."

"I've never been married," he said, looking down to study his beer bottle.

"Why not?"

He shrugged and picked at the label on the bottle. "Never met the right girl, was busy establishing my business. You know, the usual reasons."

She watched him as he spoke. Something didn't ring true, but their truce was fragile so she left it alone.

"I brought cheesecake," she said, noticing the relief that crossed his face when she changed the subject. Yes, there was definitely more to the story than he was letting on. *That's okay. I'm not exactly baring my soul, either.*

"I love Diana's cheesecake."

"The woman is a culinary goddess."

He groaned in ecstasy when he took the first bite.

I wonder if he makes that same sound when he... For God's sake, Clare. Get a grip!

"Tell me about your kids."

Clare cleared her throat and her dirty mind before she answered him. "Jill's the oldest. She's a sophomore at Brown. She's my overachiever."

"I'd say so, if she's at Brown."

Clare smiled. "She says she wants to be an attorney. She's a great athlete. She played field hockey and lacrosse in high school, and she's on the lacrosse team at Brown. She can't wait to get up here to go skiing."

"Does she look like you?"

"Nope. She's a dead ringer for her dad. She has dark hair and gray-blue eyes. They're all tall like him, too. I'm a shrimp next to them. Even Maggie, my youngest, is almost as tall as me. But Kate and I could be twins. She looks exactly like me."

"Lucky girl," Aidan said without looking up from his cheesecake.

Clare's stomach took an odd dip at the unexpected compliment. "And you surprise me yet again, O'Malley."

His sideways grin was all charm. "I'm just full of surprises."

"Apparently so."

"Kate's the one in Nashville?"

"Yes. She called me the other day to tell me she's been hired as a singer with a popular band that plays house parties in Nashville. I guess it's a big deal because you never know who'll be at the parties. Lots of people get discovered that way."

"That's great."

"I'm happy to see her making progress. Her father gave her a year to land a recording contract or she has to come home and go to college."

"He doesn't think she can do it."

"What makes you say that?" Clare asked, startled by his bluntness.

"He's indulging her for a year so he can say he was supportive. If he really believed she could do it, he wouldn't have given her a time limit."

Clare hadn't thought of it that way. "I don't think that's why he did it," she said, but suddenly she wasn't so sure.

"What about Maggie?"

"Maggie was my surprise. I thought I was out of the baby business when she came along. She's got her father's dark hair and my eyes, and this kind, generous heart that just astounds me sometimes. Her stepbrother's deaf, and she's become fluent in sign language. She's amazing."

"So he's remarried?"

"Huh?"

"Your ex-husband."

"Yes."

"Ah, I see." His knowing look said he had the whole thing figured out.

"Are you jumping to conclusions again? Because you'll end up apologizing twice in one day."

He laughed. "Why do all mothers have that particular look and tone mastered?"

"What tone?" she asked haughtily.

"*That* tone. Can I ask one more question?"

"I don't know. You're starting to irritate me again."

For some reason, that seemed to please him. "Then I'll make sure it's a good one." He waited for her nod of approval before he said, "Will you have dinner with me?"

Clare tried to hide her shock at the question. "I *am* having dinner with you."

"I mean a real dinner with waiters and tablecloths. Maybe even candles, if you're extra nice to me."

She sat back, stunned. Okay now *that* would be a real date. No denying it. "I thought you didn't date."

"Where'd you hear that?"

"Bea said—"

He hooted with laughter. "You've been checking up on me, haven't you?"

"Don't flatter yourself," she said, startled by how laughter softened his hard edges. "She *volunteered* the information."

"Whatever you say."

"She said you've got women in this town falling over themselves to go out with you. Why would you want to go out with me?"

"Because I like sparring—I mean talking—to you. Besides, you seem to have a very low opinion of me, so there's no way I can disappoint you."

"Have you disappointed lots of women?"

"Scores. The stories are legendary, but I'm sure you've already heard them all."

She'd heard just the opposite, but she wasn't about to tell him that. "You're doing a hell of a job selling yourself, O'Malley."

"So?"

"I'll have dinner with you, but it's not a date. Not a real date."

He unfolded himself off the floor and stood up. "You know what? I think I'll hold out for the real deal. How about you let me know when you're up for it."

Once again he surprised her. "All right, but it might be a while." *If ever.*

"Lucky for you I'm a patient man. I've done as much as I can in the kitchen until the cabinets come in, so I'll be starting on the downstairs bathroom. I'll see you tomorrow."

"Okay."

At the door, he turned to study her with those sleepy, sexy green eyes of his. "I don't know what happened to you, Clare, but you don't need to be afraid of me."

She held his gaze for a long moment. "I like talking to you, too."

He smiled and waved on his way downstairs. A minute later, she heard the front door close quietly behind him.

CHAPTER 16

$\mathcal{K}$ ate stepped to the microphone, and a hush descended upon the crowded room. It was her first official appearance with the Rafters, and she'd been sick with nerves all day. But the butterflies disappeared when the band played into her cue. Then she did what came so naturally it was like breathing. She lost herself in a sultry rendition of Bonnie Raitt's "I Can't Make You Love Me." Kate's black silk cocktail dress moved with her as she swayed to the music. The dynamic with the band had been magical from their first practice together. As part of her deal with them, she would be performing her own material during their breaks. They were playing tonight at an estate in Hendersonville, just north of the city.

The first song ended, and the lead guitarist, Billy Weston, moved to the microphone. "Give it up for our new lead singer, Kate Harrington."

The crowd erupted in applause. "Thank you," Kate said without showing the relief she felt. By the time their first set ended, Kate owned the room, and she could tell the band was pleased with her.

"We're taking a short break, but Kate's going to keep the music coming, so don't go away," Billy said.

Kate picked up her guitar and sat on the stool Billy put on the stage for her. She adjusted the microphone and plugged in her guitar. When she looked up, she saw Reid come into the room wearing a tweed sports coat over a cream-colored shirt.

He smiled and winked at her but was forced to look away when someone said hello to him.

Kate tried to recover her bearings as her heart pounded with excitement. The very sight of him left her breathless and light-headed. She hadn't seen him in more than a week, during which time she'd been rehearsing with the band ten hours a day and he was out of town on business. They'd spoken almost every day, usually late at night and sometimes for more than an hour. When she mentioned she would be making her debut with the band, Reid surprised her by telling her he had been invited to the party.

In the twenty minutes she played without the band, she felt Reid's eyes on her the entire time. But like she always did when she was performing, she tuned out everything and let the music take over. She had honed that skill at the hotel over the summer, and it came in handy now. It also helped to be playing for a receptive audience that was generous with its applause.

She was exhausted by the time the band finished its final set at midnight.

"You're one helluva singer, little lady," an inebriated older man said.

Kate took a step back when he got too close to her.

Reid came up behind her, took her by the elbow, and guided her away from the overeager fan. "Quite a show, little lady," he whispered in her ear.

She giggled. "Give a little lady a ride home?"

"Where's your car?"

"At home. I rode with Billy."

"Let's go."

They said good night to the hosts, who were effusive in their praise for Kate's performance.

Outside, Reid helped her into the Mercedes.

Kate leaned back against the soft leather seat and kicked off her high heels. "God, I'm so tired. I used to do four-hour shifts at the hotel, but I don't ever remember being this tired."

"You worked hard tonight."

"I've been working hard for two weeks. I'm ready for a break."

"When do you play again?" he asked as he drove south toward the city.

"Next weekend. We're not practicing again until Wednesday, so I have three blessed days off."

"That works out well."

She turned her head so she could see him. She never got tired of looking at him. "Why's that?"

"I have to go to Memphis for the day on Monday. I wondered if you might want to come along. There's something there I think you might enjoy seeing."

She gasped and sat up straight in her seat. "Graceland? Can we go to Graceland?"

He chuckled. "I don't think you really want to."

"Don't play with me when it comes to Elvis, baby," she said, affecting the King's accent.

"So I'll take that as a yes."

She reached for his hand. "I'd love to go to Memphis with you. And not just because of Elvis."

He squeezed her hand. "Good."

When they arrived at her apartment, he pulled into a parking space, shut off the car, and turned to her. "You were wonderful tonight, Kate."

She hadn't let go of his hand. "Thanks. It helped to have you there."

Later she wouldn't remember who moved first, but they came together in an explosive meeting of lips and tongues and heat. The only conscious thought she had was that no kiss had ever felt like this one. Her entire body hummed as she buried a hand in his hair to drag him closer.

When she moaned, he tore his lips free.

"I'm sorry," he said. "I shouldn't have done that."

"Don't. Please don't ruin it."

He closed his eyes and took a deep breath.

"Reid?"

"Yeah?"

"Would you do it again? Please?"

He reached out to touch her face and leaned in to kiss her softly.

The fire between them flared anew, and Kate was aware of the exact moment when his control snapped. One of his hands cupped the back of her head while the other caressed her leg under the hem of her short dress. His tongue explored every corner of her mouth, and when she responded in kind, he groaned.

"Kate, honey, we have to stop," he said breathlessly as they stared at each other. "I can't do this."

She sat up and smoothed her skirt with an unsteady hand.

He got out of the car and went around to open her door.

The cold air hit her like a slap to the face. The parking lot was dark and still as he walked her up the stairs to her door.

She rested her head against his chest. "I need…"

"What, baby?"

Tears welled up in her eyes. "Will you hold me? Just for a minute?"

He wrapped his arms around her.

She kissed his neck and then his jaw. "I know you're going to beat yourself up for this all the way home," she whispered. "But I want you to keep one thing in mind."

"What's that?"

"No one has *ever* made me feel the way you do, and everything that's happened between us has happened because I wanted it to."

He cradled her face in his hands and kissed her gently. "Good night."

"Call me tomorrow?"

He nodded.

"No regrets?"

He kissed her again and was gone before she realized he hadn't answered her question.

NO REGRETS? *No regrets?* Was she kidding? Reid was riddled with regrets. He had practically attacked her. What kind of man kissed an eighteen-year-old girl like that? This whole thing with her was totally out of hand, and he had to put a stop to it. As he barreled south on Interstate 65, the speedometer reached eighty, but he didn't notice. The ringing of his cell phone jarred him out of his stupor. Realizing how fast he was driving, he backed off the accelerator and reached for the phone.

"Hello?"

"Are you beating yourself up?"

"You could say that." Why was it so easy to be honest with her? Why was *everything* so easy with her?

"Don't."

"I can't help it, Kate. I shouldn't be letting this happen."

"I'm sorry you feel that way," she said stiffly.

"Sweetheart, it's got nothing to do with you. You're absolutely perfect, but I was almost twenty-eight when you were born. How do you expect me to forget that?"

"You're the only one making an issue out of it."

His laugh came out harsher than he'd intended. "Do you honestly think I'm the only one who'll make an issue out of it? Are you really that naïve?"

"I guess I am."

He knew he was hurting her, but maybe it was better now instead of later when the stakes would no doubt be higher. "Have you spent even one minute imagining what your father would have to say about this?"

"Why would he have to know? I'm not going to tell him. Are you?"

"Oh yeah, I'm going to call him up and say, 'Hey, Jack, your daughter's got a man in her life, and oh, by the way, it's me.' I imagine that would go over really well with him."

"I don't know why you're getting so upset over a couple of simple kisses."

He swore under his breath when he realized she was crying. "If you think those kisses were simple, you're more naïve than I thought. Go to bed, Kate. It's late, and you're tired."

"I'm sorry you're mad with me. I don't want you to be mad."

All the fight went out of him. "I'm not mad at you, baby. I'm mad at myself. I should've known better than to let this get so out of control."

"So you don't want to see me anymore?"

She sounded heartbroken, and he hurt, knowing he had done that to her. "I didn't say that. Let me call you tomorrow, okay? Get some sleep."

"I'll try."

He ended the call and tossed the phone into the passenger seat with a growl of frustration. *What am I going to do?* When she asked if he didn't want to see her anymore, a shaft of pain had sliced through him. As he admitted to himself that the thought of never seeing her again was unimaginable, he realized he was in love with her—completely, totally, ridiculously in love.

"God," he groaned. "What the *hell* am I going to do?"

KATE TOSSED and turned until about three when fatigue took over, and she finally slipped into a restless sleep. She was awake again at eight. At eight thirty, she reached for the phone to call Jill.

"You'd better be dead or bleeding to be calling me this early on a Sunday," Jill muttered into the phone.

"Bleeding," Kate said softly.

"What?" Jill asked, now sounding wide-awake and on full alert. "What's wrong, Kate?"

For a few minutes, Kate couldn't speak through her sobs.

"You're scaring me, Kate. Are you hurt?"

"Not physically," Kate managed to say.

"Take a deep breath and talk to me. Right now."

"This is big, Jill. You have to swear you won't tell anyone. Especially Dad. Do you swear?"

"I don't know if I can do that. If you're in some sort of trouble, I won't keep that from him."

"It's nothing like that. Do you promise? You can't tell *anyone*."

"Okay, okay. I promise. Now tell me!"

"There's this guy here. I think I'm in love with him, and I don't know what to do."

"You've only been there a month, how can you be in love with someone?"

"I just am. I don't know why or how. Well, I do know why. He's the most amazing man I've ever known."

"Does he like you, too?"

"Yeah."

"Then what's the problem?"

"He's um, well, he's older than me."

"Is it that friend of dad's son? Dad said he thought you liked him. He's only a few years older. What's the big deal?"

"It's not his son. It's him. Dad's friend, Reid."

"Are you *kidding* me? He's what? Forty-six?"

"Not yet. He will be after Christmas."

"Oh, that makes a *big* difference. Thank goodness he's only forty-five. Jesus, Kate! Dad would flip a nut if he knew this!"

"You promised you wouldn't tell anyone. You can't tell him."

"Is the guy hard up or something? What does he want with someone your age?"

"He's definitely not hard up. If you could see him, you'd never ask that. I don't know how it happened. We just clicked. I think about him constantly, and I want to be with him all the time. He makes me laugh, I can talk to him about anything, and he's *so* sexy. You can't even imagine..."

"Wow," Jill said. "So why are you so upset?"

"Because he's freaking out about the age difference, and I'm so afraid he's going to tell me we can't see each other anymore."

"I'm glad to hear he has some sense. He's right, you know. If Dad ever found out about this... I don't even want to think about it."

"He's not going to find out."

"Are you sleeping with him?"

"No, but I want to."

"You're playing with fire. I hope you know that."

"It might not even matter." Her eyes filled with new tears. "He was so pissed off last night that I may never hear from him again."

"Why was he pissed?"

"Things got kind of intense, and he freaked."

"Intense how?"

"He finally kissed me—really kissed me. It was unbelievable." She shivered, remembering how it had felt to be in his arms.

"I don't know what to say except be careful, Kate. I don't want to see you get hurt."

"You won't tell Dad?"

"No, but I want you to keep talking to me about this. Will you do that?"

"Yeah. Thanks for listening. I was having a total meltdown, but I feel better just telling someone about it."

"Be careful who you tell. This is not something most people would understand."

"I'm not going to tell anyone else."

"When are you coming home?"

"Christmas Eve, but I have to come back on the twenty-sixth. We have a gig on the twenty-seventh."

"I'll see you then. Be careful, Kate."

"I will. Thanks."

"Anytime."

KATE WAITED all day for Reid to call. By five o'clock, she was weepy again. By six she was despondent, and by seven, she had convinced herself she would never see him again. Yet she refused to give into the urge to call him. The next move had to be his. She just wished he would call. *I guess we're not going to Graceland.*

When the doorbell rang at seven thirty, her heart nearly jumped out of her chest. She ran down the short flight of stairs and flung open the front door to find Ashton on her front steps holding a pizza.

"I come bearing gifts," he said with a cheerful smile on his handsome face.

Kate ran a self-conscious hand through her hair and forced a smile. "Hi. Come on in."

"Hey." He took her chin and tilted her face up to his. "What's all this? Have you been crying?"

She rubbed her nose. "No. I have a cold."

"Now, darlin', I wasn't born yesterday. I can tell when a girl's been crying. Come on up here and tell old Ashton what's going on." He took her by the hand and led her up the stairs to the living room. Putting the pizza on the coffee table, he sat down next to her on the sofa. "Who made you sad, and where can I find him?"

Kate swallowed hard. "How did you know it's a him?"

"Because all men are scum. Don't you know that by now?"

She grinned weakly. "Except for you, right?"

"That goes without saying. What happened?"

"It's no big deal. Just this guy I met at Mabel's. It's not going to work out between us. End of story."

"Anyone I know?" he asked with genuine concern.

She picked at a piece of lint on her sweatpants. "No," she said without looking at him. "What kind of pizza did you bring?"

"Are we changing the subject?"

"Can we, please?"

"Pepperoni."

"My favorite."

"My lucky day." He got up to get some paper towels from her kitchen and served them each a slice. "I heard something about you today."

"You did?"

He nodded. "I was in the office for a while, and I got talking to one of the partners who happened to be at your party last night. He was going on and on about this girl singer who's going to be a huge star."

147

"Shut up," she said, pushing him. "You made that up to make me feel better."

"I did not! I swear to God. I didn't realize he was talking about you until he mentioned the Rafters."

"Really?"

"Really."

They shared a smile before he launched into a story about one of his diva clients who'd had him chasing his tail for weeks trying to finalize a contract for her to appear in a dog food commercial.

Kate laughed so hard she forgot she was supposed to be sad. They ate the pizza, watched a movie, and by the time he got up to leave at ten, she felt much better.

"Thanks for the company tonight," she said when she walked him to the door.

He kissed her forehead. "My pleasure. You gonna be okay?"

"I'm fine. Go home. You have to work tomorrow."

"I'm right over there if you need me," he said, pointing across the parking lot.

"I know." She waved to him before going back upstairs to clean up the living room.

The phone rang. "What'd you forget?" she asked when she answered without checking the caller ID.

"Forget?" Reid asked.

Her heart jumped. "Oh, hi, it's you."

"Who did you think it was?"

"Ashton was just here. He brought a pizza over. I thought he forgot something."

"Oh."

"What's up?" She made a huge effort to sound like she didn't care one bit that he'd called. He didn't need to know she'd waited all day to hear from him.

"I'm in town. Can I come by?"

"That depends."

"On?"

"Are you still mad at me?"

He sighed. "I was never mad at you, Kate. We do need to talk, though."

"That doesn't sound good. Come on over, I guess."

"I'll be there in twenty minutes."

Kate ran for the shower. When she answered the door twenty minutes later, she'd changed into jeans, a sweater, and the sexiest underwear she owned.

Just in case.

CHAPTER 17

Kate sat on the sofa and watched Reid pace back and forth as he concluded his speech.

"So for these and many other reasons, we can't see each other anymore. I'm sorry, Kate. The last thing in the world I want is to hurt you, but this is wrong."

If his pained expression was any indication, his words were hurting him as much as they were hurting her.

"Aren't you going to say anything?" he asked with his hands on his hips.

She chewed on her bottom lip and studied him. "Does this mean we aren't going to Graceland tomorrow?"

He let out an exasperated sigh. "Honestly, Kate, that's all you have to say?"

Realizing her nonchalance was getting to him, she shrugged. "You got me all excited last night to go to Memphis, and then you kissed me and freaked out. That doesn't seem fair, does it?"

"First, *you* kissed *me*. And I did *not* freak out. I've just had a chance today to think about it. This isn't what I want."

She didn't believe him for a minute. "I guess I'll just have to get to Graceland some other way," Kate said, biting her thumbnail to give the impression she was in deep thought about Elvis when what she really wanted was to shriek. *He can't end it now! Not when I've only just discovered that I love him.*

Reid put his jacket back on and whipped up the zipper. "Fine. If all you care about is Graceland, be at the house at seven."

She smiled. "Seven it is."

He shook his head, stormed down the stairs, and slammed the front door behind him.

As she heard his car start, she lamented that her fancy underwear had gone to waste. "Oh, well. There's always tomorrow."

WHEN KATE ARRIVED at Reid's house the next morning, he came out to meet her wearing a dark blue suit and tie, carrying a briefcase and another bag. Kate had worn jeans, a pink sweater, her new cowboy boots, and a sheepskin coat.

"I feel underdressed," she said, admiring how sexy he looked in the suit.

"I had to dress for my meeting, but I have jeans with me for later." He held the door to the Mercedes open for her.

She noticed he went out of his way not to look at her as he closed her door. To Kate's surprise, they drove around the house rather than down the driveway. "Where are we going?"

His knuckles tightened on the wheel in apparent irritation.

"You know what? Why don't we just forget about this? I can tell you don't want me here."

"I said I'd take you, and I will."

"Gee, don't do me any favors."

They drove in tense silence for several miles on a dirt road until they reached a large white metal building. He parked the car and came around to open her door. Even when he was angry, he was courteous.

"What's this place?"

"It's where I keep my plane."

"We're *flying?*"

"Of course we are. I don't have six hours to spend driving to Memphis and back today."

"You didn't say anything about flying." She looked around, noticing the runway and light towers at either end of the strip. "Where's the pilot?" she asked with trepidation.

"You're looking at him."

"No way." She folded her arms. "I'm not going."

He snorted with disgust and pushed open the hangar doors. "Thanks for the vote of confidence, darlin', but I've been flying since before you were born."

She stood back and watched him use a small Jeep to pull a gleaming Cessna out of the building. He tossed his briefcase and bag into the airplane's cabin and then took several minutes to walk around the plane, touching various parts and kicking others.

"Last chance." He held up his keys. "You can take the car back to the house if you don't want to come."

"How long does it take to get there?"

"Twenty minutes."

"Fine. I'll go, but I'm keeping my eyes closed the whole time."

"Suit yourself." He ushered her inside the plane and directed her to sit next to him. After he completed a series of preflight checks, he reached over her shoulder for the seat belt. The back of his hand brushed her breast, and her eyes flew up to meet his as he snapped the buckle into place.

Tearing his gaze off her, he focused on the control panel as the engines roared to life. He adjusted a headset and taxied to the far end of the runway.

Kate said a silent prayer as they hurtled down the runway and lifted off. Despite her best intentions, curiosity won out, and she opened her eyes. Gasping at the exquisite view of his property from the air, she saw the house, the creek where they'd watered the horses, the guesthouse, and the miles of white fence and rolling green hills.

"I thought you weren't going to look."

"Shut up and fly the plane."

He laughed. "Want to give it a try?"

"No!"

True to his word, they touched down twenty minutes later at Memphis International Airport just behind a commercial flight.

"You can look now," Reid said as they taxied to a hangar set back from the airport's main terminal.

"I'm working on breathing. Looking is next." She glanced over at him. "I'm impressed."

"With what?"

"That you're a pilot," she said, nodding to the plane's controls.

"It's just like driving a car after all these years. I have business interests all over the state. It saves me a lot of time."

They were met and driven into town by a man from Reid's Memphis office. While he was in his meeting, Kate took a walk in a nearby park and had coffee in a restaurant on the first floor of his office building. At eleven, he called her cell phone to say he was on his way down.

He came off the elevator wearing jeans, boots, and a long brown leather coat. The suit he'd had on earlier was in a garment bag tossed over his shoulder. "Ready to go?"

She hadn't seen that leather coat before, and he looked so dashing in it that she was robbed of speech for a moment, so she just nodded in response to his question.

Reid had the keys to the car that had delivered them from the airport, and as he held her door, he cast an anxious glance at the sky. "We need to keep an eye on the weather. There's rain in the forecast. If the temperature drops any more, it'll be freezing rain. I don't like to fly in that."

"It doesn't feel that cold."

He pulled the car into traffic. "I know, but the temperature can drop fast this time of year. I have to go by a couple of our construction sites before we head out to Graceland. I hope you don't mind."

"Of course not. You're here for work."

He drove to four sites in different parts of the city. When they reached the first one, he popped the trunk to retrieve a hard hat.

Kate stayed in the car at each stop and watched him be greeted like

visiting royalty. The sites were in various stages of construction. One
was going to be a high-rise apartment building, one was a shopping
center, another a restaurant, and the last a hotel. At each site, Kate, the
architect's daughter, studied the renderings of the finished buildings
posted outside the office trailers. The now-familiar RMD signs identified the jobs as a Reid Matthews Development.

She was getting a more complete picture today of the man she'd
fallen in love with—the competent pilot, the successful businessman,
the respected employer. These new traits, added to those she'd already
experienced, served to deepen her respect and admiration for him.
She watched him shake hands with the foreman at the hotel and
remove his hard hat as he walked back to the car.

He tossed the hat into the back seat. "Sorry that took so long."

"No problem."

He cast another worried glance at the sky. "I've got to be honest
with you. We might get tossed around a bit on the flight home. It's no
big deal to me, but I'd hate to scare you. We can cut our losses and
leave now or stick to our plans and take our chances with the
weather."

Kate hid her disappointment at missing out on Graceland. "Whatever you think is best. You're the pilot."

He studied her and appeared to be making a decision that had
nothing to do with Graceland or storm clouds. "I'll tell you what. Let's
grab some lunch and go to Graceland. A promise is a promise. I'll get
you home in one piece."

ON THE SHUTTLE bus ride through gates adorned with musical notes
at Graceland, Reid confessed he'd never been there before.

"*Never?*" Kate stared at him in amazement. "How often do you
come to Memphis?"

"Almost once a week for twenty years," he said with a sheepish
grin.

"You need to learn how to live, baby," she said, again in perfect imitation of Elvis's accent.

They listened to Lisa Marie Presley's voice in headphones as she showed them through the dining room, living room, Elvis's bedroom, and that of his parents. They strolled through the music room where his grand piano was the main attraction, before they saw the King's beloved pool table, his business office, and the famous "jungle" den. Kate loved every gaudy, over-the-top inch of the place.

The tension that had vibrated between her and Reid all day disappeared while they checked out an extensive collection of Elvis's gold records and giggled with delight at some of his more outrageous costumes.

Kate pointed to a white jumpsuit encrusted with rhinestones. "You'd look adorable in that one," she whispered.

"Not in this or any other lifetime."

"Stick in the mud." She was relieved by the return of their easy rapport, almost as if his speech the night before had never happened.

"Call me what you will, but you wouldn't catch me dead in a getup like that."

The tour of the house concluded in the Meditation Garden, where Elvis was buried with several of his relatives. At Elvis's gravesite, Kate curled her hand into Reid's.

"It's so sad," Reid whispered, lacing his fingers through hers. "He had everything, but look how he ended up."

"Alone and wasted," Kate said softly.

He glanced at her. "Don't let that happen to you."

"I'm hardly Elvis Presley."

"You have the same kind of talent, and it's going to take you to some of the same places it took him."

His certainty astounded her. "How can you be so sure?"

He shrugged. "Call it a hunch."

The rain began to fall harder, so they ran back inside to see the car collection. By the time they toured Elvis's airplane, the *Lisa Marie*, it was pouring and considerably colder than it had been an hour earlier.

"Shit." Reid looked up at the sky, reached for her hand, and hustled her onto a shuttle bus for the ride back to the parking lot.

The wind whipped and icy rain pinged against the windshield while they waited for the car to warm up.

"I'm not going to fly in this. Not with you."

"Would you go if you were alone?" His confident grin told her he'd done it many times before. "We can go. I'll be fine."

"No, you'd be scared. I won't do that."

"So what's the plan?"

"I guess we'll have to stay." He reached into his pocket for his cell phone and scrolled through his list of phone numbers until he found what he was looking for. "Hi, this is Reid Matthews. I'd like to book two rooms for tonight, please." He listened, sighed, and then nodded. "That's fine. I'll take it. Thanks."

"What did they say?"

"They're sold out except for a suite with two bedrooms. That'll have to do." A muscle in his cheek pulsed with tension. "A convention in town has all the hotels jammed."

He looked so upset she couldn't resist asking, "What's wrong?"

"I feel like I'm being tested here, Kate. I want very much to do the right thing by you, but circumstances keep getting in the way. Spending a night here with you is *not* a good idea."

"Why don't we just make the most of it, have a good time, and try not to worry too much?"

"I guess we don't have any choice."

His distress was so palpable that she reached over to take his hand. He surprised her when he wrapped his fingers around hers and lifted her hand to kiss the back of it. On the way to the hotel, he called his house to tell Martha they'd be staying in Memphis. She was relieved to hear he wouldn't be flying in the bad weather.

The hotel was small but elegant, and Reid seemed to be well known to the bellmen who greeted them. Kate walked with him to the registration desk.

"Good afternoon, Mr. Matthews," the woman at the desk said. "Welcome back."

Reid handed her his credit card. "Thank you."

She returned his card along with two room key cards. "You and your daughter should be very comfortable in the Presidential Suite on the sixth floor."

When Reid cleared his throat, Kate looked down to study her boots.

"Thank you," he said, his voice tight with strain.

Following him to the elevator, Kate could see the tension in his shoulders through the dark leather coat. *Damn that woman! That was the last thing he needed to hear! His daughter! Ugh!*

He said nothing in the elevator. When the doors opened on the sixth floor, he stormed out ahead of her to a room at the end of the hallway. He opened the door and held it for her. As soon as the door closed, he exploded. *"Did you hear what that woman said? What she assumed? Do you see now what I've been trying to tell you?"*

Kate knew she needed to act quickly or lose him forever. Shedding her own coat as she went, she walked over to him and slid the leather coat off his shoulders.

He fought her. "What are you doing?"

She pushed him down into a plush upholstered chair.

"Kate—"

Straddling him, she sat on his lap and felt him instantly harden beneath her. She resisted his efforts to remove her. "I'm not your daughter," she said in a husky whisper. "I know it, and you know it. That's all that matters." She wove her fingers into his hair, drew him to her, and kissed him with all the love she felt for him. At first he resisted her, but as she moved on his lap, she felt his control slip away.

"Kate, stop," he whispered against her lips as her tongue flirted with his. "You're starting something I can't finish."

"I want you, Reid. I want you the way a grown woman wants a man."

His hands came up to circle her bottom, pulling her closer to him. "I want you, too. God help me, but I want you."

They kissed again, and she shivered when his hands slid under her sweater to caress her fevered skin. A bolt of heat charged through her when he unhooked the front clasp of her bra and fondled her breasts. He rolled his thumbs over her nipples, and she shuddered. *"Please, Reid,"* she panted, bringing her lips down on his.

With a surge of power, he stood without breaking their kiss. She wrapped her arms and legs around him, her tongue tangling with his as he carried her to one of the bedrooms. When he set her down next to the big bed, her legs wanted to buckle beneath her. She reached up to unbutton his shirt, and he tugged the sweater over her head. His eyes flashed with blatant desire when he uncovered the lacy pink bra hanging open over her breasts. Easing the straps off her shoulders, he let it fall to the floor next to her sweater.

Standing half naked before a man for the first time in her life, Kate should have been self-conscious. But because it was him, and because her need for him was so great, she had no time for embarrassment. She pushed off his shirt and buried her face in the light dusting of brown chest hair. He trembled as her lips brushed his pebbled nipple while her hands skimmed over his muscular chest and stomach. When she reached the waistband of his jeans, he stopped her.

Tipping her face up, he studied her intently. "Are you sure, Kate?"

She nodded.

"I don't have any protection."

"I'm on the pill."

Surprise registered on his face.

"I did it a month before I left home. Just in case."

"I haven't done this in a long time, so I'm safe."

She pulled at the button of his jeans and swore he stopped breathing when she unzipped him.

With his hands on her face, he kissed her gently. "I love you, Kate. I don't want to hurt you."

Her heart hammered at his words of love. "I love you, too, but if you don't make love to me right now, I think I'll die, Reid."

He wrapped his arms around her and bent his head to kiss her. "What have you done before?"

"Nothing." Her cheeks flamed with embarrassment. "Much..."

Reid took a deep breath and looked up at the ceiling as if to summon divine assistance. His hands moved over her back, more in a gesture of comfort than seduction. He unbuttoned her jeans and helped her out of them, leaving her only in the tiny pink panties that matched her bra.

"God, Kate," he whispered against her neck. "You're so beautiful."

She pushed at his jeans, but he stopped her. "Not yet, honey." He lifted her onto the bed and stretched out next to her.

Under the heat of his gaze, her body hummed with tension and desire. Her nipples tightened in anticipation, and the tingle between her legs became almost painful. Sensing his hesitation, she took his hand and brought it to her breast.

He groaned and shifted so he rested on top of her. Dipping his head, he grazed her nipple first with his lips and then his teeth.

Without his weight on top of her, Kate would have levitated off the bed. The sensations spiraling through her were so overwhelming they were almost unbearable. When he sucked hard on her nipple, a spasm began between her legs and rocketed through her, sending shock waves from her toes to her fingers. She cried out in surprise and fright. "What..."

Breathing hard, Reid rested his forehead on her chest.

"What happened?" she asked in a small voice.

"You had an orgasm, darlin'."

Her cheeks burned again. "Oh. Is that normal?"

He smiled. "It's not usually that easy for women, so I'd say you're one lucky girl, Kate Harrington."

Reaching for him, she brought him up to her. "I want to do everything, Reid. Show me."

He chuckled softly. "You're going to kill me."

"At least you'll die happy," she said with a saucy smile as she pulled his mouth down to hers.

Their tongues came together in an explosive burst of passion that made them both breathless. He filled his hands with her breasts and toyed with her nipples. She tore her lips free of his and sucked in a deep breath.

He kissed her jaw, her neck, her throat, and dragged his tongue over her collarbone.

She lifted her hips, begging him for more.

Gently, he kissed the sloping curve of her breast.

Kate covered his hands on her breasts and pushed them together, asking him to focus on her nipples.

He flicked his tongue from one to the other.

She moaned and the burn between her legs again became urgent.

Moving down, he trailed his lips over her ribs and lingered at her belly, dipping his tongue into her belly button.

Kate was blinded by desire. Nothing in her life could have prepared her for this. She craved him—the feel of his soft skin, the citrus scent of his cologne, his hair tickling her belly, his tongue leaving a damp path to the tiny swatch of lace that covered her.

He nudged her legs farther apart and dusted a finger lightly along her thigh and into the gap of her panties.

Sliding his finger through her dampness, he seemed to know exactly where she needed his touch. The orgasm again took her by surprise, but this time she was too busy trying to breathe to be frightened by it. As she came down from the high, she became aware of her panties traveling over her legs. Kicking off his jeans, Reid lay on his side facing her.

Kate caressed his chest and let her eyes drift to his erection, which bobbed with anticipation. It was bigger than she'd expected it to be, and her breath hitched as she wondered how it would ever fit. A trickle of fear worked its way down her spine.

Tuning into her anxiety, Reid took her hand and wrapped it around his steely length. When she gave it a gentle squeeze, he groaned.

She let go abruptly. "I'm sorry. Did I hurt you?"

"No, no," he sighed, putting his hand over hers to show her how to stroke him.

Fascinated by the silky soft skin that covered the hardness, she watched a bead of moisture form at the tip. She dragged her thumb through the pearly fluid and felt him go rigid.

He captured her hand to stop her. "We'll be all done before we get to the good stuff if you keep that up," he whispered, bringing his mouth down on hers for a deep kiss. His hand traveled over her back to her bottom and between her legs to probe her dampness. "Kate…"

Unable to think of anything but the motion of his fingers, she could only feel.

"I need to prepare you, honey." His hand hovered at her entrance. "It might hurt just a little."

She could think only of the urgent need. "It's okay."

Moving slowly and with great care, he worked a finger into her. At the same time, he closed his lips over her nipple. The combination was overwhelming. So focused was she on the tugging of his mouth on her nipple that she barely noticed when he added a second finger. Her hips met the thrusts of his fingers in an almost involuntary motion.

She trembled violently. *"Reid…"*

"Does it hurt, honey?"

"No." She rolled her head into his chest and reached for him.

He removed his fingers and shifted so he was poised between her legs. "Look at me, baby."

She opened her eyes to find him gazing down at her.

"I love you," he said, brushing his lips over hers.

Clutching his shoulders, she said, "I love you, too."

He eased her legs farther apart. "Relax, honey."

"I'm trying."

He kissed her, a deep, passionate kiss that distracted her—momentarily—from the pressure between her legs. An instant of blinding, burning pain quickly gave way to pleasure. Oh, God, he felt so good.

Her hands coasted over his back to grip his backside.

Groaning, he flexed his hips and buried himself in her. "Okay?" he asked, holding still to give her time to adjust.

"Hmmm, oh, yeah."

Encouraged, he kissed her and reached beneath them to anchor her hips, keeping his movements small and easy.

"Oh," she gasped.

"What, honey? Tell me what you need."

"*More,*" she pleaded, pushing hard against him.

He flexed once, twice.

That was all it took to send her spiraling into yet another orgasm.

Reid saw her through the storm and then was gripped by one of his own.

WITH REID RESTING on top of her without crushing her, Kate knew she would never forget this. It hadn't been at all like she'd expected. Her friends had talked about feeling let down afterward, but Kate didn't. If anything, she was exhilarated. "Did you mean it?"

"What?" He spoke as if it took every ounce of energy he had.

"That you love me?"

He nodded against her neck.

"But you wish you didn't?"

He withdrew from her and rolled onto his side so he could see her. "I could never be sorry for loving you. I just wish things were different."

"Can I ask you something?"

"Anything."

"Was it good for you?"

He leaned over to kiss her, pulling her tight against him with one arm. "It's only been like that for me with one other woman. It's been so long, I'd forgotten it could be that good."

Pleased by his answer, Kate rested her cheek on her folded arm and studied his face, wanting to memorize every detail. "What was she like? Your wife?"

He thought about it for a moment before he replied. "She was sweet and very devoted to Ashton and me. He looks like her."

"How did you meet her?"

"We went to high school together and kept in touch during college, even though we dated other people. When I came home from Berkeley, all I wanted was to be with her. We got married a few months later and had Ashton right away. He was only two, and we were talking about having another child when Cindy was killed."

"What happened to her?"

"She'd been doing volunteer work at a hospital in the city and was on her way home when a truck crossed the center lane and hit her head on. The paramedics said she died instantly. I can only hope so."

"I'm sorry," Kate said, caressing his face in an attempt to wipe away the grief she had stirred.

"It was a long time ago."

"But you're still sad about it."

"I've come to realize you never really get over something like that. Somehow, you find a way to live with it. You know all about that, don't you?"

Nodding, Kate shifted so she was on top of him and kissed his neck and face.

He put his arms around her. "It feels good to be in love again, Kate. No matter what happens, I'll never have any regrets about that."

As she moved on top of him, she felt him spring to life beneath her. "Can we do it again yet?"

"No, honey. You'll be sore."

He groaned when she straddled him and sank down on him.

"I'll take my chances."

THEY FLEW BACK to Nashville late on Tuesday afternoon. Reid glanced over at Kate from the pilot's seat. "What're you smiling about?"

"It's a beautiful day."

"It sure is." He pushed aside the microphone on his headset so he could kiss her. "We need to talk about what's going to happen when we get home, though."

"I know."

"You can't tell anyone about this. About us."

"I wish we didn't have to hide it."

"I do, too. But people wouldn't understand, and it would cause me a lot of trouble."

"I've only told one person."

He looked at her with alarm. "Who?"

"My sister. Jill."

"Jesus, Kate. She won't tell your dad, will she?"

"I made her promise not to, and I trust her. We went through a lot together in the last couple of years. She won't tell."

"I hope not. I'm worried about how we get around Martha and the fact that Ashton's your neighbor. This could get complicated." Sensing her discouragement, he took her hand. "We'll figure it out, darlin'. Don't worry."

They touched down a few minutes later. After they had dinner together at his house, she drove to her apartment. He picked her up at ten and brought her back to his house so her car wouldn't be in the driveway. They spent the night in his room and were out the next morning before Martha got up.

"I feel like we got away with something," she said on the way back into town.

"I hate sneaking around. I don't want you to think for one minute that I'm ashamed of you, Kate. I adore you. I just don't want to put either of us through what would happen if people found out about us."

"It's okay. We need some time to get used to it ourselves before the whole world finds out anyway."

"That's my girl," he said, kissing her when he dropped her off at her apartment before heading to work.

"See you tonight?"

"I can't wait."

REID WAS in his office poring over plans for an office building in Knoxville when his secretary let him know Ashton was there to see him. Reid asked her to send him in.

"Hey. What brings you to my part of town?"

"I wanted to see my old man." Ashton bent to give his father a quick hug. "Is that okay?"

Reid smiled, delighted that his son had never outgrown the easy affection between them. "It's more than okay. What've you been up to?"

"Just working a lot, same old thing. How about you? You look beat. Are you sick?"

Since he could hardly admit to what he'd been doing the last two nights when he should've been sleeping, Reid shook his head. "I'm fine."

Ashton paced in front of his father's desk. Clearly, something else was on his mind. "I was wondering if you've talked to Kate."

Reid's gaze whipped up to meet his son's. "Why?"

"Well, I was over there Sunday night, and she was a mess. She said she'd had a falling out with some guy she met at Mabel's. But when I asked Butch if he knows the guy, he couldn't remember her dating anyone while she worked there. Then I couldn't reach her the last couple of days. She wasn't answering her cell phone, and I'm just worried that something's up with her. Do you think we should call her dad?"

"No," Reid said emphatically—too emphatically, in fact. "No," he said again in a more normal tone. "I'm sure she'd just had a bad day when you saw her."

Ashton looked so dismayed that Reid realized his son might have feelings for Kate, too. *Christ.*

"Do you know anything about this guy she's seeing?" Ashton asked, running a hand through his blond hair in frustration.

His heart raced as Reid looked his son in the eye. "I don't know anything about it."

CHAPTER 18

$\mathcal{C}$lare worked late at the bookstore on Christmas Eve. When Bea finally turned over the Open sign and locked the door, the two women flopped into easy chairs in front of the fire.

"Thank God it's over for another year," Bea groaned.

"My feet are killing me."

"I hope you didn't overdo it."

"No worries. I'll take a hot bath when I get home. I'll be good as new tomorrow."

"Speaking of tomorrow, the invite still stands. Why don't you come with me?" Bea had invited Clare to Christmas dinner at her brother's house in Burlington.

"Thanks, Bea, but I'm going to take it easy tomorrow. The girls will be up the day after, so we'll celebrate then. I need to get their rooms ready and do some cooking. Aidan dragged the old stove and fridge back into the kitchen for me."

"Are you sure being alone on Christmas is a good idea?"

"I'll be fine, but I appreciate the invite."

"Well, if you change your mind, just give me a call in the morning," Bea said as she hauled herself out of the chair to begin straightening up the store, which looked like a blitzkrieg had gone through it.

"You'll be okay without me next week? I can come in if you get busy."

"It'll be slow. Mostly returns, so have fun with your girls and don't worry about this place."

Clare had come to enjoy the job—and her time with Bea—so much that she'd been relieved when Bea asked her to stay on at least through the Winter Festival in late January. Clare tugged on her parka, hat, and gloves for the walk home.

"Thanks again for all the help this month." Bea gave Clare a quick hug. "You really saved me."

"I think it was quite the other way around. Have a wonderful Christmas."

"You, too."

Clare stepped out into the cold. The tiny village twinkled with white lights in the shop windows. The sidewalks bustled with last-minute shoppers and the usual groups of skiers. Christmas music coming from speakers in front of the grocery store added to the festive atmosphere.

From the corner of Maple Street, Clare noticed Aidan had plugged in the lights on the Christmas tree she'd put in the front window. The white lights glowed against the gold ornaments she had bought. Everything about this Christmas was foreign to her, but she was determined to make the best of it. Next year she would be back in Rhode Island with the girls. Maybe by then she'd be comfortable with the idea of spending the holiday with Jack, Andi, and their combined families. *Hey, it's a goal.* That would be best for the girls. She hated the idea of them shuttling back and forth between their divorced parents on holidays.

If she'd ever had doubt about her decision to temporarily move to Stowe, she could now say she'd done the right thing. She felt stronger every day, both physically and emotionally. Lately, she'd been surprised to find herself thinking of Jack less frequently. In fact, she'd been startled to realize her thoughts seemed to revolve around Aidan rather than Jack these days. *An interesting development*, she mused.

Aidan hadn't mentioned "the date" again in the ten days since he asked her, and Clare knew he wouldn't ask a second time. The ball was firmly in her court. They'd continued their casual dinners together and kept up the lighthearted sparring, but there was an undercurrent between them now that hadn't been there before he asked her out.

She came in through the front door to find him bent over, vacuuming the living room, and took a moment to admire the view. Clare had grown accustomed to him being there when she got home from the store. He was usually filthy from working all day, and his hair was often full of sawdust, but the grime and dust only added to his masculine appeal.

He sucked up the huge pile of sawdust he'd swept into the middle of the floor and turned off the vacuum.

"Hey," he said. "When did you get home?"

"A minute ago. I was enjoying the sight of you cleaning my house."

"I'm glad I'm available to entertain you," he said dryly as he checked his watch. "I've got to hit the road in a few minutes."

He was going to his parents' home on Cape Cod for the holiday.

"I thought you would've left by now."

"I wanted to finish one last thing in the bathroom so it'll be ready for phase two when I get back."

"You should get going. You have a long ride."

"Are you sure you won't come with me? I could have you back in plenty of time for the girls."

"I'm sure. Thanks for asking, but I'm looking forward to a nice quiet day tomorrow."

"So the idea of spending Christmas with my parents, my three obnoxious brothers, my sister, her husband, and their five kids doesn't appeal to you?"

She laughed at his pained expression. "It sounds lovely. Don't let me keep you."

Raising an eyebrow, he said, "You're awfully anxious to be rid of me. Is your boyfriend waiting outside for me to leave?" He took a peek out the window.

She smiled. "You just can't seem to take a hint."

"Do you mind if I borrow your shower? My mother will have a cow if I show up looking like this, and going home would take too long."

"Feel free. Towels are in the closet behind the door."

"Thanks." He went out to his truck for a duffel bag and took it with him upstairs.

While he was in the shower, Clare went up to her temporary kitchen to make a couple of sandwiches and brew a thermos of coffee to send with him. She was back downstairs by the time he came down fifteen minutes later.

"How long will it take you to get there?" She turned and froze at the sight of him in a brown turtleneck sweater and jeans—with no holes—that hugged all the right places. His hair was still wet, his handsome face smooth after a shave. *Holy cow.*

He held her gaze with green eyes that danced with amusement and desire. "About four hours."

Clare swallowed hard. "I made you some sandwiches and coffee."

He looked pleased and surprised at the same time. "Once a mom, always a mom?"

She shrugged as she handed him the bag and caught a whiff of cologne that made her want to drool.

He took the bag from her and rested it next to his duffel on the floor. "Thank you."

"You're welcome."

"You're sure you'll be okay by yourself?"

Touched by his concern, she smiled. "I'm sure."

"Well..." He started to turn toward the door but changed his mind so quickly that Clare had no time to gauge his intent before his lips were on hers and she was enveloped in his strong arms. To her great relief, the kiss didn't match the flash of desire she'd seen in his eyes, almost as if he knew he needed to go easy with her. When he finally pulled away from her, he looked stricken. "I'm sorry. I couldn't wait another minute to do that."

She looked up at him. "I'm glad you didn't," she said, going up on tiptoes to kiss him again. "You'd better go. It's getting late."

With great reluctance, he picked up his bag. "I'll see you in a couple of days."

"Remember—no crack-of-dawn mornings when the girls are here. They're late sleepers."

"Got it. Have a Merry Christmas."

She walked him to the door. "You, too."

With one last quick kiss, he was gone.

Clare watched him get into the truck and waved as he drove away. She flipped off the porch light, closed the door, locked it, and leaned back against it, willing her heart beat back to a normal pace. "Well," she said to herself, "that was a surprise." With a giggle, she added, "A very lovely surprise."

AIDAN CALLED his mother from the road to let her know he'd gotten a late start. The last thing he wanted was to irritate everyone at Christmas by making Colleen O'Malley worry unnecessarily. For two hours after he'd finished working for the day, he kept himself busy with menial chores at Clare's house while he waited for her to get home from the store. He'd wanted to be sure she was really okay before he left her alone for Christmas.

He couldn't deny she stirred emotions in him that had lain dormant for so long he'd forgotten he had them. The aura of vulnerability about her generated a powerful urge to protect her from whatever she was running from. He was also amazed by just how badly he wanted to know what had caused the haunted look he saw from time to time in those amazing blue eyes of hers.

Hours later, he was still thinking of her at home alone on Christmas Eve as he drove toward the Sagamore Bridge at the entrance to Cape Cod. Yawning, he reached for his cell phone and was glad he'd thought to program her number in earlier. She answered on the second ring.

"Hey," he said. "I'm getting tired. Keep me company?"

"I'd love to. Where are you?"

"Almost to the Cape, and then I've got about an hour to Chatham."

"Has your family always lived there?"

"Almost forty years, since right after my parents got married."

Clare groaned. "Oh, *God*, O'Malley, *you're not even forty?*"

He laughed. "Not quite. Is that a problem?"

"I'm six, no wait, almost *seven* years older than you?"

"Lucky for me you look about twenty-two."

"Ugh, I should cut my losses and head for the hills." In truth, he was thrilled to hear her acknowledge that "something" was going on between them. "This is just too embarrassing."

"Have I told you I *love* older women?"

"Good save," she said in the dry tone she did so well. "Tell me about your family."

"That's a story and a half."

"I've got time if you do."

"All right, let's see. My parents, Colleen and Dennis, grew up on the same block in South Boston. My dad's parents were Irish immigrants, but he was born in the city. My mom emigrated from Ireland with her parents when she was ten. Granny Fitz, my mother's mom, swore to her dying day that my mother set her sights on my father on her second day in Boston. He was four years older than her, and from what we always heard, he never stood a chance."

Clare laughed. "I like her already."

"Yeah, she's a pistol. Our favorite story about them happened when she was nineteen. She allegedly dragged our poor father out of a smoke-filled pub in Dorchester and issued an ultimatum on the sidewalk in front of his drinking buddies. 'It's either them or me, Dennis O'Malley,'" Aidan mimicked in a wicked Irish brogue. "'Take your pick.'"

"She did not!"

"Did so. According to legend, the fire in her green eyes brought young O'Malley to his knees, and with a wistful look at the lads, he said, 'Why, you, love. Of course I choose you.' She had him in front of the parish priest less than two weeks later. Right after the wedding—

and much to Da's dismay—she moved them to Chatham. Da was devastated. 'All my friends are in Boston,' he lamented."

"She was no fool."

"That's right. Mum said, 'Exactly. Now find a way to make a living here, Dennis O'Malley, because there're going to be babies. Lots of them.' So Da did as he was told, using the only marketable skill he had to build a construction business. O'Malley Construction was slow to catch on, and I remember a childhood long on love but short on frivolous extras."

"Tell me you were born right after their wedding, and you'll be forty *very* soon."

"Ten months to the day after their wedding. I'll be forty in February. Is that soon enough?"

"I guess it'll have to do."

"My brother Brandon was born a year after me. Two years later came Colin followed by Declan the next year. Brandon, Colin, and I were named for Mum's older brothers, who broke her heart by staying behind in Ireland when she and her parents moved to America. We grew up fascinated by her stories about the uncles, and for years she begged Da to fly her brothers over. The business had finally begun to make some decent money when he gave in and brought the 'boys' over for a three-week visit. Well, the *boys* had grown into men in the twenty or so years since she'd last seen them." Aidan smiled at the memory. "They tore through Chatham like a tornado the summer I was eleven. They brawled their way through every bar in town, and after they left, at least five local girls claimed they'd fathered their babies. They left a *big* impression on us, and suffice it to say, Mum never mentioned a return visit."

Clare roared with laughter. "You're making this up!"

"I am not! Oh, I forgot to mention I was nine when my sister Erin was born. Mum thanked God for finally giving her a girl. Ironically enough, though, it was Erin who turned out to be the hellion. We boys lived in such mortal fear of Mum—something we've never entirely outgrown—that we didn't dare cross her. Erin, however, made a blood sport out of defying her. From the time she uttered her first words, her battles with Mum were legendary. They went on until Erin turned twenty-one and met poor Tommy Maloney."

"Let me guess, history repeated itself?"

"You got it. Erin decided Tommy was the one for her and set out to win him over with a campaign of such ruthless determination that even though she'd tortured us boys for years, we felt sorry for Tommy. They were married within six months and had five children in five years, much to Mum's delight."

"I love it," Clare said, chuckling. "Where are they now?"

"They're all still in Chatham. My brothers and Tommy work with Da. The business became downright profitable once we were old enough to work. The year I was fifteen, Da proudly renamed the business O'Malley & Sons Construction. Everything I know about construction and restoration, I learned working summers with him during high school and college."

"He taught you well. So why don't you work with them?"

"That's another whole story," he said as he drove through the town of Chatham. "I'm almost there."

"What's Chatham like? I've never spent much time on the Cape. There wasn't much reason to leave Newport in the summertime."

Relieved that she hadn't chosen to pursue the "other" story, he said, "It's a lot like Stowe, actually. Sometimes I think that's why I feel so at home there. The seasons are opposite, though. Stowe's population swells during ski season, and Chatham's a madhouse in the summer when the roads are clogged with cars and the beaches overrun with tourists."

"Sounds like Newport."

"Thanks for keeping me company," Aidan said, reluctant to let her go. He'd talked more to her in the short time he'd known her than he'd talked to anyone in years. He had a feeling he'd never get tired of talking to her, a thought that should've terrified him but didn't for some reason.

"It was definitely my pleasure. That was the best story I've heard in a long time. The jury's still out on how much is fact and how much is fiction."

"All fact, baby," he said with a laugh. Aidan hadn't told that story in years and had enjoyed sharing it with her. "I'll talk to you soon." He clicked off the phone and pulled into the driveway at his parents' three-story Victorian. The house had started out as a ranch but became one of O'Malley Construction's pet projects over the years, expanding along with the family it housed.

Dennis nearly had a stroke over the fanciful, gingerbread paint job Colleen commissioned two summers earlier, and the boys knew better than to tease him about giving in yet again to their mother. Instead, when he thought Colleen wasn't listening, Dennis grumbled about living in a house that looked like a big, pink cake. A Christmas tree lit the front window, and the house was outlined with white lights that illuminated the ridiculous color.

As Aidan grabbed his duffel and a big bag of gifts from the bed of the pickup, the front door flew open and Colleen ran out to greet him wearing a long bathrobe over her nightgown.

"Aidan O'Malley, get over here, and give your Mum some love," she said, throwing her arms around him.

He dropped his bags, lifted her off the ground, and swung her around.

She swatted at him. "Put me down, you fool! You'll throw your back out!"

"Whatever you say, Mum. You're a real load. What're you? One-ten these days?"

She hooked a hand into the crook of his elbow to lead him inside. "Oh, hush. I haven't been one-ten since before you were born. Da just gave up on you and went to bed. He said he'll see you in the morning."

The house smelled like mothballs, evergreen, and spice. "What've you been cooking?"

"What *haven't* I been cooking? Your sister and I were at it all day."

"Fighting or cooking?"

She snorted. "A little of both." The light over the stove lit her still-pretty face. She would be sixty at her next birthday but didn't look a day over fifty to Aidan. Her brilliant red hair had faded with age to an equally attractive auburn that was mixed now with traces of gray. "Come in here and let me feed you."

He sat down at the kitchen table. "I'm good. I ate on the road."

"Junk, no doubt."

"No, a friend of mine made me some sandwiches."

Her eyes widened with interest. "A girlfriend?"

"Mum," he said, the warning clear in his tone. "How about you get me a beer before you start grilling me?"

She brushed the hair back from his forehead and leaned in to kiss his cheek. "I don't know why you have to hold out on me, Aidan O'Malley. You know I worry about you."

"You don't need to. I'm fine."

She got a Sam Adams from the fridge, opened it for him, and sat with him at the table. "Da and I drove into the city to go to the cemetery yesterday," she said, taking his hand.

He looked down at their joined hands as a pain cut through him. After all these years, that it still could take his breath away…"Thanks."

"You should go, too, you know."

He shook his head. "I appreciate that you go."

"Mrs. Gough down the street has had some heart troubles lately. Maybe you could go by to see her while you're home."

"What for?"

"Don't be obtuse, Aidan. You could make sure her doctor's doing the right things."

"I'm sure she's getting very good care."

"You're squandering your God-given talents up there in those mountains."

"That's not true. I'm using some of the other ones. So what's going on tomorrow?"

Colleen scowled at the shift in conversation away from one of her favorite subjects. "Da and I are going over to Erin and Tommy's early to watch the kids open their gifts. Then we're all going to ten o'clock mass. Everyone's coming back here after to open gifts and have dinner. You're welcome to join us at mass."

"No, thanks."

Colleen sighed. "It would break Sarah's heart to know you've lost your faith, Aidan."

Fighting the urge to snap at her, he forced an even tone. "I'm sure she'd understand."

"It's been ten years, love. When're you going to start living again?"

"I don't know." He sagged in his chair. "I was thinking on the way down here that Colin would be ten now. I wondered what he would've wanted for Christmas this year. A skateboard or a new bike? Maybe a baseball glove. Probably something electronic, too."

Colleen stood up to wrap her arms around him. "Why don't you get some sleep? Things will be better in the morning."

He laughed. "I wish I had a nickel for every time I've heard you say that."

"And I wish there was something I could say to make it better."

Patting her hand, he closed his eyes against the rush of emotion. "I know, Mum. I know."

CHAPTER 19

The night before Kate went home to Rhode Island for Christmas, Reid took her to dinner in an out-of-the way place over in Rutherford County. They'd managed to spend every night together for more than a week without anyone questioning them and had begun to feel more confident that they could exist in their own little bubble. After a candlelight dinner, he reached into his suit coat pocket and withdrew a wrapped box. He nudged it across the table to her.

"What's this?"

"Open it and find out."

"I have something for you, too, but I have to give it to you later."

He raised an eyebrow.

She laughed. "Get your mind out of the gutter."

"Open your present."

He wore a dark gray suit with a cranberry tie and was so handsome Kate couldn't take her eyes off him. "I'm nervous," she said, sensing a significant gift.

"Don't be." He took the box from her and slid the paper and bow from it. "I think this talent of yours will one day take you far away from me, so I wanted you to be able to take my heart with you." Inside the box was a gold locket with a diamond inset in the heart.

"Oh, Reid," she said, her eyes swimming with tears. When she was unable to stem the flood, she reached for his hand. "Can we go?"

He signaled for the check and had them out of there a few minutes later. As they walked to his car, he kept an arm around her. A bitter chill frosted the air, and a full moon rose in a night sky sprinkled with puffy clouds. "What is it, baby? I wanted to make you happy," he said, brushing at her tears.

"You did. I'm sorry. I just can't imagine leaving you for two days to go home for Christmas, let alone my career taking me away from you. I don't want that."

When they reached his car, he leaned in to kiss her and took the box from her. Turning her around, he lifted her hair to hook the locket and kissed his way down her neck, making her shiver. "I love you, and I'll be right here waiting for you no matter where your career takes you."

She turned to lean her forehead against his chest. "I came here looking for stardom, but I found you. The rest doesn't seem so important anymore." Brushing her hands over his lapels, she looked up at him. "At the party we played Saturday night, a producer gave me his card. He wants me to call him after the holidays."

"That's fantastic, Kate! Why didn't you tell me?"

She shrugged.

He tilted her chin up. "Sweetheart, listen to me. You can't abandon all your dreams because you fell in love with me. That would break my heart. You have such a rare and special talent, and you need to find out where it'll take you. As much as I want you here with me, I'd never forgive myself if I held you back."

"Let's go home. I want to give you my gift."

He opened the car door for her and kept his hand wrapped around hers on the ride home. At his house, Martha waited for them. Reid had told her Kate would be staying with them so he could take her to the airport early the next morning.

"Good evening, Mr. Reid, Miss Kate. The guestroom is all set for you, Miss Kate. I'll have breakfast ready for you in plenty of time to make your flight in the morning."

"Oh, you don't have to, Martha," Kate said. "I can get something at the airport."

"Don't be silly. I'll see you in the morning," she said and retired to her quarters off the kitchen.

Reid carried Kate's overnight bag up to the guest room.

"Oh, I forgot. I need my guitar, too."

"I'll go out to the car and get it."

"Thanks." Toying with her new locket, she watched him go. *God, I love him.* She wondered if it was normal to feel almost sick from the riot of emotions that stormed through her every time she was near him.

He came back with her guitar. "Let's go light a fire in my room."

"Bring that." She nodded to the guitar. "Part of that gift I mentioned."

"I'm intrigued," he said with a smile as he held out a hand to her.

Kate loved Reid's bedroom. He'd knocked out a wall to make two bedrooms into one large room. The walls were painted a rich choco-late brown that matched the leather furniture arranged in front of the fire. His laptop and briefcase sat on a small desk where he sometimes worked at night. His bed was on the other side of the room, which was connected to a master bathroom.

He took off his suit coat and tie, released his top button, and rolled up his sleeves. After he lit the fire, he joined her on the sofa.

"Are you ready for your gift?"

"I'm dying of curiosity."

"Well, it's nothing spectacular, so don't get too excited. I wanted to get you something special, but since you already have an airplane, I thought, what else can I get the man who has everything?"

"I only have everything now that I have you," he said, drawing her into a kiss.

She put her hands on his chest in a halfhearted attempt to push him away. "You're making me lose my train of thought."

"Sorry."

"So, *anyway*," she said with a stern look that made him laugh, "I thought of the one thing I could give you that you couldn't get anywhere else. This is where the guitar comes in. I wrote a song for you."

His face lit up with surprise and delight. "You did?"

She nodded, tuning her guitar and taking a deep calming breath. "I think this is the first time I've ever been nervous about singing."

"You've never had a more appreciative audience. Ever."

His smile of encouragement put her at ease. "Here goes." She launched into a complicated guitar intro that had his eyes widening with amazement.

I thought I knew
what love was,
but then there was you...
I thought I knew
how it would be,
but now I see,
And now it's true...
I didn't know
until there was you...
Until there was you...
Until there was you...
I thought I knew
And now it's true...
I thought I knew
what peace was,
then there was you...
I thought I knew
what dreams were,
then there was you...
I thought I knew
how it would be,
but now I see...
I thought I knew
what love was,

but then there was you
Then there was you...

She played the final notes of the song and propped her guitar against the sofa.

"Kate," he said, his voice heavy with emotion as he brought her into his arms. "That was the most amazing gift anyone has ever given me."

"Anytime you hear me sing that song, I'll be singing it for you."

"Thank you." He kissed her softly. "Do you know when I fell in love with you?"

She shook her head.

"That first day in the dining room when Ashton dared you to sing. For days afterward, I'd be at work or riding Thunder or lying in bed, and I'd hear you singing *Crazy*. You have the most exquisite voice. The voice of an angel."

"Take me to bed, Reid."

~

"KATE, HONEY, WAKE UP."

Kate awoke from a sound sleep to find Reid sitting on the edge of the bed. "What's wrong?" She noticed he was dressed in a black sweater and jeans. "What time is it?"

"Three thirty. Come on, get dressed. I've got a surprise for you."

Curious, Kate stretched and yawned before she got up. She dug a pair of jeans and a sweater out of the bag he had brought from the guest room.

They put on heavy coats, tiptoed downstairs and out the kitchen door. Kate was surprised to find it snowing lightly but accumulating fast enough to have coated the lawn and driveway.

Reid took her to the stable, led Thunder out of his stall and gave Kate a leg up.

"We're riding bareback?" she asked.

"We do it once in a while. He's used to it." Reid used a slat in the fence to boost himself up behind her. Wrapping his arms around her,

Reid gently touched his heels to Thunder's sides and guided the horse to a path through a thicket of trees where the click of hooves was the only sound in the otherwise still night.

"Close your eyes," Reid whispered.

Kate rested her head against his shoulder and did as he asked. She could feel the snowflakes clinging to her eyelashes.

They rode for a few more quiet minutes before Reid squeezed her hand. "Okay, open them."

Kate gasped. "*Oh!* Reid!" They had emerged from the trees into a meadow lit by a moon so full it gave the aura of daylight, the open expanse frosted with snow that sparkled in the moonlight. Thunder stood still and quiet while they took in the glorious scene.

Kate reached back for Reid. "I'll remember this for the rest of my life."

He brushed his lips over hers. "So will I."

CHAPTER 20

The O'Malley house buzzed with speculation while the family waited for Declan to arrive with his new girlfriend. Aidan thought Dec was nuts for subjecting the poor girl to the family on a holiday, but he hadn't been consulted.

"Now be nice and don't act like jackasses," Colleen warned her other three sons, who sat together on the sofa in the living room.

"We're not the ones Dec needs to be worried about," Brandon muttered under his breath when she moved past them.

Aidan elbowed him. His brother looked like hell, with a two-day beard and bloodshot eyes—a sure sign he'd been out drinking into the wee hours. Lately Aidan had heard from other family members that Brandon's drinking was becoming an issue. When they were younger, Aidan and Brandon were often mistaken for twins. They shared the wavy brown hair their father had as a young man and their mother's green eyes. The similarities between them faded as age and life had taken a toll on both of them. Their younger brothers and sister had Colleen's reddish blonde hair and Dennis's blue eyes.

Aidan and Colin nursed their beers while Brandon chugged his down. Erin's kids ran through the house, screaming with excitement.

"Freaking madhouse," Colin muttered.

Brandon stood up. "I need another beer."

"You've already had two," Aidan said.

"Butt out, Aidan. Did I say a word when you stayed drunk for a year after Sarah died?"

"What's your excuse?" Aidan asked.

"That's enough, you guys," Colin said.

Declan and his girlfriend, Jessica, arrived a short time later. Once she'd been introduced to the clan and had a drink forced on her, Colleen called the family to dinner.

Extra chairs had been jammed in to make room for everyone around the dining room table. Erin sat next to Aidan. Her youngest child was in a high chair on the other side of her.

Dennis presided at the head of the table. "Let's say the blessing so Mum can serve."

The family joined hands and bowed their heads. Aidan went through the motions to please his parents.

"Dear Lord, bless this family gathered here before you," Dennis prayed. "Keep them safe and in your care in the year to come, and bring them right back here again next Christmas. We say a special prayer today for the family members who've gone on before us, especially for our beloved Sarah and baby Colin. In your name we pray. Amen."

"Amen," the others echoed.

Erin gave Aidan's hand a squeeze before she released it.

AFTER EVERYONE HAD LEFT, Aidan helped his mother with the last of the cleanup. He returned one of the extra chairs they'd used at dinner back to his father's study and was drawn to the shelves behind the desk. Each of the five O'Malley children had a shelf in the study dedicated to their childhood achievements.

Aidan reached for the leather-bound book with the gilded gold pages that sat next to his football trophies. He took it over to the sofa where the light was better. The album cover was embossed in gold letters that read, "Aidan and Sarah," along with their September wedding date. He looked through the photos from the happiest day of his life and smiled at the picture of him standing with Sarah in front of the white Rolls Royce Dennis had surprised them with. On the next page, the four O'Malley brothers were dashing in their gray tuxedos. They wore the cocky grins of men too young to believe anything bad could ever touch them.

And Sarah. She was so breathtaking, with her mane of thick dark hair and hazel eyes. Aidan's gaze lingered on the photo of her in her wedding gown, with the sun setting over the water behind her. He was stunned when his eyes filled with tears, and he closed the photo album abruptly.

He'd lied to Clare when he told her he'd never been married. The lie had been told so often in the last ten years, he almost believed it himself. He found it easier to lie than to talk about it. Only when he was here at home did he ever hear her name or that of their son who would now be ten years old.

AFTER ATTENDING AN EARLY MASS, Clare kept herself busy on Christmas Day preparing for the girls' visit. She made lasagna, cooked a turkey, and baked several batches of their favorite cookies. The phone rang all day. When the girls called a second time, Clare got to say hello to Frannie and Jamie. When Jack came on the line to say Merry Christmas, Clare wanted to cheer when she felt no physical reaction to the sound of his voice, but she realized she missed him. It was an odd mixture of relief and sadness.

She also spoke to her mother, her sister Sue, and brother Tony, as well as her nieces and nephews. The nonstop calls gave Clare little time to be lonely, and by nightfall she was proud of herself for getting through Christmas alone for the first time in her life.

At nine, she curled up on the sofa with *Christmas Vacation*, which made her laugh like she'd never seen it before. The phone ringing again at ten surprised her. Who was left?

"Hello?"

"Hey," Aidan said. "How're you doing?"

Delighted to hear from him, Clare smiled. "I'm fine. How are you? How was the O'Malley Christmas?"

"To quote my brother Colin, it was a freaking madhouse. I just took a second dose of Advil."

Clare laughed. "Sounds like fun."

"Don't get me wrong, it's nice to see them all, but I live alone. It's always a shock to my system to come home. How was your day?"

"The phone rang off the hook, but in between the calls, I cooked, cleaned, made beds, and wrapped a few last-minute presents."

"You sound good."

"I feel good."

"Well, I just wanted to check on you."

"I'm glad you did. Now don't let this go to your fat head, O'Malley, but I miss you. It's awfully quiet around here without you banging and crashing about."

"Lordy, Ms. Scarlet," he said in a dramatic Southern drawl. "You sure know how to make a guy feel special."

She laughed. "Thanks for calling."

"I miss you, too. I'll see you soon."

Clare clicked off the phone and held it against her chest for several long minutes. She'd meant it when she said she missed him, and suddenly she couldn't wait for him to get back.

In Rhode Island, Kate was counting the minutes until she could return to Nashville. She'd spoken to Reid twice during the day, but it was no substitute for being with him. It was nice to see her family, but in six short weeks, Rhode Island no longer felt like home. Two nights away from him felt like an eternity. She couldn't believe how quickly he'd become as essential to her as air and music.

Kate was lying on her bed at her dad's house talking to Jill late on Christmas night when someone knocked on the door. "Come in."

"I just wanted to say good night," Andi said. "Do you guys need anything?"

"We're fine," Kate said. "Thanks. You must be beat."

"I am. I'm going to bed now. Is everything all right, Kate? You've been so quiet since you got home."

"I'm zonked from working nonstop the last couple of weeks. We had Christmas parties almost every night."

"What've you got there?" Andi asked with a nod at the locket.

Kate hadn't realized she'd been playing with it. Unable to bring herself to take it off, she had kept it hidden under her clothes during her trip home. "Oh, just something the band gave me to thank me for the hard work over the last month." She was startled by how easily the lie rolled off her tongue.

"It's lovely. Well, I'll see you in the morning." Andi turned back when she reached the door. "You know you can talk to me if you need to, right?"

Kate nodded. "Thanks, but I'm fine. Really."

"Good night, then."

"Merry Christmas," Kate said.

"You, too, sweetie. Night, Jill."

"Night," Jill said. When the door closed, Jill looked at her sister. "Dad will kill you if he ever finds out about this, Kate."

"He won't." Kate rolled onto her side and clutched a pillow. It was a lousy substitute for what she really wanted.

REID SPENT a quiet day with Ashton. They exchanged gifts and enjoyed an early dinner Martha had prepared for them before she left to spend the day with her own family. Later that evening, after Ashton had gone into the city to visit some high school friends who were home for the holiday, Reid poured himself a brandy and sat listening to Mozart on the stereo. The fire cast an amber glow on the ten-foot Christmas tree.

He missed Kate with an intensity that almost frightened him. After

Cindy died and a respectable amount of time had passed, the women in his social circle got busy trying to find him a new wife. He'd sat through countless dinner parties and blind dates with a progression of "perfectly suited" women who wanted nothing more than to take care of him and his precious little boy. Well, a few of them were probably more interested in his money, but he didn't keep any of them around long enough to find out. Not one of them had stirred in him what Kate did.

After a while his friends mercifully gave up on him. Reid buried himself in his work and taking care of his son, and the invitations stopped coming as one by one his friends quit calling. He hadn't even realized how isolated he'd become until Kate stormed into his life and made him see what he'd been missing all these years.

Reid heard Martha come in through the kitchen door. She had finally begun to slow down over the last year, and he worried about her driving at night. But whenever he broached the subject, she would give him the withering look that had worked on him since he was a child, and he would drop it.

"Hi," she said. "Did Ashton leave?" She tended to drop the formality she used around guests when they were alone.

"He was here all day, but he wanted to see his friends. How was your day?"

She sat down across from him. Every snow-white hair on her head was perfectly in place—as always—but he could see weariness in her soft brown eyes. "Tiring. The whole crowd was at Buddy's," she said, referring to her son.

"Can I get you a drink?"

"Heavens, no. That'd be the living end of me. Thank you, though." She studied him intently.

He raised an eyebrow. "Something on your mind, Martha?"

"As a matter of fact, there is. You know I care for you like my own, and I know my place in this house, but I can't stand by and say nothing when I see what you're doing."

"What am I doing?" he asked casually, but his heart began to beat faster.

Her eyes narrowed with anger. "Reid Matthews, you know *exactly* what I'm talking about. I may be old, but I wasn't born yesterday. I don't know what you think you're doing with that girl."

He kept his gaze steady and even. "I love *that girl*."

"You can't be serious!" She shook her head with disbelief. "Your parents and your dear wife must be rolling in their graves, bless their souls."

Unable to stay seated, he surged to his feet. "Damn it, Martha! Look at how I'm spending Christmas—by myself. My son has a life of his own now, so where does that leave me? I'll tell you where—alone —like I was all the time until *that girl* came into my life. I've been alone for more than twenty years. Surely you can't sit there and say I don't deserve some happiness."

"Not like this," Martha whispered. "Her father is your friend. He trusted you to take care of her."

"Do you know what *that girl*, who's wise beyond her years, once told me? 'Reid,' she said, 'people love who they love. It's not always a choice.'"

"When you're more than twice her age, it *is* a choice. You're damned right it's a choice."

"I'm sorry you don't approve."

"Does your son approve?"

Reid looked away from her.

"You know this is wrong, or you would've told him." She shrugged and stood up. "I can't tell you how to run your life. I can only tell you how disappointed I am. I'll pack my things in the morning."

He closed the distance between them and rested a hand on her shoulder. "Don't do this, Martha. I don't want you to leave. You've been a part of my family for more than forty years."

With tears in her eyes, she turned to him. "You're not the man I helped to raise. That man is honorable and decent. I don't recognize you anymore. I'll be gone in the morning."

After she left the room, he poured himself a stronger drink. Maybe if he got good and stinking drunk, he could stop the roaring in his ears.

~

JACK DROVE Kate to the airport the morning after Christmas. "I wish you could've stayed longer," he said.

"I know, but the band is playing tomorrow night. I was so lucky they hired me."

"They're the lucky ones."

"You have to say that," she said with a smile. "I can't get over how big the babies got in just six weeks."

"They're growing like weeds. At least they're sleeping through the night once in a while now. It's always a surprise to us when they do. We wake up and fly out of bed to check on them."

Kate chuckled. "Better you than me."

"I'm glad everything's going so well for you in Nashville. I've got to admit, when I was there I kind of wondered if you had a thing for Ashton."

"What?" she said, stunned. "We're just friends."

"Yeah, well, he's kind of old for you anyway," Jack said, taking the airport exit.

Kate's stomach clenched as she looked out the passenger window. "Yeah. I guess."

"You seemed distracted while you were home. Andi said the same thing. You're sure everything's okay? There's nothing you couldn't tell me, you know." He pulled up to the curb outside the departures door.

Yes, Daddy, there are things I can't tell you. Her eyes burned with tears.

"What? What is it?"

She shook her head. "Nothing. I just hate saying good-bye to you again."

He took her in his arms. "I miss you. Come home again soon when you can stay longer."

"I will."

"You're sure you don't want me to walk you in?"

"I'm sure. I'm going right to security anyway." She had left her guitar at Reid's and just had a carry-on bag with her.

Jack retrieved her bag from the trunk and then reached out to hug her.

Kate buried her face in the warm comfort of his familiar scent.

"Love you, honey."

She kissed his cheek. "Love you, too." She watched him get back in his car and waved until the silver BMW was out of sight. Then she went inside, anxious to get home to Reid. Today was his birthday, and he was waiting for her.

PART III
COLUMN

Two or more people standing behind one another.

CHAPTER 21

*J*ill and Maggie arrived in Stowe late in the afternoon the day after Christmas. Within minutes they filled the quiet house with bags, presents, chatter, and chaos. Clare couldn't have been more delighted.

After they exchanged Christmas gifts and Maggie opened her birthday presents, Clare made them some hot chocolate. "So how was Kate?" she asked.

"She wasn't home very long," Maggie complained, poking at a puff of whipped cream. "She got there on Christmas Eve, and she went back this morning."

"She's working tomorrow night," Jill added.

"How does she seem? I haven't talked to her as much as usual the last couple of weeks."

"She was on the phone a lot," Maggie said with disapproval.

"Do you think she has a boyfriend in Nashville?" Clare asked. "She hasn't mentioned anything to me."

"No," Jill said. "So when can we ski?"

"Tomorrow if you want." Clare wondered why Jill had changed the subject so abruptly. "We're supposed to get a big snowstorm in the next day or two. We'll see what the weather does."

"Cool," Maggie said.

"Let's go for a walk in town. I want to introduce you to my new friends."

They bundled up and headed into town where Clare showed them off at McHugh's and the Book Nook. Diana and Bea were delighted to finally meet Clare's daughters. The girls dragged Clare into all the stores in town, even a few she hadn't been to yet. By the time they walked home, it had begun to snow lightly.

"*Who* is *that*?" Maggie pointed to the house.

Clare smiled at the sight of Aidan bent over the table saw on the front porch. She felt her face go hot when she remembered kissing him on Christmas Eve. "*That* is Aidan O'Malley. He's doing the work on the house."

Jill grinned. "Can't wait to see if the front of him lives up to the back."

"Oh, trust me," Clare said with a smirk. "It does."

Jill's eyes widened. "*Really*, Mother. Do tell!"

Clare shrugged. "Nothing to tell. We're friends. You guys will like him." When they got to the house, Clare waited for him to shut off the saw. "Hey, you're back."

He looked up and smiled. "I wanted to beat the snow. Got some new friends, Clare?"

Maggie giggled. "We're her daughters!"

"*Daughters?*" Aidan asked with mock horror. "You have *daughters?*"

"Very funny. Jill and Maggie, this is Aidan O'Malley. He's a carpenter with a screw loose."

"I'm offended," Aidan said.

"You'll get over it. Come on, girls. Let's get dinner started. We're having lasagna if you want to stay, O'Malley."

"I'd love to."

They left him working on the porch and went inside.

"What was *that* all about?" Jill asked.

"What?" Clare asked.

"You were flirting with him," Maggie said as if she were an authority on the subject.

"I was not!"

"He's *dreamy*," Maggie said with a sigh.

Clare couldn't deny it. "Isn't he?"

Jill's eyes went wide again. "Do you *like* him, Mom?"

"We're friends. Don't make a big deal out of it."

"Hmm." Jill took a bite of a carrot Clare got out for salad. She leaned against the bare wall in the kitchen and eyed her mother with interest.

"Hmm, nothing," Clare said, but she was rattled that the girls had zeroed in on her growing friendship with Aidan so quickly.

BY THE TIME they'd had dinner and launched into a competitive game of Monopoly, the girls and Aidan were fast friends.

"That'll be four hundred bucks," Maggie told him when he landed on Boardwalk.

He groaned. "I'm busted. You girls have driven me straight into the poor house."

"I can definitely relate," Clare said dryly.

He got up to look out the window to check the snow. "I'd better go, but I'll be over in the morning to dig you out."

"We can do it," Clare said.

"I don't mind. The skiing will be great tomorrow."

"Do you want to come with us?" Jill asked. They had grilled him about the best runs on the mountain.

"I really should get some work done."

"Go ahead," Clare said. "This place isn't going anywhere."

"I'd love to," Aidan admitted. "I haven't been yet this year."

"Good," Maggie said as she finished putting the game away. "I'm going to bed. See you tomorrow, Aidan."

"I'm going up, too," Jill said with a big yawn.

"I'll be up in a minute," Clare called after them.

"They're great kids," Aidan said as he pulled on his coat.

Clare walked him to the front door. "I like them."

Smiling, he took a step toward her. "I can see why."

"It's really coming down out there. You should go." His nearness stirred butterflies in her belly. She didn't know what made her more anxious—that he might kiss her again or that he wouldn't.

He ran his thumbs along her jaw. "I missed you," he said, dipping his head to touch his lips to hers.

Clare's senses were filled with the fragrance of Christmas pine and sawdust and a hint of the cologne he'd worn on Christmas Eve. She felt his arms close around her and relaxed against him. Under his coat, her hands found his back as he brushed his lips over hers again.

"Aidan," she whispered against his lips.

"Hmm?"

"I missed you, too. I really did."

Encouraged by her confession, he tugged her closer. When he nudged at her lips with his tongue, she opened her mouth to let him in. The swirl of his tongue against hers made her weak, and before long they both were breathless.

Reluctantly, he took a step back but kept a firm hold on her hand. "It's been a long time since I've looked forward to anything the way I look forward to seeing you every day." He kissed her hand and then her cheek. "See you tomorrow."

Before she could think of anything to say to that astounding statement, he was out the door.

AIDAN RETURNED EARLY the next morning with a shovel. He cleared off the sidewalk, stairs, and porch before there were any signs of life inside. More than a foot of snow had fallen overnight, and the rumble of snow blowers and the scrape of shovels filled the air on Maple Street. When he was done shoveling, he used his key to go inside. The silence told him the three ladies were still sleeping, so he quietly brewed a pot of coffee in the kitchen. He'd been impressed last night by the way Clare had made the gutted kitchen look warm and inviting for her girls. She'd dragged the kitchen table back in from the living room and covered it with festive placemats. An arrangement of evergreen, holly, and winterberry sat in a jug on the table.

He took a cup of coffee with him to the downstairs bathroom. As he worked, he thought about the evening he'd spent with Clare and her daughters. The girls surprised him. He had expected typical teenagers, but they were exceedingly polite to their mother, even solicitous—jumping up to get something for her or to refill her glass without being asked. He'd seen none of the usual teenager attitude he'd learned to expect from girls their age by watching his sister in action. It was almost odd, really.

He was also more curious than he'd been before about their father, since the only sign of Clare in either of them was Maggie's spectacular blue eyes. The girls were gorgeous, and Aidan felt an unexpected stab of jealousy when he imagined what their father must look like.

By the time he heard stirrings upstairs, he'd applied a coat of paint to the bathroom walls. The new floors in the bathroom and kitchen would be installed next week. The job was slightly ahead of schedule, which worried him. He needed to slow it down so he would have more time to get to know Clare before she went back to Rhode Island. He didn't like to think about her leaving. He'd been taken aback by how badly he'd wanted to kiss her last night and couldn't wait to do it again.

"Morning," Jill said from the doorway.

He turned to her. "Hey. Did you sleep well?"

"Yeah, I was tired after driving all that way. That's the farthest I've ever driven in one day."

"Plus it's through the mountains, which can be stressful."

"My fingers hurt from gripping the wheel," she admitted with a grin. "What time do you want to go skiing?"

"Whenever you guys are ready."

"I'll go wake up Maggie. Thirty minutes or so?"

"Sounds good."

"I like that color," she said, nodding at the sage-colored paint.

"Your mom picked it."

"She has good taste," Jill said with a pointed look that told him she knew something was brewing between him and her mother.

Before he could reply, she turned and went back upstairs. Aidan laughed, ridiculously pleased by the backhanded compliment.

THE SKI AREA at Mount Mansfield wasn't as busy as Aidan had expected it to be since it was Christmas vacation week. He figured the tourists were scared off by the big snowfall overnight. *Wimps*. Within an hour, he and the girls had made three runs down the intermediate slope and were ready to move up.

They skied to the end of the line at one of the lifts for the advanced trails.

"You guys are really good," Aidan said. "I'm impressed."

"Our dad's a great skier," Jill said. "He taught us."

"Does your mom ski?"

"She used to," Maggie said. "Before."

"Before her fall?"

The girls looked at him with confusion on their faces.

"What fall?" Jill asked.

"Oh, well, she said…" Aidan felt like he was wandering into murky territory.

"I meant before she was hit by the car," Maggie said. "She's still recovering."

"Not so much from the accident but the coma," Jill added. "Three years is a long time to be inactive."

Aidan felt like someone had hit him. Hard.

They were quiet on the ride up the mountain in the chairlift. Aidan was reeling. No wonder they treated her like she was made of spun glass. *Three years in a coma? Jesus.*

Arriving at the top, they got off the lift and concentrated on skiing the challenging trail. Aidan and Jill reached the bottom a few minutes ahead of Maggie, who had waved them on when she got tired.

He knew he shouldn't ask, but he couldn't stop himself. "Tell me the rest, Jill."

"Why didn't she tell you?"

"I don't know, but she will. When she's ready. I need to know."

Jill looked down at her ski and pushed a pile of snow aside. "She was raped by a psycho who threatened to kill one of us if she told anyone."

"Oh *no*. No."

"She lived with it for a long time, and then one day, she just couldn't take it anymore. She let a car hit her right in front of us," she said, her voice catching as if the memory was still a raw wound. "She thought if she was dead, he couldn't hurt us."

His throat tight with emotion and rage, Aidan put his arm around Jill, who seemed to need the comfort after reopening an old wound. "When did that happen?"

She leaned into him. "Almost four years ago. She's been recovering from the coma since last April. The doctors had told us it was hopeless, so now they say she's a genuine miracle."

"Did they get the guy?"

She nodded. "He was already in prison for something else."

"How does your dad fit into it?"

"They're divorced."

"I know, but why?"

"You should let her tell you," she said, casting him a wary glance.

"Please, Jill," he pleaded. "Tell me."

With a deep sigh, she poked her ski pole into the snow before she looked up at him. "He met someone else when my mom was sick. By the time she woke up, his girlfriend was pregnant with twins. They got married in August, and the twins were born on the same day as their wedding."

"He just *left* her?" he asked, enraged and horrified. "He left your mother for this other woman?"

"No, she left him. She didn't want him to have to choose."

Right in that very moment, standing at the foot of the mountain with his arm around her daughter, Aidan fell the rest of the way in love with Clare.

BY THE TIME the girls left the following Saturday, they'd toured the Ben & Jerry's ice cream factory, visited the Von Trapp family lodge, and skied twice more with Aidan. He joined them for dinner every night and took them to his favorite Mexican restaurant in Burlington on their last night. The only thing that marred their otherwise outstanding visit was the nasty cold Clare came down with mid-week.

Ever since the conversation with Jill, Aidan had been tortured by thoughts of what she'd been through. He hoped she'd tell him about it herself, when she was ready. Until then, all he could do was show her how much she—and now her girls—had come to mean to him.

Aidan arrived at the house about an hour after the girls left. The door was locked, so he used his key and found Clare asleep on the sofa in the living room. He went upstairs for a blanket and brought it down to cover her. When he tugged it up around her, one big blue eye opened.

"Hey," she said, her voice reduced to a croak.

"Oh." He winced. "Sounds worse than yesterday."

"Mmm," she said, choking on a cough.

He felt her forehead. "You're burning up. Have you taken anything?"

"Not yet. Can't move."

"Do you have any Advil or Tylenol?"

"Upstairs bathroom."

He went up to get it, and by the time he returned a minute later, she had dozed off again.

"Clare," he whispered. "Wake up. Come on, you need to take something."

She woke up long enough to swallow two pills.

Aidan carried her upstairs to bed. She never stirred when he pulled the blankets up around her. He kissed her forehead and went downstairs to get some work done while she slept.

SHE WAS STILL asleep two hours later, so he decided to go to McHugh's to get her some soup. He took the truck so he would only be gone a few minutes. When he got back with chicken soup and get-well wishes from Diana, Clare wasn't in her bed. He gasped when he found her crumpled on the bathroom floor.

"Clare!" His heart pounding with fear, he shook her awake. "*Clare!*"

"What happened?" she asked when her eyes finally opened.

He checked her for injuries. "Did you faint?"

"I must have. I had to go to the bathroom."

"Shit, you're really sick. We should get you to a hospital." He knew she was susceptible to pneumonia after her coma. How he knew and why he knew were his own secrets.

"No!" Her eyes went wide with fear when she grabbed his arm. "No hospitals, Aidan, please."

A week ago he would have argued with her, but now he understood. "Okay, honey, don't worry. No hospitals. I'll take you to my house."

Clare groaned. "Why can't I just stay here?"

"Because this place is full of dust and paint fumes. That's not good for you right now." He lifted her off the floor and carried her into the bedroom. Had he ever noticed how tiny she was? "Don't worry, you won't have to do anything."

She began to cry.

"What's wrong?" He put his arms around her so she could rest her head against his chest.

"I don't want to be sick. I had big plans for when the girls left."

"What kind of plans?"

"I was going to tell you I'm ready for that date you mentioned. If you still want to, that is," she said, coughing.

Kissing her cheek, he hugged her tight against him. "You bet I do, so let's get you better, okay?"

She nodded and reclined against the pillows to watch him pack a bag of clothes for her. Before he finished, she'd drifted back to sleep and didn't stir even when he carried her outside to his truck.

WHEN CLARE WOKE up the next time, she saw stars. Literally. Looking up at a skylight, she had no idea where she was. Her head pounded, her throat was raw, her chest felt like an elephant was standing on it, and she was freezing. She groaned, and Aidan materialized from the darkness.

He ran a hand across her forehead and cheek. "How're you feeling?"

"Awful. I can't stop shivering."

Moving around to the other side of the big bed, he got under the covers and put an arm around her to draw her back against him. "Is that better?"

"Uh-huh." She could feel the warmth of him through her clothes. "Where are we?"

"My house. Remember I told you I was bringing you here?"

"Vaguely." When another thought occurred to her, she tried to sit up. "What about the girls? They'll be worried if they can't reach me. They didn't want to leave because I was sick."

"I called Jill." He eased her back down. "I found her number on your cell phone and let her know you'd be here for a few days. I gave her my number, and she promised to call Kate. So don't worry about anything but getting better, okay?"

"Are they home?"

"Safe and sound."

She relaxed against him. "Okay. Good. Thank you."

"Are you hungry? I can heat up the soup I got you at McHugh's earlier."

"Maybe in a minute," she said as her eyes closed again. "I don't want you to go."

He held her tight against him. "I'm not going anywhere. I had to get you sick to get you in bed with me. I want to enjoy it."

She made a sound that might have been a laugh, but a cough choked her. "I'll bet you've never had it so good in bed," she said when she could speak again.

Rubbing his chin against her soft hair, he said, "Not in a long, long time."

"Aidan?"

"What, honey?"

"Thanks for keeping me warm."

"My pleasure."

CHAPTER 22

lare was worse in the morning. When Aidan woke up, he could hear her wheezing in her sleep. He took her temperature with an ear thermometer and was alarmed when it reached 104.5. "Shit!" He jumped off the bed to find the phone.

He dialed the number in Rhode Island that Jill had given him yesterday. Dr. Langston's answering service took a message and promised he would return the call within an hour. When the phone rang twenty minutes later, Aidan pounced on it.

"This is Dr. Paul Langston. I got your message, Mr. O'Malley. You're with Clare Harrington?"

Aidan appreciated the sense of urgency in the doctor's voice. "Yes, I'm a friend of hers in Vermont. I think she has pneumonia."

"What are her symptoms?"

Aidan rattled off the list and provided her latest temperature.

"Are you a doctor?"

Aidan took a deep breath. "I'm an MD." He hadn't said those words in ten years. "But I don't practice. If you could call something in up here, I could administer it IM."

"Give me the pharmacy number. I'll call in a script for penicillin

206

right now and order the syringes for you so we can get it into her faster."

Swamped with relief, Aidan gave the doctor the pharmacy phone number. "Thank you."

"Do you know her history?"

"Yes. She didn't want to be in the hospital."

"I want you to promise me you'll get her admitted somewhere if she gets any worse."

"I will."

"She's more than a patient to me. She's a friend. Take good care of her."

"She's more than a friend to me. Don't worry." He hung up with the doctor and called Bea. She agreed to go to the pharmacy for him, so he wouldn't have to leave Clare alone.

"Hurry, Bea."

CLARE WAS FLOATING. The pounding in her head and the throbbing in her chest seemed far away. She dreamed Bea was there and Aidan was giving her a shot, but she couldn't make herself wake up, even when she felt someone trying to get some water into her.

So hot! Have I ever been so hot? She thrashed at the covers, trying to get out from underneath their heaviness. A nagging worry in the back of her mind kept her from falling back to sleep. What if she didn't wake up? It had happened before. Could it happen again? Tears leaked from the corners of her eyes as she fought the blackness.

She must have dozed off. Where was Jack? Was that his voice she heard?

"Clare, honey, wake up."

"Jack?" She opened her eyes. A light from across the room illuminated Aidan's handsome features, and she winced at the brief flash of hurt that crossed his face. "I was dreaming. I'm sorry."

"Don't be. Are you hungry?"

"Kind of."

"Will you be okay for a minute while I go downstairs to get you something?"

She nodded weakly.

"What sounds good? Soup? Eggs? Toast? Whatever you want."

"Toast, please."

Aidan kissed her cheek. "Coming right up. Don't run away."

She groaned at the thought of running anywhere.

He had to wake her up again when he returned with the toast.

"What time is it?" she asked as she nibbled on a piece of cinnamon toast.

"About three in the morning."

"Have you been up all night? I'm sorry."

"I slept for a few hours. Don't worry about me. By the way, Happy New Year."

"I missed it?"

"Slept right through it." He brushed back a lock of her hair and kissed her forehead. "Listen, um, I need to give you a shot."

"So I didn't dream that?"

"No."

"Do you know what you're doing?"

He nodded.

"How?"

"That's a story for another day, when you're better. For now, trust me?"

She wiggled a finger to bring him down closer to her so she could kiss his cheek. "I trust you."

"Thank you," he said and gave her the shot. "Now, I want you to drink all that water, you hear me? We can't let you get dehydrated."

"Yes, sir, but I need to pee."

He carried her into the bathroom, which was a lot like hers at home in Rhode Island, except Aidan's Jacuzzi had sliding glass doors that could be opened to the outdoors. Moonlight beamed in through skylights. "From what I've seen of it, this house is really something. Did you build it yourself?"

"Every nail. Do you think you can stand up?"

"Of course," she said, but when he set her down, the earth moved. She reached out to grip the pedestal sink.

He held her up from behind. "Get your bearings," he said. "Okay?"

"Yeah, but don't go far."

"I'll be right outside the door."

When she was done, she washed her hands and face and ran a hand through her hair. She was afraid to look in the mirror. A fierce coughing fit stole her last bit of energy.

When he heard her coughing, Aidan came in and put his arms around her.

"Can you grab my toothbrush for me?" she asked when the coughing had subsided.

"Sure. Hold on to something."

He left her gripping the sink and returned a minute later with her toothbrush. Reaching into the medicine cabinet, he grabbed a tube of toothpaste and squeezed some onto her toothbrush.

"Some kind of service at this hospital."

"We don't mess around," he said, holding her eyes for a moment longer than necessary.

Clare tore her gaze from his to focus on brushing her teeth. As she brushed, she thought that being with Aidan in his bathroom in the middle of the night seemed so natural. She'd have to ponder the meaning of that when she wasn't battling a fever.

"Ready for a ride back to bed?"

She nodded, and when he carried her back to the bedroom she curled her arms around his neck and rested her head on his shoulder as if it belonged there. He had changed at some point into an old Red Sox T-shirt and sweats.

He tucked her in under several blankets and got her to take two more Tylenols to stay on top of the fever. When he was satisfied she'd had enough to drink for a while, he got in bed with her. "Hot? Cold?"

"Just right for the moment, but can we pretend I'm cold so you'll come over here with me?"

"We can do that," he said, slipping an arm under her.

She turned toward him and used his chest as a pillow. "Thank you."

"For what?"

"Taking care of me. I don't know how a cold got so out of hand so fast." She ran a hand over his chest and stomach, discovering he was all muscle.

"It's probably pneumonia." He captured her wandering hand in his and brought it to his lips. "You'd better cut that out, or I'll be taking advantage of a sick person."

She snorted with laughter. "Oh, God, you've got to be kidding. I'm a disaster area."

He lifted her chin and kissed her lightly. "You're sexy and beautiful, and I want you, sick or not. So behave."

Her chest contracted, and not because of her illness. "Does this count as our first date?"

He laughed. "Go to sleep."

She squeezed his hand, snuggled closer to him, and was asleep a minute later.

CLARE SLEPT through most of the next day. She awoke at one point to the thwack, thwack, thwack of an axe cutting wood and assumed Aidan was outside getting some work done. She couldn't keep her eyes open long enough to check. When she woke up the next time, it was dark. Her head pounded for a moment when she pushed herself into a sitting position.

Across the room, Aidan looked up from the book he was reading. "Hey, sleeping beauty, you're awake."

She groaned. "I can't believe I slept all day."

He came over to sit on the edge of the bed. "You must be starving. I tried to wake you up to eat earlier, but you weren't budging."

"Sorry. I'm a little hungry but not starving."

"I have an idea. Why don't you take a bath in the Jacuzzi while I make us some dinner?"

"I'd love that. I feel so disgusting."

Kissing her forehead, he said, "You're very cute when you're sick."

"Jeez, O'Malley, you *are* hard up, aren't you?"

He laughed. "Yep, she's feeling better. Come on, let me give you a ride." He slid his arms under her to carry her into the bathroom. After he turned the water on and got her a towel, he went back to the bedroom for her bag. "Do you need anything else?"

"I've got everything, thanks."

"Be careful getting in and out. You're still weak. Call me if you need me."

"Thanks."

He left her alone, and she slipped off the sweats and long-sleeved T-shirt she'd been in for what seemed like a week. She moved with caution to preserve her limited supply of energy. The pulsing water in the tub felt heavenly against her aching body, and she uttered a deep sigh of pleasure. Using a bottle of shampoo that sat on a corner of the tub, she washed her hair. After soaking for a few more minutes, she started to feel light-headed again, so she eased herself from the tub and grabbed the towel he had left for her. When the simple act of getting out of the tub left her feeling drained, she sat on the closed lid of the toilet for a few minutes.

"How you doing in there?" Aidan called from outside the door.

"Fine. I'll be out in a minute."

"Okay, come downstairs when you're ready."

Clare found flannel pajamas in the bag and got dressed. She combed her hair and brushed her teeth. Before she could muster the energy to finish cleaning up the bathroom, she had to sit for another minute. She opened the door, and the smells wafting up the stairs made her mouth water. Suddenly, she was famished.

She put her bag in Aidan's room and went looking for the stairs. The house, an A-frame with several levels and rooms tucked into odd corners, was a wonder. The stairs hooked and curved, landing in the middle of a big kitchen where Aidan stirred something on the stove. The kitchen flowed into an inviting living room with a baby grand piano as the focal point.

"This house is amazing!"

He turned from the stove. "I'm glad you like it. Do you feel better after your bath?"

"I'm a new woman."

He held out a chair for her at the bar. "Something to drink?"

"Just some water, please." She watched him move with ease around the kitchen, where terracotta tiles formed a decorative backsplash over a butcher-block countertop. Shining copper pots hung above the center island that housed the stove. "This is quite a kitchen."

"I love to cook."

"Again you surprise me, O'Malley."

He smiled. "It's become my goal in life to keep you off balance." He brought two plates of steaming pasta to the bar, grabbed a beer from the refrigerator, and sat next to her.

"This smells wonderful."

"Chicken Alfredo, a specialty of the house."

"It's fabulous, and I'm impressed." After she ate half of what he'd given her, she pushed her plate over to him and he finished it.

"You look better."

"I have the energy of an infant, but otherwise I feel better."

He carried the plates to the sink and loaded the dishwasher. When he came back, he handed her the phone. "Want to call the girls?"

She nodded, touched by his thoughtfulness. The girls were relieved to hear she was feeling better, and she promised to call them again in a day or two.

After she hung up with Kate, he led her into a room off the living room she hadn't noticed before. She could tell right away that he spent most of his time here. There was a desk with a computer and piles of paper she assumed were part of his business. A woodstove occupied one corner of the room, and a flat-screen TV was mounted on the wall. Aidan settled her on the sofa and covered her with a blanket before he tossed another log on the fire.

"Warm enough?"

She nodded, and he sat next to her.

"I need to tell you something."

His handsome face was serious, and a ripple of fear went through her. At some point during her fevered state, she'd fallen in love with him and didn't want to hear anything that would spoil it. She reached for him.

He seemed relieved to move into her embrace and rested against her for several long minutes. When he finally looked up at her, his eyes were sad. "I lied to you about something, and I need to tell you the truth."

His distress touched her heart. "You don't have to," she said, caressing his cheek.

He kissed the palm of her hand, sending a jolt of desire through her. His eyes found hers. "Yes, I do. I need to tell you because I love you, Clare. For the first time in a very long time, something matters to me. *You* matter to me, and I don't want to mess this up."

She leaned in to kiss him and was startled by the hunger she felt in his kiss.

"Wait," he said against her lips. "We need to talk."

She kissed his forehead and cheek. "I love you, too, Aidan, and there's nothing you can tell me that will change that."

"Thank you," he said, his voice heavy with emotion. "Hold that thought for a moment." He got up, walked over to his desk, and came back holding a picture frame against his chest. "This is Sarah. She was my wife." He sat down and handed the photo to Clare.

Hiding her surprise, she studied the photo of the young woman with long dark hair and gentle eyes. "She's lovely," Clare said, giving it back to him. The pain on his face made his lie unimportant.

Lost in memories, he ran his thumbs over the frame. "I met her when I was twelve, and her family came to Chatham for the summer. She'd been coming for years, but somehow we'd never met before. She and her sister hung out with us at the beach all that summer, and by the time she went back to Boston, we were best friends." He turned the frame over. Taped to the back was a yellowed snapshot of twelve-year-old Aidan and Sarah, arm in arm at the beach.

"We wrote letters during the school year, and once in a while, we'd get to talk on the phone. She came back the next summer, and we picked up right where we'd left off. My brothers used to tease me something awful about her, but I didn't care. She was my favorite person in the world. They liked her, too, but they had to be jerks to me."

Clare smiled. "Of course they did."

Aidan put the photo on the table. "By the time we were fifteen, she was my girlfriend. We were stealing kisses every chance we got, and I was desperately in love with her. During that school year, my parents started letting me take the bus into the city one Saturday a month to see her. I lived for those days, and I worked the rest of the month to save the money for the bus fare."

Clare could see he was struggling to get through the story, so she took his hand.

"Sarah's dad was a doctor in Boston. He was always very nice to me and took an interest in my education. I hadn't planned to go to college because my dad wanted me to work with him. But Dr. Sweeny knew I was a straight-A student, and he encouraged me to aim higher. By then Sarah and I were doing a whole lot more than kissing, and neither of us ever looked at anyone else all through high school. The summer before our senior year, we hatched a plan to go to college together. She had her heart set on Yale, so I applied, too. It was a total shock to me—and my whole family—when I got in. My dad was disappointed about the business, but he didn't try to stop me from going to school, probably because I had three brothers coming up behind me."

"You went to Yale," Clare said in a whisper as it set in that this man was so much more than a carpenter.

He pointed to the framed diploma over his desk, above a second one just like it. "Dr. Sweeny encouraged me to try pre-med, and I was surprised to find I liked it. Sarah and I lived together after our freshman year in an apartment in New Haven. We thought we were getting away with it, but I found out much later that our parents knew but chose to ignore it. They'd learned by then not to fight what'd been happening between us since we were kids."

"It's so sweet," Clare said, touched by his story but filled with anxiety about where it was leading.

His face twisted into a small, sad smile. "We got married in Chatham right after we graduated from Yale. It was the very best day of my life, and it was almost ten years to the day after we first met. I went on to medical school at Yale. She'd gotten her degree in fine arts, and she worked in the university's art department. We were poor but happy. I decided to follow Dr. Sweeny into cardiology. I got through my internship at Yale-New Haven and applied for a residency at Mass General in Boston. We wanted to move closer to home because Sarah was finally pregnant. We'd been trying to have a baby for a long time."

Clare gasped as it registered that whatever had happened to his beloved wife had taken a child from him, too. *Oh, God. I can't hear this.* The tortured look on his face broke her heart. "Aidan, honey, maybe that's enough for now."

He shook his head. "I need to finish this." After a deep breath, he said, "She was two months pregnant when she found a lump in her breast."

Clare whimpered.

"Her father pulled strings to get her in with the best oncologist in the city. Within a day, we knew it was bad—stage-three breast cancer. She was twenty-nine." He shook his head as if he still couldn't believe it, even all these years later. "It was aggressive. They wanted to admit her right away and start her on chemo, but they'd have to terminate the pregnancy."

"Oh, Aidan." Tears spilled down Clare's cheeks.

"She wouldn't do it. I pleaded with her, but she wouldn't kill the child we'd wanted so badly. I told her it was *her* I couldn't live without, and we could have other babies when she got well." He shook his head and brushed at a tear on his face. "I yelled and screamed until I was hoarse, and then I begged, but I couldn't change her mind. Over time, I've come to understand that she knew she was going to die, and she didn't want me to be alone."

Clare wanted to touch him, but he was so far from her just then that she was afraid she would startle him.

He stood up and walked over to the window. "So I had to sit back and watch as our child grew and she slowly slipped away from me.

She insisted I keep up with my residency. The people at the hospital knew what I was going through, and they were good to me. We moved in with her parents because she couldn't be alone when I was working. I kept hoping I'd wake up from the nightmare my life had become. I was all churned up and frantic, but Sarah was so calm and serene. She loved feeling the baby grow inside her. He was busy, moving all the time." Smiling at the memory, Aidan turned back to Clare.

"What happened to him?" she asked in a small voice.

"She got to thirty-six weeks and was having trouble breathing because the cancer had spread to her lungs. Her OB scheduled a C-section, but the night before, she started to bleed. I rushed her to the hospital, and they took her right into the OR. They whisked her away so fast I can't remember the last thing I said to her or what she said to me. It's a total blank. They put her under to do an emergency C-section. The baby…" Aidan's chin dropped to his chest, and he shook his head.

Clare got up to go to him. A wave of dizziness hit her when she stood up too fast, but she fought it off and put her arms around him.

Sobs wracked through him. She held him until he finally pulled himself together and looked down at her with shattered eyes. "He was stillborn."

"No," Clare whispered.

"He was perfect with all his fingers and toes. They let me hold him, and I tried to convince myself he was only asleep. We'd already decided to name him after Colin—he was Sarah's favorite of my brothers. She never came out of the anesthesia, and she died two days later. The only comfort was she didn't know her sacrifice had been for nothing."

Clare led him back to the sofa.

After a long period of silence, he took a deep shuddering breath. "They were buried together, but I wasn't there," he said, his voice reduced to a whisper. "I couldn't go. My parents and hers took care of everything. I've never even been to the cemetery, which drives my mother crazy, but they go for me. I quit the residency. I couldn't stand the smell of the hospital or knowing that even with all my training I hadn't been able to save the two people I loved the most. It was just as well, because I spent most of the next year drunk anyway."

"How did you end up here?"

"Sarah's grandmother left her some money, and we bought this land a year before she got sick. We were going to build a weekend place up here eventually. She made me promise I'd use the money to build the house. When I failed to drink myself to death, I didn't know what else to do, so I came up here and built this place. I had planned to sell it when it was done."

"How come?"

"I figured it'd be too painful to be here without her, but we hadn't spent much time together here, and no one in town knew her. By the time the house was finished, I'd started to feel at home. I did a few construction jobs on the side, and before long word got out that I knew what I was doing. I had a business and a house, so I stayed put. The only person here who knows I was once a doctor and that I lost my wife and son is Bea. She's been a good friend, but even she doesn't know the whole story."

"Thank you for telling me. I'm so terribly sorry for all that you lost."

He kissed her hand. "I'm sorry I lied to you when I said I've never been married. I feel so disloyal to Sarah when I tell people that, but it's easier than talking about it. After all these years, the lie just comes so easily. When I lied to you, though, it was the first time it ever felt wrong. Forgive me?"

Clare reached out to hug him. "There's nothing to forgive."

He held on to her, seeming to need the comfort she offered after sharing his painful story.

"You must be getting tired," he said after a long period of quiet. "Let's get you back to bed." He took her hand to help her up and lead her upstairs.

She made it to the first landing before dizziness forced her to grip the railing.

Aidan picked her up and carried her the rest of the way. "You still need to take it easy," he said as he helped her into bed.

"I can probably go home, though. I've put you out enough."

"I like having you here. I probably shouldn't tell you that you're the first woman who's ever been here."

She smiled. "Really?"

"As you would say, don't let it go to your fat head," he said with a weak grin that was in sharp contrast to his earlier sorrow.

"Too late."

He got into bed and rolled over to face her. "Stay here for a while. Until you feel stronger."

When she ran her fingers through his hair and leaned in to kiss him, a wildfire erupted between them. His kiss was full of love and longing and need—a need so powerful it should have frightened her, but it didn't because she knew he loved her.

He pulled back to look at her, his eyes heated. "Not like this, Clare. When we make love, and we will, soon, it'll be for us. Not for comfort and not out of sympathy." He settled her into the shelter of his arms. "Stay with me for now?"

"Okay," she said, hoping she would be able to overcome her own demons when the time came.

CHAPTER 23

$\mathcal{K}$ate checked the address on the business card again and looked up at the dilapidated building with dismay. This wasn't Music Row. This was so far from Music Row it might've been in another city. Harvey Welshiemer, the producer who'd given her his card at a party before Christmas, had been delighted to hear from her and insisted she come right over to his office.

She pushed the door open and was hit by the odor of greasy food and what might've been urine. The stairs creaked as she made her way to the second floor where a small plastic sign next to a wooden door said "Harvey Welshiemer, Decade Records." Kate looked around at the dingy hallway with the chipping light green paint. The blare of a television came through one of the other wooden doors. She thought about turning around, but he was a producer, so she forced herself to knock.

Harvey answered the door, and his ugly face lit up.

"Kate, honey, you made it. Come on in."

With a wistful look over her shoulder at the stairwell, she stepped inside, suddenly aware that no one in the world knew where she was at that moment. She could tell right away this was his home, not his office.

"Um, I thought we were meeting at your office," she said as he ran around grabbing discarded clothes and scooping up dirty dishes.

"We are. Have a seat."

She cast her eyes around for a spot where she could sit without fear of contracting a disease. "I'll stand, thanks."

He pushed the front half of his comb-over back into place and lowered his pear-shaped body into a cracked vinyl chair. "I'm awfully glad you came by. You're just the kind of young talent Decade Records is looking for. I'm going to make you a big star, little girl."

Kate took a step back toward the door. "I'm not so sure about this."

He jumped to his feet faster than he should've been able to. "Where do you think you're going? I haven't even told you what I've got in mind for you."

She leaned against the door with her hand on the doorknob behind her back, knowing with every fiber of her being that she wanted nothing to do with whatever he had in mind for her.

"We'll start you off at the Grand Ole Opry. Get your name out there. Do you have your own material?" He rattled on before she could answer. "It doesn't matter. I've got a guy who'd love to write for a voice like yours."

"Mr. Welshiemer—"

"Call me Harvey, honey. We're going to be good friends. Now, let me get the contract I need you to sign before we go any further—"

"Mr. Welshiemer—"

His eyes flashed with anger. "Now, darlin', you'll hurt my feelings if you don't call me Harvey." He reached under a pile of magazines on an uneven coffee table, and pulled out a legal-size sheet of paper. "This is your standard entertainment industry contract that lays out all the ways I'll be working on your behalf to make you a star." He produced a pen from the depths of his stained shirt pocket. "Sign right here, and we'll get to work."

He was so caught up in his spiel he didn't notice Kate opening the door. She was halfway down the stairs before he caught up to her. When he grabbed her arm to stop her descent, she shrieked.

"Where the hell do you think you're going?"

"Get your hands off of me," she said in a low snarl.

He let go so abruptly she almost stumbled down the last half of the stairwell. "We seem to have gotten off on the wrong foot," he said, his sweaty face an inch from hers. "If you don't want to be a star, that's just fine with me, but if I were you, I'd get my pretty little ass up those stairs and sign that contract. Do you honestly think you're any different than the million other girls who are singing their hearts out all over this city? How long have you been here? How many producers have given you their cards? I'll bet I'm the first one you've even talked to."

His words struck close to home—too close. But even if she never made it as a singer, she'd sell her soul to the devil before she would spend another minute in the company of this repulsive man.

"Our business is finished," she said with a look that dared him to lay one finger on her. "I'd rather work at the Waffle House than work for you." With that she turned and bolted down the remaining stairs.

"You bitch! Who the hell do you think you are?"

The last of his tirade was cut off when the door to the street swung closed behind her. Kate gulped the fresh air as she half ran, half walked from the building. She got to her car, jumped in, and locked the door before she allowed herself to cry. Only the fear that he might follow her motivated her to start the car and drive away.

She got to her apartment and ran for the shower. Her encounter with Welshiemer had left her feeling dirty and sick. After ten full minutes under the pulsing water, she finally managed to stop sobbing. When she thought about what could've happened in that filthy apartment, she began to shake.

In an effort to take her mind off the hellish encounter, she forced herself to think of something pleasant. Her thoughts shifted naturally to Reid and the New Year's Eve they had spent together. She smiled when she remembered what they'd been doing at the stroke of midnight, and all at once she felt better. He would freak if he knew what'd just happened, but he was working in Knoxville and wouldn't be back until the next day.

When she was finally able to breathe normally again and her hands had stopped shaking, she picked up the phone to call Ashton.

"This is a nice surprise," he said when his assistant put through her call.

"Happy New Year," she said in an effort to sound normal.

"Same to you. What's going on?"

"I was wondering if I could ask a favor."

"Of course, anything you need."

"Do you know anything about a producer named Harvey Welshiemer? Decade Records?"

Ashton gasped. "Jesus, Kate, that guy's bad news. We have three clients trying to break contracts with him. He has them signed to ironclad agreements that make it impossible for them to work *anywhere*, and he's doing nothing for them."

Kate winced. Why hadn't she called Ashton before she went over there? Thank God she hadn't signed anything.

"Kate? *What?* Oh my God, you didn't sign something with him, did you?"

"No, no," she said weakly. "I met with him, but he skeeved me out, so I split before he could force me to sign anything."

"Son of a bitch," Ashton muttered. "Are you all right?"

"I am now."

"Okay, listen to me, from now on, you don't talk to anyone in the music business—and I mean *anyone*—without me with you, you got me? The next time you see me, give me a dollar."

"Why?"

"That's my retainer. Once you pay it, I'm officially your attorney."

She laughed. "You're awfully cheap, counselor. How do I know you won't cheat me?"

"I'm serious, Kate. You could've gotten royally screwed by that guy today, and your career would've been ruined before it ever got started. This is nothing to joke about."

"I'm sorry. You're right."

He sighed. "I don't mean to be a hard ass, but you have to be so careful."

"I know that now. Thank you, Ashton. I have a dollar right here with your name on it."

"Jeez, you almost gave me a heart attack." He exhaled a long deep breath. "Why don't we grab some dinner later. Are you free?"

"I have rehearsal with the band until seven, but I could meet you after."

"F. Scott's at eight?"

"Sounds good. I'll be there. And thank you for the advice."

"Any time. Remember what I said about talking to people in the business, Kate. I mean it."

"After what happened today, you won't have to tell me again."

F. Scott's was hopping when Kate arrived five minutes late to meet Ashton. She crossed the fancy black and white-tiled floor to find him waiting for her at the bar. Since he wore a suit and tie, she assumed he had come right from work.

"Hi," he said with a kiss to her cheek. "You look great."

"Thanks," she said, embarrassed by the way his eyes skipped over her face with obvious interest. "So do you."

"Our table will be ready in a minute. Want something to drink?"

"Some water would be great. I'm always so parched after practice."

He asked the bartender for the water and got up to offer her his seat at the crowded bar. A jazz trio played on the small stage across the room.

Ashton's body formed a protective barrier around her from behind. A queasy feeling went through Kate as she came to an unsettling conclusion: this felt an awful lot like a date.

"Do you have something for me?" He held out his hand with an expectant expression.

"Oh, yes. I almost forgot." She reached into the pocket of her jeans and retrieved the dollar she'd stashed there earlier.

"Thank you. I'm now officially your attorney. Use me and abuse me," he said with a raunchy grin, his words rife with double meaning.

Kate took a deep breath. "Ashton."

"What, darlin'?"

"We need to talk."

The maitre d' picked that moment to tap Ashton on the shoulder to tell him their table was ready. They followed him to a secluded corner. When they were seated, Ashton ordered a glass of red wine. Kate stuck with water.

"What's wrong, Kate?"

He was so adorable and so genuinely concerned about her that she couldn't help but love him, just not in the way she suspected he wanted her to. "We're friends, right?"

"Of course we are. Why would you ask that?"

"Um, well, I don't want to presume anything, but—"

He reached across the table for her hand. "Spit it out, darlin'."

"I want us to be friends." She swallowed hard. "Just friends."

He held her gaze for a long moment before he looked away. "I'm sorry you feel that way. You're a real special girl, Kate, and I'd be lying if I said I wouldn't like to be more than just friends with you."

"I'm sorry. I enjoy your friendship so much. I don't want to lose that."

He rallied quickly. "Don't be silly," he said with a big smile that didn't quite make it to his eyes. "That won't happen. Besides, I'm your attorney now, so you can't get rid of me that easily."

"I'm sorry," she said again, touched by the hurt he was trying so hard to cover up.

"Don't be," he said, studying her. "Whoever he is, he's one lucky son of a bitch. I hope he knows that."

"He does," Kate said softly, sick at heart over what she—and his father—were keeping from him.

Ashton picked up the menu. "Well, then, how about you let your attorney buy you some dinner? What looks good to you?"

∼

IN KNOXVILLE, Reid ventured into the hotel bar to have a drink. It was late, and he was tired from a day of nonstop meetings for five different developments he had going in the city. Lately, he'd been thinking about phasing out some of his activities outside Nashville. The traveling was getting to be a drag, especially now that he had a good reason to stick closer to home. But then he thought, as he always did, about the many people he employed all over the state. His obligations to them kept him going.

Obligations, he thought, as he nursed a scotch on the rocks. He had half a lifetime of them behind him and years more ahead before he could conceive of retiring. Sometimes when he let himself think about what he really wanted, he pictured a tiny house on the beach in the Caribbean—a house he could take care of himself. He'd never had any choice about where he lived, and that had begun to rankle him. Recently, he'd begun to imagine Kate with him in his daydream. They could sail and swim and make love on the sandy beach.

He sighed. With a home that'd been in his family for generations, a business that employed three thousand people, and the economies of several Tennessee cities reliant upon his contributions, the idea of chucking it all for a shack by the sea was at best frivolous, at worst irresponsible.

Reid snapped out of his introspection when the room began to buzz with an undercurrent of excitement. A hulking figure plopped down on the next barstool, and Reid did a double take when he glanced over at him.

"Well, wadda ya know?" said Buddy Longstreet. "Look at what the cat dragged in."

The bartender shot a dirty look to a group of women who were working up the nerve to approach Buddy at the bar.

Reid laughed and clapped his oldest friend on the back. "Of all the gin joints in all the world..."

"Yeah, yeah, yeah, whatever." Buddy tilted his black Stetson to reveal the sleepy golden eyes and neat goatee that'd driven his female fans crazy for years. "How are ya, man? I've been meaning to call you to find out what the hell happened between you and Mama. She's mad as a wet hen, and she won't tell me why."

Reid took a long sip from his drink. Buddy was Martha's son and a country music giant. He and his wife, Taylor Jones, were among Nashville's royalty, mostly because they were two of the nicest people in a town not always known for nice people. When Reid told Kate he knew people in the business, he wasn't kidding. "Let's call it a difference of opinion," Reid said in answer to Buddy's question.

"Must've been some kind of dustup if neither one of you is talking. What're you doing here anyway?"

"City council meeting. Trying to get approval for an office building we're doing out by the airport. I knew it would run late, so I'm staying over. What about you?"

"That barbeque chain I'm into with Freddy Perkins and George Gentry," Buddy said, rattling off two other big names in the music business. "We're opening our tenth franchise here next month. I came over for a look-see."

"It's good to see you, Buddy. It's been too long." They'd grown up like brothers in different parts of Reid's house.

"We're either on the road or hibernating with the kids."

He and Taylor toured only together and only three months a year so their four kids could have a somewhat normal life. Reid had a lot of respect for the way they handled two high-powered careers but still kept their priorities straight.

"So your mama's really pissed, huh?"

"Yeah, she is. I'd been after her for years to retire to that house I built for her on my property, but she always said she couldn't leave you alone. Then one day she shows up and moves into the house like she'd been planning to forever."

"It was time for her to slow down anyway. I'm just sorry she left the way she did."

"You oughta come by and see her. Kiss and make up. Taylor would love to see you, too."

"Yeah, maybe," Reid said, but he didn't think he'd be welcome with Martha in light of the way they'd left things.

They drank in silence for a few minutes while Reid mulled over another thought that'd been running around in his head since he looked over to find Buddy sitting next to him. *She told me not to pull any strings. But I could make it so easy for her. It's not like she doesn't have the talent... But she told me not to, and she meant it. Oh, what the hell?*

"Say, Buddy, there's this girl I know. She's the daughter of a college friend of mine, and she's come to town to chase the dream."

Buddy groaned. "Oh, *come on*, you're not going to pull that shit with me, are you? Do you know how many times a day I hear about someone's little girl coming to town with stars in her eyes?"

"This one's different."

Buddy sat back to study his old friend. "How so?"

"She's got a huge talent. You just can't believe how good she is."

"Oh, yeah? What makes you such an expert?"

"I'm no expert, but when she sings I get goose bumps, if that's any indication."

Buddy chewed on a small plastic straw. "What's she look like?"

"What the hell does that matter?"

"Ya ever see a total dog on stage at the Opry?" he asked with the big smile that'd made him a fortune.

"She's a drop-dead gorgeous blonde with the most incredible blue eyes I've ever seen."

"Hmm," Buddy said. "She's that good, huh?"

"Honest to God."

"How old is she?"

"Eighteen."

"Hmm," Buddy said again.

"What does that mean? Hmm?"

"I'm just wondering if this eighteen-year-old goddess with the voice of an angel has anything to do with why my mama's so fired-up pissed with you."

Reid kept his expression blank, but inside he churned. He should've known Buddy would see right through him. "I don't know what you're talking about. I said she's my friend's daughter. She's talented. I thought maybe you'd have an idea of how she can get a leg up. That's it."

Buddy studied him in silence for another charged moment. "Okay, if you say so. Where can I find her?"

"She's playing with a band called the Rafters. They've got a gig at Mabel's next Thursday. Are you in town?"

"Yep. I'll stop by. If she's as good as you say she is, I'll see what I can do. No promises though, ya hear?"

"I got it. And keep this between us, will you? She's hell-bent on making it on her own. She doesn't want any help."

Buddy chuckled. "Just a friend's daughter, huh?"

Reid got up and tossed two twenties on the bar to pay for both their drinks. "Good to see you, Buddy."

Buddy held out his hand. "You, too, brother. Don't be a stranger."

Reid shook Buddy's hand and walked to the elevator with a tight feeling in his chest. Kate would kill him if she ever found out about what he'd just done.

～

THE NEXT AFTERNOON, Reid called Kate from the air to tell her he'd be home in twenty minutes. As he shot the final approach to the runway, his heart melted when he saw her riding Thunder down the dirt road to the hangar. He couldn't remember the last time he'd been met by anyone after a trip, and he couldn't get the plane down fast enough.

She pushed open the doors to the hangar for him, and he taxied the plane into the building. By the time he cut the engines, jumped down from the plane, and locked up the hangar, she was back on Thunder waiting for him.

"Hey, baby, this is a nice surprise." He tossed his briefcase and overnight bag into the Mercedes and walked over to pet the horse. "I go out of town for one night, and you're already making time with my best buddy?" The horse nuzzled Reid's cheek.

"He likes me better than you. He told me so."

"He's got good taste in women."

Thunder whinnied, and they laughed.

"I swear to God he's human." Kate reached down to Reid. "Ride with me?"

"I'd love to."

She took her foot out of the stirrup so he could swing himself up behind her. When he wrapped his arms around her and kissed her neck, she sighed with pleasure.

"I missed you," she said. "You've spoiled me. I can't sleep alone anymore."

He groaned. "I missed you, too."

She tilted her head back to kiss him, and the passion flared between them despite the awkward position and the movement of the horse.

"I want you," he whispered in her ear, sending a shiver through her.

She urged Thunder into a gallop. "Let's go home."

CHAPTER 24

*T*he morning after Aidan told her about Sarah and Colin, Clare woke up with a sick feeling that had nothing to do with her pneumonia. The fight they'd had weeks earlier came back to haunt her when she remembered the awful words she'd hurled at him. *It's easy to say what you would do when you've never been a parent.* She winced. *I can't believe he ever spoke to me again.*

Watching him sleep next to her, she was filled with love for him. How could this have happened so fast? Not all that long ago, she'd wondered how she would ever live without Jack, and now she couldn't imagine life without Aidan.

She knew it was time to tell him about what'd happened to her, but she'd moved so far beyond it since she'd been in Stowe that it made her ill to think of revisiting it, even briefly and even if Aidan deserved to know. The possibility he might look at her differently after he heard her story was terrifying. The last thing she wanted was anyone's pity, especially Aidan's. She knew she was probably selling him short, but she just couldn't talk about all that, not now when she was standing on the precipice of a whole new life with him. *I can't. I can't spoil this by letting that horror touch it.*

She reached over to stroke his hair, and a green eye fluttered open.

He smiled.

"I'm sorry. I didn't mean to wake you."

"I'm glad you did. Feel better?" He rested a hand on her forehead. "You're still warm, but the fever might come and go for a few more days yet."

"I feel better, but not perfect. My head is pounding and my chest still hurts."

"We'll take it easy today."

"I'm keeping you from your work."

"I have a great client right now. Not only is she very, very cute, but she's also very understanding."

"Who is she, and where can I find her?"

His eyes lit up with delight. "Jealous?"

"Don't flatter yourself, O'Malley."

He cracked up. "Whew. Things are getting back to normal. What a relief."

"Aidan?"

He turned to look at her. "Yeah?"

"I'm sorry for what I said that day about you never being a parent. That was an awful thing to say."

"It's okay. You didn't know."

"It was awful, and I'm sorry."

"I asked for it by criticizing you. Don't worry about it."

"How do you feel after talking about it last night?"

"I'm glad you know." He reached for her hand. "It's always a gamble to tell that story because I don't want to be defined by what I've lost. I don't know if that makes sense, but it's one of the reasons I like being in Stowe. No one here knows, so I don't have to suffer through the sympathetic looks I get when I'm at home in Chatham or when I see Sarah's family in Boston. To them I'll always be the guy who lost his wife and kid."

"I do know what you mean, and if I ever look at you that way, I'm sorry in advance."

He kissed her hand.

"You know, that first day we met, I saw it in your eyes," she said. "It was so odd, but I could tell you'd had some kind of terrible loss. I never imagined how terrible, but I saw it just the same."

"Are you going to tell me why I see the same thing when I look at you?"

His question startled her. "Someday maybe, but right now I just want to enjoy this. Is that okay?" she asked, but she could see the disappointment on his face.

"Sure." He leaned over to kiss her before he got up. "Bea called yesterday while you were sleeping. She wants to come by to see you today if you feel up to it."

"That'd be great," Clare said as she watched him pull on jeans and a long-sleeved T-shirt.

"I'll make us some breakfast," he said on his way to the stairs.

Clare felt like she'd somehow failed him. He had bared his soul to her, but she hadn't been able to do the same for him and wasn't sure she'd ever be able to.

BEA CAME OVER AFTER LUNCH, and they visited in Aidan's den. He built up the fire in the woodstove for them before he went out to the garage to work on a vintage Porsche he was restoring.

"I'm so glad to see you up and about," Bea said.

"Thanks for coming. And thanks for the books."

"My pleasure. We're reading this one for book club next week, if you feel up to coming."

"I hope I can. I got the check you sent. I told you I didn't want you to pay me."

"Don't be ridiculous. Of course I had to pay you. So are you feeling better?"

"Yes, finally."

"You gave us quite a scare."

"I can't believe how fast I went from having a cold to having pneumonia. Thank goodness Aidan knew what to do."

Bea raised an amused eyebrow. "You two seem pretty cozy."

"I love him," Clare confessed. "He's amazing."

Bea clapped her hands with delight. "I knew it! I knew you two would be perfect for each other. What did I tell you?"

Clare chuckled. "You were right."

"That's wonderful, Clare. You both deserve it after all you've been through."

"He told me about his wife and son. It's so sad."

"I know. Have you told him what happened to you?"

"Not yet."

"What're you waiting for?"

Clare wasn't sure exactly why the idea of sharing her past with Aidan was so frightening. But Bea was right. He deserved to know. Now she just had to work up the courage to revisit her painful past one more time.

IN THE GARAGE, Aidan turned on the kerosene heater and propped open the hood of the old car to peer in at the banged-up engine. He'd found the car in a scrap metal yard a year ago and was slowly bringing it back to life.

He was coming back to life, too. With each day he spent with Clare, he could feel it happening a little more. He couldn't remember the last time he'd hoped for anything, but his relationship with her had helped him see he'd been just getting by since he lost Sarah, not really living. Now he wanted more again—he wanted a life with Clare and her girls but not with secrets between them. Even though he understood her reasons better than most people would, he was frustrated by her refusal to level with him. He knew she trusted him—but apparently not enough to tell him her story.

Banging his fist on the workbench in aggravation, he remembered all of a sudden that Maggie had called for her when she was in the shower. He walked into the house through the kitchen, and came up short when he heard her talking to Bea in the den.

"I want to tell him," Clare was saying. "I do. But am I wrong to want this time with him without making that part of it?"

"No, sweetie, you're not wrong. It's a terrible thing, an ugly thing, and I can see why you wouldn't want to pollute something beautiful with something ugly. But you can't keep it from him forever. It's part of who you are now, whether you want it to be or not. What if he heard it from someone else before you could tell him?"

Aidan almost stopped breathing when he realized Clare had already told Bea. Hurt radiated through him.

"Who would tell him?" Clare asked. "The girls would never mention it. They hate talking about it almost as much as I do."

"You're sure of that?"

"Positive."

Aidan moved around a bit so they'd know he was in the house and then poked his head into the den. "Hey, I forgot to tell you Maggie called when you were in the shower."

Her smile warmed his heart. It told him everything she felt for him, and it was a balm on the hurt.

"Thanks, I'll give her a call in a bit."

Bea got up. "I need to get back to the store. I left my niece in charge for an hour, but we've been busy this week, so she's probably ready for some relief."

"I'm glad you came, Bea. I should feel good enough to work if you need me during the Winter Festival. Kate and Maggie are supposed to be up that weekend."

"Don't worry about working. Just come by to visit with the girls." She kissed Clare's cheek.

Aidan walked Bea out and then came back to check on Clare. "Need anything?"

She held out her hand to him. "Just one thing."

He took her hand and sat down next to her. "What's that?"

"You," she said, leaning in to kiss him.

He took her in his arms and kissed her until he was crazy with wanting her.

She moaned. "*Aidan.*"

He lay back on the sofa and without breaking the kiss, dragged her with him so she was on top of him. Running his hands over her ribs, he caressed her breasts through her shirt, making her gasp. "Do you want me to stop?" he managed to ask.

She leaned down to kiss him again. "No."

He slipped his hands under her shirt and found warm, soft skin. She raised herself up to give him access.

"Oh, God, Clare," he sighed against her neck, his hands full of soft breast. But then, like cold water had been thrown on him, he remembered what'd happened to her and that he needed to be careful with her. He was afraid he'd frighten her if she knew how badly he wanted her.

She let out a whimper when he removed his hands from her breasts and smoothed her shirt back down. "What?" she whispered.

"I don't want this to happen on the sofa." He kissed her forehead, her nose, and then her lips while resisting the urge to plunder. "And I should probably buy you dinner first, no?"

Laughing, she looked down at him. "I love you. I love you so much."

"I'm very glad you do," he said, but deep inside he hurt because she didn't love him enough to tell him her secrets.

WHILE AIDAN GRILLED steaks on the deck, Clare called Maggie back. The girl was full of news about school, her friends, and the twins. She was looking forward to the upcoming weekend in Vermont. Clare planned to meet Jack in Boston a week from Friday to pick her up.

"Will Aidan be there?" Maggie asked.

"Yep." Clare wondered if her daughter had developed a crush on Aidan.

"Is he your boyfriend?"

"I think so." Knowing this was new territory for Maggie, she knew she had to ask. "Is that okay with you?"

"Yeah. He's nice."

"He is." Clare looked out the window to where he stood on the deck lost in thought. "Listen, baby, I've got to run. Give me a call tomorrow?"

"Will you still be at Aidan's?"

"Yes, for now. The dust at Uncle Tony's house isn't good for me after having pneumonia. Aidan's going to be stripping the floors next, which is really dusty."

"Makes sense. Love you."

"Love you, too."

Aidan came in with the steaks. "Everything okay with Maggie?"

"She's great, full of news, as always."

He smiled. "She's adorable."

Clare followed him into the kitchen to help set the table. "Can I ask you something?"

"Sure."

"Do you ever think about having other children?"

He turned to her. "No."

"Never?"

He shook his head. "Why?"

She bit her bottom lip. "Well, I was just thinking if you had your heart set on having children someday, maybe you'd want to be with someone younger."

Aidan walked over to put his hands on her shoulders. "I have my heart set on you," he said, kissing her lightly.

"But if you changed your mind about having kids—"

"I'm not going to. I could never stand to go through that again."

"It wouldn't be like that again, Aidan. You have to know that."

"I don't want kids. I want you. If all I ever had was you and your girls, I'd be perfectly satisfied."

"I have to go home to Rhode Island before much longer, you know."

"I know."

"What'll we do then?"

"Why don't we take it a day at a time and see what happens?"

She nodded, and they sat down to eat.

"Can I ask *you* something?" Aidan said.

"Of course."

"What was your husband like?"

Clare hadn't expected that question. She put her fork down and sat back in her chair. "He's a good guy. I think you'd like him, actually. I know he'd like you. Jill looks *just* like him."

"I remember you saying that once before. What does he do?"

"He's an architect who'd totally *love* this house."

"How'd you meet him?"

"I was working on Block Island as a bartender. He came in one night, we started talking, and one thing led to another. We spent a week together while he was there on vacation. We were pretty much together from that point on, and we were married six months later."

Aidan looked amused. "I'm trying to picture you as a bartender."

Clare grinned. "Only in the summer. The rest of the year I taught third grade in Mystic, Connecticut, but I gave up teaching when I moved to Boston to live with Jack. When Maggie went to school, I became a Realtor."

"That I can see, definitely."

"I don't do that anymore," Clare said and was relieved when he didn't ask why.

"Was he successful as an architect?"

"Very. He started out working for Neil Booth in Boston."

"Wow."

"Neil's son Jamie was Jack's best friend at Berkeley. They worked for Neil for seven years, and then they started their own business in Newport. The firm was more successful than we ever imagined it would be."

"I'll bet you have a fabulous house of your own, don't you?"

"I do. He built it as a surprise for me. It sits right on the coast. When I first got to Stowe, it took me a couple of weeks to get used to sleeping without the roar of the ocean."

"He sounds like a hell of a guy."

"He is."

"So what happened? How'd you end up divorced?"

He'd given her the perfect opportunity to tell him the truth, but when Clare opened her mouth, nothing came out.

"I'm sorry. You don't have to answer that, but there is one other thing I really need to know."

"What?" she asked.

"Are you still in love with him?"

Clare thought for a moment. "No," she said, startled to realize it was true. "Not anymore."

THAT NIGHT, Aidan carried Clare up to bed after she dozed off while watching a movie. Hours later he was asleep with her in his arms when the phone woke them up. He reached for the extension next to his bed and sat up when he heard his brother Colin's voice.

"Aidan," Colin said. "Da's had a heart attack."

CHAPTER 25

*B*uddy Longstreet was grumpy. He and Taylor were enjoying a rare lull in their schedules before rehearsals started for their summer tour. Other than a joint appearance on the Ellen DeGeneres show next week, they were free and clear for the next little while. He'd rather be home in bed with his gorgeous wife than trucking into Nashville to be fawned over at Mabel's.

Back in the day, Buddy would've sold his soul to be famous. Now it was just a pain in the ass. They couldn't go anywhere without the three-hundred-pound hunk of meat who was driving them into the city in Buddy's Cadillac Escalade. Buddy tolerated the meat only to keep Taylor safe from the crazies. When he was by himself, he usually left the security at home.

He reached for Taylor's hand, and she rewarded him with the hundred-watt smile that still turned him to mush after ten years together. She'd insisted on coming with him tonight to keep him company, and he was glad she had. He hated going anywhere without her.

No one but Reid Matthews could have gotten Buddy to Mabel's tonight to see some unknown singer. But Reid was the one person from his life before stardom—other than his mother—who'd never asked him for a goddamned thing after he struck it rich. In fact, Reid had given Buddy the money to record the demo that led to his first record deal. There was nothing Buddy wouldn't do for that son of a bitch.

Buddy also had to admit he was curious about this girl singer after the way Reid had talked about her. There was definitely more to the story than Reid was letting on, which was just one more reason Buddy was on his way to Mabel's.

"What's the matter, baby?" Taylor asked. "You're all tense."

"I'd rather be sweet talking you into bed than going to town."

When she leaned over to kiss him, her silky dark hair brushed against his face and sent a jolt of desire straight down to where he lived. "Don't start anything, sugar, we're almost there."

He put his arm around her to bring her closer to him. She was the best thing that had ever happened to him—better than all the success and money, better than the music and the fame. None of it would mean anything to him if he didn't have her to keep him grounded. The luckiest day of Buddy's life occurred when his opening act came down with mononucleosis right before they were scheduled to hit the road. His tour manager tapped the then-unknown Taylor Jones to take her place. Buddy took one look at her and he was done—flattened, struck down, *gone*. She'd given him a run for his money that summer, but fortunately he'd won her over.

The pairing had been a personal and professional home run. They'd scored five number-one hits with their duets, in addition to a dozen solo records between them that had gone platinum, and in a few cases, double platinum. And despite what the tabloids incessantly reported, they were more devoted to each other and their four children than ever.

"Here we are, Mr. Longstreet," the meat said.

Buddy pulled his signature black Stetson down over his eyes and helped Taylor from the car. Mabel had her own side of beef working the door, and his meatball eyes almost popped out of his head when Buddy and Taylor emerged hand in hand from the black Escalade.

Buddy slipped the bouncer a fifty. "Keep it cool, man. My wife and

I just want to have a good time. Can you get us a corner by ourselves where we can watch the Rafters?"

"Sure thing, Mr. Longstreet. My pleasure."

Buddy's own security guy followed behind them, and the two refrigerator-size men paved a path through the star-struck crowd. A minute later, Buddy and Taylor were settled at a secluded table in the back corner of the second floor. Buddy's guy stood off to the side in case anyone got too close to his boss.

"Shit, I remember playing here when I was in high school, and no one gave a flying fuck about me," Buddy said. "Now it's a goddamned production to walk in the door."

"Well, we're in, so relax and enjoy it," Taylor said. "When was the last time we were out on a date? You can start things off right by buying your best girl a drink."

He tipped his hat back so he could see her. "How do you do that?"

"Do what?"

"Chase away my foul mood without breaking a sweat."

"I know how to handle you, that's all."

He guffawed. "*Shit!* Handle me. I'll give you something to handle."

"Not 'til we get home, baby," she said in the little-girl voice that drove him wild.

Buddy laughed until his sides ached, and all at once he was thrilled to be out on a date with his best girl.

BACKSTAGE, Kate was having a meltdown. The whole place was abuzz with the news that Buddy Longstreet and Taylor Jones had come to see the Rafters. *What the hell do they want with us?* Billy and the guys in the band were flipping out. They were due on stage in thirty minutes, and Kate was hyperventilating. She rummaged around in her bag for her cell phone and called Reid.

"You're *not* going to believe it," she said, still disappointed that he was working late and couldn't come to the show.

"Believe what?"

"Guess who's here? At Mabel's?"

"Who?"

"Buddy Longstreet and Taylor Jones!" Kate shrieked.

"Get out, really?"

"I swear to God. And we heard they asked for a table where they could see us!"

"Wow."

"I can't."

"What?"

"I can't go out there with them here."

"What do you mean? Of course you can. This could be a major break for you."

"What if I freeze when I get on stage?"

"Has that ever happened before?"

"No."

"So what makes you think it'll happen tonight?"

"Reid! It's *Buddy and Taylor*! How am I supposed to sing with them watching? I'm not good enough to sing for them." Her eyes flooded with tears.

"All right, now you're making me mad. You're just as good as they are. So you're going out there to do what you do best, you got me? I don't want to hear another word about you not being good enough."

"Okay," she said in a small voice.

"You're fabulous, you're talented, and I love you. You can do this."

"Yes. I can do this. Okay, I'm taking a deep breath. Thank you."

"Will you do one thing for me?"

"Anything."

"Sing my song for them?"

"I will. I wish you were here."

"I do, too. I'll be waiting for you at home."

REID'S HEART raced as he ended the call. He'd stayed away from Mabel's on purpose, even though he was dying to see Kate perform for Buddy and Taylor. He knew Buddy was suspicious of his involvement with Kate, and Reid didn't want to confirm it for him by being there tonight.

Feeling like he was the one about to perform for royalty, he got up to pour a scotch to calm his nerves.

"Come on, Kate," he whispered, sending her every ounce of love and support he could muster. "Do your thing, honey."

THE RAFTERS HAD NEVER PLAYED BETTER. They created pure magic from the first note to the last, and by the time they came off-stage just after midnight, they were sweating and euphoric.

Kate wiped a towel over her face and neck, trying to come down from the high of performing. She was higher than usual tonight as the guys jumped all around her, calling for beers and celebrating their successful night.

Billy Weston, the band's lead guitarist, came over to hug Kate. "Great show, Kate," he said with a loud kiss to her cheek. "You picked the right night to be on fire, baby!"

"Thanks. You, too." She wanted nothing more than to kick off the cowboy boots that felt like hundred pound weights and get the hell out of there. As she watched Mabel's manager, Charlie Sledge, push his way through the crowd of band members, their friends, and stage crew, Kate plotted her escape so she could get home to Reid.

"Kate!" Charlie called. "Kate, come here."

She tossed her towel into her tote bag and took a long drink from a bottle of water before she turned to Charlie. "Hey, what's up?"

Charlie leaned close to her ear and spoke in a low tone. "Buddy and Taylor want you to come by their table for a drink."

"They do? Let me tell the guys." Her heart galloped with excitement. *Holy shit!*

"Just you, Kate," Charlie whispered.

Kate looked over to where the other five band members were partying. "But the guys—"

"Just you. Come on, they're waiting."

Following Charlie to the table in the corner, Kate heard Ashton's voice telling her not to talk to anyone in the business without him. *Surely he didn't mean people like Buddy and Taylor, did he?*

"Buddy, Taylor, this is Kate Harrington," Charlie said.

Buddy jumped up and extended his hand to Kate. "Great to meet you, darlin'. That was a damned impressive show you put on tonight."

"Thank you," Kate managed to say.

Taylor shook Kate's hand. "Have a seat, honey."

Still trying to catch her breath, Kate saw Charlie signal to Butch behind the bar to bring them a round of drinks.

"Well, I'll leave y'all to get acquainted," Charlie said. "You let me know if y'all need anything."

"Thanks, Charlie." Buddy turned to Kate. "I gotta tell ya, darlin', I'm blown away. You were *smokin'* up there tonight."

Kate felt her cheeks get hot. "Thank you, Mr. Longstreet."

"Oh, please, honey, call me Buddy."

"You've got an amazing voice," Taylor said. "Buddy and I are hoping you might want to work with us."

Stunned, Kate stared at her. "Are you kidding?"

They shared a laugh. "Hell no, we're not kidding," Buddy said. In the same casual tone a regular person might use to ask the time of day, he added, "How about you let us make you a star. Would you like that?"

Kate's mind went blank. She'd fantasized about how this might happen. Would she meet someone at a party? Would there be a message one day from a producer who received a copy of the demo she sent to every record company in town? She never could've imagined this.

"Darlin'? Y'all right?" Buddy peeked out from beneath the famous Stetson.

"Um, yes," Kate stammered. "I just… I don't know what to say."

"Well, then how about I do the talking for a minute?" Buddy said.

"That's one thing my Buddy's good at—talking," Taylor said with a grin.

He scowled playfully at his wife before he continued. "Here's what I'm thinking. Every summer, Taylor and me, we take a new act on the road to open for us. We've been auditioning people for weeks, but we haven't found anyone who speaks to us the way you did tonight. We'd like to take you along if you'd like to come. We'll work with you and get you ready. We're also real impressed with your songs, and we'd like to release 'I Thought I Knew' on our label to get you some buzz ahead of the tour."

Kate's head was spinning. Was this really happening? Or was she going to wake up to find she'd dreamed the whole thing?

"Buddy, honey, you're overwhelming her. Kate, why don't you think about it and come out to the house in the next week or two. We'll hash it out when you've had a chance to process it."

Taylor Jones was inviting her to come to her house? "That would be great. I just... I don't know what to say. Thank you. I'm so honored you want to work with us."

Taylor and Buddy exchanged glances.

"Sweetheart, we want to work with *you*," Buddy said. "Not the band."

"But I can't do that to them," Kate protested.

Taylor put her hand over Kate's. "Honey, the band's great. Y'all are fantastic together. But the reason Buddy and I are still sitting here right now rather than on our way home is because of you. We want to work with *you*. I want you to think really hard about this. I admire your loyalty to the band, but if one of them were being offered what we're offering you, they'd take it and run. They'd never look back. That's what you need to do." Taylor turned to her husband. "Buddy, honey, give Kate your card, and put our home number on the back. I'm ready to go."

"Give us a call, darlin'." Buddy handed Kate his card and stood up.

Kate took the card and got up to shake their hands. "Thank you. Thank you both so much."

"Think about what Taylor said, Kate. She's right. We'll take good care of you."

They were whisked away by their huge bodyguard.

Billy came running up to her. "What the hell was that all about?" he asked, excitement dancing on his face.

"Nothing," Kate said with a sinking sensation in her stomach. "They just wanted to say hello."

SHE MANAGED to hold it together until she got home to Reid's house. Since Martha quit, Kate had all but moved in with him. He hadn't said much about what happened with Martha, but Kate suspected it had something to do with her.

He met her at the front door, and she rushed into his arms.

"How'd it go?"

She couldn't get a word past the sob that closed her throat.

"Honey, what is it? What happened?" He led her into the drawing room to sit.

"Everything," she finally managed to say. "Everything happened."

He wiped the tears from her face. "Tell me. I'm dying here."

"Buddy and Taylor want to take me on the road to open for them this summer. And they want me to record your song so they can release it as a single."

He gasped. "Are you *serious?*"

Nodding, she sniffled. "But they don't want the band. Just me." Tears rolled down her cheeks. "How can I do that to them?"

Reid tightened his hold on her. "You have to do what's best for you, honey."

"But they've done so much for me. I owe them everything. The only reason Buddy and Taylor came in tonight was to see the band. I can't screw them over like this."

"You don't have to decide anything tonight. Why don't you get some sleep and think about it some more tomorrow?"

"It's not just that."

"What?"

"The whole summer on the road," she whispered. "Away from you."

"Kate, *Buddy Longstreet* and *Taylor Jones* want you to tour with them. Come on! This is the dream come true." He tilted her chin up so he could see her eyes. "Remember what I told you before? I'll be right here waiting for you. It's time to fly, baby."

She smiled. "That's my song."

"It's your time."

"I love you. I want to be with you always."

"You will be." He touched his lips to hers. "Let's go to bed. You're exhausted."

"HOLY SHIT, man, you weren't kidding," Buddy said without preamble when he called Reid the next morning.

"I told you."

"We were just blown the fuck away!"

"I heard you offered her the whole ball of wax."

"It was either going to be me or someone else, real soon. She's amazing."

"I know," Reid said with a sigh. "You'll be careful with her, won't you?"

"Reid, you know I love you, man. We were raised like brothers, am I right?"

"You know you are."

"I'm going to ask you something, and I want you to tell me the truth, all right?"

"Okay." Reid knew what was coming and decided to be honest with Buddy. Hiding what he felt for Kate was becoming harder by the day.

"What's she to you?"

"Everything."

Buddy paused before he asked, "Who else knows that?"

"Your mother and Kate's sister. I'm trusting you to handle her with care, Buddy. I mean it."

"You have my word."

CHAPTER 26

*A*fter Reid left for work, Kate saddled up Thunder and took him for a long ride along the creek. She loved Reid's horse almost as much as she loved him. As they galloped along, Kate marveled at how at home she felt in his world after just a few months with him. He'd changed everything for her. Living with him, talking to him, sleeping next to him, making love with him, everything with him. That's what mattered to her now, but she was torn, so torn by what Buddy and Taylor were offering. It was what she'd thought she wanted —until it was handed to her, forcing her to choose between the career she'd dreamed of forever and the man who made her life complete.

Slowing Thunder to a walk so he could stop for a drink at the creek, Kate remembered the picnic she'd had there with Reid on the day she first realized how important he would be to her.

When Kate returned to the stables, Derek wasn't around, so she rubbed Thunder down, refilled his water and feed, and put his saddle away in the tack room.

Back in the house, she went upstairs to Reid's room to find the business card Buddy had given her. Lying on the bed, she held the card in her hand for a long time, turning it back and forth. Buddy

Longstreet, President & CEO, Long Road Records. On the back, Buddy had scrawled their home number. Buddy Longstreet and Taylor Jones had given *her* their *home* phone number. The longer she held the card, the more absurd the whole thing became, and suddenly she was giddy. *Buddy Longstreet and Taylor Jones want to work with me! Kate Harrington is going to be a star!*

She got up from the bed to find her cell phone and called Ashton's office.

"I need my attorney," she said when he came on the line.

"Hello to you, too. What can your attorney do for you today?"

Kate was relieved that he seemed happy to hear from her. She hadn't talked to him since the night at F. Scott's. "Well, it seems Buddy Longstreet and Taylor Jones want to work with me."

Dead silence.

"Ashton?"

"How'd you get hooked up with them?"

"They came into Mabel's last night when the band was playing, and afterward they asked me to have a drink with them. They want me to open for them this summer, and they want to release one of my songs as a single before the tour."

More silence.

"Ashton? What's wrong? Isn't this a good thing?"

"It's a very good thing. Congratulations. They're two of the finest people in this town. You can't go wrong with them."

"Then what's the problem?"

"Nothing. I have a meeting in five minutes. Can I call you later?"

"Sure." Kate wondered why he didn't sound happier for her.

ENJOYING a rare night off from the band, Kate snuggled up with Reid to watch a movie in bed.

"I can't keep my eyes open," she said with a yawn.

"Don't bother. It's not that good anyway." He shifted a pile of contracts he was reviewing so he could kiss her. "Why don't you get some sleep?"

She pushed his papers aside. "I don't want to sleep."

"Well, what else is there to do?" he asked with a sly grin.

She pulled him down to her. "I'm sure we can think of something."

A crash downstairs startled them.

"What was that?" Kate asked.

Reid got up and pulled on a pair of jeans. "I don't know."

"Dad?"

"Shit!" Reid moved fast to zip up his pants and get to the bedroom door.

"Dad, wake up. I'm coming in."

The door swung open before Reid or Kate could move.

"Well, well, well. What do we have here?" Ashton's face twisted with anger as he looked from his father to Kate in the bed. "What a fucking idiot I am!"

"Ashton, wait." Reid held up a hand to stop his son from coming any farther into the room.

Ashton pushed his father aside. "No, you wait. What the *hell* are you doing? She's younger than *me!*"

"Ashton," Kate said as tears rolled down her face.

"You *knew* I cared for you, Kate. You must've gotten a real kick out of having a father and son competing for you."

"No," she said. "I cared for you, too."

"But not enough to level with me, huh? Is this the guy you were so heartbroken over, the one you cried about?"

Kate looked away from him.

He snorted with disgust. "You both had ample opportunity to tell me about this. Instead you made a fool out of me. You two liars deserve each other." He turned and stormed out of the room, slamming the door behind him.

"Stay here," Reid said to Kate. He chased Ashton down the stairs and out the front door. Reid was bare-chested and bare-footed, but he never felt the cold, just the chill in his heart over the searing pain on his son's face. "Ashton, stop!" He grabbed Ashton's jacket and spun him around. "Don't leave like this."

"I asked you *point blank* if you knew who she was involved with, and you said you didn't. You lied to my face. Is that how it's going to be between us now? I can't trust a goddamned word you say?" Ashton's voice broke along with Reid's heart.

"Wait, son." Reid put his hand on Ashton's shoulder to stop him from walking away. "Talk to me."

Ashton shook him off. "Would you happen to have *any* idea how Buddy and Taylor found her?"

Reid didn't answer him.

Ashton released a harsh chuckle. "Does she know?"

Reid looked down at his bare feet. "No," he said softly.

"I didn't think so. Are you being truthful with *anyone?*"

"I'm sorry. I hated lying to you, but I love her, and I knew you wouldn't understand."

"Maybe you could've let me decide that. Instead you lied to my face. Now I'll never believe another fucking thing you say." Something else seemed to dawn on him. "This is why Martha left, isn't it?"

"Martha retired."

"More lies, Dad? Are you so out of your mind you don't even recognize the truth anymore?"

"I know you're mad right now, and you have every right to be—"

"I'm so far beyond mad I don't even know what it's called."

"Be careful what you do with this, Ashton. Remember all the people who depend on me for their livelihoods. If you set out to hurt me, you'll only hurt them."

Ashton leaned in so he was an inch from his father's face. "Maybe you should've thought about them before you started banging an eighteen-year-old." With that he spun around and walked to his car. He was gone a minute later in a cloud of dust and rage.

WITH A HEAVY HEART, Reid trudged back upstairs to find Kate dressed and crying.

"I'm sorry, Reid," she said between sobs. "I'm so sorry."

He took her in his arms. "It's my fault. I lied to him. He asked me straight out if I knew who you were involved with, and I said no."

She pushed her way out of his embrace. "He's your son."

"And you're my life, Kate."

"You need to go to him."

"He doesn't want to see me right now."

"I have to go."

Reid reached for her. "Don't. Don't run away."

Kate brushed the tears off her face. "I've come between you and your son."

"We'll work it out. Come here, baby. I need you." He stretched out next to her on the bed. "I love you. Nothing's changed." But as he held her close to him, he couldn't help but worry that everything had changed.

WHEN ASHTON GOT HOME, he went straight to the liquor cabinet. With two shots of Jack Daniels burning their way through his gut, his heart finally stopped racing.

"*How could I not have seen this?* I've got to be the stupidest asshole in the goddamned world."

When Kate called about her meeting with Buddy and Taylor, the whole thing clicked into focus with such stunning clarity it had taken his breath away. Buddy was like an uncle to him, and he was the godfather to Buddy and Taylor's oldest two children. Since Ashton joined the law firm, Buddy had sent so much business his way that Ashton was already on a fast track for partnership.

After he talked to Kate earlier, Ashton left the office and walked along the river for hours trying to figure out what to do. When he couldn't wait another minute to find out for sure if it was true, he went to the house.

A sigh shuddered through him as he plopped down on the sofa. Resting his head in his hands, disgusted by the memory of the cozy scene he'd interrupted in his father's bedroom, he cringed when he realized he could've walked in on worse.

He really cared about Kate. He could've even loved her, but she'd never given him an ounce of encouragement. At least now he knew why.

"Son of a bitch," he muttered as he got up, walked over to his desk, and rifled through a pile of paper until he found what he was looking for. He studied the business card for a long time before he picked up the phone and dialed the number in Rhode Island.

CHAPTER 27

$\mathcal{A}$idan tore through his bedroom, throwing clothes into a duffel bag.

Clare got up to put on jeans and a sweater.

"What're you doing?" he asked as he zipped his bag.

"Coming with you."

"You don't have to do that. You've been so sick. I'll be all right."

Clare met his gaze with determination. "I'm coming with you." Seeing that his eyes were shiny with tears, she went to him. "He's going to be fine. Colin said he's alive, right?"

Aidan nodded.

Clare hugged him. "It's going to be okay. Let's go." She picked up her bag, grabbed her toothbrush from the bathroom, and followed him downstairs.

Holding his hand, she rested her head on his shoulder as they hurtled south in his truck through the mountains. Except for a couple of semis, they had the road to themselves. Colin had reported no change a short time ago.

"Hanging in there?" Clare asked.

"Yeah," he said, but his jaw was clenched with tension.

"Talk to me. What are you thinking?"

"I'm not ready to lose my father."

"You aren't going to." Clare unbuckled her seat belt so she could move closer to him. "He's where he needs to be, getting the care he needs."

He lifted his arm to let her in. "I hope you're right. Thanks for coming. I'd be flipping out by now if I was alone."

She kissed his cheek. "You're not alone anymore."

He leaned in to kiss her, and the spark of fire surprised them both. "How is it possible that even in the midst of a crisis and even at eighty miles an hour, I still want you?" He kissed her again. "I hope you're prepared for what'll happen in Chatham when I show up with you."

"And what's that?"

"They'll be all over you."

"I can take it," Clare assured him.

He chuckled. "We'll see what you're saying in a day or two when you hear my mother and sister planning our wedding."

"Wedding?" Clare stammered.

"You have no idea what you're in for."

"Maybe I can stay in the truck the whole time. They won't see me."

"They'd sniff you out. You do know that you'll be, officially, the second woman they've ever seen me with, right?"

"Yes, I'm getting that picture." But it didn't bother her nearly as much as it probably should have.

THEY ARRIVED at the hospital at five in the morning. Clare had watched him get more and more anxious the closer they got to Chatham.

Aidan grabbed Clare's hand, and they ran inside. She was proud that she was able to keep up with him, which she took as a sign that she'd made more progress in her recovery from the coma. The tightness in her chest and the occasional coughing fit reminded her of the more recent bout with pneumonia.

They were directed to the third floor where a large group had congregated in the waiting room. From Aidan's vivid descriptions of her, Clare recognized Colleen O'Malley right away.

"Mum, where is he?" Aidan asked. "I want to see him."

Colleen stood to hug her oldest son. "I'm glad you're here in one piece, love." She bent around him to get a better look at Clare. "Who've you got there?"

"This is Clare Harrington. Colin, introduce Clare while Mum takes me to see Da, would you?"

Watching Aidan walk away with Colleen, Clare felt all eyes in the waiting room land on her. "Hello, everyone," she said.

Thankfully, Colin stepped up and did as his brother asked. Clare met Aidan's brothers Brandon and Declan, his sister Erin, and brother-in-law Tommy. Brandon might've looked like Aidan at one time, but his bloodshot eyes and weathered face put ten extra years on him. The other three siblings closely resembled each other.

"Pleased to meet you all." Clare took the seat next to Tommy.

"Are you Aidan's girlfriend?" Erin asked.

Colin shot his sister a dirty look. "Erin."

"Yes, I guess you could say I am." Clare maintained eye contact with Erin, who seemed shocked that Aidan had brought someone with him.

"Well, how about that?" Brandon said with a nasty edge to his voice. "The old boy isn't dead after all."

"Shut up, Brandon," Declan snapped.

"How's your father?" Clare asked Colin, recognizing a friendly face in the tough crowd.

"They think he's going to be fine," Colin said. "It was a mild heart attack. His biggest problem right now is my mother."

"She's forced him into retirement, effective immediately," Declan added.

Clare winced. "Well, at least the heart attack wasn't as bad as it could've been."

"My father would rather be dead than retired," Brandon said.

Something about him made Clare nervous.

~

OUTSIDE DENNIS'S ROOM, Aidan grilled the cardiologist. When he was satisfied that everything had been done to his satisfaction, he went in to see his father.

He stood by the side of his father's bed with the older man's work-roughened hand in his.

"I'm sorry you came all this way for nothing," Dennis said in a weakened voice.

"It wasn't for nothing, Da. I'm glad you're okay."

"He is *not* okay," Colleen chimed in. "The man had a heart attack."

"The doctor said it was mild and more of a warning than anything," Aidan said. "You got lucky, Da."

"How about you give me a minute with my boy, Mum. Go tell the kids they ain't getting rid of their old Da today, and send 'em all home."

She kissed her husband's cheek. "Don't let him get worked up, Aidan."

After Colleen walked out, Dennis sighed. "You gotta get me out of here, son. The heart attack didn't kill me, but she's going to."

Aidan's knees wanted to buckle with relief at his father's feistiness. For the first time since Colin called, he was able to draw a deep breath. "You're not going anywhere until the doctors say you can."

Dennis groaned. "You were my last hope."

Aidan laughed. "No luck with the others, huh?"

"Bunch of ingrates. Honor thy father, my ass. Not a one of ya minds me, and you never have."

"So are you wondering how you got rid of Mum so easily just now?" Aidan asked, raising an eyebrow.

"That *was* kind of easy, now that you mention it."

"I brought someone with me."

"Did you, now?" Dennis said with a glint in his eye. "A girl?"

Aidan snorted with laughter. "What do you think?"

"And you've left her out there by herself to face your mum and your sister?"

257

"Shit, you're right. I'd better get out there before they run her off."

"Listen, son, before you go rescue your lady, there's something I need to ask you," Dennis said seriously.

"What?"

"I think your mum's serious about this retirement thing."

"I'm afraid you might be right."

"I want you to come home to run the business."

Aidan shook his head. "Da—"

"You're the only one with a head for business. The others will run it into the ground in six months' time. I need you."

"I'm sorry, Da. There's nothing I wouldn't do for you, but I can't come back here. I'm just starting to finally get my life together. Coming home would be a step back for me—an unhealthy step."

Dennis studied his son for a moment. "I understand. I shouldn't have even asked you, but I'm desperate. I can't let forty years of my hard work go down the drain, and I won't have them fighting over it."

"What about Colin?"

"I just skip over Brandon?"

"He's not equipped to run a business. Not right now, anyway."

"We're going to have to do something about his drinking."

"Yes, but let's get you better first. Take another look at Colin, Da. He's the best of all of us. Sarah always said so. He's got what it takes, and he has the balls to stand up to the boys. He's got a lot of Mum in him."

"Yes, you're right, he does. I'll think about that. You'd better go rescue your lady, son. Bring her back to see me later?"

"You got it." Aidan leaned down to kiss his father's cheek. "You scared me."

Dennis patted his son's face. "I'm not going anywhere."

"Good," Aidan said gruffly. "I'll see you later."

Aidan walked into the waiting room and groaned when he found Clare and his mother holding hands, their heads bent together in deep conversation.

"*Mum*, what're you telling her?"

"Don't be fresh, Aidan," his mother said with a pointed look at her son.

Clare choked back a laugh.

He shot Clare a warning glare to let her know that laughing right now would *not* be a good idea. "Where is everyone?"

"They went home to get some sleep," Clare said.

"We're going home, too," he said. "Clare's been really sick, and she's been up all night."

"Yes, I heard you took *very* good care of her when she had pneumonia," Colleen said with a hopeful glance at her son, the former doctor.

Clare hugged Colleen. "Your husband will be just fine. Try not to worry."

"Thank you, honey," Colleen said with a wink over Clare's shoulder at her son.

"Mum, why don't you come home for a bit?"

"No, love, I'm staying here with Da. I'll be fine. Go on ahead."

Aidan kissed his mother and held out a hand to Clare. "We'll be back later."

They walked out to the parking lot, where the sun was coming up on another cold winter day. The windshield of the truck had frosted over, so they waited for the heat to kick in.

"Did it take you all of five minutes to bond with my mother?"

"She's lovely."

Aidan snorted. "Just don't cross her. You'll find out how lovely she is then."

"I can't imagine that. How's your father?"

"Full of piss and vinegar, which is a good sign."

"Thank God."

"He's anxious to meet you."

Clare muffled a yawn. "I want to meet him, too."

"First, you're going to sleep. I don't want you having a relapse."

"Yes, Doctor O'Malley," Clare said with an impish grin.

His eyes clouded. "Don't call me that, okay?"

"I'm sorry. I was only kidding."

He kissed her hand. "I don't mean to be a jerk, but I just can't hear that."

"I understand."

They drove through the picturesque town of Chatham on their way to Aidan's parents' home. He took a left onto Shore Road. "I'll take you to see Chatham Light after we get some sleep."

"These houses are amazing."

"None of this was here when my parents moved in. It's gotten really built up and swanky, but the O'Malleys keep the neighborhood humble. I have to warn you that the paint job on our house was *not* my father's idea," he said as they pulled into the driveway of his parents' colorful home.

"Oh, it's adorable!"

"It's ridiculous," Aidan grumbled. He grabbed their bags and led her inside. They went straight upstairs to Aidan's old room, where he immediately pulled off his shirt. "God, I'm beat."

"Um, Aidan, where am I sleeping?"

"Right here with me."

"I am *not* sleeping with you in your mother's house. No way."

"You've *got* to be kidding me," Aidan groaned. "I'm almost forty years old, for Christ's sake."

Clare winced. "You have to keep reminding me you're not even forty yet, don't you?"

He dropped his jeans. "That's not the point."

Clare's eyes drifted over him with appreciation for his muscular chest and belly.

"You're really going to look at me like that and then tell me you won't sleep with me?"

She walked over to caress his chest. "Uh-huh."

He captured her mouth in a searing kiss. Molding himself to her, he left no doubt in her mind about how badly he wanted her.

"Aidan," she gasped. "Stop. Not here."

He wrapped his arms around her so she couldn't escape and kissed her again like she hadn't said a word.

"Where am I sleeping?" Clare asked when she managed to extricate herself from his kiss.

Groaning with frustration, Aidan leaned his forehead against hers. "If a man could die of want, I'd be stone cold dead right now, do you hear me?"

"Soon," she said with a nervous giggle. "I promise. But not here."

He released a tortured sigh. "Okay, come on. You can have Erin's room. My mother will be totally in love with you when she hears about this. But you already know that, don't you?"

Clare smiled. "What was it you once said? Once a mom, always a mom?"

He gave her a gentle push into Erin's old room. "Get some sleep, smart mouth. When I get you alone again, you'll need to be well rested. *Very* well rested."

Clare shivered with anticipation. Despite the fears that still gnawed at her, she couldn't wait.

AFTER A FULL DAY with the O'Malleys, Clare felt like she'd known them forever. She was halfway in love with Aidan's father, who made her laugh until she cried as he plotted his escape from the hospital. When she sneaked him a Snicker's bar from the hallway vending machine, she earned a permanent place in his fragile heart.

Colin and Declan were friendly and courteous in the short amount of time she spent with them, and Erin was frazzled as she dashed in and out of the hospital whenever she could find someone to stay with her children. Brandon disappeared for much of the day, and Clare heard rumblings that led her to believe he had a problem with alcohol. The family was anxious about where he had gone.

Colleen took Clare under her wing, sending the message to the rest of her boisterous family that Clare had been accepted by the only one who mattered. As Aidan predicted, Clare won Colleen over forever by insisting on separate bedrooms. The two women sat up talking long after Aidan went to bed.

"I almost had a heart attack myself when Aidan walked in holding your hand," Colleen confessed. "I've been waiting for years to see that again."

"It might've never happened if Dennis hadn't gotten sick."

"Oh, I think you're wrong. I see the way my boy looks at you. He'd have brought you here before much longer."

Clare smiled. "Maybe."

"He's fragile, you know. Life hasn't been kind to him."

"I wouldn't describe him as fragile. At least I wouldn't want him to hear us using that word."

"I wouldn't be his mother if I didn't ask you to be good to him."

"I love him, Colleen. You don't have to ask me to be good to him. He makes it easy."

Colleen blinked back tears. "Thank you for saying exactly what I needed to hear," she said in her lilting Irish brogue. "Let me ask you, has he sung for you?"

"He sings?" Clare asked with amazement.

"Beautifully, but not since everything happened with Sarah and the baby. It's something else in him that seemed to die along with them. He used to play the piano, too. You've seen the piano in his house?"

"Yes, but I never thought to ask him about it."

"It was Sarah's. She played, too. When I realized he had a talent, I insisted he take piano lessons when he was a boy. He pretended to hate it so his brothers wouldn't tease him, but I knew he didn't really. I keep hoping he'll find his way back to it again."

Clare shook her head. "There's so much to him. It astounds me sometimes."

Colleen smiled in agreement. "I love all my children, but I have a special place in my heart for that boy."

"So do I," Clare said, returning her smile.

"I'm going up to bed. Can I get you anything?"

Clare had been fed to the point of explosion earlier. "Not a thing. I'm going up soon, too."

"Good night, love." Colleen hugged her and went upstairs.

Clare listened to the house settle as she thought about Aidan. She loved him even more after seeing him with his family. He'd carried on a wicked banter with his brothers and sister, let his nieces and nephews crawl all over him, and had such genuine affection for his parents that it touched her heart. All combined, it painted a more complete picture of him for Clare.

She was jolted out of her thoughts by a crash in the kitchen and got up to investigate.

Brandon stumbled around in the dark.

Clare flipped on the light, and he turned to her, startled.

"Scared the shit out of me," he slurred.

Clare took a step back. She could smell him from across the room. He opened the fridge to get a beer.

When Clare turned to leave the room, he lunged at her and grabbed her arm. "Don't leave me to drink alone."

Clare tried to pull her arm out of his grip, but he tightened his hold on her.

"Let go of me," she said as her heart began to pound.

"Too good for me?" He leered at her. "Saving it all for big brother?"

"I said to let go of me, Brandon. Now. Before I scream my head off and wake up the whole house."

But instead of letting go, he backed her against the counter and held her prisoner with the weight of his body. "I'll bet you're a screamer. Does my brother make you scream?"

Clare couldn't breathe, and the dots floating in front of her eyes reminded her of the other time a man had held her captive. This could *not* be happening again. "Please," she whispered. "Let me go."

She almost fell to the floor when Brandon suddenly released her as Aidan's fist connected with his face.

"*What the hell are you doing?*" Aidan gathered Clare into his arms. "*Have you lost your fucking mind?*"

Blood poured from Brandon's nose.

Colleen appeared at the kitchen door. "What's going on?" She gasped when she saw Brandon on the floor covered in blood and Clare shaking in Aidan's arms. "Aidan, take her upstairs," Colleen said with a look of disgust for Brandon. "Now."

Aidan picked Clare up and carried her upstairs to his room.

"God, Clare, I'm so sorry." He curled around her on his bed.

"I can't stop shaking."

"I'm going to kill him."

"No." Clare clung to him. "Don't leave me."

"Never."

"I'm sorry."

"For *what*?"

"You hit your brother. Because of me."

"He's lucky that's all I did to him. I'd kill him before I'd let him hurt you. You know that, don't you? I don't care who he is."

"Don't say that."

Colleen came to the door. "How is she?"

"How do you think she is?" Aidan was clearly trying to contain his rage. "He practically attacked her right there in the kitchen. He's totally out of control, Mum."

"I know," she said, her cheeks wet with tears. "Colin's coming to get him."

"He needs help," Aidan said.

"Yes." Colleen brushed the hair off Clare's forehead. "I'm so sorry, love. That's not our Brandon. We don't know what's happened to him lately. Are you all right?"

"I will be," Clare said as the trembling gave way to chills.

"I want you to stay right there with her tonight, do you hear me, Aidan?"

"You don't have to tell me that, Mum."

"I'm sorry, Clare." Colleen closed the door behind her when she left the room.

Thinking about what might've happened if Aidan hadn't shown up when he did, Clare began to cry. Five minutes of fear had brought back all the horror she thought she'd put behind her forever. But she refused to let it ruin what she had with Aidan. She wouldn't be afraid of him.

"Please don't cry, honey. I'm right here with you." Aidan kissed her hair, her face, her neck. "I'm right here, and I love you. I'm so sorry."

When she could talk again, she looked up at him. "Aidan?"

"What, honey?"

"How did you know I needed you?"

"I don't know. Something woke me up, and I was downstairs before I knew it."

"I was so glad to see you." She tilted her face up to kiss him. "I love you."

"I don't ever want you to be afraid like that again."

"Kiss me, Aidan. I need you."

He crushed his lips to hers, and she kissed him back with everything she had.

AIDAN AWOKE at dawn and left Clare sleeping in his bed. Downstairs, he found his mother having a solitary cup of coffee in the kitchen. She seemed to have aged overnight.

"Where are you going?" she asked.

He pulled on his coat. "I've got something I need to take care of. Please don't leave for the hospital until I get back. I don't want Clare here alone."

"Aidan… What are you going to do?"

"Something that should've been done a year ago."

On the way to Colin's house, he worked on getting his rage under control. *Of all the people Brandon could've pinned into a corner in a drunken stupor, why did it have to be Clare? And just when she was starting to make some progress in putting the past behind her.* Aidan banged his sore hand on the steering wheel in frustration. His knuckles were black and blue from where he'd connected with his brother's face.

He walked into Colin's house through a back door that was never locked. Colin had been the first of them to buy his own house, a six-room cottage with a view of Oyster Pond that had been falling down when he found it. Aidan didn't stop on this morning to admire the gleaming hardwood floors or comfortable furnishings. He was a man on a mission.

In the spare bedroom, he found Brandon sleeping facedown wearing the same clothes he'd had on yesterday. Aidan punched his brother in the ribs.

"*What the fuck?*" Brandon said with a groan.

"Get up."

"What do you want?"

Aidan grabbed Brandon's shirt. "Get on your feet. *Right now.*"

Holding his head in his hands, Brandon slowly sat up to face his seething brother. "What crawled up your ass and died?"

Taking in the double shiner and the crusted blood on his brother's face, Aidan realized Brandon had no memory of what'd happened the night before.

Colin came into the room.

"He doesn't remember," Aidan said to Colin.

"He never does."

"Remember what?" Brandon sounded like his tongue was stuck to the roof of his mouth. He touched his nose and winced.

Aidan grabbed his brother's shirt and pulled him to his feet. "Let me give you an update, little brother. Last night you stumbled into Mum's kitchen and backed the woman I love into a corner, where you scared her so badly that she shook for two hours afterward."

Brandon gasped. "*What?*"

"It might also interest you to know that she's already been raped once in her life, so I'll see you or any man dead before that happens to her again, you got me?"

"Jesus Christ," Colin muttered.

"Yeah, Jesus Christ is right." Aidan released Brandon so suddenly he fell back onto the bed. "I want you to listen to me, because I'm only going to say this once. The *only* reason you're not sitting in a jail cell right now is because you're sick. You have until five o'clock this afternoon to check yourself into a program—nothing less than thirty days. If I hear you so much as lip off to those people while you're there, I'll see to it she presses charges, and I'll happily testify against you. Am I clear?"

"Yeah," Brandon said in a strangled voice as tears filled his eyes. "I'm sorry, Aid."

"So am I. She's the first woman who's meant *anything* to me since Sarah died. Hell of a way to initiate her into the family."

Brandon shook with sobs. "I'm so sorry."

As tears coursed down his brother's bruised, bloodied face, Aidan felt himself soften but only slightly. "Get some help, Brandon. This isn't an idle threat I'm making."

"I'll get him there," Colin said. "I know of a place."

Surprised, Aidan glanced at him.

"I've been looking into it."

Aidan turned back to Brandon, who was crying on the bed. "Since Da's fine, I'm taking Clare and getting out of here today. But I'll be checking to make sure you do what I've said. I won't hesitate to call the cops."

"You won't have to," Brandon said.

AFTER A QUICK STOP at the hospital to see Dennis, Aidan and Clare left Chatham.

"He looks much better," Clare said on the way out of town. "Your mother was delighted that he's coming home later today."

Aidan grunted in agreement.

"Are we back to that?"

That got his attention. "What?"

"Grunting."

"Did I grunt?"

She nodded. "Are you okay?"

"I will be. I'm sorry. This whole thing with Brandon has me really upset. I hope you'll come back here again."

"Of course I will. He needs help, and you're making sure he gets it. It's over and done with. Can we move on? Please?"

"I guess if you can, I can."

"I was wondering, are you in a big rush to get back to Stowe?"

"I need to get back to work on your brother's house, but otherwise, no. Why?"

"Well, since we're this close, would you mind if we went to Newport for a day or two? I'd like to see Maggie."

He looked over at her. "You know what? I'd love to go to Newport."

PART IV
ABOUT FACE

A one-hundred-and-eighty-degree change in direction.

CHAPTER 28

The morning after the blowup with Ashton, Kate's eyes were gritty from crying. As Reid came out of the bathroom with a tie hanging loosely around the collar of his crisp white shirt, Kate lay in bed still feeling sick over the horrific scene.

"I wish you didn't have to work today." Even though it was Saturday, he was due in the city for an important meeting with potential investors in his next Nashville development.

"I'm hardly in the mood for this today. I'd cancel it if I could, but they're coming in from out of state."

"Can you give me fifteen minutes?" She got out of bed. "I want to hitch a ride into town with you so I can do a few things at home."

He stood in front of the mirror to knot his tie. "Sure, baby, take your time. My meeting isn't until ten."

She walked over to him, massaged his shoulders, and rested her face against his back. "Did you sleep at all?" she asked, wrapping her arms around him.

He reached down for her hands. "Not really."

"Are you going to try to see Ashton today?"

"He needs a day or two to cool off."

"What if he doesn't cool off?"

"He will. We've never had any problems between us. This'll blow over."

"Maybe we should take a break for a while until he gets used to the idea." Kate's stomach knotted with anxiety at the very thought of being without Reid, even temporarily.

He turned to her. "No. We have to stay strong together, or what's the point? We're out on a limb here. We have been since day one. I don't want to be out there alone."

Kate wound her arms around his neck to draw him down to her. "You're not. We're in this together. If you were all I ever had, you'd be enough. That's how much I love you."

"Me, too," he said, kissing her as he ran his hands down her ribs.

When he cupped her bottom to lift her to him, she tugged at his tie. "You said you have until ten?" she asked with a sly grin.

"Uh-huh." He leaned in to kiss her, but she dodged him. Groaning, he said, "What are you up to?"

"Put me down."

He let her slide slowly down the front of him.

With her eyes fixed on his, she unbuckled his belt.

"Kate…"

She freed his erection and urged him down onto the bed and knelt before him. Closing her hand around his throbbing shaft and running her tongue over the tip, she smiled at the groan that rumbled through him.

He reached for her. "Baby, come here."

"In a minute." She slid her tongue over the hard length of him before she took him deep into her mouth the way he liked it.

"Oh, God, Kate." He sighed. "*God.*"

His obvious pleasure fueled her enthusiasm as she worked him over with her hand and mouth.

"That's enough," he said through gritted teeth. "Kate, come on. Stop."

The excitement of yet another new experience kept her going until he moaned and came with a surge of his hips.

"Christ almighty," he whispered when she crawled up to rest on top of him.

"Is that a good thing?"

"Yes," he said with a chuckle as he tightened his arms around her. "Definitely a good thing. You are the most amazing woman, and I love you so much."

Pleased with herself, Kate touched her lips to his and was startled when he suddenly flipped her over.

"Your turn," he said with a gleam in his eye.

REID DROVE like a race-car driver on the way into town. He took the Green Hills exit and looked over at her with an amused expression. "How did I go from being early to running late?"

"Well, first I kissed you *right here*," she said, reaching over to him.

The car swerved. "Kate!" he gasped. "Quit that."

She laughed. "You're so jumpy."

"Keep your hands to yourself," he said as he pulled into the lot at her apartment complex and parked.

"You don't really want me to keep my hands to myself." She ran her hand up his leg and nibbled on his ear. "I know better."

"Katherine, I've turned you into a regular sex fiend. I already let you have your way with me, and now I'm going to be hideously late."

"I love when you get all proper like that and call me Katherine," she purred, burying her hands in his hair and kissing him with abandon.

"Keep that up and you're going to end up with your skirt tossed over your head in broad daylight, *Katherine*."

She laughed. "Bring it on." Her laughter froze in her throat when she looked out the car window and saw her father watching them. "Oh, shit."

Reid stopped kissing her neck long enough to ask, "What?"

"My dad."

Reid gasped and pulled away from her.

Kate's stomach lurched, and her heart pounded. Her father wore the tight-lipped expression he saved for only the most extreme circumstances, and this certainly qualified.

Reid squeezed her hand and got out of the car. "Jack—"

Jack held up a hand to stop him. "Don't talk," he said in an icy tone as his other hand curled into a fist at his side. "Don't say a single word."

"Dad," Kate said as she came around the car to him.

"Get in there and pack your stuff. *Now!*"

"Dad, come in, let's talk, *please,*" Kate said with tears rolling down her face.

Jack's lips got thinner and whiter, and his wild-looking eyes made her wonder if he'd been up all night. She'd never seen him like this.

He grabbed her arm. "Pack your stuff, Kate. You're coming home with me."

Reid took a step toward them. "Jack, let her go."

"I told myself I wouldn't hit you. But if you don't *shut up,* I'm going to flatten you."

"I won't let you treat her like this."

Jack's face turned red. "You won't *let me? You won't let me?* She's my *daughter,* you son of a bitch. *My daughter.* I trusted you with the most precious thing in the world to me, so I'm going to say this once more, and I urge you to listen this time: *do not talk.*" Jack dragged Kate with him up the stairs to her front door. "Let's go."

With shaking hands, Kate unlocked the door.

Reid followed them into the house.

"You've got ten minutes to get anything you can't live without, and then you're coming home with me," Jack said. "Your little adventure is over."

"No," she whispered.

"What did you say?"

"No."

"Kate, you really, really do *not* want to screw with me right now. You're going to do what you're told."

"I'm not going home," she said softly. "I'm eighteen. You can't make me."

"I don't know what's happened to you here, but the one thing I do know is you'll be on that flight home even if I have to drag you onto the plane."

"I love him," she whispered.

Jack snorted. "You love him. Isn't that precious?"

Suddenly furious, she crossed her arms in defiance. "Aren't you being a bit of a hypocrite?"

"What the hell does that mean?"

"When Mom was sick and you fell in love with Andi, who supported you? All I ever wanted was for you to be happy. Why can't you want the same thing for me?"

His gray eyes flashed. "Because two months ago I could've had him thrown in jail for this. Does that answer your question?"

"I fell in love," Kate implored. "I'm sorry if that hurts you, but I didn't do it to hurt you. I'd never hurt you. People love who they love. Isn't that what we learned from everything that happened to us?"

"Don't you *dare* try to compare my relationship with Andi to what you're doing with this *pervert*. I never should've let you come here. It's the biggest mistake I've ever made in my life. No wait. It's the second biggest. The first was to think I could trust my *friend* to keep an eye on my daughter. That was a *much* bigger mistake."

Reid shook his head and appeared to be making a supreme effort to stay quiet.

"You gave me a year to get a recording contract, and I've done it in two months."

"Any deal you and I had went up in smoke the minute I found out what you've been up to here."

"Dad, listen to me! Buddy Longstreet and Taylor Jones have asked me to open for them on their summer tour. I'll be recording one of my songs on their label before the tour."

He dismissed her with the wave of his hand. "If you don't come with me right now, I'm through with you. Do you understand?"

"But I've done what I came here to do! My career is just getting started. You can't ask me to walk away now." She went to Reid, and he put his arm around her.

Jack's eyes went hot with fury as he studied the two of them for a long, tense moment. "I've already canceled your credit card, and you can figure out how to pay your lover his two-thousand-dollar-a-month rent. You're on your own, and I want you to stay the hell away from my other children. I don't want them poisoned by your sordid life."

"Please," Kate whimpered. "I love you. Don't make me choose."

"You've already made your choices, Kate. Now you can live with them." He pushed past her on his way to the door.

"Daddy!" she shrieked, chasing him down the stairs.

He never stopped, and he never looked back on his way to the rental car.

Kate chased the car as he drove away. "*Daddy!*" When he'd driven out of sight, she sank to her knees on the pavement and sobbed.

Reid came up behind her, urged her to her feet, and helped her inside. "I cannot *believe* Ashton did this."

"You still think it's going to blow over?" Kate asked between sobs.

"No," he said with a grim expression as his cell phone rang in his suit pocket for the third time. "Damn it. I've got to get this. They're wondering where I am." He kept one arm around her when he took the call. "I'm sorry," he said into the phone. "We're going to have to reschedule."

Kate wiped her face and shuddered as she relived the confrontation with her father.

"I'm sorry they feel that way." Reid's jaw clenched with tension. "I had an emergency that couldn't have been avoided."

Overnight their whole world had become an emergency that couldn't have been avoided. She didn't understand how something so beautiful to her was ugly to others. It just wasn't fair. Nothing had ever hurt more than having her father cut her out of his life. It had hurt even more than losing her mother for three years. She gasped. *Oh, God. He'll tell her, and she'll hate me, too! And I just got her back!* She began to cry again in deep, gulping sobs that only intensified when she thought of Maggie, Eric, and the twins.

Reid was in the midst of a heated argument on the phone. "I can't do this right now. I'll call you when I can." He slammed his cell phone closed and threw it across the room. It hit the wall and shattered into pieces. With a deep sigh, he dropped his head into his hands.

His rare display of anger startled Kate.

He reached for her. "I'm sorry."

"Reid," she said, crying again.

"What, baby?"

Tears coursed down her face. "He said I can't see Maggie or my brothers. Do you think he meant that?"

"He's mad right now. When he has time to calm down, he'll change his mind."

"I don't think he will. I've never seen him like that before." Another thought occurred to her. "I'll call Andi. She'll talk to him."

Kate went into the kitchen to get the phone and dialed the number in Newport as she went back to sit next to Reid. "Andi, it's Kate."

"Hello, Kate."

The warm comfort of her stepmother's voice brought new tears to Kate's eyes. "Have you talked to Dad?"

"He's very upset."

"Yes."

"So it's true? You've become involved with a man your father's age?"

"It's not what you think. I love him."

"Did he give you that locket you had on at Christmas?"

"Yes."

"And you felt you had to lie to me when I asked you about it?"

"I'm sorry," Kate said, weeping again. "Dad is so mad. I don't know what to do. He said I can't see Maggie or the boys. He can't mean that."

"He does mean it. You've hurt him very much, and by hurting him and lying to me, you've hurt me, too. I don't think you have any idea what you've done."

"All I did was love a wonderful man. I thought you of all people would understand that."

"What kind of wonderful man takes a girl who's nearly thirty years younger than him to bed? No, I don't understand at all. And if you're hoping I'll run interference for you with your father, you've vastly underestimated me."

Kate brushed at new tears. "I'm sorry. I love you, Andi. I'm sorry I lied to you."

Andi's voice broke. "I'm sorry you felt you had to. Take care of yourself, Kate."

"Andi—" Kate said, but the click on the other end told her she was gone. Kate dissolved into tears, and nothing Reid said or did brought her any comfort.

CHAPTER 29

"Are you *serious*?" Aidan said as he followed Clare into her house in Newport. "*This* is where you live?"

Clare laughed at his reaction. "Your house isn't exactly a shack."

He checked out the ocean view from the back of the house. "I never pictured this."

"I told you my ex-husband is an architect."

"This is a work of art."

"Come see the rest."

Clare led him upstairs to the girls' rooms.

"I can tell just by looking which room is Jill's and which one is Maggie's, so I guess that one's Kate's."

"That's right. I can't wait to see her next weekend."

"I'm looking forward to meeting this lookalike daughter of yours." Aidan pointed to the spiral staircase. "What's up there?"

"Come see." Clare led the way up the stairs and braced herself for an onslaught of emotions that never materialized. All she felt now was pride as she showed Aidan the house that meant so much to her.

He stood in the middle of the empty circular glass room and turned to take it all in. "This is unreal."

"I should call Maggie to let her know we're here."

"In a minute." Aidan put his arms around her. "It must've been very hard to lose the person who did this for you."

His insight startled her. "It was," she whispered.

"You have me now," he said with a fierce look of love that made her heart contract.

"I know." She reached up to kiss him and was taken aback by the intensity of his response, as if he was trying to chase away all her pain with one kiss.

He held her close and changed the angle so he could delve deeper. "I want you, Clare," he said against her lips after several long, hot kisses. "I can't wait anymore."

She felt a flutter of fear go through her. What if she couldn't do it? What if the moment arrived and she couldn't go through with it? But when she looked up at him and saw only love and naked desire on his face, she knew that she was safe with him. Only him. "Come downstairs with me."

He followed her to her bedroom in the first-floor study. "Why's your room in here, rather than upstairs?"

"I couldn't manage the stairs after...after my fall."

He put his arms around her. "I love you, Clare. You know there's nothing you could tell me that would change that, right? Nothing."

She nodded. "Aidan?"

"What, honey?"

She wound her arms around his neck. "Would you please, please make love to me?"

He looked deep into her eyes as if he was trying to find her secrets before he lifted her and kissed her with new urgency. Under her shirt, his hands were cool against the heat of her skin, and Clare shuddered when he lowered her to the bed. Determined not to let fear ruin this perfect moment, she pulled him down with her. He landed on top of her without surrendering her mouth. His muscular body molded to hers, sending a storm of sensation through her. She didn't remember desire quite like this—the need to rip at clothes, to kiss, to bite, to possess. Madness... *Now*, she thought, pushing at his shirt and tugging on the button to his jeans.

He broke the kiss long enough to tear the shirt over his head and then turned his attention to her neck, kissing his way down to the top button on her shirt. He fumbled with the buttons, letting out a frustrated growl as he pulled the shirt over her head. When she succeeded in unzipping his pants, he uttered an oath under his breath.

Steeped in the woodsy, outdoorsy scent she associated with him, she ran her hand along the length of him, and he swore viciously when she applied pressure in just the right place.

"Sweetheart, *stop*"—he gasped—"or this'll be over before it starts."

She pushed at his jeans but lost her train of thought when he ran his tongue along the tops of her breasts. Through her satin bra, he rolled her nipple between his lips, making her moan.

"So beautiful," he whispered as he chased the straps down her arms with his lips. "So perfect." He kissed her everywhere but where she wanted him most.

"*Aidan.*" She combed her fingers into his hair to pull him to her chest.

Chuckling, he pushed her bra aside and laved at first one nipple and then the other. He kissed, suckled, and bit until she was crazy with wanting him. Then his eyes made slow love to every inch of her as he worked her jeans down her legs and discarded his own pants.

Floating on a cloud of sensation, she lost the capacity to think or breathe when he bent to drop hot, wet kisses from her calf to her thigh, stopping finally to press his lips against her silky panties. The heat of his mouth was almost enough to tip her over the edge.

Clare tugged at his hair to bring him back up to her, and his soft chest hair made her skin tingle as she pushed at his boxers. "Aidan, I need you, *please.*"

He moved fast to divest them of the last of their clothing and was inside her in one swift movement.

There were no ghosts, no fears, no thoughts of anything but him when his eyes claimed hers, all but daring her to look away.

"I want to go slow," he said, his face pinched with the strain of fighting for control. "I want to remember this, but I—"

"Don't," she pleaded. "Don't go slow."

He gave her what she wanted in hard, urgent thrusts that quickly had them both slick with sweat. A climax claimed her in fast, almost violent waves, dragging him into the abyss with her.

Drawing in ragged deep breaths, he rested on top of her. "*Jesus*," he whispered.

She giggled. "He can't help you now."

"I don't think anyone can. I'm sorry I didn't last longer."

"I don't know if I could've taken much more."

He lifted his head to give her a lecherous look. "We're *just* getting started, baby."

"Is that a threat or a promise?" she asked with a grin.

"A promise." He kissed her and rolled them over so she was on top. "Very definitely a promise."

MUCH LATER, after they sent out for pizza and ate it in bed, Clare remembered she had never called Maggie.

"Tomorrow," Aidan said, yawning as he nestled her against his chest.

"I feel kind of bad being here and not calling her."

He raised her chin. "Can we have tonight, just this one night for us? We can spend all day tomorrow with Maggie, okay?"

"It's getting late anyway," she said with a deep sigh of contentment, but something still nagged at her. "Would you mind terribly if I called her now to make plans for tomorrow?"

He smiled and lifted his arm to let her up. "Of course not."

She leaned over to kiss him. "I'll be very quick. I promise."

"Good, because I'm already getting lonely."

Reaching into her closet for a robe, she tied it around her on the way to the phone across the room. She felt Aidan's eyes on her as she dialed Maggie's cell phone.

"Hey, honey," she said when Maggie answered.

"Hi, Mom."

"Hey, guess what? Aidan and I are in Newport for a day or two, and we're hoping you're free tomorrow."

"What're you doing here?"

"Aidan's father had a mild heart attack, and I went with him to Cape Cod to check on his dad. Since we were so close, we came to see you."

"Oh, good," Maggie said but without the enthusiasm Clare had expected.

"What's wrong, honey?"

"Have you talked to Kate?"

"Not in a couple of days, why?"

"Well, um, something's going on, but I don't know what. Dad got a call last night from a friend of hers in Nashville, and he flew down there today. He's on his way back now. I don't know what's going on, but he was really mad about something. Andi seems upset, too."

Clare's stomach dipped with anxiety. "Is she there? Can I talk to her?"

"Sure, I'll get her."

"Call me in the morning?"

"I will. Here's Andi."

"Hi, Clare."

"Hi, Andi. Do you know what's going on with Kate?"

Andi hesitated. "Jack is on his way home from the airport now. Why don't I have him call you when he gets in?"

"Is she all right? Is she sick?"

"It's nothing like that."

"Andi, you're making me very nervous. I'm in Newport. Can you ask him to come by the house before he goes home?"

"I'll do that. I'm sorry, I don't mean to be evasive, but you really should talk to him."

"Okay. Thank you."

Aidan sat up in bed. "What's wrong?"

"I don't know. Something's happened in Nashville." Clare pulled on her jeans. "Jack's coming over here."

Aidan got up to find his shirt. "I'm sure if it was something bad, they would've called you by now, right?"

"Yeah, but Jack's wife sounded really odd and so did Maggie."

They got dressed, and Clare cleaned up the remnants of their pizza picnic. She tried twice to reach Kate but got her voice mail both times.

Aidan followed her barefooted into the kitchen, where he stretched and ran both hands through his hair in an attempt to bring some order to it. "Do you think he'll take one look at us and know what we've been up to?"

"If something's going on with one of the girls, he won't be thinking about anything else."

"You never have a bad word to say about him," Aidan said, studying her. "You compliment him without even meaning to. It's admirable."

"He's a good father." She rested her head on Aidan's chest. "I'm sorry this is happening tonight of all nights."

"I understand. You have kids, and they come first."

The doorbell rang.

Clare's stomach twisted with nerves.

"I can make myself scarce if you want me to."

"No, come with me." She reached out to him, and they walked hand in hand to the foyer. Clare released his hand and reached for the door only to be startled by the ravaged look on Jack's face. "Jack! What's wrong?"

He stepped inside and stopped short when he saw Aidan.

"Jack, this is Aidan O'Malley. Aidan, Jack Harrington."

Sizing each other up, they shook hands.

"Pleased to meet you," Aidan said.

"Likewise."

Clare watched Jack's eyes travel down to take in Aidan's bare feet.

"What's wrong with Kate?" she asked.

Jack released an exhausted sigh and went into the family room to sit down.

Aidan and Clare followed him.

"I made a terrible mistake letting her go there." He dropped his head into his hands with despair.

Clare put a hand on his shoulder. "What is it, Jack? You're frightening me."

He looked up at her with broken eyes. "She's having an affair with Reid Matthews."

Clare gasped and recoiled. "What? *What?*"

"Yes, my good *friend* from college, the one who was going to keep an eye on her for me. Ironic, huh?"

"Um, maybe I should leave you guys alone," Aidan said.

"No, stay, please." Clare held out a hand to him. Her legs rubbery with shock, she sat down hard. "How do you know?"

"I got a call last night from Reid's son, Ashton. He'd just put the whole thing together himself. I gave him my card before I left there and asked him to call me if he saw her heading for any trouble. I guess this counts as trouble."

"But did he see them together? Did *you?*"

"Yes, on both counts. Ashton had a big confrontation with his father and Kate last night before he called me. He said it's been going on for months, almost since the very beginning. I didn't want to believe him because I thought he liked Kate himself. Turns out I wasn't far off on that front, but it wasn't *him* she was interested in." Jack ran a hand through his hair, agony marring his handsome face. "This is all my fault. I never should've agreed to let her do this."

Clare reached over to clutch his hands. "You can't blame yourself. You did everything you could to make sure she'd be safe."

"Apparently I did a little *too* much by hooking her up with Reid." He released a deep, rattling sigh. "I've got to tell you, Clare, I didn't believe it. Not really. That's why I didn't call you right away." He shook his head when his eyes filled. "But then I saw them. They didn't know I was watching. They were all over each other in his car."

Clare shook her head with disbelief. "Did you talk to her? What did she say?"

"That she loves him. I think she honestly believes that."

"Maybe she isn't actually sleeping with him."

Jack snorted. "Of course she is. You should've seen them in the car. I told her I was taking her home with me, but she refused. She said she's eighteen, and I can't make her do anything. The bitch of it is, she's right. I took her there, but I can't make her come home."

"How did you leave it with her?"

"I cut her off financially and told her to stay away from the rest of the kids. I don't want them finding out about this, especially Maggie."

"You can't cut her off!"

"I'm not bankrolling her affair with a man old enough to be her father, Clare. No way. Besides, if what she said is true, she won't be needing my money for much longer."

"What do you mean?"

"Buddy Longstreet and Taylor Jones have asked her to tour with them this summer. Do you know who they are?"

"Only the biggest names in country music," Aidan offered.

"She really did it, didn't she?" Clare asked with amazement.

"Apparently, they're going to produce a single for her, too."

"Wow, she must be thrilled. It's what she's always wanted."

Jack sighed. "What the hell was she thinking, getting involved with Reid?"

"I can't imagine," Clare said, filled with dismay.

"What're we going to do, Clare? I left there so convinced I'd done the right thing by cutting her off, but now I don't know. All during the flight home, I just kept wondering if I'd ever see her again."

He was so distressed that Clare's heart went out to him. "You did everything you could today. Why don't you go home and try to get some sleep? We can talk more tomorrow and figure out what we're going to do."

Jack agreed and stood up. "Sorry to be airing the dirty laundry, Aidan. Good to meet you."

Aidan shook his hand. "You, too."

Clare hugged Jack at the front door. "Thanks for going to Nashville. I know it couldn't have been easy for you."

"You look good, Clare," he said softly.

"I feel good."

He kissed her cheek. "I'll talk to you tomorrow."

She closed the door behind him and rested her head against it.

Aidan came up behind her to massage her shoulders. "Are you okay?"

"I'm stunned. In the course of half an hour, I found out my daughter's having sex, she's involved with a man who's my age, and she's possibly going to be a big star. It's a lot to take in all at once."

"Heavy stuff." Aidan put his arm around her to walk her back to the kitchen. "He seemed devastated."

"He's blaming himself because he introduced her to Reid." She reached for the phone to dial Kate's number again. "I just wish she'd answer her damned phone."

"What're you going to do?"

"I think I'll ask Maggie to come to Vermont another weekend. I need some time alone with Kate next week. I'm sure she's terribly upset after seeing Jack."

"You guys can camp out at my place, since the floors will be a mess at your brother's by next weekend."

"Thanks." She reached up to kiss him. Trying to recapture their lighthearted mood from earlier, she said, "You do know I won't sleep with you while she's there, right?"

He groaned and steered her into the bedroom. "Why did I know you were going to say that?"

"I didn't say you couldn't visit me."

His face lit up. "Now, we're talking." He pulled off his shirt. "I've gotta tell you one thing."

"What's that?"

"You weren't kidding when you said Jill looks just like him. It's crazy."

"I know. Wait until you meet my mini-me."

He kicked off his jeans. "I can't wait." After a long pause, he looked over at her. "I wasn't expecting him to be so, so..."

"What?"

"Perfect. I mean the guy could be a freaking movie star."

Clare smiled, touched by the hint of insecurity. "I need to be very careful here because your fat head is always a concern to me, but have you looked in a mirror lately, O'Malley?"

He seemed far too pleased by the compliment. "You really do love me, don't you?"

"I'm afraid so."

"He's a nice guy, Clare."

"Yes."

"Now that I've met him, I'm more curious than ever about how you ended up divorced."

She shrugged as she stepped out of her jeans. "It just didn't work out between us."

Aidan's disappointment showed on his face when she once again dodged an opportunity to open up to him. Clare knew she was hurting him by holding back, but everything between them was going so well and felt so good, the last thing she wanted was to dredge up the past. Still, she couldn't help but feel like she was living on borrowed time. He knew she was keeping things from him, and he wouldn't wait forever to hear the truth.

CHAPTER 30

*S*ince Aidan had been to Newport only one other time many years earlier, Clare and Maggie spent the next day showing him the highlights. They walked on the beach, window shopped on Thames Street, drove around Ocean Drive, and ended the day with New England clam chowder at the Black Pearl. By the time they dropped Maggie off at Jack's house, Clare felt like she'd caught up with her youngest daughter.

Maggie didn't know what was going on with Kate, just that all the adults were upset about it, so she understood when Clare said she needed some time alone with Kate. Clare and Jack agreed she should go forward with her plan to see Kate in Vermont. He hoped Clare could talk some sense into their daughter.

Clare tried several times to reach Kate during the day, but her voice mail picked up each time.

"I hope she calls me back soon," Clare said as Aidan drove them home.

"After the showdown with Jack, I'd think she'd welcome a call from you today. Maybe you should try the boyfriend's house."

"Ugh, I can't think of a man who's my age as my daughter's *boyfriend*."

"Well, what would you call it?"

"Sicko and pervert come to mind."

Aidan laughed. "He's probably a nice guy. I mean, he was Jack's friend at one time, right?"

"You can't be condoning this."

"I'm not condoning anything. I'm just thinking that things like this tend to flame out sooner rather than later. Plus, Jack said she's going out on tour this summer. If it's not over before she goes, it will be then."

"That's true."

"And since she's already sleeping with him, what's the worst that can happen between now and when she leaves?"

Clare shot him a withering look. "She could get pregnant."

"At least he's old enough to know how to keep that from happening."

"So you're saying we should just wait it out and hope it goes away on its own?"

"That's what I'd do. If you overreact, you make it more appealing."

"You would've been good at this, Aidan."

He shrugged. "I've wondered how I would've done if I'd been left to raise Colin on my own. I was such a mess after Sarah died, I probably would've screwed him up."

"I have no doubt you would've been a wonderful father."

"I hope so."

"Do you have one of those sexy black dresses all women keep in the back of their closets for special occasions?" Aidan asked the next morning after they'd slept much later than planned.

"I might," she said, intrigued.

"How about a pair of heels about, oh, say, this high?" He spread his fingers apart by three inches.

"Perhaps. Why?"

"Well, since you finally agreed to go out with me, I was thinking you'd want to be prepared when we get back to Vermont."

"So we're not talking about pizza and beer, then, huh?"

"You insult me."

Clare laughed and rolled on top of him to kiss away his pout. "You know I don't need all that, don't you?"

He wrapped his arms around her. "Maybe I need to give it to you."

She dipped her head to kiss him, and it was nearly noon before they came up for air.

"So much for getting an early start," Aidan said when they were finally on the road to Vermont.

"If you'd let me get up the first time I tried, it wouldn't be after-noon now."

"I didn't hear you complaining," he said with a cocky grin.

"That's not the point."

He laughed. "What *is* the point? I can't wait to hear this."

"We said we were going to leave early because you wanted to work this afternoon, and then I couldn't get you out of bed."

He reached for her hand. "It was time well spent. Very well spent."

"Are you okay to be missing all this work? I don't care about when the house gets done. You know that. But between me being sick, and then your dad—"

"Don't worry about it."

"Okay, I won't," Clare said, surprised by his curt tone.

Several moments of uncomfortable silence followed.

Aidan glanced over at her and appeared to be wrestling with something. "I don't work because I have to," he finally said.

"You don't?"

"Remember when I said Sarah's grandmother left her some money?"

She nodded.

"Did I mention it was five million dollars?"

Clare choked. "No, you didn't say that."

"We didn't know what to do with that kind of money, so we used some to buy a place in Boston and the land in Vermont. Sarah's dad invested the rest of it for us. After she died, I tried to give it back to her parents, but since they'd gotten plenty themselves from her grandmother, they wouldn't take it."

Clare cradled his hand between both of hers.

"Besides, her grandmother always liked me, and her parents insisted she'd want me to have the money. After everything happened, I didn't care about anything, let alone money. I had all but forgotten about it until about a year later when her father came to see me. He said it had grown to more than seven million, and I needed to do something with it or lose a big chunk to taxes."

"Is that when you built the house?"

"Yeah. I also paid off my parents' mortgage and gave them and each of my siblings two hundred and fifty thousand. I paid off all the debt for my father's business, which still left me with almost five million. So I gave two million to breast cancer research and invested the rest. It's grown again to something like five and a half million, but I never touch it. I live on what I make with my business, but knowing it's there gives me the freedom to do whatever I want."

"You have all that money, and yet you still work twelve hours a day," Clare said, amazed.

"What the hell else was I going to do? I couldn't just sit around and think about how screwed up my life was. I had to find a purpose, and my business gave me that. It got a little out of hand in the last couple of years, and right around the time we met, I decided to scale back on the new construction part. It just wasn't fun anymore. It was too hectic."

She smiled. "I remember. Whenever I think of the first time we met, I'll picture cell phones and a pager."

"I do *not* miss them."

"You helped me to see I don't want that kind of life anymore, either. That's why I'm not going back to real estate."

"What're you going to do?"

"I'm not sure yet, but I have a few things I'm considering." She leaned over to kiss him.

"What was that for?"

"You're a good man, Aidan O'Malley. You've made the best of the hand you were dealt. And even in the midst of your own pain, you thought of others. You made life easier for your family, you gave all that money to cancer research, and you work so hard even though you don't have to."

"I still feel guilty sometimes about how I came to have it."

"It's much more important to consider what you did with it."

He took his eyes off the road long enough to glance over at her. "You're very good for me. You somehow manage to always make me feel better."

She smiled. "You do exactly the same thing for me. While we're talking about your millions, I guess I should tell you the house wasn't the only thing I got out of my divorce, even though it was the only thing I asked for."

"What else did you get?"

"Three million. Jack made a fortune while we were married, and he made sure I'd never have to think about money again."

"Which was only fair. You raised his children for him."

Clare shrugged. "That was the very best time of my life, when my girls were small. I didn't expect or even want that kind of money. He did it without telling me."

Aidan sighed. "That guy is just too much. I can't compete with him."

She squeezed his hand. "There's no competition, Aidan. He's my past. You're my present, and I hope my future."

"I hope so, too."

"Do you mind if we stop to stretch?" Clare asked when they reached the outskirts of Boston. "I'm getting stiff from sitting so long."

"No problem. I'm a little hungry anyway." A few minutes later, he took a rest stop exit and held her hand as they jogged through the frigid cold to a restaurant complex.

Aidan carried a tray with deli sandwiches and sodas to a table. While they were eating, Clare noticed him watching a boy sitting with his parents at the next table. He was about eight or nine, and his hands danced through the air as he talked with animation to parents who hung on his every word. The boy wore a Red Sox hat and jersey with high-top sneakers. A hand-held electronic game sat on the table next to a can of Dr. Pepper.

Only when Clare reached for his hand did Aidan seem to realize he was staring.

"I see boys that age, and I wonder about Colin," he confessed.

"It's only natural."

"I wonder all the time what he'd be like. Would he be a Red Sox fan like I am? Like that boy over there? Would he play football? Would he have read all the Harry Potter books by now or loved Star Wars?"

"You know, you can make him into anything you want him to be. He can be a Red Sox fan who plays football and reads Harry Potter. And then whenever you want to, you can visit him in your mind."

"I like that."

"Good."

He was quiet while they finished their lunch.

On the way back to the truck, he stopped her. "There's something I need to do, something I've been putting off for a long time. I feel like I'm ready to do it now. Do you mind a detour into Boston?"

Clare shook her head. "I don't mind."

WHEN CLARE ASKED him how he knew where he was going, Aidan said Sarah and Colin were buried with her grandmother. His fingers gripped the wheel as he brought the truck to a stop in the cemetery.

Clare rested a hand on his shoulder. "Are you sure you're up to this?"

He nodded. "Will you come with me?"

"Of course."

They walked hand in hand to a hilltop grave, marked by a head-stone with the name Sweeny in large block letters. Flowers and a teddy bear sat at the base of the well-tended grave.

The marker read, "Sarah Sweeny O'Malley, beloved daughter, wife, mother." Under Sarah's name, Colin was remembered: "Colin Sweeny O'Malley, beloved son, grandson."

As he stared at the stone marker, Aidan's face might have been made of granite. The slight tic of a muscle in his cheek was the only indication of the war he waged with his emotions.

"It's a beautiful spot," Clare said after several long moments of silence.

He squatted down to brush some dirt off the base of the stone. "Yes."

When he finally stood up again, his face was wet with tears. She put her arms around him and held him close.

"I'm sorry," he said after several minutes. He wiped his face with the sleeve of his coat.

"For what, love?"

"I thought I was ready to see this."

"Is anyone ever ready to see this?"

After another long look at the gravestone, he put an arm around Clare to walk back to the truck. "Let's go."

AIDAN WAS SUBDUED during the ride through the mountains, and Clare left him alone with his thoughts while she tried a few more times— unsuccessfully—to reach Kate. They arrived in Stowe just after five.

"Do you mind if I go get in a couple of hours at your brother's house?"

"Of course not." Clare sensed he needed to work through some things by himself. "I'll make us some dinner and do the laundry."

"Don't worry about mine. I'll do it later."

"Don't be silly. I don't mind."

Lingering over the good-bye kiss, he caressed her face. "I'll be back in a little while."

"Take your time."

He couldn't seem to end the kiss, and when he finally tore himself away, his gaze was fixed on hers. "I love you."

"I love you, too." She gave him a gentle push. "Now go to work."

He smiled and was out the door a minute later.

Clare kept herself busy for the next few hours doing laundry and making a beef stew for dinner. While she worked, her thoughts were never far from Aidan. She remembered back to the day she met him and pondered all the discoveries she'd made about him since then.

Clare had to admit that part of his initial appeal had been that he seemed to be nothing like Jack. But the more she got to know him, the more she realized he was a lot more like Jack than she could've imagined. Despite her first impressions, he was no simple carpenter. He was a Yale-educated doctor who happened to also be a gifted carpenter and, from what she'd been told, an equally gifted musician. Her eyes drifted to the baby grand piano in the living room and understood in that moment that the room had been built around the piano in silent tribute to the wife he'd loved and lost. When this man loved, he loved big, and Clare knew how very lucky she was that he loved her.

All at once, she wanted to tell him everything. She wanted to let him into her private world the way he'd taken her all the way into his. *Tonight*, she promised herself. *Tonight I'll tell him.*

CHAPTER 31

The day after the terrible confrontation with her father Kate sat on the back veranda at Reid's house. She tilted her face into the unusually warm winter sun.

The door opened, and Reid came out to join her. "Your cell phone's been ringing," he said, handing it to her.

She checked the caller ID. "It's my mom."

"Why don't you call her back?"

"She's probably going to jump all over me, too."

"Maybe not."

"Do you honestly think he hasn't reported everything to her by now?"

"She might not feel the same way about it that he does."

Kate snorted. "Yeah, right. They're the ultimate tag team on something like this. They always have been."

Reid leaned back against the railing that framed the big porch. "Can I ask you something?"

"Sure."

"Yesterday you told your dad you're going on tour with Buddy and Taylor. Does that mean you've made up your mind?"

Kate looked at him, filled with sadness over everything that had happened in the last few days. "I didn't realize I'd made a decision until I said it. I needed to show him that I've done what I came here to do."

"I just hope you're doing it for yourself and not to prove something to him."

"Would I be wrong to do it for both reasons?"

"I guess not."

She reached out to him. "I'm really hoping you meant it when you said you'd be here waiting for me if I go. I'm counting on it."

He took her hand. "I meant it." But his eyes were filled with sadness that hadn't been there a few days ago.

KATE DROVE into Nashville the following afternoon, on her way to the old warehouse where the Rafters practiced. Her heart was heavy when she thought of the conversation she needed to have with her band.

Reid had stayed by her side all weekend, and judging from the phone calls he'd been fielding, Kate suspected he had a lot of cleanup work to do after missing the important meeting on Saturday.

She was full of mixed feelings. Instead of celebrating her big break, she was gripped with pain whenever she thought of her father. It was also hard to watch Reid struggling to figure out how to mend the rift with Ashton. Everything was suddenly a huge mess, which made celebrating a low priority.

She'd left a message at Buddy and Taylor's house that morning. They were in New York but were due back tomorrow. *Once I say yes to their offer, there's no going back*, Kate thought as she parked at the warehouse. All that was left to do now was tell the band she was leaving them. Since she would be rehearsing and recording for the next few months before the tour, she was also going to have to drop the classes she'd barely begun at Belmont University.

Kate walked into the big building through a side door. The guys were already there and greeted her warmly as they tuned guitars, adjusted drums, and plugged in keyboards.

They got down to business a short time later, but the practice was a disaster from the get-go. Kate kept missing her cues, and after the third time, she held up a hand to stop the music.

"What's with you today, Kate?" Billy asked, clearly aggravated.

"Can we take a break? I need to talk to y'all." The word was out before she realized she was beginning to sound like a native Tennessean.

They put down their instruments and sat on the stairs that led to the platform where they practiced.

"What's going on?" asked Mike, the drummer.

Kate got teary eyed when she tried to find the words to tell them she was leaving them for bigger and better things.

The others exchanged worried glances.

"Remember the other night when Buddy and Taylor asked to see me after the show?"

They nodded.

"Well, they made me an amazing offer. They asked me to open for them on their tour next summer and to record 'I Thought I Knew' on their label."

Kenny, the keyboard player, whistled.

"Holy smokes," Mike said.

"Yeah," Kate said.

"Just you?" Randy, the bass player, asked.

Kate nodded. "I tried to tell them you guys are my band, but they want just me." In that moment, the emotional roller coaster of the last few days caught up to her, and she began to cry. *Why does this have to be so hard?*

Billy stepped away from the others and hugged her. "We always knew you wouldn't be with us for long, honey."

Kate looked up at him with surprise. "You did?"

He nodded. "We talked about it the day you first auditioned for us. You have star written all over you, and we agreed when we hired you that we'd never hold you back when you got your break. We hoped it would take a little longer, but you can't say no to Buddy and Taylor, Kate. Chances like this don't come along every day."

The other band members chimed in their agreement, and each of them hugged Kate and offered congratulations.

"I promise you guys, if there's ever an opportunity to hire my own band, I'll come right back to you."

Mike put an arm around her. "Don't make promises you can't keep, darlin'. We're making a nice living doing what we love. You don't owe us anything."

"You guys are great. I'll never forget you."

"I think practice is a bust today," Billy said. "What do you say we go celebrate?"

Since it was high time she finally did just that, Kate agreed.

AFTER SHE SPENT a few hours watching the guys down drinks in celebration of her big break, Kate stopped at her apartment to pick up her mail. In the parking lot, she saw Ashton leaning into the trunk of his car. Without giving herself time to think about it, she walked over to him.

"Ashton."

"What do you want?"

"I need my attorney."

"You're going to have to get yourself a new one." He slammed the Saab's trunk closed.

"Why?"

"Are you seriously asking me that?" He hardly resembled the kind, generous man she'd come to know.

"It's just business. It has nothing to do with the other stuff. I'm going to have to sign stuff with Buddy and Taylor. I just thought—"

"You thought wrong."

She sighed. "Are you ever going to talk to your dad?"

"That's between him and me. You need to stay out of it. Before you showed up, we'd had twenty-five years of smooth sailing. In just a couple of months' time, you've managed to undo all that."

"Sure, blame me for everything. But maybe you can tell me why you had to call my dad."

His face flushed to an angry red. "Why'd you have to screw mine?" He stormed away, leaving Kate's mouth hanging open in shock.

WHEN KATE GOT HOME to Reid's, she learned he too had struck out with Ashton. They made dinner together, but the easiness between them was gone. After they cleaned up, they went upstairs to hang out in his room as they did most nights. Kate practiced her guitar while he did some work he'd brought home with him.

Her cell phone rang, and Kate saw it was her mother calling again. This time she took the call.

"Hi, Mom."

"Kate! Where have you been? I've been so worried."

"I'm sorry. I've had a rough couple of days."

"So I've heard. Are you all right?"

"I guess so, except Dad's not speaking to me."

"He's beside himself."

"Are you calling to tell me you're through with me, too?"

"I'm calling to make sure you're all right and to tell you I want you here this weekend as we planned."

"You do? So you're not mad?"

"I'm not thrilled, Kate. But we'll talk about it this weekend, okay?"

Just hearing her mother's voice made her want to weep like a baby. "Okay," Kate said, choking back a sob.

"Everything's going to be all right, honey. I promise. I'll pick you up in Burlington on Friday night."

"See you then." Kate ended the call and wiped her face.

Reid came over to sit with her and put an arm around her. "What'd she say?"

Kate wiped away more tears. "Not much. She said we'll talk this weekend when I go up there."

He kissed away the rest of her tears on his way to her lips.

Kate put her arms around him, and he stretched out next to her on the sofa. The fire crackled in the background as they kissed. But when he cupped her breast and ran his thumb over her nipple, Ashton's ugly words came to mind. She pulled free of Reid's embrace.

"Kate?"

"I'm sorry. I'm just not in the mood." For the first time, making love with him didn't appeal to her at all.

CHAPTER 32

*C*lare was ready when Aidan got home just before eight. Beef stew simmered on the stove, and she was in the den folding the last of the laundry when she heard him come in. *This is it. You love him, you trust him. You're going to tell him.*

"Something smells really good." He leaned over to kiss her and brought the scent of fresh air and sawdust with him.

Wrapping her arms around his neck, she drew him down to the sofa.

"I missed you," he said, holding her tight against him.

His passionate kisses soon had her trembling and needy. "You were only gone a few hours."

"I missed you," he insisted as he reached under her sweater. "I want you."

"Now?"

"Now." He kissed his way up her neck before he reclaimed her lips. "Always."

She smiled. "Are you going to come home in this mood every night?"

"Maybe." He kissed her again and tugged at her sweater. "Help me."

Clothes flew through the air and landed in a pile on the floor.

Clare pressed her lips to his chest and teased his nipple with her tongue.

A hiss of desire escaped his clenched jaw. He quickly took control by easing her onto her back. "I love having you here when I get home," he whispered against her breast. "I couldn't wait to get back to you."

Riding a wave of longing fueled by his words, Clare arched into him.

As if he had all the time in the world, he gave first one breast and then the other his full attention.

"Aidan," she sighed, her fingers tunneling through his hair.

He looked up at her with his heart in his eyes, and her own heart contracted with the kind of love she'd never expected to feel again. The surge of emotion took her by surprise, bringing tears to her eyes.

His hands, which had been caressing her breasts, went still. "What's wrong, honey?"

"Nothing at all. Don't stop."

"Are you sure?"

She nodded.

He slid down farther and eased her legs apart.

When the anticipation became too much, she closed her eyes and held her breath. At the first swipe of his tongue, her eyes flew open.

"Mmm." His lips vibrated against her most sensitive place. "I could die right now, and I'd go happy."

"Don't die just yet."

His chuckle combined with the swirl of his tongue took her right over the top.

She was still in the throes when he entered her in a powerful surge.

His tongue swept through her mouth in tantalizing strokes that, combined with the rocking of his hips, quickly took her up again. Abruptly, he withdrew from her and rested his cheek on her chest.

"Aidan? What's wrong?"

He shuddered under the hands that caressed his back. "You make me feel like I'm sixteen again and have no control. I need to catch my breath for a second."

Tipping his chin, she molded her mouth to his and ran her tongue over his bottom lip. With her hands on his hips, she guided him back inside of her. "You don't need control. Not with me." His back was soon moist with sweat, his eyes closed, his lips parted. So complete was his abandon that Clare could only hold on tight and go flying with him.

After, his breath was heavy and warm against her neck. "Clare... I love you."

She massaged his back.

"I never imagined this would happen to me again."

Moved by his softly spoken words, she whispered, "Me, either."

He raised his head to look at her, and she was surprised to find his eyes wet with tears, too. His lips were soft and gentle as they glided over hers. What had earlier been frantic now became sensual. Cradling her face with his hands, he kept his eyes open and fixed on hers as his mouth slid back and forth, denying her the deeper possession she craved.

She sent her tongue to seek out his, but still he held back. All at once she realized his hips were moving again.

He withdrew almost completely, then went deep again.

"*Oh*, this is what I get..."

"For?"

She raised her hips to meet his. "Robbing the cradle."

He laughed, a rumbling sound that shook them both. "We young guys have *lots* of stamina. Now that you've taken the edge off, I'm all set." As he spoke, he looked down at her, keeping up an easy in-and-out motion. He touched his lips to hers. "So I'm waiting for you."

She groaned. "I don't think I've got anything left."

He arched an eyebrow. "Is that a challenge?" His hand slid down between them.

Her gasp was one of surprise and then shock when he set out to prove her wrong.

"Oh, *God*," she sighed. "Note to self—no more younger men."

"Note to you—no more men, period." His fingers kept up a persistent, determined stroke. "You're all mine." When he dipped his head to draw her nipple into his mouth, the orgasm tore through her, sucking the air from her lungs.

The power of her climax milked another from him. He shuddered against her, his face tight with tension that she soothed away with her hands and lips.

~

BY THE TIME they finally took the stew upstairs to eat in bed, it was after nine.

"Hi, honey, I'm home," Clare joked when she snuggled up to him after they ate.

Aidan laughed. "See what happens when I'm away from you for just a few hours?"

"What will you be like after one of those twelve-hour days?"

"You can only hope I'll be tired."

Clare was relieved to see the light back in his eyes. He'd been withdrawn after the trip to the cemetery, and she'd worried about him. He seemed much better after a few hours alone, but it didn't feel like the right time to get into the emotional discussion she needed to have with him. Since she'd made up her mind to tell him the truth, she figured it could wait another day or two until the time was right.

"What are you doing tomorrow night?" he asked with a mysterious smile.

"I don't know. What am I doing?"

"Going out with me."

"Are you *finally* going to buy me dinner?"

He laughed. "Yes, I am."

"Well, it's about time."

"You have a very sassy mouth, you know that?"

"You love my sassy mouth."

He kissed her. "Yes, I do. So I want you downstairs at seven o'clock in that sexy black dress I saw you sneak into the truck this morning, you got me?"

"I'll see what I can do. Can I ride into town with you in the morn-

ing? I need to get my car and a few other things at Tony's house. I've
got a hot date to get ready for."

"Oh, I like the sound of that." He pulled her closer to him by
hooking a strong leg around her as his finger traced its way up her
spine.

When she realized he was aroused again, she let out a wail. "You've
got to be kidding me! I'm an old lady. I can't keep up with you."

He rolled on top of her. "Sure you can."

CLARE COULDN'T BREATHE AS she ran through the empty house. Her
heels made a frenetic staccato on the hardwood floors. From one
room to the next, the monster followed her. His eyes, once friendly,
were now evil. He was going to hurt her if she let him catch her. She
ran but couldn't find the door.

He chased her into a corner. The face that had seemed handsome
was now twisted with ugly rage. Her clothes were torn and hanging
from her. He lashed out at her, knocking her to the ground where he
was heavy on top of her. She gasped for air.

"*No*," she moaned. "No. Please."

Someone called to her.

The monster shoved his way inside her. She screamed.

"Clare! Wake up!"

She came to, awash with sweat and tears, knowing right away that
she'd had the same dream she'd had for months after the rape—the
dream that led her to remember everything after she awakened from
the coma.

Aidan held her as she sobbed. "I'm here, honey. I'm right here.
You're safe."

That face—Sam Turner's face—had haunted her for months after
he attacked her. His threats against her girls had tormented her days
while the nightmare plagued her nights. Jack never knew about the
nightmare because she was so terrified that she never made a sound,
even in her sleep.

"Want to tell me about it?" Aidan asked. He stroked her hair and held her close to him.

She shook her head. Her heart hammered, and she struggled to take a deep breath. "I need to get some water," she was finally able to say.

He stopped her when she would have gotten up. "I'll get it. Will you be all right for a minute?"

She nodded. After he left the room, Clare lay back against the pillows, willing the trembling to stop. She was so tired of being afraid. With a few deep breaths, she managed to slow her heart to a steadier beat.

Aidan came back with the water.

Clare took a drink and handed the glass to him. "Thanks."

He got back in bed and gathered her close to him.

"I'm sorry I woke you."

"I'm sorry you were scared. Will you be okay?"

Would she ever really be okay again? "Yeah."

Clare appreciated that he didn't push her to talk about it. After a while, the steady sound of his breathing told her he'd fallen back to sleep. She lay awake for a long time wondering what it meant that she'd had the dream again now.

CHAPTER 33

On the way into town with Aidan the next morning, she knew he wanted to talk about her dream but was again grateful that he didn't push her.

At Tony's house, she went upstairs to pack up a few things to take to Aidan's. When she heard the floor sander go on downstairs, she picked up the phone to call Dr. Baker, her psychiatrist in Newport. He was with a patient, so she left a message with her cell phone number.

She carried a small bag downstairs.

Aidan turned off the sander and raised his goggles. A white mask dangled around his neck. "Come on outside." He led her to the porch. "I don't want you breathing this crap."

"Should you be breathing it?"

"I didn't just have pneumonia." He tilted her chin to bring her eyes up to meet his. "Are you okay, hon?"

She bit her lip and nodded.

"Do you feel up to going out tonight? We can do it another time if you want."

"I want to go."

He kissed her. "I'll miss you today."

She smiled. "Not as much as yesterday, I hope."

309

"Maybe more," he said with a sexy grin that stopped her heart.

"I've got to get a body double." She walked down the front stairs to the sound of his laughter.

THE TOWN BUSTLED with preparations for the annual Winter Festival, which started on Friday. After quick visits with Diana and Bea, Clare decided to treat herself to a haircut and manicure. By the time she emerged from the salon an hour later, she felt better. It wasn't every day a girl had a first date with the guy she loved, so Clare made an effort to get into the right mood for what would no doubt be a special evening for them. Not that every night with Aidan wasn't special.

Her cell phone rang, and she saw it was Dr. Baker returning her call.

"Hi, Clare. I was just thinking about you the other day. How are you doing?"

"Much better. The time in Vermont has been just what I needed."

"I'm glad to hear that. What can I do for you?"

"Well, I've met someone. A man."

"Really? Is it serious?"

"It is. He's wonderful."

"Are you ready for something serious?"

"I think so. I met the right guy."

"I'm happy for you, Clare."

"Thank you. It's just that, well, I had the dream last night. I think it's because I've been putting off telling Aidan, the man I'm seeing, about everything that happened."

"Do you think he wouldn't understand?"

"I think he'd understand better than most people. He's been through some heavy stuff himself."

"So then why the hesitation?"

"I don't know. I was all set to tell him last night, but it wasn't the right time. And then I had the dream, which has me afraid again. For the first time in months, I'm afraid."

"Clare, the man who attacked you is in prison. You have nothing to be afraid of."

"Intellectually, I get that. But the dream, it was so real, like it was happening all over again."

"Maybe the dream is telling you it's time to level with Aidan so you can stop thinking about it once and for all."

"I start to tell him, and nothing comes out. I freeze."

"When the time is right, you'll know, but do it sooner rather than later. Your subconscious is telling you something in the form of the dream. You need to listen to it. Will you be coming back to Rhode Island soon?"

"Probably in the next month or so." She didn't like to think about what that would mean for her and Aidan.

"Come see me, okay?"

"I will."

"Give yourself permission to be happy, Clare. You've certainly earned it."

"Thank you," she whispered.

AIDAN LOOKED for something to smash. Surely if he could break something it would relieve some of the impotent rage he'd felt since Clare's nightmare. He let her believe he'd gone back to sleep, but he was awake next to her for hours. He knew she'd dreamed about the rape, and the fact that he couldn't talk to her about it had him searching for something to throw against a wall.

He was running out of patience. She needed to trust him with the truth soon. Otherwise, he couldn't see how they could have the future he wanted so desperately with her.

CLARE SPENT the rest of the afternoon getting ready for her date. She took a long bath in the Jacuzzi, spent extra time on her makeup, and giggled to herself when she imagined Aidan discovering the scandalous black underwear she'd bought earlier in the day. She rolled on sheer thigh-high black hose before she slipped into the skimpy black dress he'd requested.

When she checked the complete ensemble in the full-length mirror, she was pleased with what she saw. "Not bad for an old girl," she said, spinning on one of her three-inch heels.

On the way downstairs to wait for him, she was surprised by a flutter of nerves. This definitely felt like a first date, even though they'd been together for weeks. He came in a short time later and ran for the shower, calling out that he'd be quick.

While she waited, she walked over to the window. Aidan's house was built on one of the hills that formed the base of Mount Mansfield. The rising moon cast a silvery glow upon the village of Stowe below. She must have been daydreaming, because he was back before she knew it.

"Hey," he said from behind her. "Are you ready?"

She turned to him, and all the blood rushed from her head when she saw him in a dark suit over a light blue shirt and tie. "Oh, boy, look at you." She closed the distance between them, and slid her hands inside his suit coat.

"Look at *you*. I love your hair." He kissed her, and the fire between them ignited.

After several minutes spent wondering why they were bothering to go anywhere in the first place, Clare came up for air. "We'd better go before we forget we're going somewhere."

"I've already forgotten."

"You're not getting out of this, O'Malley."

He groaned. "You've got me all worked up."

"I'm starting to wonder if you're ever *not* worked up."

"Not when you're around," he whispered in her ear.

She pulled away from him. "I'm putting my foot down. This time you're buying me dinner first."

He laughed. "All right, if you're going to be that way about it. Let's go."

"Where're we going?"

He held her coat for her. "You'll have to wait and see. Let's take your car. The truck is dirty."

Clare handed him the keys, and he opened the car door for her. She liked how he did that even when they weren't on an official date.

He drove them to the base of the mountain, where the parking lot was full of cars belonging to nighttime skiers.

She glanced at him with a quizzical expression.

He took her hand to lead her inside. "Don't give me that look."

"I've never skied in heels before."

"There's that smart mouth again."

They walked up the stairs to the gondola station.

"Evening, Mr. O'Malley."

"Hi, John. Thanks for staying late."

John opened the door to a large gondola for them. "No problem."

Aidan helped her into the heated car and sat close to her as John sent them on their way. The moment they left the station, Aidan pulled her close enough to kiss.

"Where are we going?"

"Up," he said, running a hand up her leg. He sucked in a sharp breath when he encountered the lacy top of hose that ended abruptly at mid-thigh. "Oh, Jesus, I'll be thinking about that all night."

Clare giggled. "Have some self-control, will you?"

"I have none. Zero. Zippo."

"Look at the view." Clare directed his face to the skiers on the well-lit trails below.

Aidan returned his attention to her neck. "I've seen it before."

The gondola moved slowly up the mountain and delivered them to the top after a brief ride through the darkness. The operator at the top of the mountain also knew Aidan. They walked across the wood deck into a restaurant, where again he was greeted like an old friend.

"How do you know all these people?"

"I renovated the home of the owner, and we got to be friends."

They walked into the quiet dining room. "Where is everyone?"

He gestured to a sign that read "Closed for Private Party."

Clare gaped at him. "You reserved the *whole place?*"

He leaned down to kiss her. "I didn't want to share you with anyone."

A tuxedoed maître d' came out to meet them. "Good evening, Mr. O'Malley. Right this way." He seated them at a candlelit table for two next to a window overlooking the mountain. "Your waiter will be right with you."

"I cannot *believe* you did this."

Aidan moved his chair closer to hers. "Since you were only expecting pizza and beer, the bar was set awfully low."

"You continue to surprise me, O'Malley."

"My goal in life." He grinned as their waiter poured champagne and left the bottle in an ice bucket next to the table.

Aidan lifted his glass and looked into her eyes. "Here's to you and me and the last first date of our lives."

Clare touched her glass to his. The implication of his toast hung in the air between them as they were served an elaborate meal that Aidan admitted wasn't on the restaurant's regular menu.

"You must've done a hell of a job on his house," Clare said as she finished her filet mignon.

He gave her his now-familiar offended look. "Of course I did. You can ask him yourself. Here he comes."

Aidan introduced her to Michael Donnolly, the restaurant's owner and head chef. Clare could tell by the banter between the two men that they were good friends. Michael confirmed that Aidan had, in fact, done a spectacular job on his house.

"See, I told you," Aidan said to Clare.

"Was everything all right with your dinner?" Michael asked.

"It was excellent, thanks, Mike," Aidan said.

"Nice to meet you, Clare," Michael said and left them alone.

They were served a sinful chocolate dessert, and Clare fed Aidan the first bite.

"I need to check something," he said with a serious expression.

"What?"

Under the table, he ran a hand up to where lace met leg. "Yep, still there," he said with a deep sigh of frustration.

She pushed his hand away. "You're like a twelve-year-old boy. When are you going to be forty anyway?"

"Two weeks." He put his hand back on her leg and nuzzled her neck.

Laughing at his antics, Clare tilted her head to give him better access to what he wanted. "Maybe you'll act more like a grown-up then."

"I wouldn't count on it. Can we go home now? Please?"

"I'm not ready for our first date to be over, especially since you went to all this trouble."

"Our first date is *not* over, don't worry."

"There's more?"

"Haven't you learned not to underestimate me?"

"Apparently not," Clare said, dying to know what else he had up his sleeve.

On the gondola ride down the mountain, Aidan made good use of the time alone to further explore the silk and lace that had preoccupied him all evening. By the time they reached the bottom of the mountain, Clare was breathless with wanting him.

"I'll bet you have other surprises for me under there, don't you?" he asked, pretending to peek under her skirt.

She slapped his hand away. "That's for me to know and you to find out."

"Oh, that mouth of yours. It's going to get you in so much trouble one of these days."

"I can't wait."

He gave her a look that was full of promises and helped her off the gondola. They walked downstairs to the parking lot, where a horse-drawn sleigh awaited them.

"Your chariot, madame," he said with a dramatic sweep of his hand.

Speechless, Clare stared at the sleigh and then at Aidan.

He took her hand to help her into the sleigh and bundled heavy blankets around them before he signaled to the driver they were ready to go.

"I'll never underestimate you again," Clare said softly.

He put his arm around her. "You'll ruin all my fun."

She kissed him and rested her head on his shoulder. "This is the best first date I've ever had."

"I'm glad," he whispered. "Are you warm enough?"

She nodded and looked up at the dazzling array of stars in the moonlit sky. The horse's hooves beat in time with the bells around its neck as the sleigh glided over the snow, and Clare knew if she lived to be a hundred years old, she would never forget this.

THE SLEIGH DELIVERED them to Aidan's house, and Clare was surprised to see her car already there.

"How did my car get here?"

"My buddy John, the gondola operator, did me a favor."

"Did you think of everything?" Clare asked with amazement as he held the door and followed her into the house.

He took her coat and went to hang it up. When he returned to her, he had shed his suit coat.

Clare put her arms around him and snuggled into his chest. "Thank you."

"You're welcome. I'm sorry it took me so long to buy you dinner."

Clare laughed. "It was well worth the wait. I love you, Aidan O'Malley."

"I love you, too."

"Will you do something for me?"

"Name it."

"Will you sing for me?"

Startled, he said, "How do you know I can?"

She smiled.

"My mother has a big freaking mouth," he muttered, shaking his head.

"She has a bigger heart. So?"

He looked away, focusing on the wall. "I don't know. It's been a long time."

She brought him back to her with a finger to his chin. "For me?"

He studied her for a long moment. "What do you want to hear?"

"Surprise me," she said, tugging on his hand to lead him to sit next to her on the piano bench. When Clare lifted the cover, Aidan stared at the keys as if he was seeing them for the first time.

He finally lifted a hand and played a few notes of what Clare recognized as Chopin. Then he added his other hand, and tentatively played a familiar tune Clare couldn't name until he added the words to "We've Got Tonight."

He gave her a small smile as he played the music between verses and continued in a voice that sounded an awful lot like Bob Seger himself.

"Aidan," Clare whispered after he played the final notes. "That was beautiful."

His hands rested on his knees. "I love that song, but I'm all done searching. I hope you know that."

"And you know my plans *do* include you."

"I hope so," he said, slipping his hand around her neck to draw her closer to him. He touched his lips to hers with none of the urgent need he'd shown her earlier. Instead, this kiss was full of tender restraint.

"Aidan."

"Hmm?"

"I need to tell you something."

He pulled back to look at her. "Now?"

She bit her lip and nodded.

CHAPTER 34

*B*uddy Longstreet returned Kate's call the day after he returned from New York. He asked her to come see him at his Music Row office later that afternoon. This time, Music Row meant Music Row. Long Road Records was smack in the middle of the action, sitting between EMI and Sony on Music Square East. Kate took the elevator to the fifth floor and, per Buddy's instructions, used the code word "flower" to be buzzed into his suite of offices.

A young woman wearing jeans, a T-shirt, and boots met Kate at the door and introduced herself as Buddy's assistant Christina. She had the thick Tennessee accent that Kate had become so accustomed to she hardly noticed it anymore.

"Come on in, Kate." She shook Kate's hand. "Buddy's expecting you."

Two walls in the large corner office were all glass with a view of downtown Nashville. Buddy reclined in a leather chair as he talked on the phone. His signature black Stetson was firmly in place, and his black cowboy boots were perched on the desk. He gestured for Kate to have a seat.

"Well, listen, I've got a meeting," he said. "You betcha. You'll be hearing from me, don't worry. Right-o." He dropped his feet to the floor when he hung up the phone.

"How are you, Kate? Did Christina offer you anything?"

"I'm fine, thanks." Kate wanted to pinch herself. *I'm in Buddy Longstreet's office!*

"Well, darlin', Taylor and I were real glad to hear you'd called while we were in New York. The kids had a blast in the Big Apple. Have you been there?"

"Yes, I love it there," she said.

He came around the desk and plopped down in the chair next to her.

Suddenly, Kate was sitting close enough to touch a man who'd inspired thousands of women to throw their panties at him. It took supreme effort to not show him how star struck she was.

"We've got a lot to talk about. I take it you've decided to accept our offer?"

"Yes."

"I'm happy to hear that. You had us wondering when we didn't hear from you right away."

"I had a crazy couple of days. I'm sorry it took me so long to call you. I can't thank you both enough for taking a chance on me. I won't let you down."

"Of course you won't. You'll be great. But before we get into all that, I want to tell you some things I wish someone had told me when I was sitting where you are right now." He got up and went over to a small bar in the corner, where he fixed himself a short drink of what might've been bourbon. "This is a tough, tough business, Kate. You have to be willing to commit to your career one hundred and ten percent, at least at first. You're either rehearsing or recording or on the road. There's no time for a life. There's no time for anything but work. The first couple of years will probably suck. I'll be honest with you about that."

"Sounds glamorous," Kate said with a grin even as her heart ached when she considered what it would mean for her and Reid.

Buddy snorted out a laugh. "It's hard-ass work is what it is. I have no doubt you'll be a sensation if you work really hard. You're the whole package—you're young and beautiful, and you have a voice that'll take you anywhere you want to go. Plus you write your own songs, and you play the guitar. I can make you a huge star, but I want you to be prepared for the reality of what that means. You with me?"

Kate swallowed hard and nodded.

"First, everyone will want a piece of you. People you didn't even know you knew will call and ask for money. Their kids will be sick, their mother will need an operation. They'll break your heart, and you'll want to help them all, but you can't. Second, the day your single hits the charts—and it *will* hit the charts—your life as a private citizen is over. You won't be able to set foot out your front door without security. Third, the demands on your time will be staggering. Publicity, music videos, appearances, performances, recording, writing, rehearsing. It's nonstop."

Kate studied the floor as she listened to him.

"Sweetheart, you need to look me in the eye and tell me you want all that. There'll be no hard feelings between us if you just don't have it in you. Not everyone does. I've seen a lot of talented people hit it big and then run for the hills when they get everything they thought they wanted, and it turns out to be a big pile of shit."

He gave her a moment to consider that. "Before we go one step further, I need to hear you say you want this with everything you've got. If you say those words, if you say, 'Buddy, make me a star,' I promise I'll take care of you. I'll get you the best of everything—management, lawyers, accountants, musicians, publicists. And—this is important, now, darlin'—I promise you can trust *every* word that comes out of my mouth. I'll never tell you anything but the truth, and neither will Taylor."

Kate's heart beat so fast, she wondered how it stayed in her chest. She thought about Reid and what they had together. The life Buddy described left no room for Reid or anyone else. It came down to a choice—one or the other, but not both. But maybe, just maybe, they could make it work. He promised he would wait for her. As she looked into Buddy Longstreet's golden eyes, she hoped to God Reid was as good as his word. She was about to bet on it.

"Buddy," she said softly. "Make me a star."

WITH THOSE FIVE WORDS, Kate's life shifted into high gear. Buddy's tour manager, Riley Shea, wanted to hear every song she'd ever written to be sure she had enough material to fill her thirty minutes as the opening act. He approved of five songs but tossed the rest aside. She'd either have to write more, or they'd find other material for her. She began rehearsing with studio musicians to prepare for the recording of "I Thought I Knew," and had meetings with people from publicity, wardrobe, and even a makeup artist. She met with a lawyer Buddy recommended, and her heart ached when she thought of Ashton. He should've been the one hammering out the agreement with Buddy and Taylor that would pay her more than a million dollars for the tour plus royalties for anything she recorded on their label.

It was overwhelming, but the constant activity helped to keep her personal worries on the back burner. She didn't have time to think about Ashton or her dad or the tiny cracks that had appeared in her relationship with Reid during the last tumultuous week. And she still had to face her mother when she flew to Vermont on Friday evening. Until then, she pushed all her problems to the side so she could focus on her work.

On Thursday afternoon, Buddy dropped by the studio on the fourth floor of his office building to see how her rehearsals were going.

"Sounds real good, darlin'," he said when Kate stopped to take a break. "Listen, we're playing a benefit a week from Saturday, and we'd like you to open for us. It's a smaller crowd, but it'll give you a good feel for the concert venues."

"How small?"

"Five, maybe six thousand. No biggie."

Kate choked. "Five or six thousand *people?*"

Riley laughed at her reaction. "Should we tell her how many come to a show on the road, Buddy?"

Buddy smiled. "Nah, let her find out. Well, I've gotta get home. Oh, Kate, Taylor wants you to come out to the house the day after the benefit to meet the kids. She makes everyone we work with part of the family."

"I'd love to. Tell her thanks for me."

"I'll let you get back to work," Buddy said. "Just holler if you need anything."

"Buddy?"

"Yeah?"

"Thank you. For everything."

"My pleasure. Have a good time in Vermont."

KATE ARRIVED at home before Reid, so she started dinner. When her mother was ill, she and Jill had helped out around the house, and Kate had become a proficient cook. Jill had called earlier in the week to find out why their father had been so cranky since his trip to Nashville, and Kate poured out the whole story to her stunned sister. Kate desperately wanted to fix things with her dad, but she knew that was impossible as long as she was still with Reid. She stirred the sauce she'd filled with vegetables for primavera and buttered some Italian bread.

Reid came in through the kitchen door, which meant he'd been to the stables to visit Thunder and the other horses before he came in the house. "Hey, baby."

Determined to put things back on track with him before she left for Vermont, she greeted him with a big smile and a kiss. "Hi. Are you hungry?"

"Starving. What're you making?"

"Pasta primavera."

He put an arm around her and peered into the pot. "Smells fabulous."

She reached up to kiss him again and lingered when his arms tightened around her.

"Will it keep for a little while?" he asked as he lifted her onto the counter and kissed her ear, her neck, her throat.

"It's better if it simmers for a bit," she said with a coy smile.

Kissing her, he eased her back on the counter.

Startled, she looked up at him. "Here?"

"Right here."

As he hovered over her so handsome and sexy, Kate wondered how she would ever live without him—without *this*—when she was on the road for months on end. But as he set out to drive her crazy with kisses to her neck, she ceased to think of anything but him.

CHAPTER 35

*A*idan tossed another log into the woodstove and joined Clare on the sofa. He'd taken off his tie and rolled up his shirt-sleeves.

Clare caressed his arm as she searched for the words she needed. "The first thing I want you to know is I love you so much. Every day I wake up with you and feel so lucky that I found you—that we found each other and now we have this amazing second chance at love. I know I've hurt you by not opening up to you before now, and I'm sorry for that."

He clutched her hand. "You don't have to be sorry."

"I'd never hurt you intentionally. I hope you know that. I wanted us to have some time together without making everything that happened to me part of it. I'm not sure if you can understand..."

"Of course, I do."

"I don't even know where to begin," she said with a sigh.

He drew her into his arms and kissed her forehead. "How about the beginning?"

She rested against his chest. "Well, you know I was a Realtor. Because of Jack's business and the girls' school, we knew a lot of people in town, so I did pretty well. I was on phone duty at the office one Saturday when I got a call from a guy who was relocating to Newport from San Diego. He told me he was divorced with two kids and that he was coming to town the following week to look for a house. Sam..." She paused to take a deep breath.

Aidan tightened his hold on her.

"His name was Sam," she continued, determined to get through this. "He was tall, blond, and very good-looking. The other women in the office joked that they'd fight me for him. While we were out house hunting, we talked about our kids, and he showed me pictures of his. The second day, we looked at three houses." Tears rolled down her face, and she wiped them away. "The third house was near the beach, and it was empty. We went upstairs. There was a great view of the beach, and I went over to look at it. He came up behind me and lifted me off my feet. I didn't know what he was doing. And then I was on the floor, and he was on top of me."

"Stop, Clare, stop," Aidan hissed through gritted teeth. "That's enough."

"I need to tell you."

"No. I already know."

Stunned, she sat up and turned to look at him. "How?" And then she knew. "Oh, oh, *God*, the girls told you?"

He nodded. "Unintentionally."

"You've known all this time?"

Again he nodded. "That's one reason why it was all I could do to keep from killing Brandon."

Clare freed herself from his embrace and stood up. "I just... I can't believe you knew and never said anything. I've been trying to work up the nerve to tell you, and you already knew?"

"I figured you'd tell me when you were ready."

All the fight went out of her. "What else do you know?" she whispered as tears spilled down her cheeks.

"I know about the accident and the coma. I know you're one of the most selfless people I've ever met because you let your husband go rather than make him choose between you and another woman. I

325

know that last night you dreamed about the attack. And I know I've only ever felt that helpless one other time in my life."

Clare brought her hand to her mouth, hoping to muffle a sob.

Aidan was on his feet so fast she had no time to react before she was surrounded by his love.

"I'm sorry," she said.

He brought her down onto his lap. "What in the world do you have to be sorry about?"

"You must've thought I didn't love you enough to tell you, or I didn't trust you enough. After you shared everything with me. What you must've thought."

"What I thought is that you went through a terrible thing and maybe you just couldn't talk to me about it no matter how much you loved me or trusted me. But I hoped you'd tell me. When you were ready."

"He threatened my babies, Aidan," she whispered. "He said he'd kill one of them if I told anyone."

He wiped away her tears. "I know, honey. I know."

"He could've said anything else. I could've lived with anything else."

Aidan held her and rocked her as she cried.

"I never told anyone, and when that car was coming at me, all I saw was a way out. I did an awful thing to my girls by letting it happen right in front of them."

"It wasn't your fault, Clare."

"I didn't even remember any of it until a couple of months after I recovered, when I had the same dream I had last night." She wiped at the tears rolling down her face. "I had to confront all those memories of the attack and the accident on top of the fact that my husband of twenty years was in love with someone else and expecting twins with her."

"I can't imagine."

"I was really, really mad. For a long time."

"Who wouldn't be?"

"But once I stopped being mad, I actually thought I could do it. For a while, I thought we could go on with our lives, and I'd just eventually accept that he had children with another woman."

"But you couldn't?"

"I might've been able to, but he loved her. Really loved her."

"So you let him go."

She nodded sadly. "I wanted better for myself than a life with a man who wanted to be somewhere else. In a way, I wanted better for him, too. He would've stayed with me. I have no doubt about that, but we would've ended up hating each other. As heartbroken as I was, that would've been worse."

"What's his wife like?"

"She's lovely. She was wonderful to my girls, and they love her very much. I can see why he does, too."

"What brought you to Vermont?"

"I found that being home without him was just unbearable. What seemed like such a good idea when I was still in the hospital wasn't so great when I got home. My brother needed help with the house, so as soon as Kate left for Nashville, I came up here. I felt sick about leaving Maggie, but I knew if I didn't get out of there for a little while I'd never get over losing Jack."

Aidan swore under his breath. "And then I busted your chops about living away from her. I'm so sorry."

"Believe me, I was already busting my own chops about it. But I did the right thing coming here. I knew for sure when we were in Newport this week, but that was probably because you were with me."

"It's probably because you're stronger now."

Clare shrugged. "Possibly."

"I'm so proud of you."

"Why?"

"Because you survived. This terrible thing happened to you, and yet still you can laugh and joke and love. You didn't let him win."

"He took so much from me. As bad as it was to lose three years of my life and then Jack, too, you know what was worse?"

Aidan shook his head.

"I lost the thing that defined me—my life as a mother. I left three little girls and came back to two adults and a teenager."

"But they still need you, especially Maggie. You've got more than four years with her before she goes to college."

"Yes, and I'm going home to her. Soon. But it's not the same. I have to share her with a stepmother she loves—the stepmother who gave her three brothers, who saw her through her first period and middle school, and God knows what else. Maggie doesn't belong just to me anymore."

"What about Kate? She needs you more than ever right now. And even Jill's certainly not all grown up yet."

"It's not the same. It's not like it was when they were younger and relied on me for everything. I've never felt more fulfilled by anything than I did then. Losing that has left a gaping hole inside of me."

"Maybe you'll feel better about it when you get back to Rhode Island. You can be more involved in Maggie's daily life again."

"Maybe," Clare said, but she wasn't convinced. "Thank you for listening."

"Thank you for telling me." He kissed her softly. "I hope you're not mad I didn't tell you I knew. I didn't want to push you."

She caressed his handsome face. "I don't deserve you."

"Oh, yes. Yes, you do." He kissed her then as if his life—and hers—depended on it.

"Wanna see what else is under this dress?" she asked with a saucy smile.

He groaned. "You have *no* idea…"

MUCH LATER, while Clare slept in his arms, Aidan was content. With no secrets left between them, they could start to make plans for their future. He already had a few ideas about what that might entail.

"Aidan?"

"I thought you were asleep."

"Almost. Thank you again for our date."

He kissed the top of her head. "My pleasure."

"I love you."

"I love you, too. And I'm really glad you came to Vermont. I'm sorry about the reasons, but I'm so glad you came here."

"Me, too."

CHAPTER 36

a light snow was falling Friday evening, so Aidan insisted on driving Clare to Burlington to pick up Kate. The roads were slick, and they arrived just as Kate's flight was announced.

Aidan gasped when he saw Kate coming toward them. "Wow, you weren't kidding! She's you all over again!"

Clare smiled up at him. "She's the tall version of me."

Seeming to be fighting tears, Kate fell into her mother's arms.

"Okay, baby. You're okay."

Kate clung to her.

Clare let the flood of people move around them as she held her daughter.

"Sorry," Kate said, her voice muffled by her mother's coat.

"You've had a rough week." Clare searched her daughter's face for signs of the changes she knew had occurred recently. But all she saw was the tearstained face of the girl she loved.

"You must be Aidan O'Malley."

He shook Kate's hand. "Nice to meet you."

"My sisters were right about you."

"How's that?"

"Oh, nothing," Kate said with an approving smile for her mother.

Clare returned the smile. "Do you have bags?"

"Just this," Kate said, referring to the bag she carried on her shoulder.

"Let's hit the road, then," Aidan said. "It's getting ugly out there."

On the ride home, Kate filled them in on everything that'd happened with Buddy and Taylor and the preparations for the tour.

"So the next time we see you, we might need special passes or something?" Clare joked.

Kate smiled. "From what Buddy says, maybe."

"You must be very excited," Clare said.

"I'm scared."

"Why?"

"Buddy says my whole life will change, that I'll be working all the time, and it'll be really crazy."

"Isn't that what you wanted?" Clare asked.

"Yes, but it's nerve-racking now that it's actually happening."

Aidan drove them up the winding road leading to his house on the hilltop.

"Wow, awesome place," Kate said.

"We're staying with Aidan because Uncle Tony's house is a mess."

"That's cool."

They settled Kate in one of the bedrooms, and Aidan built up the fire in the den for them. "I'll be in the garage, if you ladies need me."

After he left the room, Kate turned to her mother. "Okay, spill it."

"What?"

"Oh my God, Mom! He's *hot!*"

Clare smiled. "So I've noticed, but I don't want to talk about him."

Kate's smile faded. "Uh-oh, here it comes."

"I'm worried about you. What's going on with you and this older man?"

"I love him. I told Dad that, but he didn't want to hear it."

"Kate, you're eighteen. He's forty-six. What did you expect Dad to say? What do you expect *me* to say? It's horrifying to us."

Kate's face crumpled. "Don't say that. How is it any different than you and Aidan? You love him. I can tell by the way you look at him."

"It's very different. We're both adults."

"I'm an adult, too. Look at what I'm doing, what's about to happen to me, not to mention all we went through after your accident. How can you say I'm not an adult?"

"Honey, listen to me. I don't know this man you claim to love. I only know that Dad once thought of him as a friend, so he must have some admirable qualities. But being involved with an eighteen-year-old at his age is not admirable. It's wrong."

Tears flooded Kate's eyes and slid down her cheeks. "It doesn't feel wrong. Not to me."

"I don't want to ruin our visit with tears and arguments. I love you. I'll support you no matter what you choose, but I don't approve of this relationship, Kate. I want to be crystal clear on that."

"What am I going to do about Dad? And Andi? She's mad at me, too. I lied to her about Reid when I was home at Christmas. She's really disappointed."

"If you felt you had to lie, what does that tell you?"

"That's what she said, too."

"Come here," Clare said, reaching out to her daughter.

Kate fell into her mother's arms. "I don't like disappointing you. Any of you."

"You've got a lot to think about. We can talk about it some more tomorrow. How about a cup of hot chocolate before bed?"

"I'd love some."

CLARE GOT Kate settled and went upstairs to Aidan's room to get her pajamas. When she was ready for bed, she went down to one of the other bedrooms. From there, she could hear power tools running in the garage.

As she got into bed in the unfamiliar room, she wondered why Aidan had built a house with so many bedrooms. Then she remembered he'd planned to sell it.

She thought about Kate and almost felt sorry for her daughter who was in love with a man no one approved of. *Thank goodness for the tour. At least it'll keep them apart for a while.*

Clare must have dozed off, because she awoke with a start when Aidan kissed her. He smelled like shampoo and shaving cream, and when she reached for him, her hands landed on his bare chest.

"Aidan," she whispered.

"Shhh," he said, kissing the words off her lips. In the pitch darkness, he drove her wild with his hands and lips, making slow, quiet love to her.

KATE SLEPT late in the morning and then took a walk with Clare on the trails around Aidan's house, where the sun had already melted most of the new snow from the night before. They were having lunch with Aidan when they heard a car pull up outside.

"Who's that?" Clare asked.

Aidan shrugged and went to find out.

Kate shrieked when he came back with Jill and Maggie. She leaped up to hug her sisters.

"What're you guys doing here?" Clare asked, raising an eyebrow at Aidan. "And how did you find us?"

Jill and Aidan exchanged guilty glances.

"We wanted to see Kate and surprise you," Jill said. "Aidan might've helped us out."

"Aidan's quite sneaky," Clare said, hugging Jill and Maggie. "Does your father know where you are?"

This time, Jill and Maggie exchanged glances.

"Where does he think you are?" Clare asked Maggie.

"Visiting Jill at school. For some reason that *no one* will tell me, he's really mad at Kate, and he told me not to talk to her."

Kate winced at that.

"Call him." Clare pointed to the phone. "Right now."

"Do I have to?" Maggie asked.

Clare gave her a look that left no room for negotiation.

Maggie shuffled over to the phone.

Aidan held up his hands in defense. "I didn't approve that part of it."

"I'll deal with you later, buster," Clare said under her breath.

"Oh, goodie," he whispered.

~

AIDAN WENT OUT to the garage the following afternoon to work on the Porsche so Clare could have some time alone with the girls before Jill and Maggie headed home to Rhode Island. Kate was flying back to Nashville the next morning.

Aidan marveled at how the girls had filled the house with noise, laughter, and chaos. Oh, and music, too. Clare told Kate he could sing, and she had cajoled him into playing the piano and singing with her. He couldn't believe her voice. No wonder Buddy Longstreet was out to make her a star.

The door from the kitchen opened, and Maggie came out wearing a scowl.

"Hey," he said. "What's up?"

"They kicked me out."

"Ouch. Why don't you give me a hand? You're not one of those prissy girls who's afraid of a little dirt, are you?"

She snorted. "No."

He handed her a distributor cap with instructions on how to work the gunk out of the part's spidery legs.

"Do you know why everyone's mad at Kate?"

He studied her bright blue eyes and tried to decide how he should answer that. "Maybe."

"That's not fair! I'm thirteen now. I'm old enough to know whatever it is."

"Thirteen *is* practically an adult." Aidan thought the light dusting of freckles across her nose was about the cutest thing he'd ever seen.

"See? You get that, so why don't they?"

"Maybe because sometimes being an adult isn't as great as you think it'll be when you're thirteen."

"I just wish they'd tell me. I can take it. I'm not your average thirteen-year-old, you know. I had to grow up a lot when my mom was sick. They shouldn't treat me like a baby."

"You're absolutely right, but can I tell you something?"

She nodded and worked a greasy rag over the engine part with determination he admired.

"Would you believe me if I told you this thing with Kate is really and truly something you don't want to know?"

Maggie thought that over for a minute. "So it's kind of gross, then?"

"Way gross."

"But she's not hurt or sick or anything like that, is she?"

"No," he said. "I promise."

She worked in silence for several minutes before she turned those potent blue eyes on him again. "Could I ask you something else?"

"Shoot."

"Are you going to marry my mom?"

He hadn't seen that one coming. "I don't know yet." Leaning against the workbench, he studied her. "Adult to adult, though, let me ask you this—do you think she'd marry me?"

Maggie chuckled. "Duh. *Yeah.*"

"You think so?"

"If she doesn't, maybe I will," Maggie said with a big grin.

Aidan roared with laughter. "I should be so lucky."

CLARE SURPRISED AIDAN with a trip to Boston for his fortieth birthday the following weekend. When they checked in at the hotel, he was annoyed to discover she'd reserved adjoining rooms.

"What the hell?" he fumed. "You're not sleeping over here. It's my birthday. I should get to sleep with who I want to."

"Relax, honey," she said, patting his face as she unpacked in her room.

He was still ranting about the separate rooms when someone knocked on the door of his room.

"You'd better get that," Clare said.

"You're sleeping with me, and that's the end of it."

"Get the door."

He swung open the door and was startled to see Jill, Maggie, and his entire family—minus Brandon, who was still in rehab.

"Surprise!" they said in unison.

Stunned, Aidan stared at them. "What're you guys doing here?"

Colleen O'Malley kissed her son's cheek and pushed past him into the room. "Happy birthday, love. But don't be telling people you're forty. That makes me sound so old."

Aidan fielded hugs from the girls and the rest of his family before he turned back to Clare as his nieces and nephews jumped on the king-size bed. "Been keeping some secrets?"

"Maybe," she said with the coy grin he adored.

"She rented out the whole floor and invited us all to come," Dennis told his son. "Mighty nice of her, if you ask me."

"Yes." Aidan put an arm around her and kissed her in front of everyone. "Mighty nice."

Clare's cheeks flushed with embarrassment. "Stop it." She extricated herself from his embrace. "You're all invited to dinner downstairs at seven o'clock."

"We're taking the kids to the pool," Aidan's sister Erin said to Jill and Maggie. "Do you want to come along?"

"We'd love to," Maggie said.

The room emptied as fast as it had filled, and the moment they were alone, Aidan turned to Clare. "*Very* sneaky," he said, backing her up to the bed. "Tell me the extra room is for the girls."

Nodding, she pulled him down with her. "Surprise," she said with a smile as she reached up to kiss him. "I had to celebrate that you're finally in my decade."

"But I won't be for long."

Her eyes widened, and her mouth fell open in shock. "Oh! I can't *believe* you said that!" She pelted him with her fists.

He laughed so hard he had tears in his eyes.

TWO NIGHTS after they got home from Boston, Aidan made dinner for Clare. She came downstairs at his house to find candles on the table. "What's the occasion?"

"Come have a seat. It'll be ready soon."

"Champagne, too? What are we celebrating?"

"Sit down, and I'll tell you."

She did as he asked and was startled when he knelt in front of her. He rested his head against her chest for a moment before he looked up at her with his heart in his eyes. "I love you."

She combed her fingers through his hair. "I love you, too."

"Before I met you, I had nothing. No love, no laughter, no joy, no hope. Nothing. Now I have you, and I have everything. I love you, I love your girls, and I want us to have a life together. I'll move to Rhode Island so we can be with Maggie, and we can come up here on weekends. I want to be wherever you are. Will you marry me, Clare?" He held up a large, sparkling diamond ring.

Blinking back tears, Clare looked down at him. "I want to. I want so much to marry you, Aidan."

"Why do I hear a 'but' in there?"

"Because there's something else I want, too. Something I'm not sure you want."

"What?"

"I want to have another child."

He shook his head as if he hadn't heard her right. "You'll think I'm taking aim at your age—"

She held up a hand to stop him. "I don't want to give birth, but I *do* want to be a mother again."

"You *are* a mother."

Clare sighed as she stared into the candlelight. "You did all this, and I'm ruining it."

Aidan got up to sit next to her and took her hand. "Tell me what

337

you want."

"I want to adopt a child who's maybe three or four and has no one. People only want babies, so there're lots of kids who need good homes. I want to find a child who needs me and give him—or her—a good home and a big loving family."

"I know what you're doing." His face tightened with distress. "You think I'd be a good father, and you're trying to replace the son I lost."

"No, Aidan. You *would* be a wonderful father, but that's not what this is about."

He gave her a skeptical look.

"One of the things I needed to do when I came up here was to figure out what I'm going to do with this second chance I've been given. When I look back on my life before everything happened, the only thing other than being a wife that gave me any real fulfillment was being a mother. Jack gave me all that money, so I have the freedom to do whatever I want. This is what I want. If I'd never met you, I'd still want this for me. Please believe me."

He studied the floor, and Clare's heart skipped a beat as a jolt of fear went through her.

When he finally looked up at her, his eyes were flat and lifeless. "I can't," he whispered. "I just can't."

"Oh, Aidan. You *can*. You're so great with the girls, and they already love you. I know they do. I want you so much. I want that ring and everything it stands for. We can do this together. Please."

"I can't give you what you want, and I won't ask you to live without it." He got up to turn off the stove.

"Aidan," Clare cried as she followed him. "If it's a choice, I can live without another child. I can. I don't want to live without you, though."

He shook his head. "I'd never ask you to make such a sacrifice. Someday, you'd resent me for it. You're an amazing mother, and some little person out there is about to get very, very lucky."

She put her arms around him. "Not without you."

"I'm sorry." He pulled away from her and left the room.

"Aidan!" When he didn't come back, she dropped into a chair and wept.

PART V
PARADE REST

A relaxed position of attention.

CHAPTER 37

Kate drove out to Buddy and Taylor's estate in Rutherford County the day after the benefit concert. Playing for six thousand people had put Kate on a high she'd yet to come down from. She relived the exciting night as she followed Taylor's directions to a long road that ended at the driveway to their large two-story brick colonial. Behind it, Kate could see a lake and boathouse.

She parked next to a minivan and a Cadillac SUV. Before she could open her car door, two little girls appeared. She opened the window. "Hello, ladies."

"Hi." The older of the two had light brown hair and Buddy's golden eyes. "I'm Ashley Nicole Longstreet."

"Hello, Ashley Nicole Longstreet. I'm Katherine Anna Harrington, but my friends call me Kate. Is this your sister?"

Ashley nodded. "She's Chloe Ann Longstreet."

"Hi, Chloe."

Chloe buried her face in her big sister's shirt.

Kate chuckled. "Do you guys mind if I get out of the car?"

"Ashley, Chloe, let Kate come in!" Taylor called from the front door.

Kate had the girls by the hand when she met Taylor at the door. She held a dark-haired baby on her hip and wore a fashionable black sweat suit over a hot pink T-shirt. Her hair was in a ponytail, and she hardly resembled the glamorous star she'd been the night before at the benefit.

"That's our sister, Georgia Sue Longstreet," Ashley said. "She's fourteen months old."

"I have twin cousins who are just a little bit older than Georgia," Kate said.

"Twins?" Ashley asked with big eyes as they followed Taylor into the house.

"Yep. And I have twin baby brothers, too."

"Two sets of twins?" Taylor asked.

"My dad and his sister, a year apart almost to the day." Kate was pleasantly surprised to find herself in a home where children came first. Toys and dolls were strewn about, the furniture was comfortable, and pictures of the family decorated every surface.

"Sorry for the mess," Taylor said. "I don't clean up for guests anymore. It's pointless."

Kate smiled. "It feels like home to me. My dad has six kids, so his house is just like yours." She ached when she thought of her dad and wondered if she would ever see him or his house again.

"Mom!"

Taylor turned when a boy ran into the room. He was the image of Buddy minus the goatee.

"Harry, we have company. Can you say hi to Kate?"

"Hi," he said impatiently, turning back to his mother. "Have you seen my skateboard?"

"Not since I almost fell over it yesterday. Did you look in the garage?"

"No," he said and was gone in a flash.

"That's my Harrison," Taylor said with a smile. "He's eight, Ashley's six, Chloe's four, and then there's this person." She tickled the baby and was rewarded with a giggle.

"They're beautiful."

"They're a handful." Taylor put the baby down to play on the floor. "So have you recovered from last night?"

"It was amazing. I'm still pumped."

"You did a terrific job. You do know it was a tryout, don't you?" Taylor asked with amusement.

"Tryout?"

"Buddy wanted to be sure you wouldn't freak out on the tour."

Kate laughed. "I was freaking on the inside."

"Well, it didn't show. They loved you."

Buddy strolled into the room.

It was the first time Kate had seen him without the Stetson, and she had to work at keeping her mouth from falling open. He was absolutely gorgeous.

"They ate you up, darlin'. You should feel damned good about what you did."

"Don't swear in front of the baby, Buddy," Taylor said.

"Damn is not a swear."

His wife scowled at him.

"You did a real good job, Kate," Buddy continued. "I was very pleased."

"Thanks. It was fun, and you guys were incredible. I'd never seen you live before. I don't think I'll ever forget the sound of that applause."

"It gets addictive," Taylor admitted.

"I can see how it would."

"You'll find out for yourself, but don't let it go to your head," Buddy said. "I'm starving, Tay. Can we eat?"

"It's ready. Call the kids."

Kate was treated to the kind of boisterous meal that made her miss her own family. With no sign of any hired help, Taylor served the meal of pulled pork, salad, hush puppies, and corn bread herself.

"I'll clean up." Buddy wiped Chloe's chin and pushed Ashley's milk in from the edge of the table.

When Buddy caught her eye, Kate realized she was staring.

"What?" he asked.

"I just never pictured you like this."

"Like what?"

"Wiping chins and doing dishes."

He laughed. "This is what I do when I'm not working. We only have help on the road. I work so I can do this the rest of the time."

"It's cool."

"It's *life*. It's what matters. The rest is just crap."

"Crap," Georgia said.

"Buddy!" Taylor said.

Flashing her the grin that made his female fans drool, he said, "Baby, why don't you take Kate for a walk? Show her the lake."

"Watch your mouth in front of the kids, Buddy. I mean it."

Propping Georgia on his hip, he planted a kiss on his wife and patted her ass. "Scram. Daddy's in charge."

Taylor took Kate by the hand. "Get me out of this zoo."

They pulled on coats to walk out to the lake. The sun was warm, but the breeze off the water put a chill in the air. Taylor pointed out the stables and Buddy's mother's house off in the distance. She referred to the fence that lined the lake as her security blanket.

"I'd be a wreck worrying about one of the kids drowning without that fence."

"I grew up on the water in Newport. My dad has a sailboat."

"Ours is a powerboat. Buddy loves to water ski."

"This is a great place."

"It's our haven. No one bothers us out here. The people around here protect our privacy. They'd never think of giving anyone directions to our place."

Taylor hooked her arm through Kate's as they walked. "So Buddy told me he put it all out there for you. You know what to expect over the next couple of months?"

"I think I'm as prepared as anyone can be."

"You can come here if you ever need to hide out. We've got tons of room. It's loud and busy, but you're welcome any time."

"You and Buddy have been so good to me. I'll never be able to thank you for everything."

"Well, honey, I've got to tell you, when Reid first told Buddy about you, we were skeptical. I mean people are always telling us about this one or that one. But once we saw you perform, we were your biggest fans."

The world had tilted on its axis. "What?" Kate whispered. "What did you say?"

Taylor stopped walking. "Honey, why do you look like you've just seen a ghost?"

"What did you say about Reid?"

"What? That he told Buddy about you? That's how we found you."

"No," Kate whimpered. "*No.*" Her stomach surged with nausea.

Taylor stared at her, confused. "I don't understand."

Kate clutched her stomach. "How does Buddy know Reid?" she managed to ask.

"Buddy's mother, Miss Martha, was Reid's housekeeper. They grew up together."

"Oh, no! *Oh my God.* No."

"Sweetheart, you're scaring me. What's wrong?"

"I'm sorry, Taylor. I have to go." Kate fought tears as she ran for the house. She found her purse in the living room and was headed for the front door when Buddy stopped her.

"What's wrong, darlin'? Are you crying?"

"Reid told you about me. That's how you found me. Is that true?"

"*Shit.*" Buddy groaned.

"*She didn't know that?*" Taylor cried as she came up behind Buddy. "Why didn't you tell me, Buddy?"

Certain she was going to be sick, Kate had to get out of there. "I've got to go. Thank you," she said softly. "You were real nice to me." Blinded by tears, she bolted out the door.

"Kate!" Buddy called. He stopped her before she could open her car door. "Listen to me!"

"There's nothing you can say. Let me go."

"*Listen!* Do you remember when I told you that you can trust everything I tell you?"

Wiping at her face, she nodded.

"Then *hear* this. Reid told me about you. I won't deny that. But *you* sold me. *You.* Do you honestly think you'd be coming on tour with us or having dinner at my house if I didn't think you have what it takes to play in the big leagues? Do you?"

She shrugged.

"I love Reid like a brother, but you're where you are right now because of *you.* Don't blow it, Kate."

"May I go now?"

He stepped back so she could open her car door.

She managed to keep from getting sick until she was a mile from Buddy and Taylor's house. After pulling the car off to the side of the road, she vomited and then sobbed until there was nothing left. When she was finally able to function again, she drove to Reid's house and ran upstairs, her heart thudding.

He was out riding Thunder. She was supposed to call him when she was on her way home, but she had nothing to say to him. Apparently Buddy did, though, because she heard Reid come pounding up the stairs a few minutes later.

Kate was throwing clothes into a bag when he stormed into the bedroom.

"Kate, honey…"

The sound of his voice, which had become so familiar and so dear to her, sent a shaft of pain coursing through her as she pulled open drawers and tore clothes off hangers.

"Baby, come on," he said, taking her arm.

"Don't touch me," she seethed. "Get your hands off me."

As if she'd hit him, he took a step back. "I love you, Kate. Talk to me. Please."

"You want to talk? Fine. Let's talk. Was I speaking English when I told you not to pull strings for me? Was I speaking Spanish or French or some other language you didn't understand?"

"No."

"Then all I can think is you didn't respect me enough to do as I asked."

"I respect you more than anyone in the world."

Kate laughed harshly. "You have a strange way of showing it."

"What does it matter, baby? Buddy and Taylor love you, and you're in good hands with them."

Incredulous, she stared at him. "You really don't get it, do you?"

"I guess I don't. You wanted a career in the big time, and you're going to have that."

"But I'll never know if I could've gotten there on my own. You took that away from me, and there's no getting it back."

"I ran into Buddy when I was in Knoxville. We got talking. I didn't seek him out, it just came up."

"When I called you to tell you they were at Mabel's, you knew they were coming, didn't you? You told them I'd be there that night."

Taking a sudden interest in his feet, he nodded.

"Does he know the rest? Does Buddy know about us?"

He nodded again.

Kate shook off his attempts to touch her. "It doesn't matter, because there is no more 'us.' We're done." She picked up the bag of clothes and her guitar.

"I don't want you to go. We can get past this—you love me, and you know I love you."

Her tears were gone. The love was gone. All that remained was the anger. "I'll never forgive you for this. I destroyed my relationship with the most important person in my life for you, and you weren't even worth it."

He grimaced in unabashed pain.

"You know what the most ironic thing is? Everyone disapproved of us because you were supposedly too old for me. Funny how *I* ended up being the adult in this relationship." She turned and left the room.

He followed her downstairs. "Kate. I'm sorry. I was wrong."

"So was I."

KATE SPENT two days alone in her townhouse, ignoring the constant ringing of her home and cell phones. She checked the caller ID to

347

make sure her family wasn't trying to reach her and discovered that most of the calls were from Reid. The rest were from Buddy.

She stayed in her pajamas and watched one episode after another of "Behind the Music" on VH-1 as bitterness roiled through her. She'd been so close to having everything she wanted, but it was all built on lies.

The doorbell rang late on the second day. Worried that Reid might've brought his campaign to her doorstep, she peeked out the window to find a young man in a courier's uniform holding a large envelope. She went down the stairs to answer the door.

"Kate Harrington? Sign here."

Kate signed for the envelope and took it back upstairs. Inside was a handwritten letter from Buddy on Long Road Records stationery, along with another smaller envelope.

Dear Kate,

Taylor and I are real sorry for what happened the other day. (If it makes you feel any better, she's furious with me...) Anyway, we've come to think of you as our friend, so we hope you'll forgive us for our role in all of this.

I know this won't sound very friendly, but I'm going to do you the biggest favor anyone will ever do for you by threatening legal action if you don't comply with the terms of our agreement. You're a talented girl with a big future ahead of you, and you'd be a total fool to walk away from it. So I'm not going to let you. You have forty-eight hours to lick your wounds, and then I want you back in the studio rehearsing. Otherwise, you'll be hearing from my attorneys.

Enclosed is your first paycheck. Pay your taxes (so you don't end up like Willie Nelson), pay your rent, and get your life in order, because things are about to get crazy for you.

I know you're hurting, darlin', but in our business broken hearts lead to number-one records. Now, get your ass back to work.

Sincerely,

(Your Friend)

Buddy Longstreet

President & CEO
Long Road Records

KATE SMILED and wiped away tears as she reread Buddy's letter. She opened the smaller envelope to find a check for two hundred thousand dollars.

CHAPTER 38

*C*lare marked the one-year anniversary of her recovery in late April by spending a quiet morning at home in Rhode Island. All things considered, it had been an interesting year—she'd gone from being bedridden to reclaiming her life. She had been married, divorced, and then almost engaged.

She hurt whenever she thought of Aidan and what might've been. Her brother was thrilled with the work Aidan had done to the Stowe house. He'd moved on to other clients, but not a day had gone by in the two months since she last saw him that she hadn't thought of him and their time together. In truth, she longed for him. But because they wanted different things out of life, Clare believed they'd done the right thing by breaking up. Every so often, though, she'd catch a whiff of sawdust or experience vivid memories of making love with him. In those moments, she knew her heart was truly broken.

She checked her watch. The social worker from Child Services was due any minute. This was it. She would find out today if she'd been approved to adopt, and her heart skipped with excitement when she thought about finally meeting the child they had in mind for her. He was a biracial two-year-old with a drug-addicted mother who'd signed away her rights to him. As soon as Clare cleared all the hurdles with the state, he would be hers. She had fantasized about bringing him home for weeks and had a bedroom all ready for him. The girls had been supportive of her decision to adopt but were puzzled about what'd happened between her and Aidan. However, they respected her wishes by not pushing her to talk about it.

The doorbell rang. Clare took a deep breath to calm her nerves and went to open the door to Janice Nunes.

She followed Clare into the family room.

Janice's usual smile was missing today, and Clare felt a sinking sensation. "It's not good, is it?"

"I'm so sorry, Clare. I've fought so many battles over this application, I'll be surprised if I still have a job when it's done."

"Why did they say no?" Determined not to cry, Clare bit her lip.

Janice sighed. "Well, I warned you at the outset that your medical history would be an issue."

"But you have my file from Dr. Langston and Dr. Baker. They told you I'm fine now."

"Yes, and I went over my boss's head to take it to the director, but neither of them can get past your history. It'd be different if you were married. We'd be able to make a case that should you fall ill again, the child would have another custodial parent."

"We covered that," Clare said with mounting desperation. "My sister and her husband are willing to be appointed his legal guardians, if need be."

"I know, and I think it's a perfect solution, but unfortunately it's not my decision. I get so many applications from people who're borderline cases. Half the time, I wonder if they aren't in it for the tiny bit of state aid they get when they adopt a child out of foster care. Then I have one like you—educated with a beautiful home, plenty of money, impeccable references, and lots of love to give a child, yet you get turned down."

"It's not fair."

"You're right. It's not fair, but the system is there to protect the children, and flawed or not, it's the only system we have."

"Does he have so many better options?"

Janice shook her head. "He's in foster care with little hope for adoption because he's biracial and no longer an infant."

"Maybe I'd have better luck with a private adoption."

"It's likely you'd encounter many of the same obstacles."

Clare had already lost Aidan, and now there would be no child, either.

"I'm so sorry, Clare," Janice said when Clare walked her to the door. "If anything changes, be sure to let me know."

"Thanks for all you did."

"I wish it could've been more."

Crushed, Clare closed the door and leaned against it. Now what?

CLARE SPENT a week in Nashville with Kate, who was in final preparations for her tour with Buddy and Taylor. They were all riding high on the success of Kate's first single, "I Thought I Knew," which debuted at number five on the country charts and sailed straight to number one, where it remained three weeks later. Clare and Kate had dinner one night with the two superstars, and once she got over being star struck, Clare found them to be down to earth and fun. She was relieved that such good people were guiding Kate's career.

During her week with Kate, there'd been no mention of Reid. Clare didn't ask, and Kate didn't offer, so Clare was cautiously optimistic that something had happened between them. Recalling Aidan's advice to play it cool, she held her tongue on the subject.

Once she returned home, though, Clare had to admit she was adrift. Ever since the state denied her petition to adopt a month ago, she'd been trying to figure out what to do next and was thinking about getting a job to pass the long, empty days when the girls weren't around.

She'd been home from Nashville for a week when she received a frantic call from Jack, telling her Maggie had been hurt in an accident.

"What happened?" Clare cried.

"She fell off the ladder to the attic, and she's unconscious," he said, his voice tight with fear. "Andi found her. They're taking her to Newport Hospital. Can you meet me there?"

"I'm leaving right now."

"Hurry, Clare. Andi said it looks bad."

With her heart in her throat, Clare raced to Newport Hospital. Jack arrived at the same time, and they ran into the emergency room together.

Andi was in tears as she waited for them with her son, Eric, Maggie's special pal. The twins were asleep in a stroller.

"What happened?" Clare asked, her mouth dry with fear and her hands shaking.

"I came home about half an hour after she got home from school." Andi's eyes were red from crying. "I went upstairs and found her lying in the hall under the ladder to the attic. The paramedics said she broke both her arms, one of them badly, and she wouldn't wake up."

Jack slipped an arm around his wife. "Has the doctor been out yet?"

"No, the nurse said they're trying to get her stabilized."

"Oh, God," Clare said.

Jack put his other arm around her, and the three of them sat to wait.

"We should call the girls," Clare said.

"Let's see what the doctor says first," Jack said, his face devoid of color as a tearful Eric crawled into his lap.

They waited a long time before a doctor came to find them.

"Mr. and Mrs. Harrington?"

They all jumped up.

"We've got her stabilized, but she's not out of the woods. We're concerned about the head injury, so we're sending her upstairs for a CT scan right now. She broke a rib, and it punctured a lung, but we've got that under control."

Andi gasped and sat back down when her legs seemed to fail her.

Clare clutched Jack's hand. "What about her arms?"

"The right arm was a clean break, but the left one was messy. She'll need surgery and pins. The next twenty-four hours will be critical. I'll keep you informed."

"Thank you," Clare whispered.

After the doctor walked away, Jack turned to Clare. "We should call Jill and Kate."

KATE WAS REHEARSING at the studio when one of the technicians came in with her cell phone.

"It's been ringing like crazy," he said, handing it to her.

"Thanks, Kenny." Her mother's cell phone number appeared repeatedly on the caller ID. Kate called her back. "Hey, Mom, what's up?"

"Oh, Kate, thank God you called. Honey, Maggie's been badly hurt in an accident. You need to come home."

Shocked, Kate grabbed her purse and ran for the elevator. "What happened?"

Clare filled her in quickly. "Can you get a flight today?"

"I'll call right now."

"Let me know when you're coming. Someone will meet you."

Kate's voice caught as she ran off the elevator. "Mom? Is she going to die?"

"I don't know, honey. I really don't know."

Sprinting to her car, Kate could hear the tears in her mother's voice. "I'm coming. Don't let her die." While battling the downtown Nashville traffic, Kate grew more frantic when she called every airline that flew into Providence only to learn nothing was available for the rest of the day. Without a moment's hesitation, she called Reid's cell phone.

"Kate?" He sounded shocked to hear from her.

She was having trouble seeing through her tears to drive.

"Honey, what's wrong?"

"Are you in town?"

"I'm at my office."

"I need help. My sister's hurt, and the airlines are booked." She choked on a sob. "Can you fly me home?"

"Go to my house. I'm on my way."

"Thank you."

THIRTY MINUTES LATER, he came tearing down the dirt road in the Mercedes, leaving a cloud of dust in his wake. He got out of the car and rushed over to hug her. "Are you okay?"

Tears slid down her cheeks as she looked up at him. "It's bad. We need to hurry."

He opened the hangar doors and got the plane ready. "We've got to stop for fuel at Nashville International, but I called ahead. They're expecting us. Let's go."

Forty-five endless minutes later, they were cleared for takeoff from Nashville International.

"There's an airport in Newport," Kate said. "Can we go there?"

"No, I checked. It's too small for the plane. How far is it to Newport from the airport in Providence?"

"About forty minutes."

"My office is arranging for a car to meet you."

"Thank you," she said softly.

"What happened to your sister?"

Kate told him what she knew. "I should call my mother to let her know I'm on my way. How long will it take?"

"About two and a half hours."

She whimpered.

He reached for her hand and linked their fingers. "Hang in there, baby. I'll get you there as fast as I can."

AFTER FLYING through some rough weather that slowed them down, Reid and Kate landed at T. F. Green Airport almost three hours later.

The latest report from her mother was that Maggie still hadn't regained consciousness. Hearing that, Kate was in tears again as Reid taxied the plane in from the runway.

"The car's meeting you at the hangar. Just a few more minutes."

"Will you come with me to Newport?"

"I don't think your dad needs to see me right now. Not with your sister in the hospital."

"Just for the ride? I don't want to be alone right now."

"Okay."

The limo was waiting for them. Reid secured the plane and held her hand as they ran across the tarmac to the car.

In the car, he put an arm around her, and she rested against him. "Hurry," he told the driver.

They crossed the Newport Bridge in record time. "This reminds me too much of my mother's accident," Kate said, weeping into his chest. "This is just what it felt like."

He smoothed her hair and kissed her forehead. "She's young and strong and healthy. She'll be just fine."

They pulled up in front of the hospital, and Reid followed Kate out of the limo.

"Thank you so much," Kate said, wiping tears off her face.

He hugged her. "Let me know how she is."

"I will."

"What the hell are you doing here?" Jamie asked.

Reid and Kate turned to find her Aunt Frannie and Uncle Jamie on the sidewalk. Kate ran into her aunt's outstretched arms.

Reid put his hands up to fend off Jamie, who once was his good friend at Berkeley. "I just gave her a ride."

"You've got some nerve showing your face around here," Jamie said, his jaw pulsing with anger. "Especially right now."

"Don't worry, I'm leaving. I'll pray for your sister, Kate."

"Thank you," she said with a last glance back at him as her aunt and uncle each put an arm around her to escort her into the hospital.

Frannie, Jamie, and Kate rode the elevator to the third-floor intensive care unit.

"You need to prepare yourself, sweetie," Frannie said. "She looks pretty bad."

"Is she going to die?" Kate asked in a small voice.

"No," Jamie said gruffly. "We won't let that happen."

They stepped off the elevator, and Kate ran to her mother.

"I'm so glad you're here," Clare whispered.

"Tell me she's better."

"She's no worse, but they say that's good news."

"Can I see her?"

"Dad's in with her now. They want us to take turns."

"Will he mind that I'm here?"

"Of course not."

Kate exchanged tearful hugs with all her grandparents, who had driven up from Connecticut. Jill came through the swinging door and dissolved when she saw Kate. They clung to each other for several long minutes.

"This feels far too familiar," Jill whispered through her tears.

Kate nodded, and her eyes filled again when Andi came over to hug her. "Are the boys here?"

Andi shook her head. "We sent them home with a sitter."

Jack came out of Maggie's room, his eyes red and his shoulders stooped.

"Daddy," Kate whispered.

He looked up, and his face softened when he saw her.

Kate went to him. His arms tightened around her, and she clung to him as sobs hiccupped through her.

"Kate," he said, his voice tight with emotion. "My girl. I'm so glad to see you."

Since she couldn't speak, she just held on to him.

∾

IN THE MIDDLE of the night, Kate went with Jill to get coffee in the cafeteria.

"I've been thinking," Jill said.

"About?"

"Aidan. He'd want to know about Maggie."

"Don't you think that's up to Mom to decide?"

"She's not thinking clearly. I'll bet she'd be happy to see him right about now."

"I don't know, Jill. She might not appreciate that."

"I'm going to call him anyway." Jill reached for her cell phone. "I still have his number in my phone."

"If this goes bad, I had nothing to do with it," Kate said.

CLARE WAS SITTING with Maggie at six o'clock the next morning when the girl stirred.

"Maggie? Honey? Open your eyes." Clare cried out when one magnificent blue eye fluttered open, followed by the other. "Oh, baby. Can you hear me?"

Maggie blinked and grimaced when she tried to move arms encased in plaster.

"Stay still, honey," Clare said, tears tumbling down her cheeks. "You took a bad fall. You hurt your head and broke your arms. But you're going to be just fine. Let me get Daddy, okay?" Clare ran to the door, calling for Jack and the doctor.

Jack rushed into the room. "Oh, thank God," he said when he saw Maggie's eyes were open.

"Daddy."

"Oh, baby, you scared us," he said.

The doctor checked Maggie's eyes with a flashlight. "You have a severe concussion, Maggie, so you need to stay really still for a while to give your brain time to recover. Okay?"

"Okay."

The doctor turned to Jack and Clare. "We got very lucky," he said and left the room.

"What happened?" Maggie asked.

"You fell backward off the ladder to the attic," Jack said. "Do you remember?"

When she tried to nod, her face tightened with pain.

"What were you doing up there, honey?" he asked.

"I was putting away my Barbies."

"Why?" Clare asked. "You love them."

"They're for babies."

Her parents exchanged glances over her bed.

"No one thinks you're a baby," Clare said.

"You all do! Everyone treats me like I'm a baby, so I thought if I stopped acting like one..."

Jack hung his head. "Is this because we wouldn't tell you about Kate?"

"Sort of."

"I'll tell you what," he said. "When you're feeling better, Kate can tell you all about it herself."

"She can? Really?"

He nodded. "She's here. She came home to see you."

Maggie's eyes widened. "She did? Wow, you guys must've been freaking out."

Jack's entire body sagged with relief. "Yes, baby," he said, his voice tight with emotion. "We were definitely freaking out."

Clare smiled at him and nodded in agreement.

CLARE SPENT an hour with Maggie until the nurses shooed her out so they could care for Maggie. Leaning against the wall, she tipped her head back to say a silent prayer of thanks.

Aidan burst through the swinging doors, his eyes wide with fatigue and fear.

Clare gasped. "What are you doing here?" *Had anyone ever looked so good?*

"Jill called me. I got here as fast as I could." He wrapped his arms around her. "Tell me she's okay."

Clare clung to him, wallowing in the familiar scent of sawdust and cologne. "She will be." As she said the words, she felt the tension ebb from his big frame.

He released a ragged sigh. "That was the longest five hours *ever*," he said, still holding her close to him.

"I can't believe you're here. I've missed you so much."

"Me, too." He brushed a light kiss over her lips. "Can I see Maggie?"

Clare looked into Maggie's room, where the nurses were settling her against fresh pillows. "In a minute. They're almost done."

"I have stuff I need to tell you."

"What kind of stuff?"

He shook his head in dismay at the sight of Maggie with the big casts and the pale face. "I realized something in the last five hours when I didn't know if that little girl I love so much would be alive when I got here."

Clare couldn't take her eyes off him. "What did you realize?"

"I'm already a father." His eyes were riveted to Maggie as he spoke. "Maybe it's just a stepfather, but I can't imagine any father could've been more scared than I was when I heard about what happened to her. You and those girls of yours are already mine."

Clare's eyes stung with tears. "Aidan."

"You were right, Clare," he said, focused now on her. "I *do* have it in me. I'm sorry I was such a fool and that it took something like this for me to see it."

She tugged him down and kissed him hard. "Do you remember the question you asked me that last night at your house?"

Wincing at the memory, he nodded.

"I'd like to change my answer."

EPILOGUE

"*A*idan, hurry up," Clare called up the stairs. "It's on!"

"We're coming," he said from upstairs.

Clare put out a big bowl of popcorn, opened a Sam Adams for Aidan and a light beer for herself. The TV was tuned to the Academy of Country Music Awards on Country Music Television.

Aidan came downstairs carrying their son, Max. "*Someone* didn't want to get out of the tub."

"Give me that boy." Clare held out her arms and breathed in the scent of baby shampoo coming from Max's soft coffee-colored skin and curly dark hair. His big brown eyes danced when she tickled him.

Max pointed to the television. "Kate!" he squealed. He was almost three and smart, funny, and so full of joy.

"There she is!" Aidan said with a big smile as they watched Kate alight from a limo with Buddy and Taylor. "She looks amazing."

Clare knew the silver gown was Chanel couture, the shoes were Manolo Blahnik, and the jewelry was on loan from Harry Winston. A team of stylists had worked for weeks to prepare Kate for the big night. She was up for best new artist and song of the year for "I Thought I Knew."

Jill and Maggie had flown to Los Angeles the day before to accompany their sister to the award ceremony. They'd called earlier from inside the auditorium and were having a blast hobnobbing with the biggest stars in country music.

Aidan put his arm around Clare. "I'm so excited."

She smiled and kissed him. They'd been married almost a year ago in a small ceremony at his house in Stowe. Their marriage had cleared the way for the adoption of Max a month later. Lately, they'd been talking about finding him a companion.

Jack had passed along a few leads to Aidan, and before he knew it, he was firmly established in the restoration business in historic Newport. Clare knew she shouldn't have been surprised when her new husband struck up an unlikely friendship with her ex-husband. Her goal of holidays together was now a reality, and Max referred to "Uncle" Jack's sons as his cousins. Her life had come full circle, and Clare was content—again.

"This is it," Aidan said.

Martina McBride and Alan Jackson announced the nominees for best new artist.

Clare buried her face in Aidan's shirt. "I can't stand it."

"Look!" Aidan hollered. "There they are! Jill and Maggie!"

Max clapped his pudgy hands with glee at the sight of his sisters on TV.

"And the award goes to…Kate Harrington," Alan Jackson said.

The arena went wild, and Clare finally looked up in time to see Kate hug her sisters, Buddy, and Taylor on her way to the stage. As she accepted the award and a kiss on the cheek from Martina, Kate's blue eyes were wide with excitement and tears.

"Oh, my goodness," she said with a hand on her chest as she tried to catch her breath. "There're so many people I need to thank. Buddy and Taylor, you've been so much more to me than mentors. You're my Nashville family, and I love you both."

Buddy and Taylor wiped away tears and blew kisses to Kate from the front row.

"I want to thank our crew from the tour, the gang at Long Road Records, and everyone on my team. You all work so hard to keep me sane, and I can't thank you enough. But mostly I want to thank my family for their love and support. Thank you to my sisters, Jill and Maggie, who are with me tonight. Thank you to my mom, Aidan, and Max, to Andi, Eric, Johnny, and Robby, and…" Kate paused to collect herself. "I want to thank my dad, who had the courage to say yes to this grand adventure of mine. Thank you, Daddy. I love you all very much. Thank you."

Clare and Aidan cheered and cried and hugged each other as Max squealed between them.

Kate had done it, Clare thought. She'd really done it.

In a beachfront bar on St. Kitts, Reid nursed a scotch on the rocks and watched the show on satellite TV. Kate looked so amazing as she accepted her award for best new artist, and his heart swelled with pride. As a nominee for song of the year, Kate performed "I Thought I Knew" shortly after she received her award. Reid wondered if she still thought of him every time she sang his song. He remembered her giving it to him as a Christmas gift on the same magical night they rode Thunder in the snow.

He looked out over the water as the sun set in a big ball of fire on the horizon. Nine months earlier, he'd finally chucked it all for his shack on the beach. Two days after he decided to sell his business, a conglomerate out of Austin, Texas, snapped it up with promises to retain all his employees. He'd had to laugh at how ridiculously easy it had been to shed the business after all the years he'd spent trying to figure a way out. He closed up the house in Tennessee until Ashton wanted it for his own family, took enough clothes to get by on the beach, flew his plane to St. Kitts, and never looked back.

The day before he left Nashville, he'd taken Thunder over to Buddy's stables with a note for Kate. He sold his other horses, but

Thunder was hers now. She was right—the horse liked her best anyway. After he got Thunder settled, he spent a couple of hours mending fences with Martha, and she promised to come visit him in St. Kitts.

Ashton slid on to the barstool next to Reid's. "Did she win?"

"Best new artist. Song of the year is next."

"Like there was ever any doubt."

Reid smiled at his son. They were slowly getting back on track, and this week together was a big step in the right direction.

"What do you say we take one of those deep-sea fishing trips tomorrow?" Ashton asked.

"Sounds good to me."

"There's a guy selling tickets at the marina next door. I'll go buy a couple."

"I'll be along in a minute." Reid returned his attention to the television, where Tim McGraw and Faith Hill were announcing the nominees for song of the year.

"And the award goes to…" Tim handed the card to his wife.

"Kate Harrington for 'I Thought I Knew.'"

Reid watched Kate make her way to the stage to accept her second award of the evening. She hugged Tim and Faith, and turned to absorb the audience's thundering applause.

"Thank you," she said when the applause finally died down. "'I Thought I Knew' is a song that's very close to my heart, and I'm so grateful for this award. I wrote this song at a special time in my life, a time I'll never forget. Just like I'll never forget this night. Thank you all so much."

Half a world away, Reid raised his drink in silent tribute to the girl he loved.

The story continues in Starting Over, *which begins on Brandon O'Malley's first day of alcohol rehab. Follow Brandon's journey as he picks up the pieces*

of his shattered life and finds two new loves who give him a reason to stay sober.

Turn the page to read Chapter 1 of Starting Over!

STARTING OVER

Chapter 1, Day 1

*B*randon O'Malley lay on the narrow bed, counting the cinderblocks that made up the sterile room. Ten up and twenty across, painted a boring, flat shade of tan. In addition to the bed, he had a beat-up dresser and a tiny bathroom adjoining the room. A small window overlooked the parking lot of the Laurel Lake Treatment Center, home sweet home for the next thirty days.

When his brother Colin brought him here two hours earlier, Brandon commented that the place looked more like a country club than a dry-out facility.

"It's not a country club," Colin had snapped. "The place costs a fortune, so don't forget why you're here."

Leave it to oh-so-perfect Colin to cut him down to size. He was sick to death of all three of his brothers and the way they talked down to him just because he liked to get loaded every now and then. Brandon touched the bridge of his nose, tender since his older brother Aidan's fist connected with it the night before.

To hell with them, he thought as a vicious burst of pain from his battered face stole the breath from his lungs. *They don't understand me. None of them ever has.*

Brandon checked his watch. After the most thorough physical of his life, he'd been brought to this boring room and told someone would come to see him in half an hour. That was forty-five minutes ago.

What I really want is a beer and a shot of whiskey. Brandon broke out in a cold sweat when he realized that wasn't going to happen. Suddenly, the ten-by-twenty room felt like a cell, and he wanted out of there. He sat up too quickly. The room spun, and the meager contents of his stomach churned. Bolting for the bathroom, he vomited and was splashing cold water on his face when he heard a knock at the door.

Still holding a towel, he opened the door to a balding man of average height and build.

"Yeah?" Brandon grunted.

"Hi, I'm Alan. May I come in?"

Brandon shrugged and stepped aside.

"Do you have everything you need?" Alan asked with a smile on his round, friendly face. He wore a starched light blue dress shirt and pressed khakis.

Brandon gave him a withering look.

"Towels, sheets, that stuff," Alan clarified.

"I guess."

"Well, just let us know if you need anything."

"Do you work here?"

"I volunteer on Fridays."

"My lucky day."

"It sure is." Alan sat on Brandon's bed. "In fact, one day you may look back and realize this was the luckiest day of your life."

"Yeah, *sure*," Brandon snorted, pressing a hand to his throbbing face in a desperate attempt to find some relief from the pain.

"What happened to your face?"

"My brother punched me."

"Why?"

"He says I hassled his girlfriend."

"Did you?"

Brandon shrugged.

"You don't remember?" When Brandon didn't answer, Alan pressed on. "Why are you here?"

"My brother said it was either this or his girlfriend would press charges against me. Nice, huh?"

"It was nice of him to give you a choice."

"I can see whose side you're on."

"Actually, I'm on your side, Brandon. I was once right where you are today. I'm an alcoholic."

"Whoa, man! I'm not an alcoholic. I just like to have a few beers after work. I don't know why everyone thinks that's such a big deal."

"Have you had blackouts before last night?"

"No."

"You're sure?"

Brandon looked away from him.

"How old are you, Brandon?"

"Thirty-eight."

"Ever been married?"

"No."

"You mentioned a brother. Do you have other siblings?"

"Three brothers and a sister."

"You're lucky to have such a nice big family."

"Yeah, well, they've kind of let me down today."

"Do you really think so?"

Brandon shrugged.

"What do you do for work?"

"I'm an engineer. My family owns a construction business."

"That's impressive. Has your drinking caused you problems at work?"

"No," Brandon said as his patience ran out. "What's with the twenty questions?"

"I'm just trying to get to know you. I'd like to help you."

"I don't need your help."

"Perhaps not, but I need yours."

"What could I possibly do for you?"

"Part of my recovery involves helping others who're struggling with alcohol. Would you help me by listening to my story?"

Brandon sat on the floor. "Do I have a choice?"

"Always."

"Fine." Brandon's stomach lurched again. "Have at it."

"I started drinking when I was thirteen," Alan said. "I fell into a group of rich kids who had easy access to booze. We always had the good stuff—vodka, gin, rum. I couldn't say no to any of it, but I had a particular fondness for vodka. I drank every day of high school, college, and law school. No one ever called me on it, so I thought I was getting away with it. I got married a month after I graduated from law school, and it didn't take my new wife long to realize I was drinking all the time. If I wasn't at work, I was drunk. She hadn't signed on for that, so she left me two months after the wedding. I found out much later that she was pregnant when she left. I have a fifteen-year-old son I've never met. You see, by the time I finally hit rock bottom and admitted I was an alcoholic, I'd lost my job, I was broke, my ex-wife was remarried, and another man was raising my son."

Despite his best intentions to stay detached, Brandon was moved by Alan's story. "I'm sorry."

"Me, too. I go to my son's football games just so I can watch him for a few hours. Lucky for him, he looks like his mother, and I can tell just by watching him that he's popular with his friends. He thinks his stepfather is his real father, and since I'd never do anything to mess up his life, I have to be satisfied with a few glimpses every now and then."

"That must be really hard."

"It is, but I've managed to find a good life for myself. I'm married again, and I have two little girls who are the joy of my life. I've been sober for twelve years, five months, and thirteen days."

"You count the days?" Brandon asked, incredulous.

"Every sober day is a victory to be celebrated."

"Yeah, well, I'm sorry about everything that happened to you, but I don't see how it applies to me."

Alan stood to leave. "You will, Brandon. Maybe not today or tomorrow, but one day soon, you will." He took a card out of his wallet and put it on the bed. "If you ever want to talk, feel free to call me anytime. You're going to discover an enormous network of people who want to help. If you don't want to talk to me, talk to one of them. All you have to do to gain access to all this help is take the most important first step you'll ever take in your life."

"What's that?"

"Admit you need it." He turned back when he reached the door. "Oh, and you'll want to remember today's date."

"Why?"

"Because your new life begins today. Good luck to you, Brandon."

After Alan left, Brandon got up from the floor and reached for the card he'd left on the bed. Printed on the card was only the name Alan and a phone number. Brandon studied the card for a moment and then tossed it into the trash.

BRANDON STOOD in the circle holding hands with the people on either side of him. He fixated on a spider web in the corner of the room while the others recited the Serenity prayer: "God grant me the serenity to accept the things I cannot change, courage to change the things that I can, and the wisdom to know the difference."

When the twenty or so people took their seats, the group leader, a young guy named Steve, looked around for a volunteer to go first. Brandon kept his eyes down so Steve wouldn't connect with him.

The room reeked of burnt coffee, and the walls were papered with slogans like "Live and Let Live," "Easy Does It," and one Brandon had heard often in the last five days: "One Day at a Time."

"Danielle?" Steve said. "Would you like to share with the group?"

Danielle blushed to her blonde roots and cast her blue eyes downward. Brandon wondered if she'd been a cheerleader thirty or forty pounds ago.

"Um, my name is Danielle, and I'm an alcoholic and an addict." She twisted her hands on her lap.

"Hi, Danielle." The group replied so loudly that they startled Brandon. After five days in bed suffering through detoxification—or the DTs, as it was known here—this was his first time in group, and he had no idea what to expect.

"I, um, I've been clean and sober for twenty-two days now," Danielle said to congratulations from the others. "I know that's not very long, but it's a lifetime to me. I never thought I could go a day without drinking or getting high, so twenty-two days is a big deal. I'm just hoping I can keep it up when I get out of here. It took me the first two weeks I was here to admit my life had become unmanageable. I'm very much afraid of what's ahead for me when I get out of here. I've hurt so many people." One of the other women passed a pack of tissues to Danielle. "I'm so ashamed of the things I've done…"

"You'll have the opportunity to make amends," Steve reminded her, referring to the all-important eighth and ninth steps in the twelve-step program.

"Yes," Danielle said. "I've made my lists. I'm quite certain, though, that my husband won't want to hear my apologies. I had…I'd turned to prostitution to feed my addiction, and I know he'll never forgive me for that. I can't say I blame him."

Brandon held back a gasp. This pretty, ex-cheerleader type was a *hooker? Come on! No way.*

"I'm going to do everything I can to stick to the program, to stay sober one day at a time, and to try to get visitation with my kids. That's my goal, and every day I ask God to help me get there."

While the others nodded in agreement, Brandon resisted the urge to roll his eyes. *Yeah, count on God. That'll get you far.*

The group turned next to a middle-aged man with a potbelly and a red face full of broken blood vessels. "I'm Jeff, and I'm an alcoholic."

"Hi, Jeff."

"Today's my last day at group. I'm getting out of here tomorrow.

It's time to face the music, as they say. I'll be going to court next week
to be sentenced on the embezzlement charges. Fortunately, the bank
where I worked asked the court for leniency, but I could still be facing
two years in prison."

Dismay rippled through the group.

"The upside is that at least I won't be able to drink while I'm in
jail," Jeff said with a grim smile. "I'm ready to face whatever's ahead.
This time I'm committed to staying sober, and I've given God the keys
to my car. Whatever He has in store for me, I'll willingly take.
Anything is better than where I've been, even prison. I just want to
thank you all for listening to me all these weeks." His voice caught
with emotion. "You've saved my life, and I won't forget you."

"Just keep going to meetings, Jeff," Steve said. "Even if you end up
in prison. There're groups everywhere."

Jeff nodded. "I will."

Steve checked his watch before he called on two other people to
share their stories. There were similar threads to each of them—they
were powerless over alcohol and drugs, their lives were out of control,
and once they accepted the presence of a higher power, they found a
peace they'd never known before.

All this God talk was a major turnoff to Brandon. Leave it to
Colin the Pope to find the one program on the Cape that was all
about God.

"I want to thank everyone who shared today," Steve said. "We have
a few new members with us. Let's welcome Phyllis, Frank, and
Brandon."

"Welcome," the group said in unison.

"I'd like to invite any of you new folks to speak, if you wish to,"
Steve said, scanning the circle to include each of them.

Brandon again looked away. *There's no way I'm talking to these
people. They're all drunks and druggies. What the hell do they know
about me?*

Phyllis broke under Steve's gaze and began to sob uncontrollably.

Brandon wanted to groan. *What a freak.*

"I need a couple of volunteers to stay and talk with Phyllis when she's ready," Steve said, standing to lead the Lord's Prayer. When they were done, they said together, "Keep coming back."

Brandon couldn't get out of there fast enough. He walked through the double doors that led to a patio off the cafeteria. Breathing in the cold winter air, he tried to get his hands to quit shaking by jamming them into the pockets of his worn jeans. They said the shaking was part of the detox process.

"Hey," the other new guy, Frank, said as he stood next to Brandon and lit a cigarette.

Frank offered him one, and Brandon shook his head.

"Some crazy shit in there, huh?" Frank said.

Brandon watched Frank's hand tremble when he brought the cigarette up for a drag. "Yeah," Brandon said. "I couldn't believe it when that chick Danielle said she was a hooker."

"Believe it. I've seen people do everything—and I mean *everything* —for the next fix. This is my third time through this place. I'm hoping the third time's the charm."

Great, he thought. *All this and it doesn't even work.* "What happened before?"

"I failed to commit fully to the program and to my sobriety. This time I'm going to do it, though. My wife said she'd leave me and take my kids if I don't. I can't let that happen."

"Well, good luck. I hope it works."

"What about you?"

"What about me?"

"Still in denial? Most people usually are the first week or two."

Brandon shrugged. "I was never as bad off as those people in there. I get loaded every now and then, but I wasn't like them."

"You're sure of that?"

Brandon watched a group of patients walk along a trail on the back end of the property.

"Let me give you a little piece of advice I wish someone had given me when I was first here," Frank said. "Give in to it, man. Let these people help you. It'll save you a lot of time and your loved ones a lot of suffering. Both times I fell off the wagon harder than the time before. I left some serious carnage in my wake."

"I appreciate the advice, but I'm doing my thirty days and getting the hell out of here. And I won't be back. You can be sure of that."

Frank shook his head. "Keep thinking you don't belong here, and you'll be back. Mark my words." He ground out the cigarette and tossed it into the butt bucket. "See ya around."

"Yeah. See ya."

GET *STARTING OVER* NOW. Order a signed copy from Marie's Store at *marieforce.com/store*.

ALSO BY MARIE FORCE

Contemporary Romances Available from Marie Force

The Treading Water Series

Book 1: Treading Water

Book 2: Marking Time

Book 3: Starting Over

Book 4: Coming Home

Book 5: Finding Forever

The Gansett Island Series

Book 1: Maid for Love (*Mac & Maddie*)

Book 2: Fool for Love (*Joe & Janey*)

Book 3: Ready for Love (*Luke & Sydney*)

Book 4: Falling for Love (*Grant & Stephanie*)

Book 5: Hoping for Love (*Evan & Grace*)

Book 6: Season for Love (*Owen & Laura*)

Book 7: Longing for Love (*Blaine & Tiffany*)

Book 8: Waiting for Love (*Adam & Abby*)

Book 9: Time for Love (*David & Daisy*)

Book 10: Meant for Love (*Jenny & Alex*)

Book 10.5: Chance for Love, *A Gansett Island Novella* (*Jared & Lizzie*)

Book 11: Gansett After Dark (*Owen & Laura*)

Book 12: Kisses After Dark (*Shane & Katie*)

Book 13: Love After Dark (*Paul & Hope*)

Book 14: Celebration After Dark (*Big Mac & Linda*)

Book 15: Desire After Dark (*Slim & Erin*)

Book 16: Light After Dark (*Mallory & Quinn*)

Book 17: Victoria & Shannon (Episode 1)

Book 18: Kevin & Chelsea (Episode 2)

A Gansett Island Christmas Novella

Book 19: Mine After Dark (*Riley & Nikki*)

Book 20: Yours After Dark (*Finn & Chloe*)

Book 21: Trouble After Dark (*Deacon & Julia*)

Book 22: Rescue After Dark (*Mason & Jordan*)

Book 23: Blackout After Dark

The Green Mountain Series

Book 1: All You Need Is Love (*Will & Cameron*)

Book 2: I Want to Hold Your Hand (*Nolan & Hannah*)

Book 3: I Saw Her Standing There (*Colton & Lucy*)

Book 4: And I Love Her (*Hunter & Megan*)

Novella: You'll Be Mine (*Will & Cam's Wedding*)

Book 5: It's Only Love (*Gavin & Ella*)

Book 6: Ain't She Sweet (*Tyler & Charlotte*)

The Butler, Vermont Series

(Continuation of Green Mountain)

Book 1: Every Little Thing (*Grayson & Emma*)

Book 2: Can't Buy Me Love (*Mary & Patrick*)

Book 3: Here Comes the Sun (*Wade & Mia*)

Book 4: Till There Was You (*Lucas & Dani*)

Book 5: All My Loving (*Landon & Amanda*)

Book 6: Let It Be (*Lincoln & Molly*)

Book 7: Come Together (*Noah & Brianna*)

The Miami Nights Series

Book 1: How Much I Feel (*Carmen & Jason*)

Book 2: How Much I Care (*Maria & Austin*)

Book 3: How Much I Love (*Dee's story*)

Single Titles

Five Years Gone

One Year Home

Sex Machine

Sex God

Georgia on My Mind

True North

The Fall

The Wreck

Love at First Flight

Everyone Loves a Hero

Line of Scrimmage

The Quantum Series

Book 1: Virtuous (*Flynn & Natalie*)

Book 2: Valorous (*Flynn & Natalie*)

Book 3: Victorious (*Flynn & Natalie*)

Book 4: Rapturous (*Addie & Hayden*)

Book 5: Ravenous (*Jasper & Ellie*)

Book 6: Delirious (*Kristian & Aileen*)

Book 7: Outrageous (*Emmett & Leah*)

Book 8: Famous (*Marlowe & Sebastian*)

Romantic Suspense Novels Available from Marie Force

The Fatal Series

One Night With You, *A Fatal Series Prequel Novella*

Book 1: Fatal Affair

Book 2: Fatal Justice

Book 3: Fatal Consequences

Book 3.5: Fatal Destiny, *the Wedding Novella*

Book 4: Fatal Flaw

Book 5: Fatal Deception

Book 6: Fatal Mistake

Book 7: Fatal Jeopardy

Book 8: Fatal Scandal

Book 9: Fatal Frenzy

Book 10: Fatal Identity

Book 11: Fatal Threat

Book 12: Fatal Chaos

Book 13: Fatal Invasion

Book 14: Fatal Reckoning

Book 15: Fatal Accusation

Book 16: Fatal Fraud

Historical Romance Available from Marie Force

The Gilded Series

Book 1: Duchess by Deception

Book 2: Deceived by Desire

ABOUT THE AUTHOR

Marie Force is the *New York Times* bestselling author of contemporary romance, romantic suspense and erotic romance. Her series include Gansett Island, Fatal, Treading Water, Butler Vermont and Quantum.

Her books have sold nearly 10 million copies worldwide, have been translated into more than a dozen languages and have appeared on the *New York Times* bestseller list more than 30 times. She is also a *USA Today* and *Wall Street Journal* bestseller, as well as a Speigel bestseller in Germany.

Her goals in life are simple—to finish raising two happy, healthy, productive young adults, to keep writing books for as long as she possibly can and to never be on a flight that makes the news.

Join Marie's mailing list on her website at marieforce.com for news about new books and upcoming appearances in your area. Follow her on Facebook at *www.Facebook.com/MarieForceAuthor* and on Instagram at *www.instagram.com/marieforceauthor/*. Contact Marie at *marie@marieforce.com*.

Made in the USA
Las Vegas, NV
17 March 2022